PLOTTING
SUMMER

PLOTTING SUMMER

FALLING FOR SUMMER

JESS HEILEMAN

VAGABOND
PUBLISHING

First edition June 2024

Cover design by Melody Jeffries Design

www.jessheileman.com

ALSO BY
JESS HEILEMAN

Contemporary Romances

A Newport Christmess

Plotting Summer

Regency Romances

Abigail: A Novel

A Well-Trained Lady

The Nabob's Daughter

Somewhat of a Ruse

To Tawnie, Ashley, and Jennie.
Your support made all the difference.

WELCOME TO SUNSET HARBOR

Sunset Harbor is a fictional island set off the west coast of Florida. Each book in the Falling for Summer series takes place in this dreamy town and uses crossover characters and events, creating fun connections throughout the series. Be sure to read all seven books so you can fully experience the magic of Sunset Harbor.

PROLOGUE

Ten Years Earlier

On the last signature, I dot the "i" with a small heart and smile. That's the one! It's so pretty with just the right amount of loops. Too bad that, for all my practice, I'll never use it in real life. I should stick to working on my actual name—Capri Collins —but it isn't as fun to write.

The whispers of a sea breeze play with the dark brown strands of my hair. I shut my notebook on my lap, tipping my chin upward to absorb the late afternoon sun on my face. With a long inhale, I close my eyes and note the slight shifting of the water beneath the docked boat. The subtle taste of salt on my tongue. The summer humidity clinging to my skin. The quiet buzz of distant insects. It's moments like this—when I'm alone and all my senses are heightened—that my imagination finds free rein. And I never object to where it takes me. Or, more specifically, who it always brings along: Tristan Palmer. (Yes, as in the Palmer of my Mrs. Capri Palmer dream signature).

When an image of his glorious self fills my mind, a smile of utter contentment makes its way onto my lips. He is perfection personified. A modern gentleman. The best of everything. The guy of every girl's dreams (at least at Beachside High). And conveniently, my next-door neighbor.

But, like all worthy heroes, Tristan has a paralyzing weakness. His isn't any old, run-of-the-mill weakness either. It's all consuming. Or more like *she's* all consuming. Bridget Hall. The most perfect female specimen on the planet. His girlfriend and my arch nemesis.

Okay, arch nemesis is a touch dramatic. That requires her to know who I am, and she very much doesn't. Sure, she might recognize me in a line up considering we go to the same high school and I catch a ride with Tristan every day, but if she couldn't, I honestly wouldn't be shocked. Offended? Slightly. But not shocked.

You see, Tristan and Bridget have been dating for almost three years—which in high school chronology is epically long. Not as long as my secret crush on him—that dates all the way to early elementary school when I used to visit my grandparents on the island before moving here—but who's comparing? Besides me, that is? Not that I'd have a chance with Tristan even if they weren't dating. The quarterback of the football team never sets his sights on the introverted book-nerd. Not in real life.

Which is where the need for imagination comes in. Thankfully, I have loads and loads of that. Notebooks full of story ideas, in fact, as well as partially formed plots for future books I intend to write someday. Fiction is a beautiful thing.

Almost as beautiful as the current phantom-Tristan of my mind's eye.

"Capri." It's Tristan's voice, but it sounds so real. So close. Not at all like it's in my head.

My eyes fly open, and like I conjured him into being, Tristan stands between me and his family's dock, staring at me with an amused, chest-squeezing grin. Apparently, all my senses weren't as heightened as I thought. Slacker hearing!

"Tristan!" I shoot to my feet, the notebook on my lap plummeting to the floor, before I remember exactly where I am. With my abrupt motion, the small, metal fishing boat pitches to the side and bangs against the dock. True to Newton's Third Law, the force immediately sends the boat rocking in the other direction. My arms fling outward in an attempt for balance, but when the boat shifts again and hits the dock a second time, all hope is lost. The last thing I see is Tristan's wide-eyed expression before I topple backward over the metal bench I've been sitting on and land with a thunderous thud between it and the bench row behind. Wedged with my shoulders on the floor of the boat, my chin pressed against my chest, and my legs straight up in the air, I must resemble a dead bug.

I moan, half from the pain in my head and half from utter mortification. Actually, a fourth from pain and the rest from utter mortification. At least I didn't tumble into the water.

Of course, Tristan won't pretend he didn't see my fall. I'm a damsel in very apparent distress, and he's the upstanding gentleman. On cue, he appears at the side of the boat. Kneeling on the dock, he takes hold of my arm to help me up. "You okay?"

Nope. Not in the least. The memory of this moment will fester inside me for the rest of my pathetic existence if I don't die from a brain bleed first. Frankly, that might be the more humane way to go.

Once I'm seated on the bench again, I rub the back of my head where a tender lump is forming. "I think so." My thoughts seem to be developing in slow motion, which is concerning, but that could also be my proximity to Tristan. I never think clearly with him around. "I just lost my balance." Obviously. Ugh.

He presses against the edge of the boat to subdue the rocking my fall caused. "Sorry if I startled you."

I shake my aching head, attempting not to get hypnotized by the depths of his sea-green eyes. I'd like to retain what little brain functionality I still have. "It's fine. I'm fine."

"You sure?"

"Yeah."

His gaze locks on the ground at my feet before he reaches over to pick up something off the floor, and my heart lifts into my throat when I glimpse the unadorned teal blue notebook in his hands. Thank the high heavens it's closed! "You dropped this," he says, brushing off some dirt from the cover.

"Oh, thanks." I casually take hold of it and place it on my lap again like the contents aren't of the top-secret variety. Tristan Palmer absolutely cannot know what graces these pages. And I'm not only referring to the practiced signatures—Capri Palmer —filling every blank nook and cranny. This notebook is brimming with romance plot points, character descriptions, inspirational scenes, and story ideas, ALL involving him. Not that he would know that specifically because I'm not careless enough to name Tristan outright, but I have zero desire for him to discover my obsession with romance. Or writing. Or most particularly, writing romance. I need to change the subject ASAP.

Before I have the chance, Tristan takes mercy on me. "Were you taking the boat out?"

I shake my head a second time, glad the motion doesn't send pain shooting through my skull again. Maybe I won't die of a brain bleed after all. "No. I was sitting here ... thinking." My cheeks heat in complete betrayal of what exactly I was thinking about, but I keep my eyes locked with his to compensate for it.

He gives a slow nod, then tosses a thumb in the direction of his family's souped-up ski boat. "I'm headed out for a drive."

Not sure why he's telling me, I give a small smile. "Have fun."

He glances at his boat, then back to me. "You should come. If you feel up to it."

I stare at him. Tristan Palmer is inviting me to go on his boat? Just me and him? No one else? It isn't the first time he's invited me somewhere, but I'm pretty sure all the others were pity-invites—obligatory offers when other island kids would discuss their weekend plans in front of me. Maybe this is a pity-invite too—I did totally eat it in front of him—but for some reason, I don't really care.

One side of his mouth quirks up, and suddenly I realize I'm still staring. "Unless you're too busy *thinking*," he says.

"No!" The response bursts out of me with such force that his brows lift with what I hope is amusement. I remind myself to chill and try a nonchalant, one-shouldered shrug. "I mean, I'll come."

"Do you need to let your mom know?"

"My mom and grandma are at my brother's golf tournament in Orlando. They won't be home for a few more hours." Or later if Walker convinces them to stop for dinner. Which he will.

He stands up and offers me his hand. "Here. Let me help you out, then."

My gaze lowers from those gorgeous eyes to his outstretched hand. It's just like in my imaginings. Except it's real. With only a brief hesitation where I worry I might pass out from pure delight, I put my hand in his. Instantly, my fingers are alive with warmth, and the feeling shoots up through my arm until my whole body is consumed. I'll definitely be documenting every last detail of this moment in my notebook later so I can relive it for ... I don't know ... forever.

When my feet are safely on the dock, he releases my hand and starts toward his boat like he didn't rock my entire world with a brief touch. I'm obviously still reeling and need a second. Without permission, my gaze shifts from his begging-to-be touched golden locks to the soft white t-shirt contrasting his tan skin and clinging to his muscular back. I nearly let my focus drop lower when I partially return to my senses. What would he think if he caught me admiring his mighty fine hindquarters?

Pull yourself together, Capri!

I hurry and shove my notebook in the storage compartment of the fishing boat and start after him with my lanky strides. To make sure I'm not dreaming, I discreetly pinch my inner arm. *Ouch!* I'm definitely awake. But maybe I hit my head harder than I thought? I won't be the least bit shocked to wake up any moment still in dead-beetle position. Though, if that's the case, I'm going to roll with this concussion-induced fantasy as long as possible.

It isn't that Tristan and I aren't friends; we just run in different circles. But we often chat when we're both *conveniently* outside in the yard at the same time, and he always seems to seek me out at community or neighborhood get-togethers because he's nice like that. And when it comes to boatpooling (like carpooling minus the car and add in a boat) to and from school every day, of all seven island kids Tristan takes, I'm the one he trusts with manatee watch. Granted, he originally asked Beau (his younger brother who's my age) to make sure the water near the boat is manatee free, but Beau insisted I'm more fit for the task. Once I assured Tristan I didn't mind, he allowed it. That's trust.

I've held the position for the last three years. One, because I absolutely love manatees, and though it isn't super common, manatees have been spotted in the canals that connect several of the island houses' docks to the bay. To ever cause harm to one of the gentle giants would be beyond devastating. But also, manatee duty kept me from having to interact with my peers as much. It's not like I don't enjoy being around people. I simply prefer watching to socializing. That's especially true when I'm in group settings with people a few rungs above me on the social ladder—which is basically everybody.

So, all of that to say, I would consider me and Tristan to be *friends*. Yes, I might be a bit more invested in our friendship, but that's because Tristan has so many friends whereas I have Jane ... and sort of him. But I'll take what I can get when it comes to Tristan.

I climb into the boat after Tristan and take a seat in the very front. It's my usual lookout spot and apparently the one I feel most comfortable in. He doesn't mention how far away I've chosen to sit but starts the engine. We putter along the canal, my gaze glued to the water, searching for manatees. Then we make our way out to the bay and eventually around the island's southern tip.

"I've always wanted to see the view from the top of that," he says.

I glance over my shoulder to find him pointing at the lighthouse. Since it's high tide, the sandy walkway out to it is currently covered, so it looks like an island. "I bet it'd be awesome."

We watch it pass, the boat moving into open ocean.

"Ready?" he asks, his eyes lighting with excitement so palpable it's like his spark of electricity jumps to me.

I brace myself and nod, my grin stupidly big.

Suddenly we're soaring over the water. The slight lift of waves are small bumps beneath us. My hair is whipping in my face, and I'm laughing and squealing in unexpected delight. Tristan is also beaming, his eyes on me, but I'm too nervous to meet them for longer than an occasional moment here and there.

The boat slows, then stops.

There's no one else around us and only a glimpse of Sunset Harbor in the distance. My imagination begins churning out an impressive number of potential scenarios as to where this boat ride could go if my life were a romance novel. But it's not. And with my quickened heart rate, I know it's time to rein in my unhelpful thoughts.

Tristan drops on the cushioned bench connected to where I'm sitting before stretching out his legs toward me and leaning back with his arms behind his head. "This is where I go to think," he says, sending me a conspiratorial look.

I glance at the pink-and-orange-tinted clouds that hint at a spectacular, upcoming sunset. The water is calm, the slight waves gently rock the boat, and the distant calls of seabirds add to the peaceful ambiance. "I can see why." Though what I can't understand is his reason for inviting me to come along.

We sit a while in silence, Tristan closing his eyes, and me using every strategy I can think of not to watch him. First, I work on untangling a few knots in the ends of my now wind-blown hair before moving onto chipping the remaining pink polish off my fingernails. It's a mindless task, so it's not until I see pink flakes scattered across the white bench seat that I realize my error. I'm about to brush it off but decide it probably isn't much better to have it sprinkled on the white floor, so instead, I sweep it into a small pile with my fingers, pinch it, and stuff it in my pockets to clean out later. It takes me four attempts to get most of it.

Tristan bumps his foot into my thigh, making me startle. "You looking forward to Beau taking you to school this fall?"

With Tristan headed to college, his younger brother (by a whopping thirteen months) will be my new ride to school. It's a fact I'm not the least bit excited about. Mainly because Beau isn't Tristan, but also because he's not quite as level-headed as his older brother, so having him behind the wheel of a speed-boat seems a reckless way to start each day. Though it's prefer-able to leaving the house an extra thirty minutes early to ferry over to the mainland and catch the bus.

But a small part of me wants to tease Tristan and tell him I'm thrilled for Beau to drive. Both Palmer boys have a healthy competitive side, so I know that answer would bring out a more playful reaction from Tristan. But that's unfortunately not my relationship with him, so my attempt will probably miss the mark. Or worse, Tristan might think I have a thing for his brother. "It'll be ... different," is the response I settle on, tucking up my legs beneath me.

"I think that's the phase of life we're moving into—everything being different." There's something about the way he says it, like he wants to say more.

I haven't spent much time with Tristan alone, but I've watched him enough to become a proficient reader of his cues. And Tristan definitely could use a good heart-to-heart. Well, his heart to mine, anyway. One direction. There's no reason to ruin this rare moment by having him discover what's going on in my heart. Hint: sailing off into the sunset together seems a reasonable solution to most any problem he's facing. Which is a very strong indicator I make a better sounding board than a conversationalist at present. "You can talk to me." I shrug. "If you want."

He doesn't say anything, and I try not to be disappointed I won't be allowed into his confidence, but then he lets out a long exhale. "Bridget and I broke up a few days ago."

What?! My heart attempts to free itself from my sternum and fall at his feet to proclaim its allegiance, but I clasp a hand over my chest to prevent it. This isn't about me. This is about Tristan. And he's obviously hurting. "I'm sorry. I didn't know."

He swings his legs off the bench and leans his elbows onto his knees, his head down and his gaze darting around the floor of the boat. A floor that thankfully isn't littered with remnants of pink polish. "It makes sense with us going to different colleges..." His voice trails off.

"It doesn't make it easy though," I offer.

He gives a slow shake of his head. "Maybe it'll be a good thing. It's just..." He stops again, and his gaze lifts to mine.

"We've dated for so long, it feels like I've lost sight of who I am without her."

I take in the doubt in his expression. Suddenly, a strange desire to do more than listen bubbles up from the depths of my soul. No! I'm a sounding board. An unbending, knows-my-place, sounding board. I don't give advice. Especially not to Tristan.

But it technically isn't advice I want to share. Simply a slight confidence boost. A miniscule reassurance that Bridget isn't the one that makes him who he is—the wonderful, thoughtful, fun-loving, extremely attractive guy I've been secretly crushing on since my formative years. I'd obviously need to scale down that last bit a million percent if I say something. Actually, it's best to not say anything.

"I know who you are." The words spill out of me, and I'm positive I'm more surprised by their escape than Tristan.

"You do?" He smiles, though it's likely to do with how apparent it is that I want to take back my admission.

"No. I mean, yes, but ... never mind." I shake my head, pressing my lips together to stop any more condemning blurtations.

He leans forward ever so slightly in his seat. "I think I need to hear what you were going to say."

"It's nothing." I shove my hands between my thighs in an attempt to help me get control of myself. "You're a good guy. That's all."

His smile widens. "Wow. Thanks for that."

I know he's teasing, but the generic *good guy* comment likely did less to reassure him than if I'd kept quiet. My chest starts buzzing, and I already know I'm going to attempt to fix it. "At the end of last football season—that super close game against Century," I say, and he nods. "Instead of celebrating with your teammates, you immediately went to talk with the kicker who missed the extra point. You're always seeking opportunities to help—putting up chairs for assemblies, holding open doors for people, handing change to someone in need. Sometimes, when my brother hasn't gotten around to mowing my grandma's grass or pulling her weeds, you do it without saying anything. That's who you are."

The way his eyes rove over my features at a slow, intentional pace makes it difficult to breathe. Or think.

And then all at once my head clears enough to realize my error. Not only was my little monologue more than a slight reassurance, but it was extremely revealing of how often I watch Tristan. *Stalker much, Capri?* Now I need to make this better too. "I like to watch people. Not just you. Lots of other people as well." Nope. I'm pretty sure that didn't help my cause.

Tristan's expression is now unadulterated amusement. "You watch me?"

I open my mouth to clarify but close it again. There's no explaining my way out of that admission. "On occasion."

The glory of Tristan's full smile lights his face. "Speaking of watching people ..." He draws in a slow breath, making his broad chest rise. "What were you thinking about in the fishing boat when I first walked up?"

His question's so completely out of left field, I not only didn't see it coming, I didn't even realize what game I was playing. It's like I'm standing on home plate with a tennis racket in my hand and wearing roller-skates. Then without warning, like my menopausal mother, I'm experiencing a personal summer so intense, I consider jumping ship to cool myself down. "Nothing."

He laughs. "Come on, Capri Sun." He says Capri like the Italian island I'm named after (Ca-pree) and not the short pants variation of the word that's used in the name of the actual kids' drink (cuh-pree). "What brought a smile like that to your face? You looked so ... perfectly happy."

With the warmth creeping up my neck, I can sense my skin

starting to blotch. It's like my own form of Pinocchio's nose—a there's-something-I'm-not-saying, reddening décolletage. But even the use of his little nickname won't work on me. I'll be buried with my secret. "I can't remember."

He chuckles. "That's convincing."

In desperate need of reprieve from the heat, I gather my hair and lift it to allow for airflow, completely forgetting the golf-ball-sized lump on the crown of my head until my hand grazes over it. I wince.

Tristan's teasing brow lowers. "What's wrong?"

I cup a hand over the tender spot. "It's where I hit my head on the fishing boat."

Tristan is directly in front of me now. "Here. Can I?" Unable to form words, I nod, holding my breath as his hands settle over mine. My skin is pulsating with energy from his touch. His face is inches away and his mesmerizing eyes hold my gaze. "You probably need to move your hand," he says, a slight smile pulling at his lips.

I'm fully aware he doesn't mean for me to intertwine my fingers with his like I want to do. In my seventeen years of life, I've never felt so alive. So entirely in tune with my entire body. What a sad existence I've endured until this moment, and I never knew it. But all reason isn't lost in my hopelessly romantic notions, because I lower my hand to my side.

His fingers are gentle when they locate the lump, and his face crinkles with concern. "You really hit your head. Are you dizzy or anything?"

"No. I feel fine." Honestly, I'm slightly dizzy, but not because of my head. I don't think so anyway. I'm pretty sure it's a wicked combination of Tristan's proximity and my shallow breathing causing the world to feel off-kilter. Or maybe it's the movement of the boat.

His hands move to my neck, and I go completely still. He

tilts my chin upward, his attention focused. "Your eyes are so dark. I can barely see your pupils."

I give a small laugh. "Are you checking for a concussion?"

"Something like that. I need a little more light though." Tristan stands and gingerly pulls me to my feet. "Here, can you face the sunset?"

The motion of the rocking boat is definitely more noticeable standing. I step around Tristan and then turn back to face him, feeling slightly unsteady. With a new swell of waves, I scramble to find my balance when Tristan takes hold of me and draws me to him. His hard body and sturdy stance act as a mighty fine anchor point.

"Careful. Don't fall."

"Thanks." My voice is a breathy whisper.

Obviously not affected by our closeness like I am, Tristan keeps one arm secured around my waist and settles his other hand below my chin to tip it upward again. He positions his body to block the diminishing rays of light before leaning to the side to allow them to reach my face, his gaze shifting from one of my eyes to the other as he does so. "Your eyes are dilating fine." With his medical opinion voiced, I expect him to step away. He doesn't. And his hand doesn't move from beneath my chin.

I swallow down my nerves, convincing myself the way he's still looking at me—with continued focus and ... admiration?— doesn't mean what I want it to mean. "That's good news."

His gaze shifts again, but this time it sweeps across my face. "You're beautiful, you know." It's not a question. Then, with a dip of his Adam's apple, his gaze drops to my lips.

What in the world is happening right now? Tristan freaking Palmer just called me beautiful, and now he's staring at my lips! The exact way the hero does in every romance movie ever before he kisses the woman he's falling for.

Warning signals ping through my head. And not only ones

about what my breath smells like, and whether I'll be able to remember my best friend Jane's nuanced lessons about kissing. Bridget and Tristan just broke up. He isn't falling for me. I'm obviously a rebound. Kissing him will strictly place me in that category. For forever. Do I want that?

The answer takes me exactly two milliseconds to come to: heck freaking yes, I do! This is a once in a lifetime opportunity. If I don't take it, I'll never experience what it's like kissing Tristan. I'm instantly and thoroughly convinced I'll die a happier woman having checked the previously unattainable goal off my bucket list. In fact, I already know it'll become one of my go-to stories when, as an old woman, I share the best parts of my life with my posterity. It will be its own chapter in my autobiography for heaven's sake. From here on out, it'll simply be known as *The Kiss*.

Completely settled on accepting my new role as a rebound, I close my eyes, thankfully recalling that Jane mentioned it's weird to kiss with your eyes open. If I'm only going to get one shot at this, I can't make it weird. I lean forward slightly, my lips soft and supple (or what I assume soft and supple implies). Eagerly, I wait for the feel of Tristan's lips on mine and the subsequent explosion of fireworks that all the greatest romance stories assure me will follow, but after a few seconds of nothing, I open my eyes again.

Tristan's expression is like a knife to my heart. He doesn't look grossed out or anything, just totally unsure. As in, he has no idea how he got himself into this mess with his crazy, easy-lipped neighbor.

Humiliation like I've never known—and I've clearly been no stranger to humiliation—floods through my entire body. I wish I could drown in it. Instead, I take a step back, hugging my arms around my middle.

With my retreat, Tristan's hands drop to his sides. "Capri, I ..." He runs a hand through his hair, apparently lost for words.

"No. It's fine. You and Bridget just broke up, and ..." I moan inwardly. Why did I say that? The truth is so distressingly obvious now—there's no way whatsoever that Tristan would've kissed me even if Bridget didn't exist. How did I read things so wrong? He was probably just being his kind self and returning the favor of boosting my confidence with his beautiful comment. He must've glanced at my mouth for another reason. Oh my gosh! Do I have something stuck in my braces? I swipe my tongue across them, wondering if this moment can get any worse.

"Capri, I think you're incredible—"

"Can we pretend this never happened?" I blurt, not letting him finish. I don't want to be let down softly. I'm way too close to tears for that. And that's the last thing he needs to witness because once I start crying, I also start talking—or more like blabbering—and it's nearly impossible to stop. I can't risk one of my floodgate confessions. Not when I might accidentally mention my lifelong secret crush on him.

He holds my gaze for an uncomfortable moment before his shoulders drop, and he nods.

"How about that sunset?" My tone is overdone, but I don't have the bandwidth to care. I point behind him to where the sky is alive with colors—oranges, pinks, yellows, blues, and purples —and the sun is about to disappear beneath the horizon. When he turns to look at it, I swipe a hand across my pooling eyes.

"It's amazing." He sends a smile over his shoulder like all the awkwardness has vanished and everything is completely normal between us again.

And for the sake of keeping it together, I'll pretend it is too, though my attention remains on him after he looks back at the sunset. "It really is." My heart physically aches knowing Tristan will always be out of reach for me.

We don't linger much after the sun goes down, and despite his casual comments and friendly smiles on the boat ride back,

I'm sure Tristan is eager to get me home. We're puttering our way through the canal when I notice a figure on the Palmer's dock. "There's someone waiting," I say, looking back at Tristan from my place up front.

His eyes narrow, attempting to determine who it is. "Is it Beau?"

I set my gaze on the figure again, trying to make out more than a general shape in the growing darkness. The boat's light doesn't do much from this distance, but as we move closer, the shape begins to clarify. Long legs, cut-off shorts, a snuggly fitted crop top, and waist-long blond hair that's been curled to perfection despite the humidity.

Bridget Hall.

We're close enough now that she might hear if I say something, but judging by Tristan's look of surprise, he's recognized her too.

He steers the boat to the side, it's trajectory moving toward the dock, and cuts the engine. "Hey, Bridget. What are you doing here?"

Her arms are crossed, her glare pausing on me before returning to Tristan. "I've been thinking about what you said—us trying the long-distance thing—and I came to talk to you about it. But if you're busy ..." Those ellipses hold a lot of accusation.

Tristan ties up the boat and his gaze discreetly slides to me, an apology in his eyes. "Capri and I went out for a ride. That's all."

Her scoff is audible. "At sunset? Just the two of you?"

I consider chiming in and assuring her that, to my great disappointment and complete mortification, it was a very platonic experience, but words have not been my friends today. So instead, I sit quietly, trying not to draw any more of Bridget's ire.

"You thought about what I said?" Tristan asks, and I can't

help but think a change of subject is the right move. Even if I have zero desire to see where this goes.

She purses her lips, her sandaled foot tapping on the dock like she's not sure if she'll let him off so easy. But when her appraising gaze flicks to me again, I know she will. She realizes I'm not a threat. "The last few days have been unbearable," she finally says. Bridget climbs into the boat and steps in front of Tristan, her arms snaking around his waist. "I don't know exactly what it'll look like, but I want to make this work. I want to make *us* work."

And that's my signal. I carefully step over the side of the boat with one foot so my exit doesn't draw attention.

"You headed home?" Tristan's voice stops me mid-escape. And I mean that very literally. With a foot on the dock and a foot still on the boat, I'm one solid thigh slap away from squatting-sumo-wrestler status.

I physically lift my *boat leg* over the side and onto the dock before facing him. "Yeah. I figured you'd want to talk. Alone."

"We do," Bridget says, snuggling into Tristan's chest. "Thanks, Cali."

I stiffen. I'd typically be impressed she managed to get that close to my name, but Tristan had just said it. Not that I'll say anything. "Of course. Night." I give some sort of *wax-on wax-off* kind of wave.

There's a flash of indecision in Tristan's expression, and I know he's feeling bad about how this all went down because that's who he is. "Night, Capri." Tristan accentuates my name, but all I notice is the way his arms loosely settle around Bridget's back. Those arms that were just wrapped around me. Yes, it was to keep me from falling, but for a brief moment, I had a glimpse of what it was like being held by Tristan.

And you know what? That's more than I ever expected.

Would I change any of the last hour if I could go back for a do-over? Absolutely! A heart-resounding yes! Please! But if it meant I'd have to give up the memory of Tristan's skin against mine, the gentle way his fingers searched for the lump on my head, and the way his voice sounded—deep and breathy—when he called me beautiful, I wouldn't change a thing.

Sure, recalling *The Incident* (formally hoped to be referred to as *The Kiss* until everything went entirely wrong) will forever make me cringe, but I can't imagine it will affect anything with Tristan. He appears every bit as eager as I am to pretend it didn't happen. Besides, he's leaving for college soon.

So I'll take what I can from tonight—the inspiration gold that Tristan gave me.

In the real world, girls like me don't get kissed by the most sought-after guy in school. And girls like Bridget Hall always win. But in the world of fiction, I create the story. With ideas already flowing through me of how differently this sunset boat-ride could have gone, I smile and head toward the little fishing boat to retrieve my notebook.

This story-writing book-nerd is about to get her man!

Right after I go inside to take some ibuprofen and find an ice pack for my head. And possibly have a good cry.

CHAPTER 1

I'M ENTIRELY CONVINCED there's no sweeter sound in this world than the rapid clacking of keys on a keyboard. Specifically, my keyboard. More specifically, my keyboard when I'm nearing the end of an epic love story I plotted months ago.

Yes, my fingers are begging for reprieve from the onslaught of catching each detail of the unfolding scene in my mind. And yes, my back is in near spasms from sitting for hours in this supposedly-ergonomic luxury chair I fully regret purchasing. But I can't stop. I intend to take advantage of every glorious moment the words are flowing. Not just because I'm on a deadline. But mainly because I'm on a deadline. And it's a tight one.

Brant's eyes are warm and alluring, making the choice to step closer effortless. "I always knew it was you." His voice comes out rough as gravel, but the sensation of it against my skin is …

I tap my index finger mindlessly on the H key, conjuring up the right word. Welcome? Pleasant? No, I need something with more intensity. Exhilarating? Maybe a bit too intense for what I'm going for.

My finger tapping grows more pronounced.

Oh! How about intoxicating? I consider the word a moment.

I do like it, but I'd have to change the *rough as gravel* to a more applicable metaphor.

Mid deliberation, I sense my state of flow coming to an abrupt halt.

Intoxicating it is.

Until edits.

… intoxicating.

My legs grow heavy and my head spins. "Always?" There's a waver in my voice with the rise of emotions—

My phone buzzes on the desk next to me. Without even a glance, I silence it. Where was I? Oh yeah. Rise of emotions.

… swelling inside me. He couldn't know what his admission meant. He couldn't know how deeply my very being longed to—

Buzz. Buzz.

I glare at the phone like it needs to understand how intensely I resent the interruption. But then I see the name on the screen: Tala. Of course it's her. My sister is on a three-person list of permitted callers (along with my mom and my best friend, Jane) when my phone's set to concentration mode, and her second attempt to reach me might mean it's important. Like it was last fall when I didn't answer either of her back-to-back calls only to find out hours later that Grandma had been admitted to the hospital with a heart scare. I haven't ignored a repeat call from Tala since.

Reluctantly bidding my state of flow farewell, I accept Tala's call. "Hey! Is everything okay?"

"Do you have a minute to video chat?"

Her tone is light, but I'm also aware she doesn't answer my question. "Sure." I exit concentration mode and the phone immediately beeps with the incoming video call.

When I accept it, Tala's dark eyes and rosy cheeks fill the screen. It's uncanny how much we look alike—down to the similar smatter of freckles across our nose and cheeks—except my chestnut brown hair still hangs to the middle of my back while Tala recently chopped hers off just below the chin. Drastic hairstyle changes must be a step in her postpartum recovery because she's undergone one after having each of her three kids.

She lifts my newest nephew, Lucas, into view, setting him against her shoulder. "Are you still working?"

My gaze flits to the flashing cursor on my laptop before I stand with the phone in hand. All the muscles in the lower half of my body protest the movement. "I need to take a break anyway."

"I totally interrupted you, didn't I? I can call back later."

"Really, you're fine." I mosey into the kitchen and open the fridge. When deadline mode hits, I rely on meal kits to lessen any food-prep required as well as visits to the store, so there's unfortunately not many options for a quick snack. Instead, I snag a can of Diet Coke to distract me from my hunger for the time being.

"What scene are you working on?"

"The final kiss."

Tala brightens at the news. "So, you're basically done?"

I manage to not roll my eyes at the all-too-familiar sentiment and take a swig of carbonated heaven. I can literally feel my dopamine stores rising as the bubbly liquid slides down my throat. "Not all romances end at the final kiss."

"But they should."

Though the creative in me cringes, I'm grateful my sister is a summation of most of my readers squeezed into one blunt package. Between her and Jane, I know exactly what my audience wants and when I've deviated from it.

Lucas wiggles on Tala's shoulder like a pudgy little caterpillar searching for his next meal, and she gently pats his back until he settles.

"He's getting so big," I say.

She peers down at his tiny hand clutching her shirt with a look of complete adoration. "I can't believe he'll be three months on Monday."

"Three months already?" It's not until the words are out that I realize my mistake. I hold my breath, waiting to see what she'll do with my admission. I've not come to see them since my brief visit to the mainland hospital when Lucas was born. And I'm entirely aware of what a terrible person I am, being that I live less than two hours away.

"Yep." She pauses briefly, and I'm certain she intends to mention my *worst aunt ever* status. "When do I get to read this new book of yours?"

My shoulders relax with her mercy. Tala is literally a saint. "As soon as I'm done writing it. Like always."

"No guess when that'll be? I fully intend to clear my calendar for the entire day to binge read it."

I can't hide my delight at her declaration, and I'm partially still relieved at having dodged a shame bullet. "I should have it finished in the next few days, but I also need to double check that my main male character's arc is sufficient."

"I'm sure he's perfect."

"That's actually what I'm worried about. I want to make sure he isn't too perfect."

Tala's brows lift. "Isn't that the point? Women have to deal with men falling short of our ideals constantly—the last thing we want is to spend our spare time reading about another guy that disappoints us."

"Hey, now." Heath walks into view and carefully grabs Lucas from Tala. "That comment felt a bit pointed."

"I have no idea what you mean." Tala tosses the burp cloth at him with a smile. "I was speaking in general terms."

He chuckles. "I'm pretty sure I heard an *us*, *we*, and some *ours* in there."

She looks back at me, her smile intensifying. "Capri, please assure my husband that my ideal man is one who eats my leftovers without asking and donates brand-new items to the island charity raffle with zero reservation."

Heath leans into view of the camera, his toothy grin filling the screen. "It was one item, Capri. And I'd argue that most people don't leave a rug they actually want rolled up and sitting in a garage for months after they move in." He eases away and glances at Tala. "How was I supposed to know you didn't intend to donate it?"

"By asking me." Tala's gaze follows him off camera. She gives a brisk nod and scrunches up her nose playfully before returning her attention to me. "I was trying to decide where I wanted it," she says, loud enough for him to hear wherever he disappeared to. "All that wasted money, and he thinks we should *laugh about it*."

Heath steps back into view, no longer holding Lucas, and takes a seat next to Tala at the table. He drapes an arm across the back of her chair and leans in close to her. She looks away with crossed arms and pursed lips. He doesn't relent, and after a moment, she lifts her cheek to allow his apologetic kiss.

"Think how happy I made the bidder who scored a hundred-dollar rug for thirty bucks," he says.

"I always admire your generosity." She smiles. "But it was a *three-hundred-dollar rug.*"

"Three hundred," he mouths, looking back at me with widened eyes.

I can't suppress a smile. For all the romance scenes I write, this is what real love actually looks like.

Tala cozies up to Heath, the rug apparently forgotten. "Anyway, I actually did call to talk to you about something."

With our casual chat, I nearly forgot her double attempt to

get a hold of me, and my stomach tightens at the reminder. "What's up?"

She fidgets with something clasped in her fingers and doesn't look at the camera. Shoot. That's not a good sign. "Heath and I were hoping you'd come grab the boxes of Grandma and Grandpa's books. With all Lucas's baby stuff, we're overrun, and the extra closet space would be amazing."

At the mere thought of returning to Sunset Harbor, my heart rate doubles. It isn't that I don't love it there. I do. I miss it every single day, but I can't go back. Not now. "Can we store them at Mom and Stan's until they get back from Europe in August?"

Tala shakes her head. "With Walker staying there, I'm not sure he'll appreciate six large boxes taking up the place. Especially since he probably brought all of his golf equipment."

That's right, my older brother's back on Sunset Harbor for the time being. If only he weren't still healing from back surgery, I'd attempt to bribe him to bring me the boxes. But I assume carrying anything heavy is currently out of the question for him, so that's not going to work. Besides, we don't have a super great relationship, so I'd feel more comfortable asking Heath. My gaze shifts to Heath on the screen, and I debate if I can make the request of him. The way my gut twists is a pretty clear indicator I shouldn't. With loading and unloading and the drive here and home again, it would take up a whole day. With limited free time, a new baby, and two other kids, Tala needs him right now. "Can you mail them? I'll pay for it."

"Besides that getting them to the post office will be a huge pain, they'll cost an arm and a leg to ship." She leans toward the screen. "It'll be easiest if you come get them."

Is it bad that in my panicked mind, an arm and a leg seem a reasonable trade-off? "I know. But I ..."

I can't say what I want with Heath listening. It isn't that I don't trust Heath, I do ... for the most part. It's just that for one reason or another, I've postponed telling him (along with the rest of my family, sans Tala) about my being an author. Yes, he knows bits and pieces of the truth, but only as much as is required to make Tala feel like she's not outright lying to her husband—which is basically that I write books for fun. And it's absolutely true. I do. I love writing. But Heath views me as a hobby writer. Someone who will eventually, in the far and distant future, submit one of my silly romance stories for publishing.

The truth is, I'm actually already published. I have been for almost nine years, having written my first book as a seventeen-year-old senior in high school and self-publishing it the summer after I graduated. But I'm not just any author. I'm the recent social media sensation, now *New York Times Bestselling Author*—Sunny Palmer.

SUNNY PALMER!!

As in a combination of Tristan's previous nickname for me—Capri SUN—and *his* last name! I foolishly chose that pen name when I was a young, naive debut author seeking poetic justice for unrequited love. Go ahead, roll your eyes and scoff. I've cursed my stupid choice repeatedly since Sunny Palmer became a household name for romance readers.

In my defense, when I first published, I honestly didn't think anyone would ever read my book (or any other books I'd write). I put the first one out there for me. To prove to myself I could, and, probably equally so, to satisfy my best friend Jane's constant harassment to do something with my manuscript. It surprisingly did okay for an unknown debut author. Nothing amazing, but I gained a steady flow of readers. Then, with each subsequent book release, the traction continued until I was making enough money to scale back on the free-lance editing I did to pay the bills and write full-time. And I was perfectly content with that.

So, it was catastrophically unfortunate that at the end of last summer my very first book randomly went viral and overnight the trickle of a following I'd managed to build throughout the years, multiplied exponentially. That number has continued to grow to ridiculously unforeseen proportions.

And as anxiety inducing as that is, it's not even all of it. That same book, *Secret Crush*, is *my* story. Or, more accurately, my fictional *choose-my-own-better-ending-with-Tristan* story. Down to the freaking boat ride at sunset!

The fact that no one on Sunset Harbor has made the connection yet is in part thanks to Maven Chase, my literary agent/manager/women of all business who specializes in helping authors with pen names remain anonymous, and in part a testament to how utterly out of my league Tristan Palmer was. And still is. Even with my main characters' minor name adjustments—Tristan and Capri to Trenton and Cali (yes, the idea for my name change was courtesy of Bridget), it won't be long until someone connects the very apparent dots. Once that happens, my life is going to turn into a dumpster fire. I'll never be able to live down the embarrassment. Ever. And to think of Tristan getting dragged into any of it because of my mistake makes me physically ill.

So there it is. My big, awful, mortifying secret. The reason that going home with the Sunny Palmer madness still going strong is completely out of the question and why I enacted the Sunset Harbor Avoidance Protocol (which I've strictly adhered to for the past six months). Especially now that Tristan is back on the island to run his family's senior living center, Seaside Oasis. The very same center where Heath works as the in-house physical therapist and where Grandma now lives. See the complications?

So, all things considered, as bad as I feel about not being upfront with my family regarding my writing career, I can't help but think it was solid intuition that prevented me from sharing. The fewer people that know, the better. Which means, for the foreseeable future, that privileged group consists of three people: Tala, Jane, and Maven Chase—two who've taken an oath of absolute secrecy and the other who's signed a legally binding non-disclosure agreement.

"I don't think I can get there right now," I finally say. "I've got a lot going on."

As if my thoughts are transparent to her, Tala's return look is a perfect response—*no one is going to find out, Capri.*

She might be correct, but there's a slight chance she's not, and that's enough for me to keep my distance until I can figure out a good way to proceed. Plus, with the risk of running into Tristan, it's simply not worth it.

Heath shrugs. "If it's easier, we can donate the books to the next charity auction."

"No!" I hardly register his playful grin as my mind shifts through some of the books packed away in those boxes—absolute classics like hardcover copies of *The Count of Monte Cristo* and *Les Misérables*. There's even a third edition *Jane Eyre* (which had been Grandpa's favorite book when he was alive) along with every one of Nicholas Sparks and Jojo Moyes' books. It was Grandpa who taught me to love reading the classics and Grandma who introduced me to the glory of romance novels. For the sake of their book collection, I can put on my big girl pants. "I'll find a time to come get them. Soon. I promise."

"How soon?" Tala's gaze locks on me, and I'm well aware she's using her uncanny human lie detecting skills to verify my honesty.

"This Thursday is when I'm finished with my current project." Code for I'm sending my manuscript to the editor and I'll have over a week off until I get the developmental edits back. I pause, hardly able to believe what I'm about to agree to. "I'll head that way Friday morning."

Tala stares at me, taking in every last detail of my expression through the camera. "If you don't come, I may just let Heath donate the whole collection."

I doubt she means it, but with my *worst aunt ever* status already working against me, I hate to tempt fate. "I'm coming."

After a moment, I receive a nod of acceptance from Tala, and she smiles. "You can stay with us for the weekend. The kids will be thrilled to get some extra auntie time."

I don't break the news that I won't be staying the night. Not yet. I'll be in and out before anyone outside of my family and Jane knows I'm there. A quick day trip—even a half-day if I can manage it. My conscience pings slightly, but what other choice do I have? Literally none.

I assuage my guilt by promising myself I'll make it up to all of them somehow. Maybe a day at Disney World is in order. Or I could sponsor a family cruise. Wow. I am desperate. But it really is for the best if my visit to Sunset Harbor is as brief as possible. Tala will understand once I tell her. She always does. "I can't wait to see all of you!"

CHAPTER 2

AS I MAKE my way along the sidewalk, the wicked combination of humidity and heat has me wishing I'd called Tala for a golf-cart ride from the ferry station. It's one of my favorite things about Sunset Harbor—no cars—though it isn't always convenient and it definitely takes longer to get where you need to go. Though I suppose that's the exact reason I walked. I'm a master of procrastinating the hard conversations, and I'm all too aware of the conversation that awaits me when I get to Tala's.

I turn onto the street I grew up on, and in an attempt to delay a little longer, and possibly to wrangle in my rising emotions of being here again, I pull out my phone to text Jane.

CAPRI

> I know you're busy, but I had to let you know that I'm officially back on Sunset Harbor! And I'm only freaking out a little bit.

> Okay. I'm freaking out a lot.

It's only been six months since I last visited, but it feels so much longer. Probably because even when I moved off the island several years ago, I've made frequent visits. Like, exceptionally frequent. So I've felt the void intensely.

JANE

> Yay!

I mean, yay you're here. I'm sorry you're freaking out though.

But everything will be fine.

I'll drop by after I'm done helping with the flowers for the wedding tonight so don't you dare leave before I see you.

CAPRI

I can't wait to see you!

JANE

Same!

I tuck the phone in my bag and pause a moment on the front lawn to take in the sight of Grandma's house, letting it fill every homesick crevice inside me. I'm not sure how long it'll be until I venture this way again. Our family lived in a few different places in the years before Mom, Tala, Walker, and I moved in with Grandma, but nowhere feels as much like home as this two-story, aqua blue house with its white trim and wrap-around porch. Naples, Florida, where I live now, is a close second, considering that's where we lived before Dad died. Since I can't be here, it seemed like the next best option. A way to stay close to his memory. Though, with how often we visited Sunset Harbor, Grandma's house is equally full of memories of Dad. As well as Grandpa.

Except now that Grandma's chosen to move into the Seaside Oasis Senior Living Center, it isn't her house anymore. It's Tala and Heath's. Not that I'm not thrilled for them. I am. But even positive change sucks sometimes.

Without permission, my gaze slides to the Palmers' house next door. Their previous house, anyway. Another change. Except with the way my limbs start to tingle at the sight of it, I'm slightly relieved Tristan's parents moved across the street from Seaside Oasis the year after Beau and I graduated. The fact that I'm not going to run into any of the Palmers is a huge factor in my willingness to come today. The nice older couple they have renting out the place know less about me than I do about them, and basically all I know is they are mainlanders soaking up their retirement days here on Sunset Harbor.

"Auntie Capri!" Serenity darts out the front door, and when she gets to me, I wrap her in a hug. At nine, she's getting too big to scoop up anymore, but I plant a kiss on the top of her head to make up for it.

"How's my favorite girl on this planet?"

She beams up at me, and I'm struck again at how dominant Tala's and my genes are (or Mom's genes, though her hair is now streaked with silver)—the dark hair, smear of freckles, and dark brown eyes. "I'm excited you're here!"

"Not as excited as I am to be here."

She takes my hand and pulls me toward the open front door. "You have to see the house! And my room! Mom painted my walls pink, and Dad is going to build a window seat for me when he can find the time."

"Did you know that used to be my room?"

She nods her head, her eyes bright. "That's why I picked it."

Her excitement at wanting my old room heals a part of me that I didn't know needed healing.

We're up the porch steps when Tala opens the door with Lucas in arm. "You're here!" Tala wraps me in a hug, sandwiching Lucas between us.

"I am! And hey, *you*," I say to Lucas, nabbing him from my sister when she releases her hold on me. I nuzzle him, and he gives a little smile. "Oh! You have smiles!"

"Aren't they adorable?" Tala's attention remains on Lucas, a smitten look on her face, before she glances back to me. "Why didn't you call when you got off the ferry? We were planning to give you a ride."

"I didn't want to bother you. Besides, it's a quick walk."

"It isn't a bother at all. Even a quick walk feels a lot longer in this heat, especially with luggage." Tala searches the porch behind me, then her focused eyes settle back on me. "Where's your luggage?"

I shift my body to reveal my laptop bag, as though that will help my case.

She stares at me, her arms crossing in front of her chest. "That's all you brought?"

Here it comes. The moment I fretted over for the whole two-hour trip. "I'm sorry. With prepping for the upcoming book release—" I silence mid-poor-excuse. The reasoning sounded a lot more convincing when I was alone, talking the situation through on my walk here. But now that I'm actually with Tala, I'm aware there's no way she's going to buy any of my bogus reasons for not staying.

You see, Tala is a hybrid sibling. Being ten years older, she sometimes gets confused about what role she's supposed to occupy—cool big sister or second mom. Most of the time I don't mind the pendulum back and forth, but in this moment, the utter disappointment on her face is excruciating to endure. I'm already feeling bad enough for taking the coward's way out, but her added *mom-guilt* sits heavily on me.

"You aren't staying?" She asks it in a way that makes me want to curl up with my shame right here on the front porch.

"What about the talent show?" Serenity glances from me to her mom. "You said Auntie Capri will be there."

My icicle heart nearly shatters at the announcement. "There's a talent show?"

"Tomorrow." My sister pauses like she's considering something. "I was going to tell you, but we wanted it to be a surprise."

How can I possibly miss Serenity's talent show performance? I can't. Not when I'm already here. And not unless I want to tattoo "worst aunt ever" across my forehead to make it official. I glance at my sister, the wheels in my mind turning. Tala and I wear the same size of clothes, so I can definitely borrow a pair of pajamas and an outfit for tomorrow, and I'm confident she has an extra toothbrush I can have. It's only one night. I'll sneak into the back of wherever it's being held to watch, and I can go home right after ...

The way Tala is chewing her bottom lip gives me pause. "Where's this talent show at?" I ask.

"Dad's work," Serenity says before her mom can stop her. "They've been doing lots of fun things this summer."

My gaze locks with Tala's guilt-ridden one. "The talent show is at the retirement center? Interesting." My words are dripping with sarcasm. It's a good thing I didn't speak my pajama borrowing plan aloud. "I can't think why you didn't tell me about it."

"Because I want you to come." She tilts her head to the side in that motherly way of hers. "We all do."

"Auntie Capri!" Jack comes sprinting out the door in perfect seven-year-old fashion and throws his arms around my waist. "Want to practice my magic tricks with me for the talent show? I have a wand I stuff with scarves—"

"She's not coming," Serenity blurts, clearly not thrilled with me in the slightest.

"What?" Jack immediately morphs into a small puppy with large brown eyes that urge me to give him whatever he wants. "You have to come."

No. What I have to do is resist the temptation to give into my darling, missing-front-tooth nephew. I hand Lucas back to Tala and squat down so I'm eye level with Jack. "I have to get back tonight, but I was thinking you and your family can come visit me soon. We'll go to the pool and the beach by my house— the one with all of the shells. And we'll go bowling ..." He narrows his eyes like he's contemplating my offer, so I know I'm close. "... and hit up the arcade."

His eyes go wide with excitement. "When can we go?"

Nice. That was easier than I thought. Still bent over with hands propped on my knees, I turn my head to look at Serenity, who's watching me with vague interest. "I was thinking that we can grab an ice cream at that shop I brought you to last time—you know, the one that had that monstrous sundae with all the whipped cream and sprinkles and the upside-down waffle cone coming out of the top. What was that thing called again?"

A smile spreads across her face. "The Unicorn Sprinkle Bomb."

"That's it. Want another Unicorn Sprinkle Bomb?"

She nods her head in an excited burst of motion.

Aha! Victory is mine! "Great! I'll talk with your mom and see when we can make it happen." Straightening again, I risk a glance at Tala.

She's giving a subtle shake of her head, but her expression is noticeably softer. "Auntie Capri and I will definitely be *talking* about this."

I swallow, feeling like the principal called home to report I was caught cheating during a test, but instead of being scolded directly, I have to wait for an adequate consequence to be decided. Not that I know this from experience, but I've thought through what it'd be like to be *that kid* on several occasions thanks to my vivid imagination.

"In fact, why don't you two go inside and practice your talents?" Tala says to Serenity and Jack. "That way you can perform them for Capri before she leaves *tonight*."

Jack darts back in the house without a backwards glance, but Serenity pauses on the threshold, glancing between us with a suspicious expression.

"Go on," Tala says. "And shut the door so the cold air stays in."

With one last look at me, Serenity huffs and shuts the door behind her.

Tala shakes her head. "That one's getting too perceptive for her own good."

Warning noted. "So ..." I know the lecture is coming and there's no point in postponing it any longer. "Let's have it."

Tala's shoulders drop like she hates having to be the all-knowing, wiser sister. "I get why you don't want to stay. I honestly do. But you can't avoid Sunset Harbor forever. This is your home. Your family's here."

I step toward her armful of cuteness and mindlessly rub Lucas's tiny fingers and toes one by one to evade Tala's stare. "I'm not going to avoid it forever. Only until I can develop a plan for how to navigate everything." A plan that involves no one discovering the truth while simultaneously making it feel like I'm not hiding some huge, opinion-altering-life-changing-secret from everyone.

Okay, with those parameters, maybe forever isn't unrealistic. I've put a lot of brain power into how I can make any of this right, and I've come up with nada. Zero. Zilch. Except to keep clear of Sunset Harbor for the foreseeable future in combination with maintaining an unwavering death-grip on the fact that I'm Sunny Palmer.

"You could start telling people. Begin with our family."

My gaze shoots to hers. "You're kidding, right?" I'm shaking my head as though my fate rests on my ability to convey how against the idea I am. "Do you think Mom or Grandma can keep that secret? Or Heath?" Walker, my older brother, might be the exception because he won't care much. "If the truth gets out, I'll never be able to come home. People will talk. And Tristan will get dragged into the mess ..." A wisp of a breath escapes me. "No one can know."

"Capri, it was a long time ago." Tala's gaze flicks to the Palmers' old house next door, but I resist following it. "At this point, I think Tristan would find the whole thing ... endearing."

"Endearing?" I stare at her. "Which part? That his romance-

35

obsessed, former neighbor wrote a fictional love story about the two of us, or that I borrowed his last name for my pen name?"

She tucks her lips between her teeth like she's fighting a smile. "Well, when you say it like that."

"Trust me. There's no way to say it that makes it sound remotely okay."

Tala quirks her head thoughtfully. "And you really can't change pen names?"

It wasn't too long ago that I had this exact conversation with Maven Chase, my agent, though I was the one asking the question. "I can. Technically. But if I republish my older books under a new name, it'll just draw more attention. The same thing will happen if I announce that I'll be going by a different name moving forward or stop writing under that pen name altogether. Besides, there's no way to change it on the books already in circulation." Millions of them! I lean back my head and moan. "It's hopeless."

Tala touches my arm, pulling my focus back to her. "It's not. We'll figure something out."

I give a grimaced smile, not willing to break her spirits further by voicing my doubt. "I hope so."

"Oh, I know it. Because I refuse to let this"—she points to my laptop bag as though it embodies my decision not to stay the weekend—"be our new normal."

"That reminds me, I have something for you." My intended peace offering isn't complete yet, and I have high hopes this next gesture will get me off the hook completely. At least for the time being. I unzip my bag and pull out a plastic-comb-bound manuscript of the book I sent to my editor this morning.

She glances at it and back at me. "You think handing me that is going to make me overlook this little stunt of yours?"

"That's the idea."

Tala looks at my offering again, unable to hold back her

smile. Then she snatches it from my hands. "Fine. You're forgiven."

See? She's a saint. "Just don't read it until I'm gone."

"Deal. Now let's get inside. Grandma and Heath should be here soon, and I still need to get lunch ready."

WITH SERENITY and Jack off practicing their talents and Tala putting Lucas down for a nap, I drift through the downstairs rooms. The whole house looks amazing. And different. I love seeing Tala and Heath make this place their own, but I also miss the way it was. The old china cabinet with knickknacks from all of Grandma and Grandpa's travels. The mismatched set of floral couches in the front room where Jane and I spent countless afternoons together, talking and laughing and watching for signs of Tristan out the window. The infamous collage of photos in the upstairs hallway with its mortifying collection of blackmail-worthy pictures of me and my siblings. Grandma's house has always been one of the most constant things in my life. But in a matter of six months, it looks like a different place entirely.

I begin perusing the newly added floor-to-ceiling bookshelf that now occupies the entire interior wall of the front room. Tala somehow managed the DIY project being seven months pregnant. Not that I'm surprised. Tala has an eye for decorating and an uncanny amount of energy for a busy mom with three kids. Certainly more energy than I have.

The shelves are colorful and interspersed with decorations, not at all like my overfilled bookcases that hold a mix of classics and a broad selection of different genres. Tala strictly reads romance, and I have to admit the aesthetic is a lot more pleasing than mine. Not that I'd trade any of my eclectic collection for aesthetics' sake, but I will gladly admire a pretty space when I encounter it. I stop at the shelf Tala has dedicated to my published books and run my finger along the spines. She has all sixteen of them, including multiple copies of several. And it makes my heart do a happy dance.

The front door opens, and I literally jump away from the shelf faster than a kid sneaking popsicles from the freezer. "Grandma!"

When she catches sight of me, Grandma throws out her arms wide. "Capri!"

I hurry to her and return her embrace as if it's been years since I've seen her and not months.

"Look at you!" Grandma pulls back and rests a hand on my cheek. "You get more beautiful every time I see you."

I clutch her fingers in mine. "Thanks, Grandma."

Heath steps in behind her and tosses a teasing smirk in our direction. "Or maybe your eyesight's getting worse, Deedee."

"Hello to you too." I whack him with the back of my hand, which only makes him laugh. "Though I'm glad to see you're leaning into the whole dad joke thing. It fits you. You know, with all that gray hair you're sporting now." I flick at his perfectly styled hair, and he bats my hand away.

"You two!" Grandma looks between us. "You're worse than siblings."

"And here I thought we were siblings," Heath says, wrapping an arm around my shoulder. "Besides, Capri knows I love her."

Grandma looks at him expectantly. "And ... ?"

I glance up at him with a victorious smile, waiting patiently for the forced compliment like I'm seven and not twenty-seven.

Heath shakes his head and flicks his eyes upward. "And she's beautiful," he mumbles like he's ten and not forty.

Grandma's expectant gaze turns to me. "Do you have anything to say to Heath, Capri?"

"I really do enjoy his dad jokes?" It's a question because I'm not sure if that's the apology she's looking for.

She contemplates my sincerity for a minute and then nods, apparently satisfied. "There. That wasn't so hard." This time, Heath gets Grandma's cheek pat. "Since Capri's only here for the day, I expect you two to be nice to each other."

Surprised she's aware I'm not staying, I glance at Heath to see if he's heard the news as well. He doesn't so much as blink at her mention of it. Tala must have texted them, which I feel kind of bad about but I'm also grateful for.

"We want her to come back more often," Grandma says, a conspiratorial grin lifting her lips upward. "Especially now that *Tristan Palmer* is back on the island."

With how hot my cheeks feel, my face must resemble a beet. My gaze flits to Heath, who's observing the exchange with way too much interest. "Please don't get any ideas, Grandma."

"And why shouldn't I? I'm pretty sure he's also single, and I know you used to have a little crush on him."

My mouth hangs open. "I did not." It was an epically huge crush. I'll admit to nothing less.

Grandma drops her chin. "I suppose you've forgotten how you and Jane Hayes used to sit in my front room for hours, watching out the window for him. Then you'd giggle like little schoolgirls when you'd finally get a glimpse."

My whole body is now uncomfortably warm, and my décolletage is definitely starting to splotch. "That should never be repeated," I say, my gaze sliding to Heath. "By anyone."

Heath squeezes his lips together and runs his fingers across them as though he's zipping them shut.

Grandma's focus remains on me. "I'm just saying, now that he's single, this might be your chance to snatch him up before someone else can. He's a mighty fine catch, that one."

I laugh at the absurdity. Not that he's not a mighty fine catch, because that's an undeniable fact, but that I'd ever be able to *snatch him up*. "I think your book club is reading too many romances," I say. Jane runs it up at the retirement center, so I know exactly what sort of books are being read. "Maybe you should suggest a biography next ... or a mystery book."

She waves a dismissive hand. "We're too old to read anything but what we love. Though I did propose *The Haunted Cowboy and Me*, but Jane vetoed it. Your Jane squirms at a little spice. But it's okay because we settled on a re-read of *Secret Crush* by Sunny Palmer in preparation for her upcoming release."

That's it. I've officially lost the battle on regulating my body temperature. If it weren't so blasted hot in Florida, I'd make turtlenecks a wardrobe staple to hide my splotching skin. Now that's an idea. Maybe I should move somewhere cold and far, far away from here. I'd hate it, but it might be my best option for all sorts of reasons.

"Have you not read it yet?" Grandma asks, apparently mistaking my blank stare and slow rhythmic blinking pattern for ignorance. "It's definitely not her best writing—a little bit on the juvenile side compared to her more recent stuff—but the story is absolutely divine. And that Trenton. Boy, oh boy! If that man weren't fictional ..."

I'm too overwhelmed to process any part of what she just said, including her unintended criticism or her mention about my Tristan-inspired character.

"Thanks for not finishing your comment, Deedee." Heath grins, then gestures behind him at the bookshelf. "And Tala has all of Sunny Palmer's books. She's weirdly protective of them, but I'm sure she'd let you borrow the *Crush* ... whatever one Deedee said."

"No, I've read it," I say, rallying myself.

"You have?" Grandma asks, clearly wanting me to share my opinion.

"Yeah. It's decent."

Grandma tsks. "Don't let the ladies at Seaside Oasis hear you say that. We've got some diehard Sunny Palmer fans over there."

"Including Tala." Heath's smile makes it apparent he actually adores this about his wife. "Her obsession is borderline unhealthy."

"It really is crazy Sunny Palmer's gotten so big," I say, attempting to play it cool. And because I'm right there with him on not understanding the appeal. Don't get me wrong, I love my stories, but it shocks me that others love them too. Especially as much as they seem to. "Is Walker coming tonight?" I turn to Heath, feeling the need for a subject change.

"He's golfing," Heath says. "But last I heard, he might stop by."

Why am I not surprised my brother will choose golf over his family? I get that as a professional, it's his career, but I'm pretty sure he can take off one afternoon. Though with Jane here, maybe it's best if he doesn't come. The two of them have already run into each other several times in the week he's been back on Sunset Harbor, and I'm not sure how I feel about it. He's an experienced flirt, and I'd hate for Jane to get the wrong idea about his intentions. Especially when he'll be off the island with the first opportunity that presents itself. He's never been a fan of Sunset Harbor.

Grandma hums softly. "If only your mom and Stan were here, we'd finally have the whole family together again." Her gaze locks on me. "But I'm overjoyed you've come home, my dear." She rubs my arm with a meaningful look, but before I can feel too bad about my prolonged absence from the island, she steps past me. "Now, where are my great-grandbabies?"

Heath follows Grandma into the kitchen and opens the back door. "Grandmama's here," he calls.

"Shhh." Tala descends the stairs, pinning Heath with a look. "I just got Lucas to sleep."

"Sorry," he whispers in time for Jack and Serenity to come charging through the door toward Grandma's open arms like stampeding, shrieking bulls.

When a wail echoes from upstairs, Tala points at Heath. "Congratulations, you're on baby duty."

"Oh, I'll do it," Grandma says, hugging Serenity and Jack to her and kissing them atop their heads. "Do either of you want to help me get your brother back to sleep?"

Jack shakes his head and darts away, but Serenity takes hold of Grandma's hand, and the two of them make their way upstairs. My gaze lingers on Grandma, noticing her careful, slow movements.

"He's still in our room," Tala calls, pulling my attention back to her. She smiles up at her husband. "You're lucky you brought reinforcements. Don't expect to get off so easy next time."

His gaze shifts to me, his hands lifting at his sides. "Do you see this welcome? No, *I'm so happy you're home, honey. Thanks for bringing Grandma. How was your day?*"

Tala wraps her arms around Heath and kisses him in a way that has me diverting my eyes.

"Much better." Heath is now grinning ear to ear.

"That's enough, you two," I say, fighting my own smile.

Heath chuckles. "Says the girl who hopes to be a romance author someday."

"And yet somehow that doesn't translate into me watching my sister and brother-in-law make out."

I don't like the twinkle that enters Heath's eyes. "If you think that was us making out ..." He grabs Tala's smiling face between his hands, but before he can prove his point, I take hold of his arm.

"Okay, okay," I say, pulling him away from my sister. "You and Tala can do that *after* I leave tonight. Right now, I need help with my boxes."

CHAPTER 3

WITH A LARGE BOX IN ARM, Heath turns sideways to fit out the back door. I follow him, boosting my own box upward with my knee. It's a good thing I emptied half the contents of this one to another box, because I'm even struggling with my half-load.

"Maybe we should make a few trips," Heath says over his shoulder. "I'd hate to sink the boat."

He might be kidding, but he has a point. Springing a hole in Grandpa's sturdy old fishing boat isn't likely, but under the weight of several boxes of books, it's also not out of the realm of possibilities. To think of losing any of my grandparents' treasured collection is spine-chilling, but to lose the entirety of it to a sinking vessel would be a travesty of greatest proportions. Especially when this book collection is one of the main things I have to remember Grandpa by.

"That's not a terrible idea," I call after him, shaking the thought away. "Do you have time though?"

"Yep. I now only work half-days on Fridays, so I'm off the rest of the day." Heath starts onto the rickety old dock that is a perfect match for the rickety old boat tied to it, his quickened pace evidence of the load he's eager to be rid of.

Unlike Heath, I can't walk any faster. My box is slipping from my grasp again, and I pause, trying to get a better hold of it. When I can't find a grip that feels comfortable, I do an awkward chair-sit squat, resting the box on my knees so I can wrap my arms around it more fully. The sides of the box protest, but eventually they give enough that I manage to clasp my hands together in the front. I try to straighten, but the distribution is off and the box begins to slide downward again. You have to be kidding me! I'm more of an at-home yoga person than a gym-rat, but this half-full box has me rethinking my priorities.

"Need some help?"

The deep, familiar voice has my head whipping to the side. My hair flies into my face just as a twinge of pain shoots from my shoulder blade to the base of my neck. The upper left of my back tightens into a ball—a hard, unyielding, horribly crampy ball.

A small whimper escapes my lips, and purely out of instinct, I release my hold on the box with one hand in an attempt to relieve the awful pain. It takes me a fraction of a second to realize my mistake, but the weight of the load of books is already shifting forward. Before it crashes to the ground, Tristan is at my side, scooping the box up into one arm and taking me by the elbow with the other.

"Got it?" he asks. Despite the platonic assistance he's rendering, my legs turn to Jell-O at his touch. And with the heat racing through from where his fingers are making contact with my skin, I'll soon be a melted pool of artificial color and sugar. *Pull yourself together, Capri.*

When I'm firmly standing on my own two feet again, I glance up and meet his gaze. I'm pretty sure I'd meant to express my gratitude, but the depths of those sea-green eyes instantly mesmerize me, exactly like they've always done. Especially when they go wide with excitement.

"Capri Sun?" With the use of his nickname for me, my ability for rational thought vanishes altogether. He's called me that since middle school when one of our classmates couldn't, for the life of him, remember my name. Tristan, in an attempt to help, said: "Think of a Capri Sun—the drink. But instead of cuh-pree it's ca-pree." The nickname stuck. And I love it. Or, more like, I love that Tristan Palmer has a nickname for me. Period. End of story. He could call me *Juice Girl*, and as long as he says it with that subtle teasing tone and wears that hint of a smile he's currently sporting, I'll happily answer to it.

Or I would have.

Not anymore.

Obviously.

I'm a full-fledged adult now and refuse to get weirdly sentimental about him having a nickname for me.

But why does he have to be so darn handsome? I'm talking about public hazard levels of handsome. Like, put this guy on a street corner with his sandy blond hair and stubbled jawline, and distracted drivers will be wreaking all sorts of havoc on the road.

"I didn't realize you were going to be here," he says.

My tongue is cemented to the bottom of my mouth, so instead of speaking, I nod my head as if it's an appropriate response to anything he said.

"Tristan!" Heath walks toward us, his arms empty but a gigantic, *knowing* grin on his face. "Fancy meeting you here."

"I saw Capri out the window—I mean, I thought she was Tala—so I came to see if she needed a hand." He gives a slight lift of the box now in his arms as if it's evidence of his story.

Out the window? My gaze shifts to the Palmers' old house where Tristan had apparently just come from. Why was he inside? Does he manage the property for his parents in addition to running the retirement center?

Obviously taking notice of how my brain is working on overdrive, Heath points at the Palmers' house, his eyes trained on me. "Now that he's back on the island, Tristan moved into his family's old house. Him and Beau, actually. They're roommates."

My sneaky, back-stabbing, secret-keeping sister! And Heath! Oh, they are in so much trouble. I bet neither of them even cared about storing my boxes of books longer. They just needed an excuse to get me here so I'd run into Tristan—their freaking next-door neighbor!

"Isn't that great?" Heath asks, and only then do I realize I haven't responded.

I give another small nod, my mouth literally hanging open as though I'm a fish gasping for air. *Close your mouth, Capri.* Like I'm an animatronic bass, my mouth shuts mechanically, but my eyes seem to be doing some weird bulging thing while I stare at Heath. Why am I suddenly so aware of my whole self?

Yes, this bomb-shell encounter with Tristan was unexpected, but I'm no longer that awkward, love-struck teenager. I'm a grown woman. A woman who communicates with men regularly and has been in several healthy relationships. Okay, several is a bit of an exaggeration, but I've definitely been in a few.

But then again, this isn't an encounter with any old secret crush. This is the man whose last name I've stolen and who has been the love inspiration for a book that involves a fictional relationship between us. A book that now has its own collection of fan-art and a number of overly-used hashtags: #MyOwnSecret-Crush #CaliandTrentonforlife #SunsetProposalorBust. I think I might throw up.

"What brings you to Sunset Harbor?" Tristan asks, pulling my attention to him again.

I keep my eyes trained on his so I don't risk ogling him like every particle of the instinctual portion of my brain wants to do. "I'm only here for a few hours." I did it. I spoke. And I didn't even sound like an idiot. Just a mature adult speaking to another mature adult. I can totally do this. With a slight confidence boost, I gesture to the box in his arms. "I came to get some books Tala and Heath have been storing for me."

"Serenity and Jack couldn't talk you into staying for the talent show tomorrow?" Tristan asks, and my heart warms that he knows my niece and nephew's names. Until I remember that we are on Sunset Harbor—population: everyone knows every-one. "It's set to be the event of the season," he says, a teasing glint in his eyes.

"I bet it is." I try not to hear what I shouldn't want to hear but also really want to hear—that he'd like it if I stayed for it. "Unfortunately, I've got a bunch of work, so I've got to get back."

Heath drapes an arm around my shoulder. "Capri owns a *very* successful freelance editing company. It keeps her insanely busy."

I drop my gaze. I don't enjoy being the center of attention ever, but even less so when it involves talking about my work. Yes, technically, in addition to being a writer, I own a freelance editing company with a handful of editors who work for me, but I've personally only kept one client so I can honestly say that I edit books when people ask me what I do. At this point, the company's a well-running machine that has required very little marketing since it got out that Sunny Palmer uses our editing services (because I do—Susan, one of our editors is irreplaceable to me). I'm proud to say the company's done well, but the success Heath is referring to—my recent home-owner-status, leather-interior-Jeep-Wrangler-driving success—has more to do with publishing my own books, including the colossal jump in book sales this past year.

"That's what I've heard." Tristan's comment pulls my atten-tion upward again. There's a teasing glint in his eyes, and I'm hoping it's not because I've been the subject of other conversa-tions involving Heath or my sister. Or my grandma. But I'm sure it is. Those traitors!

"Have you heard that she's also working on becoming a published author?" Heath continues.

I can sense the skin-splotching coming on strong, and a wave of panic rushes through me. "It's nothing." My throat is unusu-ally dry as I force the words out. "Just something I do for fun."

"It's not nothing," Heath counters. "Capri's written several stories that Tala says are actually decent."

Oh heavens! Why have I never thought to clarify to Heath that I don't want people knowing about my *so-called-hobby*? "She's biased. She's my sister."

Tristan's brow lifts. "Regardless, that's impressive. What kind of stories do you write?"

And here it is. My reddened décolletage is on full display. I put a palm to my chest in hopes of covering it partially. "Umm … all sorts."

"She writes romance," Heath says matter-of-factly, and I want to kick him in the shin. And then kick him again twice in the other shin. Romance comes with a certain stigma attached to it, especially for two guys that likely don't understand the appeal. "Tala wouldn't read them if they were anything else."

"Is that so?" Tristan asks, his amused gaze sliding to me.

I shrug, like my life isn't flashing before my eyes. "I hear there's a big market for it." As though that's my reason for writing romance and not because I'm downright obsessed. Tristan's intent gaze makes me shift, and I take hold of the collar of my tank top and start lifting it up and down to allow for some airflow. Why is it so blasted hot?

"But back to my original point." Heath looks at me. "One would think, being your own boss, you could take a weekend off. You know, stay a couple of days. See what you've been missing on the island." His gaze slides from me to Tristan. If discretion were Heath's lifeline, he'd be a goner.

I'm shaking my head before I can think of my next excuse. "I also have a date tomorrow," I blurt, glad I've already made plans with myself to celebrate turning in my recent manuscript to the editor. Actually, my whole day is booked—food deliveries from a few of my favorite restaurants, a 90s romcom movie marathon, and an hour-long reading session in a skin-reddening bubble bath. It's a tradition. And I'd be loath to break with tradition, especially since coming to Sunset Harbor has delayed the celebration an entire day.

"With who?" Heath asks, his eyes narrowing. He's onto me.

"It's none of your business," I say playfully, hoping he'll let it go. Before he can press me further, I point to the box, my gaze settling on Tristan's muscular arms without my consent. "Sorry, that's probably getting heavy."

"I'm okay. But is there somewhere you want me to put it?" When I pry my eyes from Tristan's arms, his slight smile sends my attention back to Heath.

"The fishing boat," Heath and I answer in unison.

Tristan glances at the sorry excuse for a boat and back to us. "How many boxes do you plan to haul over in that thing?"

"Just two or three at a time," I say. "We'll make a couple trips."

Tristan's gaze returns to the boat again, his expression lined with concern. "Why don't we take my boat? That way we can do it all in one trip and eliminate the risk of capsizing."

The repeated image of the third edition *Jane Eyre* slowly descending into the watery depths fills my mind's eye, but even that isn't motivation enough for me to accept Tristan's offer. Because I know one thing about myself that makes this risk-averse girl eager to hop in that metal dingy and paddle a near-sinking boat loaded with beloved books across the bay: the moment I saw Tristan again, I instantly realized that my secret crush is still alive and well. No, not only well. It's flourishing by the second. So, all things considered, even a short ride with him over to the mainland is dangerous territory.

"That's kind of you but—" I begin, but Heath cuts me off mid-sentence.

"That'd be awesome. Thanks, man."

I swallow down my rising panic. "You really don't have to. The fishing boat is sturdier than she looks, and I'm sure you're busy."

"I'm on my lunch break." Tristan glances at his watch, like the box in his arms is full of helium balloons instead of over fifty pounds of books. "I've got some time."

"We owe you." Heath claps his hands and rubs them together as if it's settled. "Our family will appreciate the extra time we'll get with Capri." He sends me a side smile. "Each minute with her is a *rare, precious* gift."

Gag me. I glare at him to indicate I'm not the least bit amused by his overdone praise. How can I love someone so completely and despise him so intensely at the exact same moment?

"Great," Tristan says. "I'll go grab my keys."

"Let me take that." Heath snags the box from Tristan. "I'll put it in your boat and move the other one over. Capri can show you where the other boxes are."

The idea is reasonable, unremarkable even, but with the proud grin Heath is wearing, I know exactly what he's up to. And though I briefly wonder if Grandma's mention of my *little crush* on Tristan is the cause of his sudden enthusiasm, the whole situation—me not being told that Tristan is currently living next door—is too orchestrated to not be pre-conceived.

"I'll wait here while you get the keys," I say to Tristan, hoping to be the bigger person, although Heath will one-hundred percent pay for this later. In fact, after this little stunt, a name-change for the male antagonist in my upcoming release might be in order.

Heath heads to the dock and Tristan toward the house. I avoid watching Tristan like the creeper I want to be until I hear his back door open. Then I peek over at him. He leans inside the house where the keys must be hanging, pauses on the threshold to look at his phone, then starts back in my direction, his thumbs moving across the screen.

Since his attention is elsewhere, I might as well allow myself a much-delayed eye roving session.

And it's official, people: Tristan Palmer only gets better with time! The softness of his boyishly handsome face has sharpened. His sandy blond hair is a shade or two darker than the last time I saw him, styled like a Pinterest Hair God with his matching set of manicured whiskers. It's more than a five-o'clock shadow but less than a week of growth. The perfect length for understated manliness. And I'm basically a certifiable expert on the subject with the countless hours I spend scrolling through men's faces for inspiration pictures. Tristan fits in among the best of them—rightly confusable with a long-lost Hemsworth brother.

He's also thicker now in all the right places, which proves that even though his football days are behind him, he's not let up on the discipline required to maintain a physique like that. Which I respect. Especially with the way that cotton polo shirt with a Seaside Oasis logo clings to his chest and abs, hinting at the glory of the present beneath the wrapping. Before my thoughts can stray too much into what it'd be like to get a glimpse of that present or how willing I am to completely objectify him, Tristan shoves his phone into his pocket and I divert my eyes.

"Sorry, I had to send a quick text." He steps up next to me. "Ready?"

I can't help but wonder if he was quickly touching base with some gorgeous Bridget-esque replacement now that the two of them aren't together anymore. But it's none of my business.

"You're fine." I flick my head toward Tala and Heath's house as if I'm functioning normally and my insides haven't congealed into a nervous blob of energy. "The boxes are inside."

He follows me, an uncomfortable silence between us. When we step through the screen door, hushed voices quiet, and my gaze falls on Tala and Grandma standing at the kitchen sink—conveniently near the window with the best view of the backyard.

"Look who I found outside," I say, aiming my overdone smile

at Tala. There's not even a tiny flick of surprise in her expression or Grandma's. Guilty. And guilty.

Tala smiles. "Hey, Tristan."

Tristan lifts a hand in greeting. "Tala. Mrs. Winn."

"How many times do I have to insist you call me Deedee?" Grandma says.

"He offered to help with the boxes," I say, hoping to make this as quick and painless for Tristan as possible. I don't need Tala or Grandma to start chatting or invite him to stay longer. I'm sure he has lots of other things to do. "They're this way."

I lead him upstairs to the extra bedroom and stop in the doorway to find Tristan looking around the long hallway. His gaze meets mine, and he's wearing an empathetic expression that makes me feel like he can somehow see the state of my heart. "It looks different in here."

A weird surge of emotion takes hold of my chest, constricting it. I take in the freshly painted walls, six-inch white baseboards, the natural wood and gold frames displaying classy artwork, and the woven jute runner on the floor. "Yeah." It's all I can muster.

"If I'm being honest," he whispers, stepping onto the threshold next to me and making my body go rigid with how close he's standing, "I prefer your grandma's collage of pictures. There were some real classics in there."

My eyes go wide, but before I can respond, he steps past me into the room.

"These are the boxes?" he asks.

Since I have no desire to hear what mortifying pictures of me he's referring to, I follow him inside. "Yep." I point to the pile—four bigger ones of varying sizes and the half-box I partially filled from the contents of the one I carried outside.

Tristan lifts the largest of the boxes, and I'm slightly relieved that it actually appears to be a struggle for him this time. "What's in here again? Just books?"

"They're deceptively heavy, right?"

He adjusts his hold on the box, and his veins bulge in a way that makes me want to run my fingers along them. Huh. I've never used that in a book before. Probably because it's a little strange, but it doesn't make the desire any less real. "Extremely."

I step toward him. "I can empty some of the—"

"And let Heath show me up? Not a chance." He throws me a boyish grin that sends my heart pounding like I'm seventeen again, then he carefully maneuvers around me. "But I'm going to head down before I drop this."

"Be careful on the stairs," I say, like an overprotective mother. "Be careful on the stairs?" I repeat under my breath when he's gone. What a dumb thing to say. Of course he's going to be careful on the stairs.

I'm literally shaking from the whole interaction, so after one attempt to pick up the other half-full box, I instead decide I'll let the men do the lifting and head downstairs to grab my keys. I don't need to make a bigger fool of myself in front of Tristan.

My laptop bag is still in the entryway, but when I search the pockets, my keys aren't there. The main compartment is also key free. I glance around, check my own pockets, then head into the kitchen where Tala and Grandma have resumed talking in hushed voices. Surprisingly, I hear them mention Virginia Sawyer's name, so their current conversation must not be about me. "Have either of you seen my keys? They have the seashell keychain."

"No." Tala walks over to where I'm standing, her gaze following mine to the kitchen countertops. "Are they not in your bag?"

I'm pushing aside the sandwich stuff that's set out and checking around the appliances in the kitchen. The first thing I did when coming inside was help Tala get lunch ready. I must have put them down in here, but I don't see them anywhere. I sift through my fragmented memories to decipher where else they might be. I had them after I got out of the Jeep. I'm certain of that. Or am I? A wave of panic rushes over me. How could I not have grabbed them? But suddenly, I can't remember.

If I left them inside the Jeep, the doors wouldn't lock, which means, if some ill-intentioned person hasn't already realized my error, they might soon. A whole scenario plays out in my head instantly: I return to the parking garage to find the Jeep gone. I call the cops to report the theft, but while they're writing up my testimony (where I have to confess to thoughtlessly leaving my keys inside), a voice comes over the radio. The Jeep was found … totaled. My stomach plummets like I'm actually living it. See, that's the problem with my author-mind—it's always eager to create a story. Even when it's overly dramatic and entirely unhelpful.

"Don't panic yet." Tala is obviously aware I'm concocting a worst-case scenario in my head. "I'm sure they're around here somewhere."

Grandma brushes past me. "Let me ask the kids if they've seen them."

Right then the back door opens, and Heath and Tristan step inside, talking about a recent game of some kind. Possibly base-ball? My gaze settles on Tristan before I can stop it. His eyes meet mine and he smiles like he knows I have no control over my gawking self. I quickly glance away and open the silverware drawer as though that's a logical place for my keys to be. The spice cupboard is next. Also a negative.

"Have you seen Capri's keys?" Tala asks Heath while I continue opening random cabinets and drawers. "She can't find them."

"Did you check the drawer in the entryway table? That's where I would've put them if I'd thought they were ours." He pauses. "Though I highly doubt I'd confuse Capri's Jeep fob with our Suburban keys."

Their Suburban is ancient, so Heath has a point about how different our keys look, but hope still rises in my chest. Maybe he didn't take a close look and slid them into the drawer when he brought Grandma earlier. I shut the fridge (yes, I checked in there) and hurry to the front entryway. I pull the drawer open, sifting through the keys inside. The Suburban keys, two sets for the golf cart, and a ring with a few smaller, unfamiliar keys on it.

"Are they there?" Tala asks, coming up behind me and glancing over my shoulder.

I shake my head.

"The kids say they haven't seen them," Grandma calls from the family room. "But I'll keep looking."

My shoulders deflate like a balloon that's sprung a leak. "They have to be in the Jeep. I'll take the fishing boat over—"

Heath steps into the entryway, leaning against the wall. "Maybe Tristan can drive you to the parking garage in his boat." He looks behind him to where Tristan must be waiting. "If you don't mind. It's just that it'd be the fastest option."

I glare at my brother-in-law with all the fury inside me until Tristan appears at his side and I'm forced to shift my expression into something more pleasant.

"I'd be happy to take you," he says.

Instantly, I'm my hyper-aware, overthinking younger self again, and Tristan is offering me another one of his *obligatory invitations*. I don't want a man, particularly not Tristan, to feel obligated to be with me. And there might also be a small part of me that doesn't trust myself to be alone with him. Not because there's any chance of a repeat of The Incident, but because of the level of awkwardness I'm currently exhibiting. That and, after what I've done, it's best to avoid any further interactions with him. Especially when the less sensible parts of me want nothing more than to further our interactions. All signs point to saying no. "Actually, now that I think about it, I could have dropped them on the walk over. I should probably retrace my steps. That way I can also ask if anyone turned in keys on the ferry."

Tristan watches me, as though he's trying to decide what to make of my refusal.

"I can take the ferry." Heath says it so casually I almost believe he isn't a master schemer at work. "That way you can get to your Jeep quicker. Make sure it's still there and someone hasn't driven off with it."

Hitting me where it counts, I see. Well played. "I doubt thirty minutes will make a difference," I say, praying desperately I'm right. Though maybe I shouldn't be offering prayers when I have murder on my mind. Karma is coming for Heath. "But if you would, Heath, can you move the boxes from Tristan's boat back inside for now? I'm not sure how long I'll be gone, and I know Tristan has to get back to work." I can feel the collective focus of the room follow me as I take my phone from my bag and slide it in my back pocket. "I'll hurry." I head to the door but pause and meet Tristan's contemplative gaze. "Thanks for your willingness to help. It was good to see you again."

And then, without waiting for a reply, I lift a hand in farewell and slip outside.

CHAPTER 4

IT'S OFFICIAL. The keys are lost.

After coming up empty-handed on the retracing-my-every-step-adventure, I spent over an hour scouring my sister's house with the help of a sincerely baffled Tala and Heath. Even Grandma chipped in when she wasn't holding Lucas. And then, out of sheer desperation, I offered Serenity and Jack a hefty cash prize if they could locate the missing keys. A small part of me hoped that one of the kids had hidden them to prevent me from leaving, but when they both came back empty-handed after a very determined search, they were as disappointed as I was.

Almost.

The silver lining: my Jeep is still in the parking garage. And it's locked, which means the keys aren't inside. So that's one place they can't be. Which only leaves an innumerable number of places they can be.

The impromptu trip to the local Jeep dealership this after-noon was also useless. It'll somehow take two to three weeks and a small fortune to get one measly little fob programmed for my specific vehicle when it only took four weeks to get my custom Wrangler ordered and delivered according to all my specifications. Go figure. I told the dealership employee to hold off ordering a new one for the time being, and I'll call Monday if the keys don't turn up.

I pull Tala and Heath's old Suburban into the parking lot of the mainland grocery store and search for a spot. After several loops, I accept my fate and park at what's possibly the furthest parking space from the grocery store entrance. It tracks, considering I've not had a bit of luck since arriving on Sunset Harbor this morning. I drop my head onto the steering wheel, still coming to terms with the fact that my brief visit to Sunset Harbor will be extended through the weekend. Likely longer. How is this my life right now? And with Tristan next door? A small whimper escapes me.

I pull out my phone to text Jane.

CAPRI

> Apparently Tristan moved back into the Palmers' house and everyone forgot to tell me! Traitor!

The three dots immediately appear, and I tap my finger on the side, waiting.

JANE

> We didn't forget. It was a very conscious choice.

CAPRI

> It's a clear violation of our BFF Code of Conduct. Where's the loyalty?

When Jane and I were in seventh grade, we created a list of rules we'd uphold in our friendship, forever and always. To make it binding, we signed it with our blood and our signatures in perfectly dramatic middle-school girl fashion. But even now, when circumstances necessitate, we refer back to it. Though we're mostly joking.

JANE

> Technically, not informing you about Tristan doesn't break any of the rules. Not like your clear disregard for Rule #9.

CAPRI

I had to move. I had no choice in the matter.

JANE

That point is very much debatable. Unlike my choice to withhold information for your benefit. And our friendship's. It's been too long since you've been home, and you wouldn't have come if you'd known.

But I will always be Team Capri.

I allow myself to bask in my wretched existence for a moment longer before looking at the dashboard clock. I've got an hour and a half until Jane will be at Tala and Heath's for dinner. Possibly Walker too. Which, now that I think about it, isn't a lot of time, so I'd better stop sulking and head inside with my mental list of basic necessities to get me through the next few days. Can I technically buy all the things I need at the general store on Sunset Harbor? Absolutely. But I have no intention of repeating the awkward run-in with Tristan from earlier. Or anyone else for that matter. Besides, I'm already on the mainland.

I turn off the ignition and ignore the momentary rattling as if a loose screw is bouncing around the engine. This beast has made odd noises for years and it's still running, so I'm not worried. Grabbing my phone out of the middle console and making sure I have the keys in hand, I lock the paint-chipped door and head inside. I take a basket and mosey along the front of the store, just past the registers, glancing down each aisle. I can count the number of times I've come here on one hand, and even then, it's been years, so I'm not familiar with where anything is. Finally, I locate the health and beauty section and start perusing the products. I grab a bristled brush, hair ties, shampoo, conditioner, and floss. I also place my go-to brand of deodorant in the basket in addition to another one that guarantees twenty-four-hours-stench-free because Florida humidity in the summer is no joke.

I pick out a tube of bright red lip gloss, some mascara, and a BB cream with sunscreen that looks to be a match for my pale complexion. Makeup wise, Tala should have anything else I need for the time being. I'm about to leave the aisle when I pass the feminine products and come to an abrupt stop.

No. No. No.

When is my period supposed to start?

I pull up the *My Cycle* app on my phone to double check, and I nearly groan out loud. This Monday?! I seriously can't catch a break. Though now that I think about it, maybe that's why I've been so out of sorts today. And grumpy.

Or more likely, my less-than-stellar mood has to do with the fact that I lost my keys, got stranded somewhere I've been avoiding, and ran into my secret crush after our fictional love story (that he knows nothing about) has been on the *New York Times Bestseller List* for months. But I can't imagine the flux of pre-menstrual hormones has helped my processing of the situation.

I glance at the array of pink and green packaged products. I briefly question whether Tala might have enough supplies to hold me over until I can get home, but a memory quickly surfaces waving red flags and blaring a warning horn. Last time I made that assumption, Tala had just had Jack, and after spending nine months pregnant, the only feminine products in the Vanderduesen household were Tala's enormous hospital pads. To say the least, it was an uncomfortable few hours until Jane came to my rescue. With Lucas only being a few months old, I grab a box of Butterfield tampons and a pack of their pantyliners, then head to check out.

There are only three registers open, and with the parking lot as full as it is, it's no wonder the lines are forever long. To kill time, I snatch a magazine and begin thumbing through it. I love celebrity gossip. It's one of my favorite ways to mine for inspiration. There are so many juicy details to work with, and I'm completely engrossed in news of the most recent breakups and rumored hookups, mindlessly stepping forward when the line moves.

My attention catches on an article about Presley James: *America's Darling, No More?* I'm curious what the A-list actress did to capture the ire of Hollywood. The piece is, unsurprisingly, way too vague on the particulars. I flip another page, and this time my gaze lands on an article that literally knocks the breath from my lungs: *The Hunt for Sunny Palmer.*

> *The hunt is on for the author behind the anonymous pseudonym, Sunny Palmer. Since her first book, Secret Crush, went viral last summer, she's hit the NYT Bestsellers List consistently with not one or two but several of her backlist books. As an independent author represented by Maven Chase, publishing houses have been scrambling to sign her. With international book deals, screen rights, and merch contracts still up for grabs, it's no wonder the search is intensifying. The problem? No one knows who's behind the best-selling sensation.*

As I continue reading, my stomach is roiling, and the last line sends a chill through me:

> *With so many hoping to get in on the potential goldmine Sunny Palmer has created, it's only a matter of time until someone cracks the code and the world discovers the person behind the now acclaimed name for romance readers everywhere.*

I think I need to sit down.

Or text Maven. She'll know what to do.

I snap a picture of the article and send it. Then I force myself to take a deep breath. This is why I pay Maven a hefty chunk of my royalties each month. Maven and I have been extremely thorough in covering my tracks: registering my books as pseudonymous works; making a Delaware based LLC under a "Does Business As" name; a digital mailbox for all documentation; and hiring a specialist to scrub the internet not once but twice to be safe. If there was something to discover, it would've been found by now. But maybe we missed something. Maybe it is *only a matter of time until someone cracks the code.*

If I'm discovered, it won't take long to figure out other things about me—about how I was the studious introvert and my next-door neighbor was the captain of the football team, exactly like the characters in my first book. How Tristan just so happens to have the last name Palmer. And then there's the whole Bridget thing.

An image of a time bomb with the numbers steadily ticking downward enters my mind. If it explodes, it will leave my entire life a mess. And Tristan's too.

This is bad. Like really, really bad. But I have no idea how to disarm it.

The squeaky wheels of a cart stop behind me, momentarily drawing my notice, but I return my focus to the magazine and my spiraling thoughts. What am I supposed to do?

"Capri?"

Literally the only thing that can force my current dread aside is the new, more pressing dread at hearing Tristan's voice. I'm already calculating the odds of it actually being him and not some man with a similar voice that also knows my name. In my preliminary analysis of stopping here, my odds of running into him were statistically insignificant. Almost non-existent. Hence the reason I chose the mainland grocery store, but apparently the world is against me—including decently sound mathematical calculations.

I don't have the bandwidth for this right now, but life doesn't seem to care about that. After way too long of a delay, I finally look over my shoulder to confirm it isn't some talented impersonator that inherently knows my hearing Tristan's voice will be the ultimate prank.

"Tristan. Hey." I lift my hand in a sort of wave, but with the magazine still in my grasp, it appears as if I'm weirdly fanning him. Quickly, I drop it to my side, removing my thumb from the page with the Sunny Palmer article to be safe. "What are you doing here?"

He gestures to his cart full of fresh produce, meats, nuts, and cheeses alongside two gallons of milk. He either eats exceptionally healthy or he's bringing a charcuterie board to the talent show tomorrow. "Grocery shopping." Healthy it is. Which makes sense considering his physique and that he doesn't seem like the charcuterie type. "What about you?"

I angle the basket hanging from my elbow behind me to block him from glimpsing the feminine products thrown on top. Apparently, I don't want to be the bearer of the news that half of the human population will menstruate at some point in their lives. Me among them. "I came to grab a few things for the weekend."

"Aren't you headed home tonight?"

"That was the plan, but I haven't found my keys."

"Still?"

I shake my head. "They seem to have vanished. So until I find them, I'm stuck on Sunset Harbor. At least for the two to three weeks it'll take to get a new fob."

His narrowed eyes rove over my expression. "That sucks."

"Yeah." I'm sure he means my losing the keys and not my being his neighbor until I find the darn things, but the unhelpful thought implants itself regardless.

"And you don't have another fob?"

"I do at my house, but my keys to the house are—"

"With your lost keys," he says, finishing for me.

"Exactly. But I'm hopeful I'll find them here soon. I'm eager to get home."

"For your date tomorrow?"

It takes me a second to recall the excuse I gave Heath and Tristan earlier—'the date' with myself and a nice hot bubble bath. "At this point, I doubt I'll make it, but it can be rescheduled." Like super easily.

He nods one of his slow, thoughtful nods. "So, if you're *stuck* on Sunset Harbor for the weekend, will you be coming to the talent show? Because if not, maybe we can—"

"Oh shoot!" I blurt, before he can finish. Which, in hindsight, is kind of crazy considering I think he was about to suggest that the two of us should hangout. Except it would've been another pity invite anyway—a courtesy of Heath and Tala's meddling. Not that I'd risk it, even if it wasn't. I need an exit strategy ASAP. "I forgot I'm supposed to get a treat for Serenity and Jack." I step out of line, backing away slowly. "I'd better go grab something."

"I can hold your place for you."

"Oh, no." I bat the same magazine-yielding hand toward him like it's my new appendage. "Thanks for the offer, but I'll be a minute." I turn to leave but remember my manners and pause briefly. "It was good seeing you ... again."

He lifts a parting hand, but he looks completely dumbfounded by my desperate attempt to flee. All these years later, I'm still a master of reading his expressions. The slight hurt and confusion etched in his features nearly has me returning to his side. But I can't. That's not an option. If my resolve to keep my distance is already weakening at the slightest disappointment on his part, I'll be absolutely hopeless against a more concerted effort. Not that I expect him to put forth any sort of effort.

Recommitted to my plan, I duck down the candy aisle and out of view of Tristan. I'll be taking my sweet time to ensure he's long gone before I head to the parking lot.

CHAPTER 5

IT'S NEARLY twenty minutes later when I exit the store with a brimming paper bag in each arm. I probably should've nabbed a cart for my hike to the boonies where I parked, or perhaps forgone the darling yellow notebook, pens, and large selection of chocolates I bought myself in addition to the treats for Serenity and Jack. Oh, and the cursed magazine I purchased to show Tala and Jane. Even if I prefer to skirt around the issue, it's time to develop a solid emergency plan on the suddenly-not-so-off-chance I'm discovered.

I finally reach the Suburban and set one bag on the back bumper, using my body to wedge it against the back door while I search my pocket for the keys. The Suburban no longer has a functioning fob, so I stick the key into the lock and turn, then pull the handle. When the door's high enough, I step back to allow the mechanism to automatically open it the rest of the way, but it slams shut. I attempt the same thing a second time before I remember Tala mentioning the lift-gate something or other not working. This must be what she was talking about.

With my armful of groceries, I glance at the cars parked next to the Suburban. The parking spaces are exceptionally tight and the burb is massive, so with how close they both are parked and the fact that some kind of liquid has recently spilled near where I'm standing that prevents me from putting the bags down, I'm not sure I have another option but to try again.

For the third time, I carefully grab the handle with the tips of my fingers and pull until the door is slightly ajar. If I can use my foot for a prop, then …

A dark gray truck stops directly behind me, but in my current position, I can't fully turn my head to see if they stopped for me. I hear a door open and close, then hasty footsteps making their way toward me. Hallelujah! It's a rescue!

"Need some help?" Tristan steps into view, and I honestly feel like, at this point, I can't even be surprised it's him. I mean, I am and I'm not. But mostly not. Apparently, his damsel-in-distress radar is in perfect working order, and for some reason, it's currently tuned in to me. Probably because I can't stop getting myself into scrapes. He takes hold of the trunk door and carefully lifts it from my aching fingers.

"Thanks." I quickly slide the groceries into the back. My arms feel like they might float right off my body with their newfound freedom, so I wrap them around my midsection to keep any involuntary movements to a minimum. "The thing that keeps the door open is apparently broken."

"Apparently." Still propping the door, Tristan gives one of his heart-stopping smiles. I nearly convince myself to look away, but I don't. Doing so is like the equivalent of glancing away from the last moments of a sunset when the sun finally dips beneath the horizon. Ooh! I'll have to remember that line—it's perfectly cheesy and something my readers will eat up. "Can I ask what your plan was?"

I give a tight laugh, not sure how exactly to handle his teasing. "Let's just say I'm not confident I possess the acrobatic abilities or the strength to have pulled it off, so it was a good thing you saw me."

He chuckles.

We stand for another few breath cycles in awkward silence before I begin phase one of my exit strategy and take a step toward the driver's side. "Well, I'm going to be late for dinner, so I'd better go." I throw a thumb over my shoulder like I'm a career hitchhiker. "But thanks for coming to my rescue. Again."

He closes the trunk and gives that look of his—the one where his brow furrows slightly and his eyes crinkle at the corners. The one that means he doesn't quite understand. Specific to this moment: he clearly can't figure out why I'm so desperate to leave. For the third time today. But I'm counting it as a good thing because if he knew, he'd be the one bolting. And, if the article I just read is correct, I'm guessing that's exactly what he'll be doing in the near future.

I turn my back so I don't have to further witness the hurt I'm causing him—even if it's a teeny tiny, miniscule wound for him—and begin to search my pockets for the keys. Except they aren't there.

"Looking for these?" he says, walking toward me and dangling the Suburban keys in front of him. "You left them in the lock."

What's wrong with me? I haven't felt this scatter-brained in … I don't know how long. "It's crazy how important those things are for driving."

"So it would seem." He gives a half smile that doesn't reach his eyes and hands them to me. "Maybe I'll see you later."

I clutch the keys, letting them dig into my palm to counter my desire to lessen his disappointment. "Maybe."

He only makes it a few feet before he pauses and faces me again. His hands are tucked in his pockets, and those sea-green eyes are locked on me. "Are you avoiding me, Capri?"

"Me?" I ask, pointing to myself while shaking my head excessively. "No." I'm usually super opposed to flat-out lying as I'm more of a partial truth girl when it's necessary, but I have no choice here.

"You are," he says matter-of-factly. He shifts and runs a hand through his hair, and I'm glad he doesn't know how entirely affected I am by that one little action. It's thankfully less potent than a truth-serum, but only just. "Does it have to do with the boat ride we took right before I left for college? Where I—"

"Nope," I blurt, stopping him from finishing whatever he was going to say. "That was so long ago. Like a *really, really* long time ago." Yes, I still daydream about it from time to time—at least the fictional version of how it might have gone had my feelings been reciprocated—but that's not my point. Any mention of The Incident needs to remain firmly in the past where it belongs.

He doesn't look completely convinced by my insistence. "Then what is it?"

I shrug. It's the best I can do considering the situation.

"If it's something I've done—"

"It's not. I mean, it's not only you I'm avoiding." Crap. I didn't intend to say that. I shake my head, thinking how to fix this. "It's everyone on Sunset Harbor … other than my family. And Jane." Why do I think I can actually fix anything by continuing to speak? I have a track record that strongly suggests otherwise. "Besides, so much has changed the last little while, it doesn't quite feel like home anymore."

He studies me for a second, as though he's trying to determine how best to respond. "I get that."

That's not the response I'm expecting. "You do?"

"Except for a few quick visits, I've been avoiding coming back since Bridget called off our engagement. Until a few months ago, that is."

I fidget with the keys in my hand. "I was sorry to hear about that."

"Don't be. Her dreams were always too big for our little island." I don't miss that he calls it *our* island, though I know he doesn't mean it the way I want him to. The way I absolutely, positively *shouldn't* want him to. "I suppose I worried that all my memories with her—the reminders of the life we were supposed to have—would drown me if I came back."

"But they haven't?"

"Oh, they completely have." The broad smile that lights his face contradicts his heartbreaking admission, and he gestures toward the store with a lifted hand. "It's been three months, and I still do my grocery shopping here to avoid running into Bridget's family. Honestly, outside of work, I avoid most people on Sunset Harbor these days if I can help it. It's like people don't know how to act around me anymore or what to say." His eyes lock on mine again. "It's not their fault, but it still sucks."

The ensuing silence presses on me. I swallow, dropping my gaze to the keys I'm still fidgeting with. I can't return openness for openness. No matter how grateful I am for Tristan's attempt to relate to me.

In my periphery, he draws a step closer. "And I didn't say all of that so you'll feel obligated to tell me anything. I don't need to know your reasons for avoiding Sunset Harbor."

Timidly, I lift my gaze to his. "Thanks. And thanks for telling me … *all of that*. It's helpful to know I'm not the only one trekking all the way to the mainland grocery store."

"What can I say?" He lifts his hands at his sides. "If you ever want someone to commiserate with, I'm your guy." I laugh until I see Tristan's gaze go distant. His expression turns thoughtful and he gives a short, "Hmm."

Oh no. This isn't good. I can sense it in the way every cell inside my body stands at attention as though it also needs to know what he's thinking. "What is it?"

His focus sharpens on me. "I have an idea."

I lift my brows in response.

His thumb beats against his thigh, and he looks like he's trying to decide how to word whatever it is he intends to say.

"For one reason or another, neither of us wants to be on Sunset Harbor right now, so maybe we need to redefine our relationship with the island. At least make it so we don't dread coming home anymore."

My heart lifts in my chest as if it's already casting a vote of confidence before it even knows what it's voting on. "And how does one redefine a relationship with an island?"

"Make new memories to replace the old ones. Start fresh. I don't know. I'm just spit-balling here."

I stare at him, attempting to wrap my mind around what he's saying. Surely he doesn't mean we do it together, as in the two of us.

"Dependent on you finding your keys, there's a chance you'll be around for a while." He shrugs. "It could be fun and give us something to do while you're here."

He does mean *us*! I'm desperately trying to rein in my runaway imagination that, at the slightest encouragement, is all too willing to envision what our children will look like and where we'll live on the island. I've literally stolen this man's name and used it without his permission or knowledge for the past nine years. There's a far better chance of my having a restraining order placed against me than my having his future children. Which is why I can't go along with his plan, no matter how badly I want to. "People will talk."

"About two old *friends* hanging out?" I don't miss the way he accentuates *friends*, as if he wants to make the boundary clear from the start to prevent any confusion on my part. It's a sound idea considering I was just envisioning our children. Not that I'll need that boundary because I'm not going to agree to any of this.

"Yes, actually." I don't counter his assertion that we were friends, regardless that we haven't seen each other in years, because I'm well aware our definitions of friendship are different. Everyone is Tristan's friend, and on the island, I have Jane. "Especially those matchmaking gossips at Seaside Oasis."

He crosses his arms over his broad chest, his smile entirely too effective. "You're going to let a few little old ladies intimidate you?"

"One hundred percent. Those women, my grandma included, are terrifying when they set their minds to something." And with the way Grandma mentioned Tristan earlier, it's wise to be cautious.

"I've already made it abundantly clear to them that I've no intention of dating anyone from Sunset Harbor again."

I ignore the way my heart flops over in disappointment at his declaration. "Oh, that's good to hear," I say, my tone bordering on sarcasm. "I'm confident they'll simply take your word for it."

He chuckles. "We'll make sure they don't get any wrong ideas about us."

With another of his soul-crushing comments, my resolve remains intact.

Mostly.

"I just don't know if it's a good idea."

He studies me for a moment. "If you really don't want to, it's fine." His expression is sincere and full of an unhelpful amount of understanding. "But whatever's holding you hostage—whatever's making you dread coming home—maybe it's time to find a way forward."

A way forward.

My chest buzzes with energy.

There's no way what he's offering is the answer to my current dilemma. After racking my brain again and again to try to figure out how I can make things right, the solution can't be as simple as becoming friends with Tristan. Can it? Developing a relationship—completely platonic, of course—so that, eventually, I can confess my transgressions against him? The truth bomb will definitely be better coming from a friend. A real, actual friend. Not a previous semi-friend Tristan hasn't spoken with in almost ten years. A friend that is helping him heal his relationship with Sunset Harbor. *Our* little island.

And maybe Tala is right—maybe Tristan will find the whole confession endearing.

HA! I barely manage to not laugh out loud. There's no way.

But wishful thinking aside, at least this is a plan—and an actionable plan at that. Knowing that there are people out there actively working to discover my identity, this puts the confession on my terms. Tristan won't have to find out what I've done through some random news source or a reporter showing up at his door for an interview. Or worse, from gossip around the island. I can tell him myself—let him ease into it gently and prepare him for the chaos that might come his way.

I momentarily wonder if my own self-interest is swaying me. Because I'm not going to lie—the idea of hanging out with Tristan is making me dizzy with excitement. But the logic is also there. I think.

"Okay," I say before my better judgment convinces me otherwise. "I'm in." The intensity of his smile nearly knocks me off my feet. "But you have to promise me one thing."

"What's that?"

My brain spits out the classic line about him promising to not fall in love with me, but I push it away before it can slip out. This clearly isn't a romance. "You can't ask about my reason for avoiding the island." I draw in a long, slow breath, hoping to quiet my pounding heart. "But I'll tell you when I'm ready." Accountability is a huge motivator for me, so offering this to him will ensure I don't forget why I agreed to this along the way.

"I can accept that." He gives a solemn nod. "And will you agree to stop avoiding me?"

That seems like a decent trade. "Agreed."

He steps forward with an outstretched hand.

I glance down and wonder if he actually means for me to shake it as though we're entering into some sort of contractual agreement. When he doesn't waver, I realize he does. Hesitantly, I put my hand in his, and the minute our skin touches, a jolt of pleasure rushes through me, and I become acutely aware I was never going to say no to his plan. Because somehow, after everything, Tristan is still my greatest weakness.

CHAPTER 6

TRISTAN'S BOAT putters along the canal, just like in our boatpooling days. And, also like those days, I'm sitting in the very front with my gaze locked on the water, watching for manatees ... and possibly avoiding conversation. It's been less than an hour since Tristan and I agreed to the idea of redefining our relationship with Sunset Harbor, and I'm already questioning my sanity.

"Hopefully you won't be too late for dinner," Tristan says, pulling my attention over my shoulder to where he's causally steering the boat with one hand, his leaned-back posture somehow full of a carefree confidence. I create a mental image of him to store away for later because he's radiating a *this-scene-needs-to-be-in-a-romance-book* vibe. Not that I intend to write another story about him—one is regrettably too many—but that doesn't mean I can't grab nuggets of inspiration here and there to jot down. The man is basically a living, breathing book boyfriend, and it would be a travesty not to continue to share bits and pieces of him with my readers.

I tuck a strand of hair behind my ear. "Tala just texted to say dinner is ready. So I'm fine. Besides, I'd be thirty minutes later if you hadn't insisted on giving me a ride from the parking garage."

His eyes glint with humor, and I know it's because of how adamant I was in regards to my taking the ferry when we saw each other back at the parking garage after leaving the store.

Tristan finally put an end to my feeble excuses by calling them what they were—an attempt to avoid him. Again.

"When should our first outing be?" he asks.

I shrug as though the idea of hanging out with him doesn't send my insides reeling. "Next week sometime?"

He pins me with an accusatory look. "Give it plenty of time for someone to find your keys?"

I open my mouth to defend myself, then close it again. "When were you thinking?"

"What about tomorrow after the talent show?"

My chest constricts. "Tomorrow?"

"Unless you have plans already?"

He's well aware I have zero commitments. Not that I'm attempting to avoid him again, I just ... Shoot. I am. Old habits die hard. "Tomorrow works. Should we make a plan for what we want to do?"

"What if we take turns planning the outings?"

"Like we each come up with something we'd want to do?"

"Or we could come up with something we think the other person wants to do."

I laugh. "That's not fair. I'm easy. Take me to the beach and hand me a book."

"Tempting, but this is about making new memories, not passing time reading on the beach. Besides, I'm confident I can think of a few things to do that you'll love."

"Really?" I pin him with a skeptical expression. Tristan hardly knows me. Not like I know him.

"Capri Sun, are you doubting my abilities?" The corners of his lips are creeping upward, and it ignites an odd desire in me to keep this going. And there's nothing to stop me. Friends can have playful relationships. Besides, I've always wished that was the sort of friendship Tristan and I had. So why not lean into it now that we're also redefining our own relationship along with our relationship with the island?

"Entirely."

He shakes his head. "Let's make a bet, then."

I narrow my eyes. "What sort of bet?"

"If I plan the most memorable outing, I want your first published book dedicated to me."

An unexpected laugh bursts out of me. Partially from my shock at the request but mostly at the irony. Done. *Secret Crush* is already dedicated to him: *The protagonist of my own love story. Thanks for the inspiration.* Since I'm going to be confessing the whole thing by the end of this, it fits in perfectly with my current course of action. "And what if I never publish a book?" I ask, hoping to play off my laughter as something other than the unhinged outburst it was.

"You will. And that dedication page is going to have my name on it."

His confidence in me is so very Tristan, and I distract myself from the unfounded warmth it causes by contemplating whether he'll still count my dedication if I didn't name him outright. "You seem pretty sure you're going to win."

He grins. "You don't seem to be putting up much of a fight."

"It's the quiet ones you have to watch out for."

His smile is now bright enough to burn a permanent imprint on my retinas. "Is that so?"

I lift one shoulder in a casual half shrug, pretending that my heart isn't accelerating with every passing comment. "I guess you'll have to see."

"I guess I will. But, so we're clear, I really want that dedication, so don't think I'm going to go easy on you." He slows the boat as we near our dock, turns the steering wheel, and cuts the engine.

Like the creature of habit that I am from our boatpooling days, I toss the attached fenders nearest me over the side while Tristan does the same with the ones in back. The boat glides sideways, and Tristan catches hold of the dock, bringing us in slowly before tying it off. When the boat's secured, Tristan walks toward me. "What do you want your prize to be on the off chance you do win?"

I laugh and shake my head, surprised at how well I'm holding up my end of the conversation despite my nerves and the constant stream of unhelpful thoughts—like the off-handed comment that surfaces about how I'll settle for his first-born child (as long as I'm the mother). Or perhaps that kiss I never got. "I'm still thinking, but I'll let you know."

"Make sure it's something worth competing for."

I swallow at the intensity of his gaze. "I will."

He draws closer, and my whole body starts to tingle with his nearness when he steps past me and onto the bench seat. "Here, let me help you," he says, offering his hand and officially ending our conversation. I step up next to him, ignoring the way my skin hums at his touch, but before I turn to climb out, he tightens his grip on my hand to pause me. "Actually"—he pulls his phone from his pocket with his other hand, unlocks it, and hands it to me. "We should probably exchange numbers first. That'll make scheduling easier." He grins. "If you're not opposed."

I've envisioned this scenario countless times—the moment when Tristan finally asks me for my number—but in all my imaginings, the reason behind his request wasn't quite so ... platonic. It's as if my heart and my brain are in a tug-of-war while the rest of my organs aren't sure which side to take. Not trusting my voice with the pulling and pushing happening inside me, I take hold of his phone, enter my number, and hand it back to him.

He types in something (I assume a text so I can have his number as well), and my phone buzzes in my back pocket as confirmation.

"Ready?" he asks, extending his hand again.

With his assistance, I carefully step over the side of the boat and wait as he hands me my bags one at a time. "Got 'em?"

I nod. "Thanks again for the ride."

He smiles. "What are friends for?"

And there it is again. The blatant expectation-setting that crushes my heart into a million little pieces. "I'll see you tomorrow, I guess."

"I guess so." He lifts a hand and steps back down onto the floor of the boat to get his own groceries.

"Capri!" Jane is running toward me from Tala's with a huge smile on her face. She's wearing a yellow sundress that makes her look like some sort of beach goddess with her tanned skin and long brown locks with golden highlights. She grabs one of my bags and wraps her other arm around my neck. "Oh, I missed you."

"I missed you," I say, letting her welcome warm me all the way through. In our friendship, she's always been the sun to my moon. The bright day to my dim night. Not only in looks but in personality—she's the life of the party, while I enjoy observing the party from the sidelines.

"Hey, Tristan," she calls, waving in his direction before sliding her arm through mine and leading me to the house.

"So … ?" Her voice is near a whisper. "Tell me everything."

"Well, I was born at St. Andrew's Hospital not thirty miles—"

"Hilarious." She nudges her hip into me. "You know exactly what I mean."

"I ran into him at the store," I whisper back.

"And … ?"

My brother steps into the doorway, forestalling my explanation. I didn't think he'd show. His blue eyes slide from Jane and me to Tristan behind us. He doesn't wave or smile at him but just stands there. I don't know what their deal is, being that Walker and Tristan were in the same grade with similar social standings (i.e. the popular kids), but the two never really got along. Though Walker didn't make a point of getting to know anyone he didn't want to. Including me.

He wasn't always that way. We went through a lot when Dad died and we moved to Sunset Harbor away from our friends and everything we knew. But unlike me, Walker didn't find a good friend like Jane to work through his emotions with. He bottled it all inside and started to push us all away. I miss the old Walker. The one that didn't think he was too cool for his dorky, book-loving sister. The one that laughed and teased and didn't care so much what people thought of him. It's been a long time since I've seen that Walker.

"Later," I whisper to Jane now that Walker's within ear shot.

She releases my arm. "Fine, but I'd better get every detail."

"Hey, Walker," I say to my brother, feeling like I should give him a side hug, but when I wrap my arm around his waist, he goes stiff. We've never had a hugging type of relationship—actually, we haven't had much of a relationship at all since Dad died —but the reminder still stings a little. "You came."

His dark brown curls are visible beneath the edges of his hat. "It ended up working with my schedule."

Of course it did. Otherwise, he wouldn't be here.

"I had to give him a ride like some hitchhiker on the highway." Jane sends him a teasing look. "But I got him here."

I don't appreciate their shared, knowing smile. Jane is strictly off-limits to Walker for so many reasons. "You guys came together?"

Walker shrugs. "I just needed a ride."

I nod, taking in his expression. He looks innocent enough, but for some reason, my internal warning signal is going off.

"Now that everyone's here, let's eat before the food gets cold," Tala calls.

Jane links arms with me again, and the two of us head inside, dropping our bags on the counter. The whole crew is assembled, and a big pot of something that smells amazing—like lemons and oregano—is steaming on the stovetop. "Sorry I'm late. After the dealership, I stopped to grab a few things at the store. It obviously took longer than I expected."

"You're fine," Tala says. The happy little smile she's wearing tells me she glimpsed who brought me home.

Serenity approaches me with a pout. "And we still didn't find the keys. Jack and I looked everywhere. We even checked the front lawn."

I run a hand down her long, chestnut hair that is only a shade or two lighter than my own. "That's okay. They'll turn up." I hope. Though I'm no longer put out by the idea of staying a few extra days. Not because I get to hang out with Tristan (at least that's what I'm telling myself), but because by the end of this, I'll have found a way forward out of this mess I've created. Hopefully. "But I got you two something as a thank you for helping me look."

Heath is already rummaging through my bag. "Did you get me anything?"

I swat him away, but then I grab the box of tampons and toss it to him. "There you are."

Laughter echoes through the room.

"You asked for that," Grandma snickers.

"Funny." He scowls, but I ignore him and pull out a large pack of Swedish Fish for Serenity and a bag of Nerd Clusters for Jack.

They both wrap their arms around me, squealing in excitement. Being an aunt is the greatest thing ever. A few inexpensive treats and I'm suddenly at favorite-person status.

"Thanks, Auntie Capri," Serenity says.

"Yeah, thanks." Jack rips open the package, but Tala snags it from him before he can get one out.

"After dinner." She gives him a pointed look and sticks his candy, along with Serenity's, on top of the fridge.

"Sorry," I mouth to Tala.

"You're totally fine." Her smile returns. "But let's dish up so we can sit and hear about your *eventful* afternoon."

If she thinks I'm mentioning anything but the barest details about Tristan in front of my family, she is sorely mistaken. In fact, this entire room is full of conspirators who knew Tristan had moved back into the Palmers' house, and not one of them told me. If I hadn't missed them all so much, the whole group would be getting the silent treatment. Or villains named after them along with Heath.

CHAPTER 7

"WOW. I had way too much of that shrimp orzo." Jane lays back onto the guest room bed, resting her hands over her stomach.

I plop down next to her and grab a decorative pillow, hugging it to me. "Seriously. And that bread. I think I ate a whole loaf on my own."

She laughs, then shifts to her side and props herself onto her elbow. "So, dish it," she says with a conspiratorial smile. "Every detail."

"You first. How is the *Summer of Jane Hayes* going?" Last weekend, Jane declared she was going to fall in love this summer. Not intended to, but absolutely, unequivocally was going to fall in love. To make sure it happens, she's attempting different romance tropes on each date to see which, if any, will lead to her happily ever after. The plan is so perfectly Jane.

I'd never tell her that tropes are just a marketing tool authors use to set reader expectations, because honestly, if anyone can find love by forcing tropes onto unsuspecting guys, it's Jane. Plus, her own parents—country music stars Tucker Hayes and Loretta Lee—had a very trope-ish romance and are still happily married almost thirty years later.

"There's nothing new to report since the choking disaster with Beau and the toolbox incident with Dax. I just haven't found the right combination of tropes yet. Or the right guy. Hey, I have a great idea." She's now brimming with excitement.

"Maybe, now that you're home, you and Tristan can act as double on a couple of the dates."

"That's not happening." I gesture to the whole of me. "This is friend-zone material. Not double-dating material."

"Yeah right. I totally saw how he helped you out of the boat earlier. It was so sweet."

"I promise you, that's Tristan being Tristan. He made it crystal clear—on multiple occasions today—that we're just friends."

She pushes herself to a sitting position, her brown eyes locked on me. "What exactly did he say?"

I give a messy explanation of our previous conversations along with the whole arrangement and how it came about, all while trying to ignore Jane's perpetual, and completely unhelpful, smile. To prove my point, I pull out my phone and show her the text he sent when he got my number.

TRISTAN

TRISTAN PALMER

That's it. No playful comment or teasing. Just his name. "See … friend zone."

Her lips purse thoughtfully. "Even if you're right, which I'm not sure you are, it doesn't matter. Now that you're spending more time together, he's totally going to fall for you and make all those dreams of yours come true." Jane's always been a glass-half-full person, and I love her for it, though I have to take her optimism with a grain of salt. Or a large chunk, depending. Her eyes go wide. "It's the friends-to-lovers trope. Oh, and obviously secret crush."

"What's the trope for my stealing his name and writing a fictional romance book about us?"

Her head quirks to the side as if she's taking my question seriously. "Definitely secret identity with a last-to-know twist. Or possibly hidden past. Though yours isn't very dark."

I groan and throw back my head. "Why didn't you stop me from using Sunny Palmer as my pen name?"

"Are you kidding me? That's the absolute best author name in existence. And the poetic justice ..." She gives a contented sigh. "So romantic."

"Unrequited love," I mumble, all too aware of what my actual trope would be if they truly existed in real life.

"More like belated love epiphany." Jane's hand comes to rest on mine. "You just wait. By the time you leave, Tristan's going to be completely smitten by you."

I laugh, but in a humorless way. "Especially once I tell him my secret identity."

Jane goes still. "You're going to tell him?"

I grab the magazine I bought at the store and open to the dog-eared page, flipping it so she can read the article, *The Hunt for Sunny Palmer*.

Her eyes enlarge as she reads it to herself. After a minute she glances up. "Do you think they'll figure out you're Sunny Palmer?"

"I have no idea, but that's honestly why I agreed to his plan. My hope is that if Tristan and I can actually become friends, I'll be able to tell him before he finds out some other way. He deserves a heads up to the kind of chaos that might ensue if anyone does figure it out." The very thought of the impending conversation has my stomach souring.

"Did you send the article to Maven?"

"Yeah. She texted back during dinner. She says not to be too concerned, though we're going to fine-tune our PR strategy on the off chance the news does get out."

Jane's eyes are moving across the page again. "This is crazy. You're in a magazine! How cool is that?" She smiles at me, but it lessens when she sees my unenthusiastic expression. "Obviously the reason for it isn't the best, but they're talking about you. I bet you'll see a huge spike in book sales."

"They're talking about Sunny Palmer, not me. At least for now. Which is why I need to figure out how to tell Tristan in a way that ..." My words trail off. For someone who writes books for a living, phrasing things in real life is no easy feat. "Basically, in a way that won't make me look like some sort of love-crazed nutjob."

"He's not going to think that. Honestly, I bet he'll be touched by the whole thing."

See what I mean about the optimism? Her and Tala both, apparently. "Yeah, in a how-sweet-but-I'm-going-to-lock-my-doors-and-never-talk-to-her-again sort of way." Which is the reaction I'm expecting, so I have to be okay with it. "I'm hoping if I lean into the 'In high school I may have had a bit of a crush on you and did something a little wild and a lot stupid' side of things, it won't go over as poorly as it otherwise could."

"Well, I honestly can't believe you're going to tell him. That's big. Like really big." She pauses. "Does this mean you're going to tell other people too?"

"Just my family, but I feel like I can't until Tristan knows. He needs to hear it from me first."

"Well, if it means you'll come home more so I don't have to travel two hours every time I want to see you, I'm all for it." She lies flat on the bed again, staring up at the ceiling. "Where do you think he's going to take you tomorrow?"

I do likewise, stretching out on the bed next to her, my legs dangling off the edge. "I don't know. It has to be somewhere on Sunset Harbor, since that's the whole point of it."

"And what are you going to do for the date you plan?"

"It's not a date."

"Fine. Your *outing*."

"I have no clue. I'm not the adventurous type. Unless the adventure consists of discovering a comfy place to read a book."

Jane's head turns toward me. "You're Sunny Palmer—

romance author extraordinaire. Your books are chock-full of exactly this kind of stuff."

"Yeah, but it's fiction."

She rolls her eyes. "Because the ideas don't come from that amazing brain of yours and you do absolutely no research to make sure things are accurate."

She has a point. I've spent hours upon hours researching and planning all sorts of events and outings for my characters. Just because I'm not the one having the experiences doesn't mean I lack the ability. "Okay. That does help to remember."

Jane lifts onto her elbow again, her eyes alight with excitement. "And when you win, tell Tristan the thing you want is to have a do-over of the sunset boat ride."

Despite that I'd had the same thought, I grab a pillow and smack her with it, causing her to roll to her other side and laugh.

"I think it's time to make a slight addition to the BFF Code of Conduct," I say, unable to resist joining in on Jane's contagious laughter. "The Incident is henceforth banned from ever being mentioned."

"You can't change the code." She sobers some. "Can you?"

"It's an amendment, not a change. The core principles are set in stone."

She doesn't look incredibly thrilled by the idea, and I wonder if this has something to do with the rule about never falling for my brother. I'd originally put it in because, at the beginning of our friendship, I was fed up with girls pretending to be my friend so they could get closer to Walker. It had always seemed a frivolous addition. Until now.

But before I can think how to ask her, she smiles. "Let's start brainstorming ideas for your dates."

"Outings."

She grins. "Right. Your *outings*."

CHAPTER 8

"LET'S give all of our participants another round of applause."
Tristan doesn't look like a man averse to interacting with his
fellow Sunset Harborians, not with the way his genuine, confident smile shifts across the applauding crowd. Whereas I'm
tucked in a seat next to the wall, close to the back, and using the
head of the man in front of me to make sure Tristan doesn't
make eye contact with me a second time. Once was enough to
set my nerves on end, and his subtle wave in my direction had
several people glancing over their shoulders. "On behalf of the
residents and the staff at Seaside Oasis, thanks for coming out
today—both those who shared their talents and those who came
to support. We truly appreciate it."

Another round of applause interrupts Tristan, and he waits
for it to die down again, then he points to the back. "Be sure to
grab a cookie and some lemonade on your way out, or stay and
hang out for a while. Oh, and don't forget our family swim night
this next Thursday from seven to nine. It should be a lot of fun."
Tristan heads to the side of the makeshift stage and hands his
microphone to a middle-aged woman I don't recognize. She
starts talking to him, and his gaze flicks in my direction, but I
quickly glance down to Serenity instead of holding it.

"You did such a great job. I've never been able to do a back
walk-over. Or the splits."

Serenity smiles. "I was so nervous."

"Well, you did amazing. And so did you, Jack." I muss his

hair, causing his darling, toothless smile to grow. "How did you make that marker disappear when you crinkled the paper?" I'm sincerely curious.

"A magician can't reveal his secrets," Jack says, folding his arms in front of his chest, clearly proud of his well-executed trick.

"Who wants a cookie?" Tala is scooting her way down the row, following Heath who has Lucas in arm and is bee-lining it to the desserts.

"I do!" Jack reaches for her outstretched hand, and the two of them head in the direction of the back tables.

Serenity doesn't follow but leans in toward me, her hand cupped by her mouth. "Jack takes the ink tube out of the middle of the marker, then there's a bend at the bottom of the lid so it folds when you crumple the paper."

"Oh, that's how he did it." Brilliant. I briefly contemplate writing a protagonist who's a magician, but then I come to my senses. That would take way too much research and it doesn't fit into my beach read niche. Unless he's a street performer and does his shows at the boardwalk ... No. That probably won't work. But if he—

"That was some pretty impressive tumbling." Tristan is standing at the end of our row of chairs, his gaze on Serenity.

"Thanks." She looks at him with all the confidence in the world, and I can't help but envy her. "Maybe by the next talent show I'll have my aerial. Or a back handspring."

"That'd be awesome." His eyes lift to mine. "Hey, Capri Sun."

I lift a hand, reminding myself that I don't need to feel awkward with him. Our last two conversations have gone ... decently well. But I suppose both of those took place with no one else around. No one we knew, anyway.

Serenity looks from me to Tristan and back again before apparently deciding a cookie is more enticing.

After she passes Tristan, he takes a step toward me. "You ready for our outing?"

I gesture to myself as if it should be apparent, but he seems to take it as an invitation with the way his gaze moves down my body at a slow, intentional pace. I know he's only considering the practicality of my outfit, but regardless, heat consumes me, and I glance around to see if anyone has taken notice. The last thing I need is people seeing the two of us together and connecting the similarities between us and my characters in *Secret Crush*. Especially now that several of the women at Seaside Oasis are currently reading it for book club and the story is fresh in their minds.

His eyes return to mine. "You're sure it's fine to get wet in that?"

Tristan texted me this morning with one line: *Wear clothes you can get wet in.*

"Yep." Technically, Tala's fine with it, since I didn't bring any clothes with me to Sunset Harbor. But it isn't the worst over-sight I've made. Tala is a lot more fashionable than I am. Not that I don't love shopping, but I also don't own anything like the perfectly fitted black one-piece swimsuit concealed beneath the soft button-up shirt. And these cut-off shorts are unbelievably flattering.

"Great. I'll go change, then come find you."

"How about we meet out front?" I say, trying to limit the occasions where people will glimpse us together. "In like ten minutes?"

"Sure." Tristan glances at his watch, then gives me a parting nod. On the way to the exit, Tristan is stopped several times by residents and their families all eager to say hello to him. He greets them all with a friendly smile or handshake, then hurries on his way. And that's the difference between us—people adore Tristan. Outside of my family, there's only a small handful of people that take notice of me, let alone are excited to see me.

Not that I blame them. Where Tristan is outgoing and charismatic, I'm quiet and easy to overlook.

"That Palmer boy is trouble if you ask me." Virginia Sawyer, Grandma's dearest friend and one of those on the small list of people that will seek me out, is at my side, following my line of sight to Tristan and studying him skeptically through her coke bottle glasses. "I know you always had a thing for him, but keep your distance. They're a sneaky bunch with their good looks and flashy smiles, but they'll kick you when you're down."

I suppress my emotions—horror that she knows I ever had a thing for him and amusement at her dislike of the Palmers. The Sawyers and Palmers have had a drawn-out family feud that once divided Sunset Harbor, but that was a long time ago. I don't know the particulars except that it was regarding the property Seaside Oasis was built on. Besides, Grandma and Mom have always been Switzerland on the matter (considering all three of our families are also neighbors), so us Collins kids have followed suit. "I'll keep my eye on him."

The purple highlights in her hair perfectly match the sardonic look she throws my way. "That's apparent."

Time to pivot. "So, Grandma tells me you're moving into Seaside Oasis?"

"That's the plan. As long as Palmer doesn't give my room to anyone else out of spite, I'll be next door to her. We've not lived two doors down from each other for over fifty years to not be neighbors now."

There's no point in defending Tristan to Virginia. Her opinion won't change. "Do you have someone helping you with the move?"

"My granddaughter, Gemma. You remember her, don't you?"

"Of course." Gemma was a grade younger than me, and our time on Sunset Harbor only overlapped for a couple of years before she moved away, but she's a hard one to forget. Even in middle school, she somehow knew her own mind and wasn't intimidated by anyone, the Palmer boys included. It probably helped that she was so pretty and never went through an awkward stage whereas my awkward stage comprised my entire middle school and high school experience. In truth, when Gemma lived here, I used to worry Tristan would fall in love with her—they had incredible star-crossed-lovers potential with how intensely their families disliked each other—but she moved away before the opportunity presented itself.

"She'll be here tomorrow."

"If she needs any help, I'd be happy to lend a hand."

"I'm not sure how much those scrawny little arms of yours could do,"—Virginia reaches out and squeezes my arms with her bony fingers as if to assess the accuracy of her statement—"but I'll pass the message along."

Serenity steps up next to me and grabs my hand. "You'd better come get a cookie. The chocolate chip ones are almost gone."

She knows me too well. Chocolate chip cookies are one of my favorites, especially the big gooey kind like they have in the back. Before I can make my excuses to Virginia, she's already making her way toward the other side of the room. That woman bends to no one, not even societal niceties. Serenity leads me to the table where I snag one of the remaining chocolate chip cookies, then we join the rest of my family in the courtyard.

"You need to come see my room," Grandma says to me when I step up to their small group. "Tala decorated it—to the envy of all the ladies." Helping Grandma move into Seaside Oasis six months ago was the only time I'd been in it. After we got her settled and Tala and Heath moved into her house, I enacted my Sunset Harbor Avoidance Protocol. It made sense considering that was about the time the Sunny Palmer craze hit the island hard. So, between that and the fact that Tristan's dad informed us Tristan was moving back to run Seaside Oasis, it was definitely time to stop visiting.

"Besides," she says, a glint in her eyes, "last time I'm not sure you had a chance to enjoy the view from my porch."

With her tone at the end, I know exactly the view she's referring to. And it has nothing to do with the gorgeous scenery and everything to do with Dax Miller's shop. Or, more accurately, Dax Miller. AKA eye candy for the ladies of Seaside Oasis. I went to school with Dax, at least the years he wasn't in juvenile detention for a series of pranks he pulled. He isn't my type at all, but I won't deny that Dax is exceptionally easy on the eyes. If I ever write a rebel as a hero, he'll definitely be the inspiration.

I glance at my watch. Tristan will be out in a few minutes, and I don't want to keep him waiting or risk him coming to find me. "I really want to see your room, but I can't right now. Maybe I can come by Monday or Tuesday since you'll be with us at Tala's tomorrow?"

"Do you have plans with Jane?" Grandma asks, as though that's the only logical answer. Typically, she'd not be wrong.

I shift. "No, not Jane."

Tala and Heath share a knowing look, so Tala must have mentioned my outing to him. Which is fine, it's not like I insisted she keep it a secret. I just don't want everyone making a big deal about it.

"Tristan, actually." Before Grandma can say anything, I hold up a finger and lower my voice. "And no, it's not a date. We're just friends."

"Sure," Grandma says, dipping her chin and sending me a you-can't-fool-me look. "Two single, attractive young people choosing to spend time alone together as friends. Got it."

I hate that I have to fight a smile. My family is not going to be any help in keeping my intentions straight regarding Tristan. "Think what you want, but it's true."

Their amused expressions and half-hearted nods are far from reassuring.

"When will you be home?" Serenity asks, and the slight pout on her face reminds me that I promised we'd paint each other's nails today.

"I'm guessing I'll be back before dinner." I didn't ask Tristan any of the details for our outing—not even where we were going —because with the lack of information, it seems like he wants it to be a surprise. But I can't imagine we'll be gone that long, considering it's only noon. "I'm still planning on our girls' time. Maybe we can make a night of it?"

Serenity brightens and nods her head excitedly.

"Tristan and I are running in the morning," Heath says with a smirk that informs me I won't like what follows. "And we tend to chat about *all* sorts of things to distract ourselves. So keep that in mind when you two are interacting today. If you try anything on him, I'll probably hear about it."

I roll my eyes and kiss Grandma on the cheek before waving to everyone else.

"Have fun," Tala calls as I make my way toward the front lobby.

Honestly, with how on edge I am, I hope I can even attempt fun.

WELCOME TO
SUNSET HARBOR

BELACOURT RESORT

GOLF COURSE

NOAH'S HOUSE

JANE'S HOUSE

NATURE PRESERVE

DAX'S DUPLEX

SEASIDE OASIS RETIREMENT HOME

SUNSET REPAIRS

PHOENIX'S OFFICE

CITY OFFICES

SCOOPS AHOY ICE CREAM

KEENE PUB

SUNRISE CAFE

TOWN

BAKERY

SQUARE

GULF OF MEXICO

BRIGGS'S APARTMENT

THE BOOK ISLE

CUTS AND CURLS

TRISTAN & BEAU'S HOUSE

CAPRI'S HOUSE

GEMMA'S HOUSE

HOLLAND'S HOUSE

BEACH BREAK BAR & GRILL

PUBLIC BEACH

N
W E
S

CHAPTER 9

TRISTAN IS ALREADY WAITING outside when I step through the lobby doors. He's wearing a pair of blue swim trunks, his classic plain tee, and some flip flops. He also has a large cooler bag slung over one shoulder. "Ready?"

A surge of excitement rushes over me, but I smother it with a healthy dose of reality. "Do I get to know what we're doing?"

"Kayaking."

I don't know why, but I'm not expecting this answer. I've only been on a kayak a couple of times, and they aren't my fondest memories. Once, the plastic kayak was unknowingly taking on water until the boat got so heavy the sides were only a few inches above the surface, making it extremely difficult to both paddle and remove from the water. Another time, I forgot to sunscreen my shins and I sported outrageous tan lines for weeks after the sunburn subsided. "Oh. That sounds ... fun."

Tristan chuckles at my lack of enthusiasm. "I promise. You'll love it. It might even become the *most memorable outing* you've ever been on."

That might prove true, but likely because I'm on it with Tristan, not because I'm sitting in a kayak. "Speaking of, who's judging this little competition of ours?"

"We are." Tristan starts toward the parking lot, and I fall into step with him.

"The two of us?"

He nods like he can't see the problem.

"What happens if I choose my outing and you choose yours? We both win?"

"Absolutely not. There will be no participation awards. The winner has to earn it. And as mature, honest adults, I trust that we'll be able to come to the same conclusion—that I planned the superior outing."

"Your non-partiality is astonishing." Instinctively, I nudge my elbow into his side in a way that, in hindsight, is borderline flirtatious. Which is totally not acceptable. Even if Tristan laughs like it's the expected response.

"Here we are." Tristan gestures to the old, familiar golf cart. It's the same one his family had when we were in high school, and that surprises me a little. In a good way. With all the money the Palmers have, and likely Tristan, it would be easy for him to upgrade, but that's what I've always liked about the Palmers. They've never rubbed their wealth in the faces of those of us with less. They had nice things, but they never needed the newest or the best. And they typically used what they had until they couldn't.

Tristan pats the roof like the golf cart is a beloved horse and not an inanimate object. "Good old Bessie."

I laugh, remembering the name the Palmers gave to their cart years ago. "I'm shocked she's still running after everything you and Beau put her through."

"She's definitely been through a lot, but I can't bear to part with her before I have to. She's full of memories."

With his distant smile, I wonder if he's talking about memories with Bridget. I witnessed the two of them drive away together in old Bessie countless times, so it seems pretty likely. It's exactly the reminder I need to keep my heart in the correct lane.

We load into his golf cart and head north. The conversation is sparse at best, but with him sitting so close to me, I'm mentally going over the ground rules I set for myself.

1) Friends. Only friends and nothing more. Ever. Not even when my imagination tries to whisk me away to secluded islands and private beach cottages with Tristan as company. Friend zone is the safe zone. That's my new motto.

2) I cannot and will not guilt-blurt my confession. Timing is everything. It'll take a little while to get to a place in our friendship where an admission of this magnitude will make sense. I'll know when the moment comes. Hopefully.

3) Don't revert into seventeen-year-old Capri every time Tristan looks at me. Or talks to me. Or smiles at me. And especially not when he touches me—platonically.

I glance down at his knee, settled so close to mine that I can almost feel his body's energy jumping between our skin. The mere thought sends a rush of pleasure through me. This is going to be difficult.

Eventually, we turn off at the nature preserve. I haven't been here in years. We took a few school trips to the preserve, and I have a vague memory of coming with my family when I was young, but all I can recall is that I was hot and hungry and that I got a collection of bug bites as souvenirs.

We park the golf cart and Tristan pays at the kiosk, then we start down the paved road on foot to a water-front shack with kayaks and canoes stacked around it. A slender woman with tanned skin and a long, blond ponytail is organizing life jackets when she catches sight of us and straightens.

Tristan waves. "Hey, Lola."

"Tristan Palmer," she says with a smile just for him. I glance at her hand and notice a gold wedding band on her finger that somehow makes me feel less insecure. "Back already?"

"I had to bring my friend ... a different friend."

That infamous word again, and this time with an added

nuance that I'm trying hard to not care about. What *friend* did Tristan bring here recently? It's not my business, but he made it sound like he didn't have a lot of friends on the island he hangs out with at present. But maybe his *friend* isn't from the island. He did say he had no intention of dating anyone from the island again, not that he had no intention of dating.

Lola looks at me like she just noticed Tristan wasn't alone. "You look familiar. Are you a Collins?"

Again, I nod, and I feel Tristan's gaze shift to me.

"I know Tala. And my husband and I are big golfers, so we're also huge fans of your brother. How's his recovery going?"

Walker's back had been hurting for years, but it finally got bad enough that he underwent a pretty extensive surgery for it this past spring. "He seems to be doing well."

"Do you know if he'll make it back to the PGA tour this year?"

"I'm actually not sure." Walker doesn't inform me about much of anything in his life. I get most of my information about him from Mom, and on occasion, Tala.

"Well, tell him he has some loyal fans here on Sunset Harbor rooting for him."

"I will."

Lola's gaze shifts back to Tristan, who's still watching me. "You reserved the clear-bottomed, double kayak for four hours, right?" she asks.

He returns his attention to her. "Yep."

"I have it in the water for you already. Paddles are in there as well." She hands each of us a life jacket. And not just any life jacket, the old-school, bright orange kind that you put over your neck. "Make sure to keep these on, and don't disturb any of the wildlife. If they come to you, that's fine, just don't touch or feed them. But you know all the rules," she says to Tristan. "Besides that, have a great time."

"A clear-bottomed kayak?" I ask, snapping the waist strap of my life jacket.

Tristan nods, leading us toward the dock. "The water is clear enough, especially in the mangrove forest, that you can see all the way to the bottom."

And suddenly, kayaking sounds like the best idea ever.

I'm about to step into the front of the kayak when Tristan grabs the strap of my life jacket, halting me. "Not so fast." I turn to face him, and he has his phone out and in selfie mode. "I think it'd be wise to document our outings—you know, compile evidence so that when I win, you can't claim the whole thing was rigged."

"Ah. The proof will be in the pictures?"

"Something like that."

We stay a decent length apart—a still-becoming-friends distance—and he lifts up his phone, but before he clicks the side button, I drop my shoulders and give an exaggerated frown. I don't know where the idea comes from, but it feels right. When he presses on the thumbnail to see how it looks, a grin spreads across his face, and he holds the picture out so I can see it.

"Wow," I say, squinting at it to keep myself from smiling. "I look pretty miserable. Is that the proof you were talking about?"

"This is what you meant about watching out for the quiet ones, isn't it? You play dirty."

I shrug, no longer able to fight my smile. "Or maybe I play smart."

"I'm keeping my eye on you." He shakes his head, tucking his phone into his pocket, then helps me into the kayak before climbing into the seat behind me. He places his cooler bag between us as a barrier. I'm not sure if it's intentional since it's the most natural place to put it, but I can't help but feel it is. Tristan points toward our destination across the bay—the shady mangrove forest he referenced—and we start off. I'm not super efficient with the paddle, but Tristan's skills more than compensate.

Tristan clears his throat behind me. "The friend I mentioned coming here with is Noah Belacourt."

"Oh." I say it like my heart isn't soaring at the news his *friend* isn't some sporty, gorgeous outdoors woman from the mainland with sun-kissed skin and blue eyes that match the sky like Tristan's match the sea. Okay, so I may have created a mental image of her in my mind. "I didn't realize he's in town."

"Just for the summer. We like to go out kayaking together."

I don't know Noah personally. I've seen him on occasion, but because he went to private school in New York, I've never actually spoken to him (huge surprise here, I'm sure). But just because I don't know him doesn't mean I don't know all about him. Besides that, the Belacourts are the wealthiest people on the island and own the fancy Belacourt Resort at the north end where celebrities and other mega rich people vacation. They also have a reality tv show, *The Belacourts*. See the recurring theme? They are a bit obsessed with themselves. Which is why I hate to admit that their show is one of my guilty pleasures.

"That's fun," I say. "I've never met him."

"I'll have to introduce you two sometime. He's a great guy."

Did Tristan casually mention introducing me to the island's celebrity billionaire bachelor as though it's no big deal? Not that I actually expect it to happen. I'm not even sure I'd want to meet him considering the freaky amount of information I have stored in my head about him and his family, but that's so sweetly Tristan of him to offer.

We pass a few kayakers who are excitedly pointing in the direction opposite of us, and before I can wonder what it is they're looking at, a dolphin jumps out of the water. "Did you see that?" I ask, glancing back at Tristan.

His gaze is set where mine was and he nods. "How about a little side competition?" His smile returns to me. "Whoever spots the most wildlife before lunch gets the can of ice-cold Diet Coke I brought."

I shift to face him more fully. My life jacket lifts awkwardly into my neck with the attempt and digs into my cheek. I'm positive it's a super attractive look on me, particularly with the bright orange color clashing with my pale skin tone. "You only brought one?"

"Technically, I brought it for you, but this sounds like more fun."

"The dolphin counts as mine, then."

He shrugs. "I mean, if you feel right about that."

I huff which makes him chuckle. "Fine," I say. "We'll start the count now."

We begin paddling again, and I keep my eyes trained to movements, but I don't glimpse any. When we finally reach the shade of the mangroves, the temperature drops noticeably. The waterway is narrow, with trees that overlap above in a sort of canopy as if we're in some kind of Amazonian tree tunnel. Then I see a turtle lounging on a log. "One." I see another just behind it and point. "Two."

"One," Tristan says, pointing to a sea bird perched on a branch overhead.

After about an hour carrying on this way—paddling and pointing out wildlife—we come to a small grove where the water widens and steer our kayaks to the side on the off-chance someone needs to move past us. But considering we've only passed three other boats this whole time, I doubt it's necessary. Apparently, there aren't many people crazy enough to be out in this heat and humidity. Or possibly brave enough to venture this far into the mangrove forest waterways.

With our approach, a bird on a nearby tree takes flight. "One hundred thirteen," I say, setting the paddle across the kayak to give my throbbing arms a minute to recoup. "And what are you at?" I ask, already knowing the answer. "Seventy-eight, wasn't it?"

"One of us had to actually paddle," he says, throwing me one of those smiles that lights my insides on fire. "And, I hate to mention it, but you have a serious advantage sitting up front."

"Excuses. Excuses." I hold out my hand. "I'll take that Diet Coke now."

"Wow. No mercy." Tristan rummages through his bag and hands me the ice-cold soda. "I didn't realize you were so competitive."

"Neither did I." When I pop open the tab, it gives a satisfying hiss, and I take a swig before looking at the can in my hand like a love-struck woman. "Apparently, I just need the right motivation."

Tristan laughs, grabbing out a water for himself. "Speaking of, did you decide what you want your prize to be if you win?"

I shake my head. "I'm still thinking of something equal to your dedication request."

"I'm eager to hear what you come up with." He opens up the cooler again and tosses me a sandwich. "If I remember correctly, peanut butter and honey is your favorite?"

"It is." I smile and accept his offering, taking a bite of my sandwich. Not only did he remember the peanut butter and honey, but he remembered I prefer crunchy peanut butter. "I'm impressed."

"At my memory or my sandwich-making skills?"

"Both, actually. But I meant your memory."

"Then you should probably know I've got salt & pepper chips, some cut-up mangoes, and a double pack of Reese's with your name on it."

My heart stutters at his list of my favorite sack lunch items—things I regularly packed in my high school lunches.

Just friends. We're just friends. I repeat it several times to myself. The problem is that Tristan's regular thoughtfulness is on par with the romantic gestures by the heroes in my books and in romantic fiction at large. So the tell-tale signs for most women—things like remembering favorite foods—don't mean to Tristan what my hopeless romantic heart is trying to convince me it means. The very reason I know his favorite sandwich is turkey and cheese with sweet pickles, he always picks BBQ chips if those are an option, he loves citrus (oranges in particular), and his dessert of choice is a brownie. Or key lime pie. At least those used to be his favorites.

A splash in the water nearby has me searching the surface as though our competition hasn't ended. "What was that? A fish?" And then, suddenly, I see it. A manatee. And not one but two. No three. "Oh my gosh! There are several of them!" I exclaim, glancing at Tristan to make sure he's seeing the same thing I am. "Manatees!"

The smile Tristan wears tells me this wasn't just part of the plan, this was *the* plan. I'm utterly speechless.

My gaze catches on a movement beneath our kayak, and I glance down to see a manatee floating, belly-up, in the water just below us. I've seen my share of manatees from a distance but never this close in the wild except for one other time, and I'm filled with an overwhelming sense of joy. And then ... grief. And suddenly, completely unexpectedly, as I'm staring into the magnificent creature's little black eyes, I realize tears are streaming down my cheeks. Not just a few but a massive wave of them like the tide coming in. Or in my case, out. Thank heavens I bought waterproof mascara. I set my sandwich on my lap and attempt to wipe away the evidence with the back of my hand, hopeful that Tristan won't notice, but they won't stop.

Then a shuddering breath escapes me.

"You okay?" he asks, and I nod, keeping my gaze down and the back of my head to him.

Another shuddering breath, this one with a small gasp.

"Capri?" His fingertips graze my arm, but I don't look at him. "What's wrong?"

I shake my head, not wanting him to see me in this emotionally imbalanced state. "I'm fine," I manage to get out in a very I'm-not-fine sort of way.

The kayak shifts, and I realize it's Tristan moving the cooler so he can scoot closer. And then he's right behind my seat, rubbing my back with his hand. He doesn't say anything, he simply sits there comforting his weirdly emotional neighbor and probably second-guessing his whole plan of redefining our relationship with the island together.

After a minute, I feel I owe him some kind of explanation for my peculiar behavior. "Manatees remind me of my dad," I manage to get out, willing myself to stop there. But that's not the way things work. I'm a floodgate that is solid and unyielding until there's a slight breech, and once it starts, there's no stopping the flow. "About a year before he lost his battle with cancer, we were visiting my grandparents. He and I were taking the fishing boat to the mainland parking garage when we spotted a manatee and her baby in the canal. Instead of just pointing it out and continuing on our way, he turned off the motor and we sat there. I don't even know how long we watched them—the two of us together." Dad always made time for me. Which, for a person who tends to go unnoticed, meant the world.

"I didn't really know him," Tristan whispers, "but I do remember that he was always outside playing with you and your siblings when your family would visit the island."

Right when I think I'm finally getting a hold of myself, Tristan's acknowledgment causes a gasping sob to escape me, and I start full on ugly crying. Releasing months of pent-up emotions. Years, even. "I miss him a lot. And my grandpa. And the way things used to be before my whole life was turned upside down." The words are now gushing out of me, refusing to be dammed. "With Grandma at Seaside Oasis, Mom married to Stan and the two of them always off traveling the world together, and Tala and Heath in my grandparents' house, it's like losing everything all over again. I'm so happy for them all, I really am, but it's not easy letting go and moving on. It feels like all the memories I'm trying so desperately to hold on to are either fading or packed away in boxes."

His hand stills on my back. "That all must have been so hard on you, having to pick up and move while you were grieving. Now to have it all change again ... I'm sorry."

I sniff and look back at him. "I'm not sure where I belong anymore."

His expression is full of sympathy, and I can see the question in his eyes that he won't ask because he'd promised he wouldn't.

Instantly my gaze drops. "It's not the reason I've avoided coming home. Well, it's not the main reason."

He sits a moment in silence, leaving me the opportunity to continue my confession if I want, but there's absolutely no way I'm going to tell him about my secret identity on top of everything else I unintentionally unloaded on him. Especially when I have snot dripping from my nose and my eyes are all swollen from crying. I've likely already done irreparable damage to our budding friendship, and I'm just hoping it won't wither up and die before it even has a chance to bloom.

"I'm sorry again for whatever that was," I say, swiping a hand under my nose.

"I knew you loved manatees, but had I understood the connection, I would've told you about them beforehand."

Oh great, now he's feeling bad for bringing me on an outing that is so epic there's no way it won't win our competition. Why do I have to be me sometimes? "No, I'm so glad you brought me. Honestly." I risk a glance at him, and he looks more concerned than convinced. "I don't know what came over me. It's probably just PMS. I become an emotional mess when I'm about to start my period."

I freeze. Did I just tell Tristan I'm starting my period soon? What is the matter with me? "Sorry, I shouldn't have told you that." I place the palm of my hand over my tear-streaked face and groan. So much for not reverting to my seventeen-year-old self. Though I'm confident this is worse, considering my seventeen-year-old self never would've casually mentioned her monthly cycle to the boy she's loved her entire life. At least not on their first outing together.

Tristan's chuckle has me peeking through my fingers. "Despite what you might think, Capri Sun, I do realize women menstruate … and what that can entail."

Of course he does. He was with Bridget Hall for more than eight years. Eight years! Almost three years of high school, four years of college off and on (but mainly on), and they were engaged for more than a year while Tristan worked on his MBA. I'm not exactly sure of all the details, but that's the gist of it.

"Imbalanced hormones aside, thanks for planning this," I say. "Really."

A loud bump and a slight rocking motion sends our attention downward again. Near to where Tristan is sitting, the manatee's mouth is open against the bottom of the kayak like it's testing to see if the kayak is edible.

Tristan slowly scoots back, giving us a better view of the curious manatee. After a few attempts, it's clearly disappointed and comes up for a breath at our side before returning to his spot beneath us.

"Incredible," I say, taking another swig of soda and picking up the neglected sandwich from my lap in an attempt to move on from my embarrassing breakdown and get back to enjoying the moment.

A second manatee joins the one beneath us.

Tristan's gaze lifts to mine, and he smiles that darn smile of his that makes me start repeating my motto again: *Just friends. We're just friends.*

CHAPTER 10

"WHAT DO you mean you started crying?" Jane asks, sharing a nervous glance with Tala as we sit around the kitchen table.

I drop my attention to Serenity's nails and the layer of pink polish I'm brushing on. "I don't know. I just started crying when I saw the manatees."

"Like a tear or two?" The hope in Tala's voice makes my stomach sink. Both Jane and Tala have observed my floodgate *sobbing* at one point or another throughout the years, so I'm sure they're hoping Tristan wasn't witness to one of these sporadic episodes that seem to be brought on by emotionally heightened situations.

For example, my eighth-grade English teacher asked our class if we could think of an event in literature where someone risked their own life for another person. When he called on me (no, I didn't have my hand raised), the first thing that popped into my head was Mrs. Weasley battling Bellatrix Lestrange in Ginny's place—the "Not my daughter!" scene. And then suddenly, I was sobbing and blabbering about Fred and Tonks and Lupin. This occurrence had as much to do with the emotional overwhelm of being called on when I wasn't expecting it as with my strong feelings about this moment in *Harry Potter*. It's lucky Jane and I were established best friends at this point because her support mitigated most of the teasing.

"Nope. Full on bawling," I say. "And then I told him it's

probably because I'm PMSing since I'm about to start my period."

Neither of them speak, but I keep painting as if my admission doesn't faze me.

"All in all, I definitely think I helped make the outing even more memorable." But not in a good way. I finish painting Serenity's last nail and begin blowing on them.

"What about the rest of the date?" Jane asks.

"It wasn't a date," I remind her for the tenth time since she dropped by to see how things went with Tristan. I screw the lid on the nail polish and lean back in my chair. "And I'm not even sure how the rest of it went. From my ugly-cry session onward, I couldn't get out of my head. I highly doubt he'll want to repeat the events of today."

"He will," Jane says resolutely.

"I don't know. Maybe I should call this whole thing quits before I embarrass myself worse."

Tala quirks her head from the other side of the table to see Serenity's nails. "Those look so pretty," Tala says. Serenity lifts up her hands and wiggles her fingers. "How about you go pick out the movie. We should probably start it soon so you can get to bed on time."

"I already decided what movie we're watching—*The Princess Bride*."

Jane smiles. "Count me in! That's one of my all-time favorites."

"Don't you have plans tonight?" I ask. "Because there will be plenty of time to watch movies with us *after* you fall in love."

"No plans." She sighs dramatically, but then brightens again. "Well, besides *The Princess Bride*."

I lean toward her, reaching for her hand. "In that case, you definitely have to stay."

"As you wish."

At the laughter that bursts out of Jane and me, Tala rolls her eyes. "It's incredible that you two are still single."

Jane and I look at each other with widened eyes and gaping, offended mouths, then we laugh harder.

"We'll start the movie in a few minutes." Tala is looking at Serenity again. "Do you want to go get in your jammies?"

Serenity hesitates only briefly, then hops up from her chair at the table. When her footsteps echo on the stairs, Tala's gaze narrows on me, silencing the last of my laughter. "I'm going to begin by saying that I love you. Every. Single. Bit. Of. You. Is that clear?" I nod, the realization of why Serenity was sent away now dawning on me—Tala's transitioning into Mama mode and she doesn't want her daughter to hear the forthcoming lecture. "But you need to stop overthinking EVERYTHING. Tristan wouldn't have come up with this plan if he didn't enjoy being around you."

"He's trying to help. That's what Tristan does."

"Or maybe he actually likes you." When I pin Tala with a look, she lifts her hands. "As a friend. But either way, stop selling yourself short."

Jane is nodding in a way that makes me think this is some kind of intervention. "Tala's right. Just be your wonderful, glorious self. He won't be able to resist falling in love with you."

"I don't want him falling in love with me." Okay, so that's not entirely true. I may have subconsciously concocted a few fictional scenarios where he does exactly that, but that's beside the point. "I just need to be good enough friends that I can tell him the truth."

Jane and Tala sober, as though they'd forgotten that monumental piece of information.

"Preferably in a way that doesn't end with me having my name on a court order." I pause. "And, after today, I'd prefer to avoid another emotional breakdown during my confession." Is that asking too much?

"You're making this a bigger deal than it needs to be," Tala says.

"I really don't think I am."

She sighs. "Fine. Have you thought out how you're going to go about telling him?"

My brow lowers, not exactly sure what she's asking. "Besides just saying it, what other way is there?"

Tala's lips purse. "How would you get a character out of this situation?"

"A *fictional* character?"

She nods as if my emphasis on the fictional aspect isn't important.

I consider her question. If I had my heroine get herself into a similarly stupid situation, how would I have her get out of it? Lying obviously won't work, readers hate that. And a solid relationship can't be built on a lie. Hmmm ... Honestly, if I were writing this story, there's a good chance I'd have the hero discover the truth before she tells him to up the angst. He'd likely be disappointed and upset that she didn't trust him enough to tell him sooner, but in the end, after some time apart and a cathartic moment, he'd come to realize her reasons for it. Because how could he not? They'd be so in love by that point, there's no way he'd let this one long-ago offense come between them. "I've got nothing," I say, well aware that my fictional solution doesn't echo my and Tristan's real-life story in the least.

"I have an idea," Tala says. "What if you were to start hinting at the truth? Drop little clues that will make your big confession seem not so entirely massive."

"Like what?"

"Start hinting at your crush," Jane says with an unhelpful smile.

I shake my head. "That's not happening. Any other ideas?"

"Heath already told him you write, didn't he?" Tala asks.

I cross my arms in a reactive motion to the memory. "He did."

"Maybe that's a good thing. What if you let Tristan see small glimpses of the author side of you—the plotting, story-driven part that makes up backstories for strangers or tucks away an interesting fact or piece of information for later? The side of you that's always jotting ideas down in your notebook. The side of you that you're way too good at hiding from everyone but us."

"Ease Tristan into it," Jane says, nodding. "It's brilliant."

It actually does make sense. Giving him bits and pieces along the way instead of unloading it all on him in one fell swoop will hopefully mitigate both my concerns: a floodgate crying situation from too many pent-up emotions and the restraining order. "Okay, I'll do it."

SPRAWLED out on the bed in Tala's jammies, with teal blue nails that match the new flair pen sitting on my open notebook, I'm staring at my phone, wishing Tristan would have texted. But he hasn't, so I'm trying to garner the courage to text him before he decides to write me off completely after today.

I draw in a long, slow inhale.

I can do this.

Hey! It's Capri.

Obviously, he has my number. I erase the last part.

Hey! I wanted to reach out to you

Reach out to you? What am I, a secretary? I delete again.

Hey! You up for another outing?

That's acceptable. I read it aloud to make sure it actually sounds okay and that I didn't miss any blatant errors, and I press send.

CAPRI

Hey! You up for another outing?

My heart is beating with an intensity that causes my eardrums to thud as I wait for his reply. Then I begin to wonder if mentioning this on the same day as our last outing makes me look desperate. Maybe I should have sent it tomorrow. Is there a way to recall a text? Before I have time to look into it, three dots appear. I hold my breath, waiting.

TRISTAN

Perfect timing. I was just about to text you to get something on the books.

I release my breath. I didn't scare him away with my crying disaster! Or he's too nice to refuse me, but I'm fine with that too, at least for the time being.

CAPRI

Do you have plans Monday evening?

TRISTAN

I do now. What time were you thinking?

CAPRI

Come by when you're off work. Wear something comfortable.

TRISTAN

Sounds good. I'll be there at five.

Also, if you haven't found your keys by Thursday, you should plan on coming to the family swim night at Seaside Oasis. There will be snow cones.

CAPRI

I have a weakness for snow cones.

TRISTAN

> I remember that about you. That's why I
> mentioned it.

I'm wearing the stupidest grin as I read his last text, but I choose to forgo repeating my motto about the friend zone. I'm not planning to see Tristan again till the day after tomorrow, so I have plenty of time to steel my resolve.

With the high from our conversation still rushing through me, I open to a blank page in my new notebook and pop the lid off my pen. Hanging out with Tristan is like an inspiration gold-mine, and I might as well keep track of the golden nuggets I find as I go.

WELCOME TO
SUNSET
HARBO

BELACOURT RESORT

GOLF COURSE

NOAH'S HOUSE

JANE'S HOUSE

NATURE PRESERVE

DAX'S DUPLEX

SEASIDE OASIS RETIREMENT HOME

SUNSET REPAIRS

PHOENIX'S OFFICE

CITY OFFICES

SUNRISE CAFE

SCOOPS AHOY ICE CREAM

KEENE B&B

GULF OF MEXICO

TOWN SQUARE

BAKERY

BRIGGS'S APARTMENT

THE BOOK ISLE

CUTS AND CURLS

TRISTAN & BEAU'S HOUSE

CAPRI'S HOUSE

GEMMA'S HOUSE

HOLLAND'S HOUSE

BEACH BREAK BAR & GRILL

PUBLIC BEACH

N
W E
S

CHAPTER 11

I'M THROWING fresh ice packs into the picnic basket when there's a knock at the front door. I glance at the kitchen clock. Tristan's almost an hour late. He did text about fifteen minutes ago to apologize and let me know that he'd be here soon, which I very much appreciated since I'd convinced myself he was going to ghost me after Saturday's outing. But now everything's back on track (for the most part), and I'm eager for another shot to prove to Tristan I'm relatively normal. That I'm decent friend material.

Light, quick footsteps tell me Serenity or Jack have beat me to the door. Sure enough, the sound of a door opening is followed by Tristan's voice. "Hey there, Serenity. I'm looking for your aunt. Is she here?"

"Auntie Capri!"

"I'm coming," I call, hauling the overloaded wicker basket out of the kitchen.

When I round the corner, I stop, taking in Tristan's khaki shorts, navy tee, and white sneakers. We are more or less wearing the exact same thing. Well, the same colors anyway. I momentarily contemplate slinking away to go change, but his gaze meets mine, then it drops to my outfit before lowering to his.

"I see you got my message about the matching outfits," I say.

His mouth quirks at the sides. "Apparently."

Serenity glances back and forth between us. "You planned to match?"

I step next to him for easy comparison. "Who wore it better, Serenity?"

She grins, and despite Tristan pointing at himself, she points to me. "Auntie Capri. I like her shorts."

Tristan throws up his hands with a laugh. "I feel like I'm kind of at a disadvantage."

"Always the excuses with you." I send him a playful smile, ignoring the way my entire body reacts to teasing Tristan. Friends tease each other. Just because that hasn't been our relationship in the past doesn't mean it can't be part of our friendship moving forward. "Serenity is a less partial judge than some of us."

"That's probably true." He winks at Serenity, then opens the door for me, but before I step through, he grabs the wicker basket. "Here. Let me get that."

I willingly hand it over, then step outside into the humid afternoon air. As Serenity closes the door behind us, we make our way down the front steps.

"Again, I'm sorry I was late," he says, glancing over at me. "My last meeting ran a lot longer than I'd expected."

"It's fine. Though we might have to shuffle a few things to make sure the timing works out." I point at him. "And you can't take off points from my outing for the food being cold."

"Noted." Tristan lifts the basket and takes a whiff. "Wow. That smells amazing. Is it BBQ?"

"Chancie's." I know it's Tristan's favorite. At least, it used to be.

"You went to the mainland to get me Chancie's?"

"I'm in this to win it." I smile. "And I hope you're hungry, because I may have gone overboard on the portions."

"I'm always hungry, especially for Chancie's."

I don't doubt that he's always hungry. It must take a lot of sustenance to maintain that exceptionally toned physique. Though, considering his shopping cart at the mainland store, BBQ ribs and cheese grits probably aren't on his daily eating regimen.

I step up to the garage keypad and type in the code.

"So, am I allowed to know the plan for this evening?" he asks.

The garage door lifts and I smile, gesturing to two beach cruisers parked next to Tala's golf cart. "We're taking a bike ride." It's the simplest of the ideas Jane and I discussed, but most of my other ideas involve water, and there's no way I'm doing any water activities on day one of my period.

Tristan's gaze roves over Heath's bright blue bike. "It has a … bell."

I barely hold in my laugh at the uncertainty in his voice. "I guessed you'd like that feature." I take the basket from him and secure it on his bike's rear rack with the bungee cords Tala set out for me. "And since yours doesn't have a basket in front like mine, I'm going to let you tote this one."

He stares at the bike and back at me. "Heath rides this thing?"

I can no longer fight a smile, and I set my hands on my waist. "You're not too cool for a beach cruiser, are you?"

"It has a bell," he repeats, as though that's the very symbol of lost manliness. "If Beau sees me on that thing he'll never let me live it down."

"I won't tell Heath you said that." I look at the bike and then back at him. "It's fine if you would rather forfeit the competition."

His gaze flies to me. "Oh, there's no chance I'm forfeiting."

I pat the seat of the cruiser. "Then you'd better get on the bike."

He chuckles, shaking his head, and closes the distance between us until my neck is craned to look up at him. "You realize you're setting a precedent right now, don't you? A precedent I fully intend to utilize in my upcoming plans if you won't back down?"

Nerves lift my stomach, and I'm not sure if it's because of his proximity or his threat to plan something I might be opposed to. "Go ahead. I'm not scared." I'm totally scared.

Tristan throws his leg over the bike, holds my gaze, then dings the bell. "Let's do this."

Once we get the bikes out and I shut the garage door, I hop on Tala's cruiser and start pedaling before Tristan realizes what's happening. "First one to the lighthouse wins," I call over my shoulder. With the way Tristan lights up, I'm thinking maybe I shouldn't have made this part a competition.

CHAPTER 12

WHEN I PULL my bike up next to Tristan's, I'm huffing and my legs are shaking with exhaustion. It's now apparent that beach cruisers are meant for exactly what they were named for—cruising, not racing. Though even on a bike meant for racing, I'd probably be dying.

"You almost had me there." Tristan, unsurprisingly, is not the least bit out of breath, and I know it's because he was going easy on me—keeping a pace I could just barely keep up with, then pulling ahead right at the end so he could collect the win. Otherwise, he'd have been here twenty minutes before me.

Unable to speak through my puffing, I drop the kickstand and walk to the basket attached to Tristan's bike to grab waters for us. I hand him his, then take a seat on one of several large rocks in front of where the bikes are parked. They're used to block golf carts from driving on the sandy walkway to the lighthouse since, being that it's situated on a tidal island, the pathway's submerged beneath the water half of the time. Thankfully the tide shouldn't be in for another hour and a half, but we should probably plan to eat after just to be safe.

Despite how my tailbone aches against the warm stone, it feels nice to not have weight on my legs. "Maybe I let you win," I say, finally catching my breath a little. I twist the lid off the water bottle and guzzle the entire thing in one go. "You seem like you needed it after the ego hit of having to ride a bike with a bell."

He dings the bell again. "I appreciate that. Especially after your Diet Coke win yesterday." He glances at the basket. "Speaking of, is there some sort of prize for my victory?"

"Unfortunately not. Though I should have pegged you as one of those people who needs to be rewarded with every success." Wow. I am on fire with this banter. I'm definitely going to have to jot down a few of these one-liners I'm throwing out there.

He leans forward on the handlebars of his bike, locking his gaze on mine. "How about I get to ask you a question, then? And you have to answer."

Right when my breaths were coming more easily, my lungs constrict again. It's honestly like this man is in possession of a manual on romance. A *question I have to answer*? Classic. "It can't be about my reason for avoiding the island."

"It won't be."

I hesitate, still not sure I want to agree, but those darn green eyes of his are hindering the signal from the logical part of my mind again. Besides, real friends are open with each other, and that's what we're supposed to be. Real friends. "Okay."

"Okay? You'll answer my question?"

I shift under his appraising gaze and lift up my index finger. "One question."

"Hmm." His gaze goes distant and he brings a hand to his chin, then his thumb rubs across his bottom lip.

I'm not staring. You're staring.

"I've got it," he says, and I hurry and pull my eyes from his lips so he doesn't notice me gawking. "The day we took the sunset boat ride—"

"It can't be about that either," I say, shaking my head. Thankfully, I'm already bright red from biking here, so my intensifying color shouldn't be too noticeable.

He lifts his hands in a calm-down motion. "I was just going to ask: *before* that, when you were sitting in the fishing boat by the dock, what had you been thinking about?"

Exactly like when Tristan asked me that day ten years ago, I'm back on home plate wearing roller-skates, with a racket in hand and wondering where in the world that pitch came from, what I'm supposed to do with it, and what game we're even playing here. I give a tight laugh, hoping to buy myself some time. "You remember that?" The whole experience is ingrained into each neuron in my brain, but I'd assumed Tristan hadn't thought about that moment a second time.

"Every so often, the memory pops into my head." He shrugs casually, as if he isn't asking me to bear my soul to him. "It seems like something worth knowing. What can cause such a look of utter contentment?"

I glance toward the lighthouse, still attempting to figure out exactly how to answer. Then I recall Tala's idea about giving Tristan hints that'll make my final confession seem less random. Nothing too condemning, but a minor revelation. "I have stories in my mind—full on scenes and characters. Sometimes, when I close my eyes, it's like I'm watching a movie."

"And what *movie* were you watching in your mind that day?"

My heart thumps as if encouraging me to continue, but I shake my head and hold up my index finger again. "Sorry, just one. You'll have to win another competition if you want that answer."

He flicks his head in the direction of the lighthouse. "First one there wins?"

"Not a chance." I laugh, glancing at my watch and standing to get the picnic basket off the back of his bike. It'd probably be safe here, but between the heat and the birds, we'll just have to tote it along. "But we should get going. We want to make sure we don't get stuck on the island at high tide."

Tristan steps up next to me and takes the basket. "I don't know, that sounds pretty memorable."

We start across the sandbar that leads to the lighthouse side. "Especially with Beverly and Bill for company."

"Who?"

"The couple giving us a tour of the lighthouse."

"Since when can you take a tour of the lighthouse?"

"You just have to know the right people, I guess."

His brows are lifted, but he doesn't say anything. Being a Palmer, Tristan is one of the most well-connected people on the island while I keep a much more intimate circle, if you will. But Tala brought her kids to see the lighthouse a few weeks ago and got to talking with the couple that were just hired as property managers for the historic site. They gave Tala and her kids an impromptu tour and were apparently super happy to do it, so Tala reached out to them on my behalf to see if they'd be willing to do another one for us.

When we're nearly across the sandy, tidal path, the lighthouse door opens. A stout woman with gray curls and a friendly face steps out to greet us. "I don't even need to ask if you're Tala's sister," she calls. "You look just like her."

"Okay, so my sister knows the right people," I whisper before lifting a hand in greeting. "I'm Capri. And this is my friend, Tristan."

Tristan waves a hand.

"I'm Beverly. It's nice to meet you both." Her kind eyes take us in. "And don't you two look cute in your coordinating outfits."

Tristan and I share an amused glance.

"It was his idea," I say, shooting a grin his way. "He likes matching when we go out in public together." I can see him shaking his head in my periphery, his laughter vibrating in the humid air between us. Success.

"Actually," Tristan says, and I'm sure he's going to explain the real reason we're matching, but instead, he holds out his phone toward Beverly. "I forgot to take a picture before we left. Any chance you could grab one for us?"

"Of course." Beverly takes the outstretched phone and

ushers us in front of the red lighthouse door. I grip my hands together, feeling all kinds of awkward now that the proximity wall has been infiltrated. "Come on, you two. If you're chummy enough to coordinate outfits, you can get a little closer than that. Closer—" She gestures for us to move in more, and Tristan places a *chummy* arm around my shoulder, but Beverly's not having it. She drops the phone and gestures to my hands. "Sweetie, you look so stiff. Why don't you put your arm around his waist?" I'm pretty sure this woman has missed her calling as a portrait photographer.

I follow directions (because that's who I am), and I try not to focus on every muscle fiber in Tristan's lower back and the way my greedy little fingertips seem to be memorizing the feel of them.

"You two are just the absolute cutest." Beverly takes a few steps toward us and grabs more pictures before passing the phone back to Tristan.

He slides it into this pocket without looking this time. "Thanks, Beverly."

"And thanks for agreeing to give us a tour," I say, eager to keep our conversation moving and my obstinate thoughts about Tristan's back muscles at bay. "Tala said it was fun to see the inside of a place we've seen from the outside for our entire lives. A really long time ago now, I also heard this guy"—I flick my chin toward Tristan—"say that he always wanted to see the view from the top."

This time when Tristan's gaze settles on me, the warmth seeps into my core, making me feel as though I might overheat. Or it's likely I'm just recovering from the impromptu photo shoot ... and possibly still the bike race.

"Well, I'm just thrilled you're both here." Beverly claps her hands together in front of her. "The last property manager was apparently quite the recluse and hadn't given a tour in over thirty years, but that's not how my Bill and I plan to go about this job—and I told the City Council as much. I said, if we take on the position of managers for this historic relic, we want people to be able to visit it. Honestly, I thought they might offer the position to someone else, but I didn't care. What's the point of keeping a historic site in such great condition when the public that's paying for all those repairs aren't allowed inside? That's nonsense. Besides, all lighthouses in the US are now automated, with the exception of the Boston Light, of course, so it's not like there's harm to be done by letting interested people have a look around." Beverly finally pauses before gesturing us inside. "But you two didn't come to hear me chatter on and on. Let's head on in. You can leave your basket just inside so you don't have to carry it to the top. Even without the extra weight, the climb isn't easy, but the view from the top is worth the effort."

Oh no, why did I think this was a good idea after a bike ride here? My legs are already protesting at the thought of it. "How many steps are there?" I ask, stepping over the threshold behind her.

"Two hundred and three."

I glance over my shoulder at Tristan and mouth, "Two hundred and three?"

Tristan sets the basket next to the door and leans in behind me, his breath tickling my neck. "You can always hop on my back if you need to."

The way his grinning face lingers near mine, I know his offer comes with a stipulation I'm not going to like. "And what will that cost me?"

He smiles. "Just one little answer."

Looks like I'll be making it to the top of the lighthouse unassisted, wobbly legs and all.

CHAPTER 13

THE SKY IS GROWING dark as we make our way home on the bikes.

"So, what'd you think?" I look over at Tristan, and a wave of pleasure rushes over me at the sight of him. My nervous system is obviously still getting used to our interactions. "Was it worth the wait?"

"Honestly?" His smile tells me his answer before he even speaks it. "It was awesome." His eyes go back to the boardwalk we're riding on. "Between the view, Beverly's detailed story about how she and Bill met, and that food you brought, I have to admit, you came in strong with this one, Capri."

"Not manatee strong."

His smile grows again. "I don't know. I'm nervous."

"It was the Chancie's key-lime pie that kept me in the running, wasn't it?"

"That was a very strategic move."

My bike bumps, and I grip the handlebar so I don't lose control. What was that? Once I feel balanced again, I glance behind me at the boardwalk, but in the dim light, I can't see what I could have possibly ran over.

"You good?" Tristan asks, following my gaze.

"Yeah. I must have hit a rock or something." I turn my attention back to him. "So, what's next for us?" My question hangs in the air for a brief moment before I think to clarify. "Outing wise."

"What's the key situation?"

"As of now—unchanged. This morning, I called every business on Sunset Harbor as well as the mainland parking garage, but no one has had keys turned in." My legs are starting to burn again, despite that we are on flat ground. They're probably near to hitting their max exertion level for the day. "Unfortunately, I'll need to call the dealership tomorrow to place an order for a new fob."

"What about your house keys?"

"I'll hire a locksmith, but I have another set inside."

"Why don't I drive you there this weekend? You said you had a fob at your house, and if you have to pay for a locksmith anyway, it'd be the cheapest option. Plus, it'll also give you more time for your keys to show up before you have to buy a replacement."

Despite his kind offer, all I hear is that Tristan is eager to see me on my way. The keys are supposed to be the indicator that our time together is almost up, but now he wants to forego the entire wait and simply take me home. "You don't have to do that."

"I'm happy to."

Of course he is.

And here I thought things were going well between us. We seemed to hit a natural flow and balance to our conversations today. It felt easy. Like ... friends. But apparently not. "Thanks," I say, my breaths coming out with more effort. "That'd actually be great. If you have time for it." Looks like my confession will also be sooner than I want. And now, despite the four-hour round trip drive I get to spend in Tristan's company, I'm dreading Saturday.

"Is your back tire flat?" Tristan's gaze is set on my back wheel.

I pull my bike to a stop and look at my back tire. Sure enough, it's deflated. No wonder it was getting harder to pedal.

I huff out a breath and get off my bike. "I'll walk it the rest of the way. We aren't that far."

"Why don't you leave it here and we'll come back for it in a golf cart."

"If I'm walking, I might as well—"

"I'll give you a ride." Tristan pats the handlebars in front of him.

With the way my stomach somersaults in absolute delight at the thought, I set my gaze forward and start pushing the bike. What is wrong with me? "I'm not sure I could manage it."

"I'll let you ask me a question."

Without permission, my feet pause. "Any question?"

"*Any* question."

I don't know why the offer's even a temptation. Not two minutes ago, Tristan basically let me know he's ready to put an end to our redefining-our-relationship-with-the-island agreement and take me home himself. But I do have a question for him. Well, technically, I have two questions for him, but I'm not even sure I truly want to know the particulars of what happened between him and Bridget. And I'm definitely not brave enough to ask.

I scoot the bike just off the boardwalk, drop the kickstand, and join a smiling Tristan. "Why don't you and Walker get along?" I waste no time spitting it out so I don't cower and ask him his favorite color or what his favorite animals is. I already know those answers—blue and otters. Cute, huh?

Tristan's brows lift. "That's not the question I was expecting."

"What question were you expecting?" I ask, too curious to resist.

He holds up his index finger between us exactly like I did to him earlier. "One question."

I cross my arms, trying to appear unamused.

"Fine." He lets out a heavy breath as if he's about to grant me some huge concession. "Because I'm so generous, I'll give you the option: your first question or your second?"

Suddenly, I really want to know what he assumed my question would be. Have I been waiting for the answer to my other question for years? Possibly. But now that Walker's around more, maybe I can finally get the truth out of him instead. Or I can win another side competition. If there is one in the time we have left. "Second, I guess. What was it you thought I'd ask?"

Tristan smiles, like he's expecting me to choose that option. "I'd assumed you'd want to know, first hand, what happened between me and Bridget."

Okay, I'm glad I picked option two. Except ... "Since you already answered my *one* question, I don't get the answer to this one, do I?"

Tristan chuckles. "Do you want it?"

I shrug as though it doesn't matter, but the way my eyes are locked on his, I'm sure he can decipher my actual feelings.

"I suppose you did win the *who-wore-it-better* competition."

"Exactly," I say, pointing at him with way too much gusto.

He just smiles at my over-the-top reaction. "I'm guessing you're probably aware we dated on and off through undergrad ... more on than off once she transferred to FSU."

I nod.

"Well, junior year, toward the end of the football season, I jacked up my knee pretty bad and had to get surgery. The recovery was brutal, and by the time I resumed regular practice with my team that next summer, the previous second-string quarterback—my good friend, Logan Phelps—was killing it. It didn't take me long to realize, going from starter to bench-warmer, that any chance for a future in football was very likely gone. Unfortunately—or maybe fortunately—Bridget felt differently. She said I was giving up on my dream to play professional. But, in hindsight, it was pretty much always her dream for us.

"I think it took her a while to recognize how drastically the new version of our life deviated from her original version. We got engaged right before I moved to Gainesville for my MBA. She stayed in Tallahassee to work, the plan being that we'd get married the next summer and she'd join me for the last year of my program. Then, after I graduated, we were going to move back to Sunset Harbor." He glides a hand through his golden hair, distracting me momentarily. "The second time she pushed back the wedding date, I finally realized something was off. With the conversation that followed, she ended the engagement. Two weeks later, she and Logan were together. Two weeks." He gives a wry laugh and shakes his head. "That was a punch to the gut."

I've overheard the entirety of that story in bits and pieces over the last few years, but hearing it from Tristan adds an extra layer of hurt that I feel for him. Logan, his *good friend*, took his place as quarterback and then took Bridget. And on top of all of that, Logan was drafted into the NFL. So apparently, Bridget got exactly what she wanted in the end—a pro football player for a husband.

"I'm really sorry," I say. "That's awful."

"It is what it is at this point. She's happy and I'm ..." His mouth quirks, and he shrugs. "And I'm finally moving on." My heart lifts briefly, and I wonder if I'm part of the reason for it, but then his gaze drops from mine to the pavement between us. He lets out an audible huff as though there's something else he needs to say but he doesn't know quite how to say it. "Capri, I'm just here until the end of summer."

As quickly as my heart lifted, it falls, crashing into the cavity of my chest with a debilitating pain. "I thought ..." My words trail off as I try to make sense of what he means. "Your dad said you were coming home to run Seaside Oasis."

"I think that's what he'd hoped originally." His chest rises with his slow inhale, then his eyes meet mine again. "But my family's decided to sell Seaside Oasis. Actually, we're selling all four of our centers."

My lips part. "And that's why you're back on Sunset Harbor? To help with the sale?"

He gives a slight nod. "I'm the point guy. I know this affects you and your family, so I want you to know that I'm being super picky with prospective buyers. We won't sell until we know the centers will be in good, capable hands. It really is for the best," he says, as if he's trying to convince himself as much as me. "Since Beau has no interest in running them, and I ..." He pauses. "Well, my old offensive coach at FSU was just hired on as head coach at a college in California. He asked if I'd be interested in being one of his assistant coaches."

"Wow," I say, hoping he can't hear the devastation in my voice. But all I can think about is how this will affect Grandma and Heath and so many other people on the island. And the fact that Tristan will be in California. But I attempt a smile. "That's exciting."

"Yeah. It is." His gaze is distant when he nods this time. "My entire life I've been a do-what's-expected-of-me type of person. Grandpa wanted me to play football, so I did. Mom wanted me to be involved in student council, so I did that too. Bridget wanted me to try for the pros, so that's where I set my sights. When that didn't pan out, I went to get my MBA like my dad suggested and never once questioned going into the family business. After I graduated, I went to Tampa to run our center there, and the plan was, with my dad's retirement, I'd move to Sunset Harbor and take over running all four centers from here. But then I got here and... I don't know. I felt stuck." His gaze meets mine with intensity. "It's like one day I woke up to realize I was living a life I didn't choose for myself."

There's a warring in Tristan's eyes that make my heart soften and my worried thoughts quiet. He clearly hasn't made the decision lightly. So, as his friend, what he needs is my support and encouragement, no matter how much I dislike the idea of him being on the other side of the country from where I am, not to mention having someone else running Seaside Oasis. "That makes sense. And, for what it's worth, I think you'll make a wonderful coach."

A slight smile touches his lips. "Thanks, Capri Sun."

We sit—well, Tristan sits on his bike and I stand an arm's length away—in silence for a minute, allowing our thoughts to wander. Then I feel his gaze settle on me, and I meet it.

He rolls the bike forward slightly so he's closer to where I'm standing. His teasing grin seems too light for my current mood, but Tristan is my weakness, so I smile in return. "What?"

"Heath said Tala's read a few of your stories," he says. "Does that mean you have more than one finished book waiting around to be published ... in need of a dedication?"

Before I have a chance to curse Heath's name for ever telling Tristan I write, I remember the new plan. It's a good thing Tristan knows. Every hint at the truth will make the final confession easier. "Something like that."

"And they're all romances?" The intensity of Tristan's smile makes me blush.

My stomach tightens, and I'm too aware of the pre-conceived notions surrounding romance in all its varying forms. My reviews have been full of them for years: *For a romance, it was decent; Three Stars! Which is as high of a rating as I'll go for a romance; Complete and utter fluff, which is expected being that it's a romance.* See the pattern? But if I intend for Tristan to glimpse this part of me, I can't cop-out and say that it's a lucrative market to write in. That's not why I write romance. "Those are the best kind of stories."

"Really?"

"Love is a universal experience. We're all seeking to love and be loved. It's something everyone can understand and relate to."

"I can see that."

"And love, or the lack of it, encompasses countless other feelings—happiness, sadness, jealousy, heartbreak, redemption, pettiness, wholeness, and on and on. Love stories are where we can see the whole spectrum of human emotions on display—in both its lowest and highest forms. That's what romance is. What's better and more impactful than that?"

Tristan's brows are raised and he gives an impressed nod. "If I were a reader, I think you might have just convinced me to pick up a romance."

I stare at him as though this revelation is more upsetting than his previous one about his family selling Seaside Oasis. Fictional Tristan loves reading as much as I do. "You don't like reading?"

"I read an occasional non-fiction if it comes highly recommended, but I can't remember the last fictional book I read. I think it was a Dan Brown, maybe? Years ago, though." I can't seem to wrap my head around the fact that Tristan doesn't enjoy reading, and he chuckles when I don't reply. "I hope that's not a dealbreaker or anything."

I shake my head a little too vigorously. "Not at all," I say, certain he means a dealbreaker for our short-lived friendship, nothing more. Because not only is he taking me home on Saturday, but he's also about to move across the country. "I'm just surprised."

"Why's that?"

I shrug, not sure I want to answer. "You seem like someone who reads."

He leans forward on his handlebars, his grinning eyes set on me. "I feel like I need to hear more of your thoughts on this."

I also lean forward, lowering my voice. "Which is why I'm stopping right there."

He laughs, shaking his head.

Ready to change the subject, I appraise the bike and his position on it before stepping closer. "Remind me how I get on this thing? The last time I rode on handlebars, I think I was in middle school." Technically, I watched a few videos of it being done when I was writing my fourth book, but that was also years ago. Though, to this day, that handlebar scene is still one of my favorites I've written. I'm not sure the specifics of the kiss were logistically possible, but again, that's the beauty of fiction —the smudging of details to make things more idealistic. But now is definitely not the time to think about the logistics of kissing on a bike.

"Why don't you—" The sound of an approaching golf cart has us both glancing behind us, and Tristan groans when he sees the souped-up police cart with his brother at the helm.

"Hey!" Beau pulls up next to us. "This man isn't bothering you, is he Capri?"

I smile at Tristan as though I'm tempted to say that he is, but instead I shake my head. "No. I got a flat tire."

Beau leans sideways to see the bike behind me, and I get a brief glimpse of his dog. It's the least intimidating dog I've ever seen—a Chow Chow with a lolling tongue hanging out the side of her mouth. But I guess if Sunset Harbor were to have a police dog, it's a Chow Chow breed kind of island. Beau puts his cart in park and heads toward the bike, intentionally strutting in a way that makes Tristan roll his eyes. "If you'd like, I can load this up and drop it off for you at your sister's."

"That'd be super helpful. Thanks, Beau."

Beau walks the bike to his cart and lifts it up onto a rack along the back. "That's my job, miss." He moseys back toward me. "To serve the people of Sunset Harbor how and where I'm able." He then dips his chin and winks at me, as if he's some sort of charming sheriff from the wild west.

"I'm much obliged," I say, dipping my own head in return, intrinsically knowing it's the correct response.

Beau offers his winning smile that looks a lot like his brother's though it doesn't do the same crazy thing to my insides. "I always liked you, Capri Sun."

At hearing Beau use Tristan's nickname for me, I glance at Tristan. His eyes are fixed on Beau, and his lips are in a straight line like he's not amused by any part of our interaction, which doesn't make sense to my brain. Tristan isn't the jealous sort. At least not when it comes to me.

"Thanks for your help, Officer Palmer," Tristan says. "Now, instead of flirting with the civilians, I'm sure there's a possum that needs to be removed from an attic somewhere."

Beau looks at me while pointing at his brother. "You sure you're going to be okay if I leave you with this disgruntled man? You can always squeeze between me and Xena if you feel the need. I'd be more than happy to take you wherever you want to go." I know Beau's trying to get under his brother's skin because they'll make a competition out of anything. And apparently, right now, the competition somehow involves me.

"That's really kind of you, but I think I can handle him."

"If you say so." Beau climbs back into his cart and gives Xena a sound pat on the head which is returned with an affectionate kiss to his face. "Down girl," he says with a smile. "We're on duty."

"See you at home." Tristan offers a wave that slightly resembles a triumphant gloat.

Beau starts his cart forward but suddenly brakes and locks eyes with his brother. "Nice bike, by the way. The bell suits you."

Tristan smiles right back at him and rings it defiantly. "I think so too."

"And if Toto escapes from your basket there in the back, make sure he's leashed. I don't want to have to write my own brother a ticket. Again."

"Your *Wizard of Oz* references never get old."

And with that, Beau laughs, flips on his lights, and drives off.

"I never pictured Beau becoming a police officer," I say, drawing Tristan's attention back to me.

"Because he was always getting in trouble?"

"Basically." I glance at his golf cart in the distance. "But it suits him. And I know the ladies far prefer him to Officer Francis." I throw out this last bit to test the waters on my jealousy hypothesis, and sure enough, Tristan's brows lift and his eyes narrow just a touch. He's jealous. Only a little. And maybe not that I think this about Beau, but that others think it as well.

"So, I've heard. Though considering Officer Francis is like eighty years old now, I'm not sure that's much of a recommendation." His gaze settles on me. "But that reminds me of another question I have for you."

"Yeah?"

"Did you ever have a crush on Beau?"

I nearly laugh out loud but resist, and instead, I take a step closer to the bike, feeling a boost in confidence at the mere possibility of Tristan being jealous about anything to do with me. "I'd really love to answer that, but you didn't earn another question."

Tristan's unable to fight his smile though he looks like he's putting in a significant effort.

"But I will say that I'm sorry if I've permanently damaged your brother's image of you by making you ride a bike with a bell."

He leans back in the seat in mock appraisal. "Actually, it's a pretty great bike. I might need to get me one. And Beau one. In pink. With a front basket and a bell for each of his handles."

"And long, streaming tassels."

"Definitely tassels."

"He's going to love it. Maybe you should also get him one of those seats that fit two people. That'd be handy right now."

"Speaking of," Tristan scoots back in his seat. "If you come stand in front of me, I can lift you onto the handlebars."

My mind needs no prodding to create an image of exactly how this will go down—me standing way too close to Tristan when his hands settle on my waist, his grip firm and ... I'm shaking my head. There's no way I'll risk falling harder for him when he's already trying to get rid of me. And he's moving. Friend zone is the safe zone. "I'm sure I can get up from the front." I straddle the front tire, facing away from Tristan, and place one hand on each side of the handlebars behind me. I give a little hop, but it's not enough to get me onto the bar. When I attempt it again, it works, but the bar is (unsurprisingly) hard to balance on, so I'm forced to lean into Tristan's perfectly firm upper body for support.

"Got it?" he asks.

"I think so," I manage to get out, despite the fact that my vital organs seem to be spasming with our proximity. The very reason I chose to climb on this way has been thrown out the metaphorical window. My back is now pressed against him, with his hands grasping my waist and the side of his face way too close to mine. Not that I'll risk it for the sake of drawing a firm conclusion, but if I turned my head, I'm pretty sure my kissing-bike-scene logistics actually weren't too far off in my book, *Summer Fling*.

Carefully, Tristan removes his hands from my body and sets them next to mine on the handlebars. Like right next to them— the inside of his hand pressed against the outside of mine—and the current flowing through my skin has an electrifying effect. But I don't let go. "Let me know if you need me to stop." He starts pedaling. "You could also face me if it'd be easier. That way you could put your feet on the middle bar."

Another image flashes through my mind—one of Tristan and me face to face—that I like less. (Well, truthfully, I like it more, which means I should like it less.) My resolve is set. I will manage the entire ride home in this position or die in the attempt. And with the way I'm teetering on this thin little bar, there is a decent chance of the latter.

CHAPTER 14

THE ACCENT COLORS of Grandma's room perfectly match the teals and blues of the bay you can see from her screened porch. Off-white, creams, and light pinks—like the color of shells—form the base color-palette. "It's beautiful," I say, taking in the decorated space I've only seen while chatting with her over the phone.

The area's small but perfectly cozy, with a sitting room that is separated from her sleeping area by a partial wall. The bathroom is immaculate, and she even has her own kitchenette. But my absolute favorite part is the simplified version of her framed-photo gallery from home in updated, light wood frames. There are only a dozen pictures or so, but they're some of the most classic: Grandpa, Walker, and me fishing from the dock at the back of the house; all three of us Collins kids on the Fourth of July with bright eyes and holding sparklers; and a picture of my whole family, dad included, gathered around me and Tala with mermaid tails made of sand.

Grandma steps up next to me, her eyes on the pictures. "The rest are in a photo album I keep in my closet. That way, whenever I'm missing one of you, I can pull it out."

I look over at her. "Do you like it here? Honestly."

"I really do." Grandma lets out a slow breath. "I'll admit the first few months weren't easy, and I've definitely had some hard moments, but it truly is a wonderful facility. There are so many classes and outings and people to socialize with. Not having to cook for myself or take care of a house that's way too big for just me, it's been … liberating. And now with Virginia next door, it'll be just like it was."

For a brief moment, I again wonder how the Palmers selling this place will affect Grandma, but I quickly push the thought away. I can't dwell on that right now, or Grandma will start prodding for information I can't give. Besides, I trust Tristan will thoroughly vet any potential buyers exactly like he said he would. So, at this point, it's needless worrying.

"I'm glad." Not being here to see how she's faring has been one of the hardest things about adhering to the Sunset Harbor Avoidance Protocol, but now that I'm with her, she does seem more carefree. Younger even. Maybe I should consider moving into a retirement center myself. Having prepared meals and a cleaning and laundry service during deadline mode would be invaluable. Not to mention that the planned activities would definitely help this introvert get some much-needed socializing in, and it'd be with one of the age demographics I feel most comfortable talking to. It's unfortunate I'm more than half a lifetime too young for a place like this.

Grandma begins to empty the bag of requested groceries I brought her from Tala. Fruit. Chips. Peanut butter and jam. A loaf of bread. Two packs of thin mints. And a package of Fig Newtons. She opens the Fig Newtons and takes one out, stuffing it in her mouth and savoring every chew until it's gone. For all the wonderful things I've heard about the food here, Grandma's exuberance over a fig-filled cookie suddenly gives me pause. Surely she's getting enough to eat.

"Want one?" she asks, stretching the package toward me.

"No thanks, I just ate breakfast," I say, and she pops a second cookie. "How is Virginia settling in?"

"There's been a slight *incident*, but I'm really hopeful it'll resolve itself soon."

"An incident?"

"Virginia isn't thrilled with a few of the rules here at Sunset Harbor." She opens her mini fridge and sticks the fruit inside. "She's convinced some of the residents to go on a hunger strike with her."

My lips part. "You aren't participating, are you?"

"Oh, only here and there. Mainly when I'm with Virginia."

So that's why Grandma requested the groceries, so she could eat in her room, away from Virginia's judgmental eyes. That woman! Don't get me wrong, I love her, but when she feels wronged, nothing stands in her way of setting things right according to her own skewed notions of justice. "You need to talk to her. A hunger strike can't be healthy for the other residents." Especially considering some of their advanced ages and medical conditions.

"She'll come around soon. Once she realizes Tristan isn't out to get her—you know how she still holds on to the whole Sawyer vs Palmer rivalry." Grandma finishes putting all the groceries into the cabinet and turns to face me again. "Speaking of Tristan, Tala mentioned you've been out together a second time." Grandma waggles her eyebrows.

"We have, but just as friends." The pinking of my cheeks isn't helpful to my cause.

"Either way, I want to hear all about it."

"There really isn't much to tell. We went kayaking Saturday, and yesterday we went on a bike ride to the lighthouse."

"For a woman who hopes to become a published author one day, I'm confident you can do better than that. I need details." When I tip my head to the side, she mirrors me. "Or I can always ask Tristan."

"Fine," I say, well aware I'll never out will-power Grandma. "But this is for your ears only. I don't want any of this spreading around Seaside Oasis. Is that clear?"

"Crystal clear. Let's have a seat." She takes me by the hand to lead me, but when she heads past the sofa, I realize she means on the porch. "I'm guessing this might take a minute, so we might as well enjoy the view while we chat."

The view of the tattooed boat mechanic, Dax Miller, that is.

I SURPRISINGLY DIDN'T RUN into Tristan at Seaside Oasis when I visited Grandma this morning (his office door was closed both when I came and left), which was sort of a relief. And a disappointment. So my heart soars when my phone lights up with his name during another Vanderduesen movie night. It's not the least bit surprising that Walker is the only one that notices my incoming text. It's like he can sense it's from Tristan from all the way across the sectional. I give him a brief smile and wait for him to look back at the screen before dimming the brightness on my phone to text Tristan back.

TRISTAN

Hey. How's your day been?

CAPRI

Good. I stopped by Seaside Oasis earlier, but your office door was closed.

TRISTAN

You should have knocked. Your company would've been a bright spot in an otherwise trying day.

CAPRI

That bad?

TRISTAN

Let's just say I still have a couple hours of administrative paperwork to do.

I've got a strange suspicion his late night has to do with Virginia Sawyer's hunger strike, and the idea to offer to bring him dinner pops into my head. But it's almost nine and he's probably eaten, and honestly, now that I think about it, that seems way too over-the-top for the friend vibes I'm striving for. If it were Jane having to stay late, I'd bring her dinner in a heartbeat, but Tristan and I aren't to that level of friendship and we likely won't ever be now. Though the most pressing reason for abandoning the idea is the thought of someone witnessing my late-night visit to his office, since it's not late enough that residents won't still be up and about.

CAPRI

I'm so sorry. That's frustrating.

TRISTAN

It is, but that's not why I texted.

I wanted to see if you're up for another outing. I have something in mind if you are.

I don't know why his request surprises me. Even if he plans to end the whole thing Saturday, he'd still feel obligated to follow through with one more outing. A part of me is demanding I proceed with caution because I'm just setting myself up for disappointment, but I apparently only take into account the *proceed* part of the warning. Weakling.

CAPRI

When were you thinking?

TRISTAN

With how long I'll be here tonight and since I don't have afternoon meetings tomorrow, I'll take a half-day tomorrow. I can come by after lunch to pick you up if that works for you.

The perks of being the boss—you can take a half-day after spending a late night at the office. Not that he'll be the boss for much longer.

CAPRI

That works.

TRISTAN

Awesome. Wear a swimsuit, but bring
something nice to change into. And whatever
you need to get ready after swimming.

CAPRI

You aren't going to tell me where we're going,
are you?

TRISTAN

No, but if it helps, I'm pretty sure you're going
to love it.

With his response, my heart does some sort of weird lifting sensation as if I'm sitting on a rollercoaster, and I can't suppress my smile.

"What's so funny over there?" Heath's gaze lands on the glowing evidence in my hands. Walker glances in my direction too.

"Sorry." I lower my phone to my lap. "I was just texting … a friend."

"Which friend would that be?" Heath asks, a knowing smile forming on his lips.

"You'd like to know, wouldn't you?"

"It's Tristan," Jack says from his seat next to me, reading the name from my screen.

My gaze catches on the subtle shake of Walker's head, and I flip the phone face down. "Hey! Whose side are you on here?"

Jack shrugs and sets his attention back on the movie.

"Are you two going out again?" Tala asks.

"Tomorrow afternoon. We don't have plans, do we?"

Tala shakes her head. "I was thinking of taking the kids to the beach, but we can do that in the morning if you want to come."

The movie pauses, and Serenity's holding the remote up, her impatient gaze shifting between all four of the adults. "Jack and I can't hear with everyone talking."

"You're fine," Tala says, pinning Serenity with a correctional look. "It's not like you haven't seen *Trolls* before."

The Vanderduesen children are as serious about their movies as I typically am. But with Tristan's texts, I'm all too aware that I'm going to have a hard time focusing my thoughts on anything but tomorrow's outing. After a solid fifteen minutes of an average C- effort, I quietly excuse myself and slink from the room.

I'm halfway up the stairs when I hear footsteps behind me, and I glance over my shoulder to see Walker standing at the bottom of the stairs. It's still odd to me that he's here, hanging out with us by choice.

"Was the movie not holding your interest?" There's a touch of accusation in his voice, as though I'm sneaking away for something more sinister.

"I've seen it before, so I figured I'd get some work done." He nods, and I can tell he wants to say more. "Is that all you wanted to ask me?"

"What's going on between you and Tristan?"

Heat instantly creeps into my face. "We're just friends."

He stuffs his hands into his pockets and leans a shoulder against the wall. "I know you've always had a thing for him, but be careful."

With my shock at Walker stepping into the role of protective brother for the first time ever, I'm apparently left speechless.

Walker shifts. "With how he is, it'd be easy to confuse his intentions."

"With how he is?" I repeat, not exactly sure what to make of his comment.

"He's one of those guys who needs people to like him. And

he'll do whatever it takes for their approval. Just keep in mind that he might not have your best interest at heart."

A wave of shaking starts to move through me. It always happens with confrontations, which is why I avoid them at all costs. "You don't even know him," I say. "We were neighbors for years and you refused to be his friend. What happened between you?"

"It doesn't matter."

"It matters to me." I hold his gaze. "And if you won't tell me, I'll ask Tristan." And this time I'll get an answer.

"Let's just say neither of us treated you like you deserved." I narrow my eyes, trying to make sense of his comment, but before I can ask for clarification, he takes a step away and starts toward the door. "Night, everyone. I'm headed out."

A muffled set of goodbyes sounds from the family room, but I just stand there, wondering what in the world that was all about.

When I get to the guest room, I open my laptop to distract myself. Seventeen email requests from publishing houses since yesterday, over a dozen agents, marketing companies promising to bring Sunny Palmer's books to the next level (no, thank you), and some foreign distributors asking about book and audio rights. Oh, and one from a screenwriter. Interesting. I forward a couple that seem legit to Maven for her to respond to, then delete the others, when a new email comes in from my editor.

Ms. Palmer,

I'm pleased to inform you that your developmental edits are complete for A Lease on Love. Once we receive the updated manuscript with all incorporated changes, I will begin on the proofread. Let me know if you have any questions. Otherwise, I look forward to hearing from you.

Susan K.
Pencil to Ink Edits

*P.S. It was such a fabulous book! I allowed myself a quick
readthrough first so I could concentrate on the actual editing.*

Susan's the best. I hit the attached file and start reading the
write-up with her broader suggestions to see how much work
I'm in for. My heart drops a little when I read over a few of the
things she's listed, including tweaking my main character's arc
and adding in a whole side character. Which makes sense now
that she says it, but it'll definitely take me longer to implement
the changes than I'd hoped. And I'm already cutting it closer
than usual to my submission deadline, considering it'll still need
to be proofread. If I hadn't already made commitments for the
next few days, I'd be tempted to rent a car to get me back to
Naples. My dual monitor setup makes editing so much quicker,
but since there's no way I'm missing out on my last outing with
Tristan (despite knowing that it's just setting me up for a bigger
disappointment) and I told him I'd be at the swim night, I'll just
have to make do with my laptop for now.

CHAPTER 15

AS WE PASS the Belacourt Resort sign, my gaze flies to Tristan in the driver's seat of the golf cart. "Why are we at the Belacourt?"

Tristan just smiles.

"This place is ridiculously expensive." The palms overhead are interspersed with banyan trees that give a nice even shade covering. "Not that I've been here before, but I've heard the prices for everything are astronomical. Even the restaurant," I say, assuming that's where we're headed. It's the only thing that makes sense.

"When it comes to our competition, are astronomical prices a bonus point?"

I look at him wide-eyed. "You can't spend that much on one of our *outings*."

"First, the way you just said outings, I'm offended. And second, sometimes you just have to know the right people." He grins at me, and I realize that he's referring to Noah Belacourt. Talk about knowing the right people.

Tristan pulls in front of the resort, and an eager young man in the most comfortable-looking uniform I've ever seen—a soft-woven purple shirt and loose-fitting tan pants—takes Tristan's place to park the cart for him. Tristan grabs both of our bags and hands him some folded bills. I can't help but think about how much just parking here probably cost him. For Tristan's sake, I hope his connection with Noah comes through. Otherwise, this is going to cost him a pretty penny.

As we approach the sliding glass door, I catch a glimpse of my windblown hair and overly casual clothing. "I can't go into the Belacourt looking like this," I say, taking a step back.

"You look great."

"No, I don't. I look as if I'm ready for a beach camping trip. Or more like I'm mid-camping trip." I appraise my reflection in the door again, discreetly trying to smooth down the flyaways in my ponytail. "Three or four days in, if I had to venture a guess."

He smiles. "No one here cares how we look."

I'm sure Tristan understands rich people a lot better than I do, but that's not what I've been led to believe through my immense study of fiction. And the people at the Belacourt are uber-rich. I glance down at my romper thrown over a swimsuit with flip-flops. "Do you have specific wording you want for that dedication page or does it just have to say your name? Like for instance: *This book is dedicated to Tristan: The man that made me walk into the Belacourt Hotel looking like a vagabond he found wandering on the beach.*"

Tristan's laughing when he steps next to me. "You're not forfeiting." His gaze slowly trails down the length of me, and it's as though he has laser vision with the way my body heats wherever his eyes touch. Then his eyes meet mine. "And like I said, you look great."

I pin him with a stare that says I very much disagree with his conclusion. "Just so you know, you've lost two points for allowing me to enter *the Belacourt* for the first time looking like this." My only consolation is that Tristan's similarly dressed, though even in swim trunks and a plain tee, with our bags slung over his shoulder, he still looks as if he belongs here.

He takes another step, causing the door to open, and he gestures me inside.

The lobby isn't like I expect. Instead of some posh, marble hall with chandeliers and gargantuan vases of fresh-cut flowers, its opulence is understated. You can still see it in the details of the light-colored furniture and rugs that contrast the wood and wicker, but the space is surprisingly inviting.

"Can I help you?" A man in khaki pants but this time a soft blue shirt watches us expectantly from the front desk, probably assuming we accidentally stumbled into the world of the rich and famous. Tristan sets his hand on the small of my back, leading me forward. My heart nearly stops at the simple gesture. It's so insignificant, and yet my writer brain translates it as a sign of possession. Not the bad kind, but the 'this is my woman' kind that makes readers' hearts patter and involuntary smiles come to their lips. I know because it does the same thing to me when I read. And it's doing the same thing to me now, despite that I'm entirely aware he's simply being a gentleman.

"We have a reservation for Tristan Palmer."

A reservation? Confused, I glance at him, and the smile he has waiting for me is full of sheer mischief.

"Here you are, Mr. Palmer." He hands over a key and pulls out a map of the resort. "You're in villa thirty-six." He points to a door across the lobby and then to the corresponding door on the map for reference. "Just take this door and follow the pathway until the end. You'll be the second-to-last villa on the right."

"Thanks." Tristan takes the key and guides me in the direction the man indicated.

"Why do we have a villa?" I whisper-hiss, ignoring the way Tristan's hand is still situated on my lower back as he directs me past a few patrons whose curious gazes follow us. They're probably also wondering why we're here. Or why I'm here. Or maybe why Tristan is here with me. So many possibilities.

Tristan leans in close. "Don't get the wrong idea, Capri Sun. I have no intention of letting you seduce me today."

My lips part, and I nudge my elbow into him.

"Fine." He chuckles and opens the door for me. "If you're going to be like that, I'll consider it." And then he winks.

Tristan Palmer WINKS! At me!

I step through the door, hardly able to take in the sight of the massive pool in front of us. My brain is using up all its energy attempting to compute what's happening right now. Not just the fact that Tristan and I checked into a private villa together, but the blatant flirting. I get that the seduction comment is a joke—Tristan's not that kind of guy—but it's not the sort of teasing we engage in. We keep all interactions strictly in the platonic zone which, as I understand, doesn't include mentions of seduction in any form. Maybe this is what Walker meant when he warned me to be careful. I'm also aware that Tristan can be a flirt, but I haven't been the recipient of it. His thoughtful remarks, yes. His knowing looks and smiles, yes. But not his flirtatious teasing, and I can suddenly see why my brother thinks I might take it the wrong way—because my heart is already throwing caution to the wind and wanting more.

Tristan must mistake my contemplation for concern, because the twinkle in his eye lessens. "Noah thought we should have a home base for today. A place to put our stuff and get ready when we need to—*separately*," he says with emphasis.

So the villa wasn't Tristan's idea. "That makes sense."

We continue down the palm-covered pathway, pointing out the different villas tucked away as we go. When we finally get to villa thirty-six, we walk up the narrow, foliaged path to the front porch, and he opens the door. I step inside, my heart taking off at a rapid gallop when my gaze falls on the single bed with white linens and thick, fluffy pillows. One wall is completely open and leads out to a patio where a small private pool is situated, surrounded by lush greenery that makes it feel enclosed. There's a wicker loveseat inside (not a full, sit-on-the-other-side-of-the-couch length sofa) and one bathroom. And the general ambiance is screaming secluded romance.

This room has way too much potential for a mouth-watering scene—two friends, sharing a secluded villa. That is, if characters from my books found themselves in this situation (which they just might after this). But because it's me and Tristan, I mute the author part of my brain for the time being. Though I do soak in the small details for future inspiration, like the tri-fold blinds that can be used for privacy and the sheer white fabric draped over the wooden four-poster bed.

"It's a shame we'll only be using this as a place to change," I say before I realize how that sounded. "I only meant—"

"I know what you meant." Tristan doesn't tease me this time. Maybe I'm not the only one with a warning siren going off in my head. Not because he actually worries about anything happening between us but because he wants to make sure the boundaries remain crystal clear. Tristan glances at his watch. "Our first appointment is in ten minutes, so we can"—he lifts his hands at his sides—"head over now if you want?"

For someone who was jokingly throwing out comments about whether he'd consider letting me seduce him, he seems pretty eager to not be alone with me. Which I completely under-stand. Situations like this—and like sunset boat rides—can confuse the logical side of people. Or, as evidenced in the case of The Incident, the logical side of me. Better safe than sorry, espe-cially when he likely regrets blurring the otherwise firm lines we've maintained with his next-level teasing earlier.

"What's the appointment for?" I ask.

The carefree, excited smile returns to his face. "You'll see."

I STEP out from the dimly lit room into the posh waiting area, my eyes adjusting to the change in light.

"How was that?" Tristan asks, glancing up from his phone. He looks straight out of one of my daydreams with his disheveled hair and the fluffy white robe he's wearing that came from our room. I know he has on his swim trunks underneath, but without being able to see them, and with the way his chest is peeking through at the top, my natural instinct is to look away. Or more like protective instinct, so I don't start drooling or staring or say something incoherent. But that's what seventeen-year-old Capri would have done, so I meet his gaze as if his Grecian lounging vibe doesn't faze me.

"Unbelievable." Never in my twenty-seven years of life have I considered paying a stranger to rub my entire body into a state of utter relaxation. But I'm officially hooked.

Tristan pats the chair next to him, and I secure my own matching robe more tightly around me before sitting. "How was yours?" I ask.

"Tony was a little heavy handed. I may have whimpered a few times."

I smile, ignoring the way Tristan's arm is draped over the back of my chair and the smell of his minty breath when he leans in. "You did not."

"Oh, I did. I kept thinking how glad I was we opted not to do the couple's massage."

Clarification, Tristan opted not to do the couple's massage, letting the pretty young woman at the counter know that we actually weren't a couple and I'd probably prefer my own room. Yes, in hindsight, I'm extremely grateful. I'm not sure I could have relaxed at all with Tristan on a massage table next to me, both of us wearing nothing but a sheet for cover. But the woman's eagerness to assist him, all while batting her thick eyelashes, felt a little pointed.

Speaking of Miss Eyelashes, she steps in front of us with two large tumblers in her hand. "Mr. Palmer, Miss Collins, if you'll follow me."

We stand up in unison, and again, Tristan's hand goes to my back. "After you," he says. Apparently the whole 'this is my woman' meaning attributed to the gesture is fictionally based, and I'm now mad at every author who has continued to push that narrative, including myself. From here on out, I vow to use it correctly—as nothing more than gentlemanly behavior.

We follow our guide into an area with tiled floor, a collection of drains embedded throughout, and several large glass doors lining the otherwise wooden planked hallway. She points at the first door. "This is the sauna and that there"—she then points to the next door—"is the steam room. We also have a cool pool and a hot pool there, and a saltwater ice bath through the last door on the right. Be sure to stay hydrated." She hands us each a tumbler, and the ice clinks around inside. "There's a refill station at the end of the hall just past the bathrooms. Please don't hesitate to ask if there's anything else you need. Otherwise, whenever you're ready for your mud baths, let me know and we can get you started on those."

"Mud baths?" I mouth to Tristan.

He shrugs as if he has no idea what Noah signed us up for. "Is there an order we're supposed to do everything?" he asks.

"Nope. It's a matter of preference." The woman flutters her eyelashes again and leans toward him ever so slightly. "Do whatever brings you the most pleasure."

Geez, lady. Can we be any more obvious?

"What will bring you the most pleasure, Capri?" Tristan's focused on me. "You're the one I'm trying to impress with all of this."

The woman's gaze flicks to me, and I try to fight my smile but I can't. I know exactly what he means—that we're here for the competition—but she doesn't know that. In her eyes, I went from being someone Tristan declared he isn't in a relationship with to being the person he's trying to impress. "How about we start with the … steamy room?" That's what it's called, isn't it? Why doesn't it sound right?

Tristan's lips tick upward at the corner. "I won't say no to that." Again, Tristan's hand goes to my back, and he gives a nod to the Belacourt spa employee. "Thanks for your help, Lisa. Oh —" He takes his phone out from his robe pocket. "Can you grab a quick picture of us?"

"Of course." She manages a tight smile and takes his phone.

Unlike our awkward posing at the lighthouse, Tristan pulls me in close, wrapping both of his arms around me, and if pictures are evidence for the best outing, he just won with the size of my smile.

"There you are." Miss Eyelashes hands the phone back to Tristan.

"Thanks again," he says, taking his phone but allowing one of his arms to linger at my waist. "We'll let you know when we're ready for those mud baths."

"Wonderful." Her gaze slides to me for another brief moment as if she's wondering why Tristan would ever attempt to impress me, then she turns and walks out the door.

I allow Tristan to guide me forward when my eye catches on the sign next to the door. "It's *steam* room," I say, blushing. "Not steamy room."

"I like your name for it better." I glance over to find Tristan removing his robe, his chiseled abs and defined pecs begging to be admired. But this time, I go with my protective instincts. Tristan with a robe on and his chest peeking through is one thing. Tristan shirtless requires a whole other level of self-discipline I don't currently possess. At least if I want to continue functioning at an optimum level.

Averting my eyes from him, I quickly remove my robe to hang on one of the unoccupied hooks on the wall. I'm glad I settled on wearing Tala's black one-piece again. With its low back but high neckline, I've never felt more confident in a swimsuit. Though I doubt Tristan has to avert his gaze from me for his own protection. That proves true when I look in his direction and Tristan's eyes are on me. Well ... on my body. And then, to my complete surprise, he diverts his gaze and rubs a hand behind his neck.

"Ready?" he asks, still not looking at me.

I smile, feeling giddy at the thought that maybe he's not entirely unaffected by me. "Yep."

Tristan opens the door, and a plume of steam escapes toward us. I mentally pat myself on the back for making the call to do this room first. The diminished visibility is exactly what I need to get my head on straight.

There are two other men already seated on the benches opposite each other, so instead of spreading out, Tristan and his shirtless body come and sit right next to me against the back of the small room. It's fine. I'm fine. Though I'd be more fine if the other two men were wearing swimsuits and not just towels around their waists. Between them and the Trojan warrior at my side, I don't have a good place to look, so I settle my attention on the floor in front of me. It feels like the safest option.

"Tristan Palmer." A middle-aged man with dark brown hair and a slim build gives Tristan a larger-than-life smile that makes him instantly recognizable. Senator Clayton Brooks. "I thought that was you."

Tristan lifts a hand in greeting. "Senator Brooks, I didn't see you there."

"I don't blame you." His smiling eyes glide to me. "Not when you have such a pretty young lady to distract you."

The other man glances up briefly, looks at me, but then lowers his gaze again. As is evidenced by his comment, Senator Brooks is a politician through and through. If there was a baby here, he'd kiss it.

"I heard Ivy's back in town," Tristan says, obviously eager to move on from his comment.

The mention of his daughter snaps his attention back to Tristan. "The blessing and curse of living in a small town—news travels fast." He's still wearing a smile, but it's definitely strained, and I'm well-aware of the reason for it. Well, not any of the particulars, but that rumors are Ivy Brooks returned to Sunset Harbor with a … bang, if you will, and ended up with a court sentence because of it.

"I just meant … it'll probably be nice to have her home for the summer."

"Oh, yes. It certainly will." He gestures to me. "So, who's this young lady with you? She looks familiar, but I don't think we've met before."

We have met before, on several occasions, actually, but I don't expect him to remember.

Tristan glances at me expectantly, as if he wants me to answer despite that Senator Brooks asked Tristan the question.

"I'm Capri Collins."

His eyes widen. "A Collins, huh? As in Faye's daughter?"

I nod.

"Why did I think Walker was her youngest?"

I'm not the least bit surprised by his question, but Tristan straightens slightly in his seat. "I'm sure Ivy would remember her," he says. "The two of them were consistently the highest academic performers in the school."

I'm staring at Tristan's profile, trying not to melt into the wood plank benches we're sitting on. Partially because I hate attention and want to avoid it, but mostly because I have the distinct impression Tristan's championing me to one of Florida's most powerful men. Or the other option is that I'm actually melting with how much sweat I'm currently losing.

Senator Brooks' brows raise slightly. "Impressive. And what do you do now, Capri?"

"I own a free-lance editing company—we focus our services on independently published authors and small press books." I take a big swig of water from my tumbler, hoping to cool myself down a little.

"She also writes," Tristan says.

At the unexpected reveal, I pull in a breath, but with my mouth full of water, I inhale some of it instead. A coughing fit ensues, and I can't seem to draw in another breath.

"You okay?" Tristan asks. His touch on my sweaty back doesn't help regulate my breathing. Not even a little.

I nod, putting up a finger to signal I need a moment.

"She must have swallowed wrong." It's the man who hasn't spoken yet. "Just give her a minute."

All three men wait in absolute silence as I attempt to hack up my lung to the point where I nearly dry-heave. I'm calling it a major victory that I don't. When the coughing subsides some and I can finally draw a few breaths, I'm dizzy from the heat and the embarrassment. "Sorry," I say with a rasp to my voice. "If you'll excuse me, I think I need some air."

The moment I step out into the steam-free corridor, my lungs seem to relax, but I'm still overheated, and my eyes are stinging.

Tristan follows me out, carrying our cups. "You alright, Capri?"

"I'm just really hot." I'm already walking toward the door across from us. "I think I'm going to take a quick plunge in the cool pool. Want to join me?"

"Sure."

I swing open the door, and to my great relief, the room is empty. Without a moment's hesitation, I step into the frigid water. With how hot I am, I'm surprised I don't hear a sizzling sound like a scalding pot being submerged into cold water. I take another step, then another, then lower down until all but my head is underwater.

Tristan sets our cups on the bench by the door and follows me into the water, dropping beneath the surface in one quick motion like I did. "Oof. That's cold."

"I didn't mean to pull you away from your conversation."

His gaze is fixed on me. "You don't want people to know you write, do you?"

He has zero idea the layers that come with that question. "Not yet."

"I'm sorry I said something."

I close my eyes again, allowing the cold to numb me and all of my confusing thoughts. "It's okay. You didn't know." My heart is pounding in my chest, and I can't help but think the moment for me to tell him the truth is here. Instead of waiting until Saturday, I'd just rather have it over with now. "Tristan?"

His gaze is already on me when I open my eyes again. "What is it?"

The words stick in my throat. Tristan put a lot of thought into our outing, and it seems unfeeling to drop this truth bomb on him now, right in the middle of it. Maybe waiting until Saturday isn't the worst idea. I'll have time for a few more hints this way, and I can more fully think about what exactly I want to say. Besides, with my current emotional state after the whole choking situation, the risk of a tear-filled confession is significantly higher at present.

"Capri?" Tristan's hand grazes my arm beneath the water, and I know my decision is solidified. I'll tell him Saturday.

"Thanks for what you said in there to Senator Brooks."

The corners of his lips lift slightly. "You're worth remembering, Capri Sun."

I'm not sure most people would agree, but Tristan believing it is enough for me.

CHAPTER 16

TRISTAN'S HEAD is leaned against the pillow in the mud bath next to mine, his muddy, muscular arms draped along the sides. If I had my phone on me, I'd take his picture and sell it to the Belacourt Resort to use in their advertisements. Or, more likely, I'd keep it to my greedy little self.

"I like that you didn't want to ride a bike with a bell but you have no problem soaking like a diva in a mud bath."

Tristan's eyes remain closed but he smiles, the white of his teeth a stark contrast to the brown mud we're sitting in. "I'm secure enough in my manhood to enjoy every minute of this." He pauses, his smile growing. "And also, I know no one but you is going to see me in my true diva state."

I laugh, lifting my arms out of the bath to rest on the sides, mirroring him. "This is amazing. I can't decide what's more enjoyable, this or the massage."

"I haven't whimpered once in here, so my vote is this."

My gaze falls on the large clock hanging on the wall, signaling that our time is up. "Do we really have to get out?"

He peeks an eye open. "We could always see what they do if we don't."

I give a relaxed smile, attempting to convince myself to sit up but to no avail. "That would definitely be memorable—being escorted out of the Belacourt covered head to toe in mud."

"It's more like neck to toe in mud. You're missing a spot

right here." He reaches over and touches the tip of my nose with his muddy finger.

"Hey," I say, unable to wipe it away since my hands are also covered in mud. "You're asking for it."

Tristan just sends me one of his I-dare-you-to-do-something-about-it smiles, but as I reach over, a lady steps to the side of my tub. She's dressed like Lisa but is a few years older with vibrant red hair that hits at her chin, and I'm worried she's going to scold me, but instead she gestures to the far side of the room. "Whenever the two of you are ready, the showers are through that door."

And that's the cue. I'm a strict live-by-the-rules kind of girl, so I lean forward and find my footing before standing to let the mud drip off me. Tala's black swimsuit is no longer black, and I really hope the mud will come clean from it or I'll be buying her a new one. Tristan follows my lead and stands, and in a desperate attempt not to stare at his body and the way the brown liquid runs down the natural crevices along the edges of his muscles, I rub my hands down my limbs to get off as much mud as possible. Okay, so I may have peeked a few times, but considering the enormity of the temptation, I feel as though I'm doing decently well.

Tristan and I look like some sort of mud-monster duo as we head toward the indicated door. When we step through, there's a small, tiled area with three other doors off of it. I can hear a shower running in the stall closest to us, so I try the next door. It's also locked. I slide down to the last one and it opens. "Looks like there's only one shower open."

"I can wait," Tristan says.

I nod and step inside before glancing back at him. The mud on his body is already starting to dry in places, and with the way my own skin is tightening where the thinnest layers of mud are drying, I can't help but think how uncomfortable he'll be by the time there's a vacant shower.

I gesture to the shower. "We're just rinsing off quick and we have swimsuits on, so if you want, you can come in with me."

His brows raise, and he looks completely uncertain—an uncanny throwback to that day on the boat all those years ago. And, just like then, my stomach plummets. Why do I always have to push things too far? I honest to goodness was just trying to be considerate. Yes, I may have had a brief image of a wonderful scene for a book, but that obviously didn't sway me. At this point in my life, I'm super efficient at separating reality from the constant stream of fiction happening inside my head. Okay, maybe not *super efficient*, but I'm much improved from the younger version of myself.

"No pressure," I say, taking a step back. "I was just—"

He shrugs. "If you're sure you don't mind."

"Not at all. Friends do things like this together." My face instantly is on fire. Why I decided to speak this particular thought aloud is beyond me. Like so, so far beyond me. It's definitely more of a seventeen-year-old Capri move, but honestly, this one's on Tristan. Planning a date ... not a date, an outing ... where he's shirtless for the majority of it and covered in mud for a part of it was a heartless thing to do. I can hardly be blamed for my brain lapse to my former love-struck, awkward self.

"We are *friends*," Tristan says, securing the friend zone boundary right along with me.

But when we step into the space together and turn the shower on, friendship is the farthest thing from my mind. And it's really, really not good. Especially after a few minutes when he lifts his now clean hand to my nose. "Here. Let me help you with that."

I swallow, holding still despite the drumming inside of me. He swipes his thumb over the spot once, but I can still see it in my periphery.

He steps closer, his proximity pushing the air from my lungs, which is probably beneficial to keep me from gasping when he places a hand on each side of my face. "It doesn't want to come off," he says, gently rubbing both thumbs across the tip of my nose as the water streams over us. Then he smiles. Just a normal, unaffected smile. "There you go."

It takes me .003 seconds to realize I need to pull myself together. I need to act as though I'm also unaffected by our nearness and that his hands on my skin do nothing to me, but I can't seem to manage it. "Thanks," I say with a frustrating amount of breathiness in my voice.

His gaze roves over my face, then he drops his hands and takes a small backward step. He puts his head beneath the running water and rubs his hands over his face and through his hair.

Unable to keep my focus from lingering on him, I decide I've gotten enough of the mud off for the time being and head out of the shower. I nab a towel from a shelf against the far wall and begin drying myself when the shower door next to ours opens and a woman steps out. Her short brown hair is wet, and she's wearing a white robe and large sunglasses ... inside? But even with her sunglasses on, it only takes me a fraction of a second to recognize her.

With one brief look in my direction, she's gone.

Tristan's voice comes from behind me. "What are you looking at?"

I spin back toward him with wide eyes. "You'll never guess who I just saw."

He glances toward the now closed door, taking a towel and rubbing it over his sculpted body in a way that almost distracts me, but I'm laser focused. "Who?"

I lower my voice to a whisper because, as a woman trying to hide her own identity, there's no way I want to be the one to call attention to her secret. I'll just tell Tristan. And Jane and Tala. But that's it. "Presley James. You know ... America's darling? The A-list actress?"

Tristan keeps drying himself as if he doesn't understand how thrilling this information is. "No one seems to know where she is, but she's here—at the Belacourt." And I just saw her!

"It makes sense. Noah says they have celebrities come here when they want to lay low."

Despite his lack of enthusiasm, I'm near to bursting with excitement. "I can't believe she was in the shower next to ours."

Tristan laughs. "When you say it like that, it does sound like a core memory—Presley James in the shower next to *ours*. I also can't wait to hear you explain that one to your family." There's that teasing again, and instantly, my celebrity sighting is all but forgotten. But before I can think how to respond, Tristan glances at the clock on the wall. "We've got about an hour until our dinner reservation. Hopefully that gives you enough time to get ready."

"It should," I say, trying for a casual, unfazed smile similar to his.

On the way out of the spa, we retrieve the robes we brought from our room and start back toward the villa with sopping hair and more than a few left-over spots of mud still clinging to us. Considering I was hesitant walking into the Belacourt in my romper and flip flops, I'm now strangely okay traipsing around looking like a wet puppy that found a mud puddle on her walk.

"Tristan!" A man in business attire waves a hand. An extremely handsome man and another very familiar face.

"Noah." Tristan smiles, lifting a hand and taking a step toward his friend. "I was hoping we'd run into you."

"How was the spa?" Noah's brown eyes skirt to me, and I'm suddenly no longer comfortable being a mud puppy. Not because I've ever harbored feelings for the man—I've been thoroughly stuck on Tristan way too long for that—but this is Noah Belacourt! And he's looking at me expectantly. What did he ask again?

"It was amazing," Tristan says when I obviously can't find

the words. The spa. That's what he'd asked about. "Do you remember Capri Collins?"

Noah's dark features settle on me. "I do. How are you, Capri?"

I'm nodding. Why am I nodding? Probably because I'm stunned he said he remembers me. I doubt it's true, but it's nice of him to say so. Noah Belacourt is a nice guy in real life. I always knew it. "Good," I say, finally finding my voice. "And you? Are you good?"

His lips tick at the sides, and I'm guessing this isn't his first encounter with a secret-reality-TV-watching star-struck fan. "I'm doing okay. Thanks for asking."

I take a step closer to Tristan, hopeful it might help ground me, or boost my confidence, or maybe just draw Noah's attention back to him. Like he realizes what I'm in need of, Tristan puts his hand on the small of my back.

Noah doesn't seem to miss the gesture, and he smiles. "So, how's the competition going?"

Tristan looks at me. "It's still close."

I shake my head. "It's not. I don't even have a shot after today. And I believe I have you to blame for that."

Noah chuckles. I just made Noah Belacourt chuckle!

"For real, thanks for hooking us up, man," Tristan says. "It's been amazing. And that villa …"

Noah waves a dismissive hand, stopping Tristan's gratitude. "It was vacant, so I'm happy it can get some use. Also, dinner is on me tonight. I already put instructions in with the restaurant staff. You can eat there or order in room service, whichever you prefer."

Tristan's gaze meets mine, and I must look like a deer in headlights at the mention of ordering in room service. Not that it would imply anything other than we'd be eating together in a villa by ourselves instead of eating dinner with a room full of people. Okay, that's sufficient reason for my unblinking, doe eyes.

"We have reservations at six," Tristan says, setting his attention back on Noah.

"They're super lax on reservations here. It's part of the tropical resort vibe—come as you are whenever you want to show up."

"That's good to know."

"Well, I won't keep you two. I'm sure you're anxious to get back to the villa and get changed. But if there's anything else you need, don't hesitate to ask. Otherwise, I'll see you soon," he says, pointing at Tristan. "And hopefully I'll also see you again, Capri."

Noah Belacourt hopes to see me again! "That'd be great," I say, the picture of calm and collected. "Thanks again for everything."

We wave goodbye, then continue along the path back to our villa. I veer off to the side as I walk, making sure there's ample room between me and Tristan. With the sensation of his hand still lingering on my lower back even through the thickness of my robe, it's probably best.

Tristan's watching me with an odd look.

"What?"

He shakes his head. "Nothing."

The tone of his 'nothing' speaks volumes, and I can feel the heat congregating in my cheeks. With how I'm hugging the edge of the pathway and dodging plant branches for the sake of distance, he must have guessed his uncanny effect over me.

"Noah Belacourt is a good guy, isn't he?" His smile is casual, but his eyes are searching mine, and suddenly, I understand his real question—what do I think of Noah Belacourt? Or more specifically, why was I acting like a twitterpated pre-teen in his presence? Though I'm not exactly sure why it matters.

"It's Noah Belacourt," I say as if that's some kind of defense. "I was just a little star struck."

Tristan laughs. "Really? I couldn't tell."

I scowl at him, pushing a small palm frond out of my path. "I'm not used to celebrity sightings, let alone two back-to-back. Three if you include Senator Brooks." Which I don't. "You're lucky I was functioning at all."

He grins. "Fair enough."

A couple probably around our age moseys past us. The man's arm is draped over the woman's shoulder, and he's whispering something into her ear, her dark brown curls concealing his face. She looks up and giggles at him, then her gaze meets mine. We share a smile before the man begins to whisper again.

When I look back at Tristan, our eyes meet. "What are you thinking?" he asks.

"What do you mean?"

He glances over his shoulder, then steps closer. "The way you were watching that couple," he whispers. "It's like I could see the wheels in your head turning."

Heat prickles my cheeks, but I know it's an opportunity to let him get a glimpse of my imagination at work. "I was just thinking about what brought them together. What their story is."

He grins as if he knew that's what I would say. "And?"

I glance behind us one more time, assessing the couple again. "I think they were co-workers, vying for the same promotion. He tried to ruin her chances by doing something awful—probably swapped her printed resume for one that listed her greatest accomplishment as owning an exaggerated number of cats and highlighted that her lifelong ambition was to start a party service where she dresses up as a curly green-haired clown people endearingly refer to as Madame Broccoli."

Amusement is written in every part of his face. "Madame Broccoli?"

I shrug. "It feels like something he'd do. And it wasn't until halfway through the interview that she discovered his interference, but instead of outing him, she decided to get even, which led to the most epic office prank war ever. It ended with them both locked all night in a utility closet where they were finally forced to face the undeniable attraction between them. They understandably got fired but started their own company together, and now they're here on their honeymoon. It's been a big year for them."

Tristan is laughing. "Did you just come up with all of that right now?"

"It's what my brain does—thinks up stories for people."

"What's my fictionalized story?"

Oh heavens! I have a plethora of stories to share about him, but doing so is completely out of the question because my default mode for fictionalized Tristan is that he ends up with me. Period. Exclamation point. "It's trickier when I know the person in real life."

He looks slightly disappointed, but it's only a matter of time until he'll have the option to read a fictionalized love story about us in real life. The thought makes my stomach churn.

"I haven't seen your parents since I've been back," I say, ready for a subject change. "How are they?"

"Great. Actually, they both mentioned on Sunday that they'd love to see you." His gaze flicks to me. "I hope it's okay, but since they're planning on being at the swim party tomorrow night, I told them they'd see you there."

Joy and Mark are the absolute sweetest, despite what Virginia Sawyer thinks about them. I get that they aren't perfect, but after Grandpa died, Mark became a regular at Grandma's house, helping to fix leaking faucets and running toilets and securing places on the outside where critters could get in. And Joy is literally the kindest with her big hugs and inviting smile that she passed on to both of her boys. "Of course. I'd love to see them."

We start up the weaving path to the villa again, and Tristan's so close to me, I'm all kinds of aware. He reaches past me to unlock the door, and we step through. In the silence of the empty room, neither of us seems sure how to proceed.

"So ... what do you want to do?" Tristan asks. "Would you prefer to keep our reservation or order in room service and eat it on the patio? Maybe take a swim?"

I shrug like my insides aren't vibrating at the very mention of the second option. "You tell me. You're the one planning it." And despite all reason, I'm willing him to say that we should order in room service.

He scans the room, his eyes pausing briefly on the bed, before looking back at me. There's indecision in his expression. "It might be smart to just keep the reservation."

My stomach drops, but I nod my head like that's exactly what I want to do. "Yeah. That's definitely the best option." I take a step back, gesturing to the bathroom. "We'd better start getting ready, then. Do you want to shower first?"

His gaze is still on me, as if he's attempting to decipher my response, but then he shakes his head. "No, you go ahead."

"I'm guessing it'll take me longer, so I really don't mind waiting if you want to go."

Tristan picks up his bag. "I'll be like five minutes." He stops at the bathroom door and glances over his shoulder. "Oh, and I was thinking you should stay the night. We have the room until tomorrow, so like you said earlier, it seems a shame for neither of us to use it. You can even invite Jane if you want."

The sheer rollercoaster of emotions of the last ten seconds leaves me reeling, but I miraculously manage a smile of sorts. "If you're sure you don't want to stay. Instead of me, I mean."

"I've got to win back those points you docked me somehow."

With one more heart-pattering smile, he disappears into the bathroom and shuts the door.

I head out to the patio to text Jane and possibly take a quick dip in the pool. After my completely inaccurate presumption that Tristan was asking me to spend the night *with him*, I need to cool myself down. Not that I would have stayed. And not that he ever would have asked, but with the way my body is flooded with nerves and anticipation, it turns out I'm not quite as efficient at differentiating between fantasy and reality as I'd thought. Though I suppose, for one brief moment, the two morphed together in an extremely unhelpful test of my friend zone boundaries. And I failed. Miserably.

WELCOME TO
SUNSET
HARBOR

BELACOURT
RESORT

GOLF
COURSE

NOAH'S
HOUSE

JANE'S
HOUSE

NATURE
PRESERVE

DAX'S
DUPLEX

SEASIDE OASIS
RETIREMENT HOME

SUNSET
REPAIRS

PHOENIX'S
OFFICE

CITY OFFICES

SCOOPS
AHOY
ICE
CREAM

KEENE
B&B

SUNRISE
CAFE

GULF OF
MEXICO

TOWN

SQUARE

BAKERY

BRIGGS'S
APARTMENT

THE BOOK
ISLE

CUTS AND
CURLS

TRISTAN &
BEAU'S
HOUSE

GEMMA'S
HOUSE

CAPRI'S
HOUSE

HOLLAND'S
HOUSE

BEACH BREAK
BAR & GRILL

PUBLIC BEACH

N
W   E
S

CHAPTER 17

BRIGHT MORNING LIGHT drifts in from the patio, but I refuse to move. The bed has chosen me as its own, and with the way it embraces my entire body, I'm not sure a hurricane making landfall can separate us.

"Come on, sleepy head," Jane says, bustling around the room as if the sunlight is contagious. "I have to get to work. And you just got a text." I peek an eye open, and she's holding my phone with a smile on her face. "It's from Tristan."

"You're just trying to get me up," I say, closing my eye again.

"He wrote: 'On a scale of 1 to 10, how comfortable was that bed last night?'" She sends me a wide-eyed grin, then gives a soft hum. "How should I respond? Maybe ... 'It would have been a lot more comfortable with you—'" I'm up before she can finish, snatching my phone from her.

To my surprise, Tristan actually did text. And he did ask how the bed was. I'm a little tempted to reply along the lines of what Jane says, just to be funny and not at all because I mean it. Okay, I'd mean it a little which is why I'll go a different route.

CAPRI

> 0 out of 10. Do not recommend.

> You should count yourself fortunate you didn't have to sleep in that heavenly embrace that might have just given me the best night's rest of my life.

Three dots appear, and my heart lifts in anticipation.

TRISTAN

That does sound terrible. It's a good thing I left because for a minute there I was tempted not to.

I suppress my unfounded hopes before they even have a chance to take hold. He was way too eager to leave last night for him to mean that comment in any way other than that he wishes he would have stayed the night himself. Without me.

"He loves you," Jane says, grinning.

My laugh sounds tired and empty. "With how fast he bolted after dinner, I'm pretty confident he doesn't. Which is fine considering my forthcoming confession."

"Are you sure you shouldn't wait a little longer to tell him? Saturday is so soon, and I feel like you two are right on the cusp of something wonderful."

Oh, sweet Jane and her hopelessly romantic heart. A heart I usually share with her, but not in this situation. "We agreed to the redefining-the-island thing *until* I found my keys."

"And you haven't found them."

"But he's bringing me home so I can get my other keys."

"Because he's Tristan and Tristan's a nice guy."

"Or because he needs an excuse to end the whole thing."

Jane sighs. "I think you're wrong, but I don't have time to argue. I've got to get you back to Tala's so I can get to work." She pushes me toward the bathroom. "And you need to brush that hair in case we manage another Presley James sighting on our way out. Or an encounter with Noah Belacourt. I'd gladly take either."

I grab the brush from the counter and start working through my tangled strands. "Noah Belacourt's on your list of potential dates, isn't he?"

"Of course. And I have high hopes, considering the billionaire trope is one of my favorites." I'm honestly not sure which trope isn't her favorite—secret baby, possibly? "I just have to figure out how to make it happen."

"Ah! Speaking of making things happen, my editor sent my developmental edits."

"So when will I have the final copy in my hands?" Unlike Tala, Jane doesn't like reading the book until it's ready for print. Years ago, she read an early draft of my third book before I had to remove an entire character she'd grown attached to. She's refused to read anything but the completed versions since. Which, considering my upcoming edits, is probably a good standard to keep. There are going to be a lot of changes, and I still have to have it proofread after that. So it'll still be a while.

"The moment it's done."

"Can I get it hand-delivered and put in one of those spiral bound notebooks like Tala got?"

"That'll depend on how things go with Tristan Saturday and whether I'll forever be banned from the island."

"He's not going to ban you from anything. As already stated, he's way too nice for that. And he loves you." Jane glances at her watch again. "But if you want to avoid having to text him or Tala for a ride home, we need to go."

I stuff the remaining items on the bathroom counter into my bag, glance around the villa with one last longing look of all the things it could have been, and follow Jane outside.

"WHAT DO you mean he was in a hurry to leave?" Tala whispers. Heath and the older kids are a good distance ahead of us in the parking lot, making their way toward the Seaside Oasis entrance.

I readjust Lucas in my arms. For only being three months,

the kid is a tank. "After dinner was over, he walked me back, grabbed his bag, and left. He did give me a hug, but it was one of those from the side kind—strictly platonic." I release an unintentional sigh. "But in his defense, I totally get it. The private villa atmosphere really wasn't conducive to two friends hanging out." Co-ed friends, anyway. Jane and I had a blast until way too late, and I yawn at the reminder.

Tala gives a slight pout, obviously not thrilled with the platonic relationship Tristan and I have maintained despite all our time together. And I feel it. Deeply. Even though I shouldn't. What I should be is relieved things are following my original plan perfectly. Tristan and I are friends, nothing more. It'll still be awful to tell him the truth, and I'm dreading it with every fiber within me, but it'll be easier now than if we weren't friends at all. Or, honestly, if we were miraculously more than friends. So it really is good that I've remained strictly in the friend zone. And if I say it over and over again, it might quiet the little part of my brain that secretly hoped Tristan would fall in love with me during our time together.

"You slowpokes coming?" Heath stops on the threshold of the automatic door with his armful of towels. "We're already twenty minutes late. At the rate you two are going, we'll miss the whole swim party." Serenity and Jack gesture for us to hurry, so Tala and I pick up our speed. When we step through the doors into the lobby, there's only a handful of people inside, most of them heading in the direction of the courtyard where a din of voices can be heard. Heath glances over at me. "I forgot to tell you, but I had a good chat with Tristan on our run this morning."

The spike of my heartbeat would likely show up on a seismograph. "What do you mean?" I ask, silently pleading that they spoke about baseball or football or even where to purchase a pink beach cruiser for Beau. But the satisfied grin on Heath's face confirms my fears—he spoke to Tristan about me.

"Don't look so panicked, Capri. It went really well."

My gaze flicks to Tala, who looks as stunned to hear about Heath's intervention as I am. "What'd you say?" I ask, and Tala takes Lucas from my arms as if she's worried I might drop him in my current state of shock. Or maybe she knows I need my hands free to strangle her husband.

"We talked about how everything is going between the two of you."

"There's no *between us*, Heath," I whisper even though there's no one directly around us to overhear. "We're friends. That's it."

"I'm aware." How he says this makes me wonder if Tristan was forced to explain the same thing, and the thought causes my legs to feel as if they might give out. "I only meant we talked about how the outings were going and ..." He shrugs. "... lots of stuff, really. I promise it was a great discussion."

"Heath wouldn't say anything you didn't want him to," Tala says, eyeing her husband. "Would you, sweetie?"

"Why are you two acting as if I did something wrong?" There's a twinkle in Heath's eye I don't like. "I did Capri a real solid. Trust me."

Serenity is standing in front of the open courtyard doors, pointing outside. "It's Grandmama. Can I go see her?"

Tala nods and Serenity disappears through the door, followed closely by Jack.

"We're not finished talking about this," I say before Heath can escape. "When we get home, you're going to tell me everything you said to him."

"I'll see what I can remember by then." His gaze focuses behind me. "But speaking of the man himself ..." Heath lifts a hand, and I follow his line of sight to Tristan walking toward us from the direction of his office, still in slacks and a Seaside Oasis polo, holding a paper in his hand. I'm suddenly lightheaded, and I'm not sure if it's just seeing Tristan or the fact that I'm nervous he might have overheard us. Probably both.

He smiles at Tala and Heath, but his gaze settles on me when he nears. "I'm glad you made it."

I smile, but with Heath's knowing grin plastered to our profiles, I'm all sorts of self-conscious. "I told you snow cones were a weakness of mine."

Tala grabs hold of Heath's arm. "We'd better go make sure the kids don't get in the pool without us there." She pulls him toward the courtyard. "We'll see you two outside."

Heath shoots one last smile over his shoulder before I turn my attention back to Tristan. I try not to think about his and Heath's conversation from earlier since I'm nervous enough with the prospect of being seen interacting together. At least the lobby is currently empty. "How's the swim party going so far?"

"I actually haven't been out there yet. I was just finishing up a few things, the last of which is pinning this"—he hands me the festive red and blue flyer—"to the bulletin board. It's for the Sunset Harbor Fourth of July Bash. Jane emailed it over a few hours ago, but Sandra's been so busy prepping for the swim party, I figured I'd print it and hang it up to save her the trouble."

That's so Tristan of him.

As we walk toward the front, I scan the advertisement—a pancake breakfast in the morning followed by the parade, games in the town square throughout the afternoon, and a dance that night with live music before fireworks. Same as always, but with the addition of food trucks. Which was Jane's idea and is so brilliant. "This is one of my favorite Sunset Harbor traditions."

Tristan reaches over the reception area for a stapler, then steps up to the bulletin board along the front wall beside the door. "Does that mean you'll be here for it?"

I hold the flyer against a vacant spot on the board while he staples it. "I've never missed one. Even when we were little, we'd always come visit Grandma and Grandpa that first week in July. So I hope so." My stomach twists a little, realizing this year is dependent on a few things—or one thing in particular now—namely Tristan's reaction to my news. At this point, I honestly can't see him getting too upset, but it still might be wise to give him some space to process it all. And with my Avoid Sunset Harbor Protocol, I'd already come to terms with this being the first year I'd miss.

"I haven't been in quite a while." Tristan closes the stapler and places it back behind the reception area desk.

"You'll love it."

He leans against the wall. "Will you save a dance for me?"

I tuck my lips inward to keep myself from blurting out an excited, *Yes!* "I don't know. The line to dance with me is usually pretty long. I'd hate for anyone to think I'm playing favorites."

Tristan smiles. "Beau said he danced with you last year. Did you make an exception for him?"

The thought of Beau remembering that he danced with me at all, let alone mentioning it to Tristan, causes my smile to break through. Especially since he was the only guy I'd danced with, and it hardly counts because it's Beau. "How was I supposed to say no to a man in uniform?"

Tristan gestures to himself. "If we're being technical, this is a uniform."

I make a show of considering him, my gaze lingering longer than is probably necessary on his well-fitted polo. "Fine. Based on my appreciation for technicalities and my desire for consistency, I'll do my best to squeeze you in." I shrug. "But that's all I can do."

"After everything we've been through." Tristan shakes his head, a smile dancing on his lips. "Maybe I'll make our next outing be to Beach Break Bar and Grill when Mo and the Kokomos are playing, and you'll have to dance every dance with me or you forfeit."

That actually sounds like the most amazing outing ever, minus that our fellow Sunset Harborians would see us together.

"Speaking of the competition," he says, leaning toward me. "Have you figured out what you want your prize to be if you win?"

There's literally only one thing that keeps coming to my mind, but there are a few very good reasons why I don't say it. Kissing Tristan is completely out of the question. "I still can't think of anything."

He smiles as if he can read my thoughts and leans in closer. He's a mere breath away from me now. "Really? Not one little thing?"

My gaze betrays me and drops to his lips. "I ..." The glass doors slide open, saving me from my near lapse in judgement. I glance over my shoulder and am stunned to find my brother strolling inside Seaside Oasis. Instinctively, I take a step away from Tristan. "Walker? What are you doing here?"

He glances over at me, apparently as surprised to see me as I am to see him. His gaze flicks to Tristan, then settles back on me. "I was told there was a family swim party here tonight."

I stare at him. "And you came for it?"

"I knew you'd be excited, but your reaction is next level, Capri."

"I am excited." I smile to prove my point. "I just ... I wasn't expecting to see you."

He puts out his arms like 'here I am' before glancing around. "Where's everyone else?"

"They were in the courtyard a few minutes ago, but I'm guessing they've made it to the pool by now."

"And where's that?"

I'm about to describe how to get there, but Tristan steps to my side. "We can show you. We're heading that way."

Walker's jaw tightens, but he gives Tristan a small nod of acknowledgment. Which is something.

In the following silence, I fully regret my choice of giving in to curiosity instead of having Tristan answer my question about the strained relationship between him and my brother. "So, how is it being back on Sunset Harbor?" I ask Walker, hoping to ease the tension.

"Better than I expected." I really hope Jane doesn't have anything to do with his response, but I'm suspecting she does.

"That's good. Tristan and I spoke with a big fan of yours the other day. She said to let you know that she and her husband will be rooting for you if you make it back to the PGA Tour this year."

"I'll actually be playing in the British Open in July."

My gaze shoots to his profile. "You're going to England?"

"Scotland. Which works out well since Mom and Stan will be there at the same time."

I wonder if Jane knows. But I can't ask Walker, at least not right now, so I paste on another smile. "I'm not at all jealous."

"No one's stopping you from coming."

"Oh man, with an invitation like that, I might need to take you up on that."

He nudges his shoulder into me. "You know you'd be welcome."

I actually don't know, but strangely enough, I appreciate him saying so.

Tristan opens the courtyard door, allowing both of us to step through before him. "So Walker, I assume you've been practicing at The Belacourt course," Tristan says, pulling Walker's gaze to him.

For a second, I worry that Walker won't answer him, but he nods once. "Yeah."

"What are your thoughts on that seventh hole?"

Despite his obvious desire not to engage with Tristan, Walker's lips lift ever so slightly at the corners. "It's a beast."

Tristan gives a commiserating nod of understanding, and suddenly the ensuing silence doesn't feel quite so intense.

WELCOME TO
SUNSET
HARBOR

BELACOURT RESORT

GOLF COURSE

NOAH'S HOUSE

JANE'S HOUSE

NATURE PRESERVE

DAX'S DUPLEX

SEASIDE OASIS RETIREMENT HOME

SUNSET REPAIRS

PHOENIX'S OFFICE

CITY OFFICES

SCOOPS AHOY ICE CREAM

SUNRISE CAFE

KEENE B&B

GULF OF MEXICO

TOWN

SQUARE

BAKERY

BRIGGS'S APARTMENT

THE BOOK ISLE

CUTS AND CURLS

N
W   E
S

TRISTAN & REESE HOUSE

CAPRI'S HOUSE

GEMMA'S HOUSE

HOLLAND'S HOUSE

BEACH BREAK BAR & GRILL

PUBLIC BEACH

CHAPTER 18

JACK HOLDS on to my arm and Serenity stands next to me, both of them searching the water for the plastic diving ring I dropped. "There it is!" Jack calls, diving with a big splash that hits me square in the face. I'm still wiping the water from my eyes when he comes to the surface with the ring in hand and a proud smile. I reach out and pull him toward me. He's a strong swimmer for his age, but we've been going at this for a while now, and with the way he's breathing, I'm confident he can use a little assistance.

"That's eleven for you and fourteen for Serenity."

"I'm at fifteen," Serenity says, readying herself for the next round.

"Oh yeah, fifteen," I lift the ring and drop it again. "Wait until it lands. Okay ... go." Both kids dive at the same time.

My gaze unintentionally catches on Tristan again. He apparently is here as a Seaside Oasis employee and not a participant since he's still wearing his polo and slacks. Which honestly makes sense. It would be unprofessional for Tristan to be walking around shirtless with his incredible abs ... and broad shoulders ... and thick, toned arms ...

I blink, pulling myself from the memory of Tristan shirtless at the spa yesterday. As I was saying, it's good he isn't swimming because, with the exception of coming outside together, Tristan and I haven't really crossed paths again. And Walker being with us at our first appearance made the whole thing a lot less suspect. If anyone even noticed me in between Tristan and my brother, they probably thought I was here with Walker.

Serenity bursts out of the water, lifting the ring above her head. "I've got it!"

I grab Jack as he surfaces when I hear Heath call my name. I search the overcrowded pool until I see him wading through the water. "I'm here to relieve you of duty," he says when he nears.

"I'm more than happy to keep swimming with the kids."

"I don't doubt that," Heath says, like he knows I'm avoiding Tristan. "But Joy and Mark Palmer are over talking to the family, so I've been instructed to send you their way to say hello."

I glance toward the group, and I can't help but feel a rush of nerves. Which is ridiculous because Joy and Mark are some of my favorites. I hand Heath the diving ring. "The score is: Jack eleven, Serenity sixteen."

"Got it," he says, freeing Jack's hand from my forearm and pulling him onto his back.

When I climb out of the pool, I wrap my arms around myself and start toward Tala and the others.

My gaze is down when I feel a touch on my arm. I look up to find Grandma standing in front of me. "Walker and I are going to get a snow cone. Would you like us to grab you one?"

Walker doesn't look super thrilled to be taking my order, but he also doesn't voice any opposition.

"Sure. Strawberry and peach if they have those flavors. Otherwise, surprise me."

"Did you get that?" Grandma asks Walker.

"One lime raspberry, coming up." Walker grins as the two of them pass me.

That combination actually sounds amazing, so the joke's on him.

When I reach Tala and the Palmers, I shiver despite the warm, humid air, and Tala tosses me a towel before I can even say hello. I wrap it around myself and smile at my onlookers.

"Capri!" Joy comes toward me with outstretched arms. The loose-fitting pants and cream-colored blouse don't look as if they mix well with water, but she hugs me all the same. She pulls back, taking a look at me. "My boys are right; you do keep getting more and more beautiful."

I'm sure she's just saying that to be nice, because I'm definitely putting off more of wet cat vibes at the moment. "Says the woman who hasn't aged a day since I was a little girl." And it's true. With the exception of a few smile lines, her skin is still glowing with a youthful radiance.

Joy shakes her head, but the flush in her cheeks only adds to her beauty. "We've missed you. Haven't we, Mark?"

"We have." Mark steps next to his wife and smiles at me. Joy's golden hair and light eyes remind me so much of Tristan, where Mark clearly passed his darker features on to Beau. "But it sounds like you're doing amazing things. Tristan mentioned you own your own editing company."

I squeeze the water from my hair with the edge of the towel. "It's really not that impressive. It's a pretty small company."

"What's the name of it?"

"Pencil to Ink Edits."

Mark gives a little shake of his head, indicating he hasn't heard of it. "Well, that's something to be proud of."

"Thank you."

"Excuse me." A woman, likely in her mid-forties with light brown hair and a tight bun that looks out of place at a pool party, steps up next to me. "Hello Mr. Palmer. Mrs. Palmer." She gives both of them a little wave before turning back to me. "I'm so sorry to interrupt, but did you just say you're the owner of Pencil to Ink Edits?

My gaze drops to her hand and my blood curdles. There, with her finger marking her place, is *Love Rising*, written by none other than Sunny Palmer herself.

Well, me.

"That is what you said, isn't it?" she asks, glancing around the group as if for confirmation.

I fight every inclination to look to Tala for help. There's no way out of this. With the Palmers' watchful gazes on me, the only option is to act as though I'm not entirely freaking out when I entirely am. "It is."

"Your company edits for Sunny Palmer?" She lifts her book, opening to the page her finger is marking—the acknowledgments section—and points to the part about Susan and her incredible editing skills. Since when do readers actually read the acknowledgments? Years ago, the very intentional choice I made to include my company's name was for the sole purpose of garnering editing leads. Not once did I regret that decision or think it might come back to haunt me. Until now.

With the heat rushing through me, I'm positive I'm turning a similar shade to the dark red color of the swimsuit Tala loaned me tonight. "Yeah, she's one of our clients. I don't personally edit her stuff though." I glance down at the page that she's still holding up between us and point to the name. "Susan does."

This woman's mouth is gaping. "Have either of you met her?"

"No. All correspondence is through email. She seems to be a very private woman."

"Sandra, this is my sister, Capri." Tala stands with Lucas in arm, her smile shifting to me. "Sandra here is the receptionist at Seaside Oasis. At book club, the two of us always tease about which of us would be the president of Sunny Palmers' fan club."

Sandra smiles proudly. "I missed last month's discussion due to a cold, but I was beyond thrilled to hear we're reading *Secret Crush* in preparation for Sunny Palmer's next release. That would have been my choice as well."

"I've been meaning to give one of her books a try," Joy says. "I've heard such wonderful things. Which is the best to start with?"

This time I can't stop from looking at Tala, my eyes imploring her to intercede on my behalf before Sandra can give her opinion.

"That's a great one." Tala points at Sandra's book. "I even have a copy I'd be happy to lend you. Or I always recommend *Summer Fling*."

"Oh, the bike scene in that!" Sandra waves a hand as if she's fanning herself, and all I can do is watch in horror. "So amazing. But even with that, I'd recommend starting with *Secret Crush*." Sandra's attention shifts back to Joy. "It's the book she's most well-known for and my all-time favorite. In fact ..." She walks from her spot in our circle to the chair she must have been occupying before jumping in on our conversation. She rummages through a brown-leather handbag until she pulls out a well-worn copy of the book itself. "Here it is!" She presents the book to Joy as though she's bestowing on her the greatest of treasures, and I resist the urge to whack it out of her hands, but just barely. "You can borrow my copy."

"Don't you need it for book club?" Joy asks.

"I've read it several times and I also own it on Kindle."

Joy looks a little stunned at the forceful offer, but she recovers and smiles at Sandra. "If you're certain. I probably won't get to it for a few weeks though. I'm absolutely determined to finish War and Peace, but I'm only halfway through it."

"That's more than fine. If you get it finished in time, you should come to book club." Sandra's gaze moves to me. "And you should come too, Capri. I'm sure everyone would love to hear about how your company edits Sunny Palmer's books. It's your own little claim to fame."

I'm already shaking my head. "I'd really like to be there, but unfortunately, I'm not going to be on Sunset Harbor that week." Do I know when the next book club will be? Not a clue. But I'll make sure I'm nowhere near the island while it takes place. And maybe I'll stay away longer now that Joy Palmer intends to read the fictionalized love story between me and her son. I just pray she's as blinded to the connections as everyone else seems to be.

"Will you be here the following Saturday? Because if you will, a different book club I attend here on the island is also reading *Secret Crush* in preparation for *A Lease on Love*. And you'd be more than welcome to join me for that one as well."

I stare in disbelief. What sort of tiny island has two book clubs? Let alone two that are reading the exact same book at the same time? This can't be real!

Tala locks eyes with me. "Didn't you say you had something going on that weekend as well, Capri?"

I nod, suddenly feeling as though I might throw up. "Yeah, I think so."

"Well, if you end up being here for either of them," Sandra says, putting her hand on mine, "we'd love for you to come."

"Thanks. I'll keep that in mind."

"She finally emerges from the pool." Tristan's sudden appearance behind me makes me jump, and I place a hand over my heart.

His expression is equal parts amusement and concern. "You okay?"

"Yeah, I just …" There's no way to explain my current state, so I just shrug.

Tala steps next to Sandra's side, and I hear her say something about author recommendations before gesturing to some nearby chairs. To my great relief, Sandra nods excitedly and follows my saintly sister.

Tristan leans in close, placing a hand on my back. "Are you really okay?"

I nod and offer him a tight smile to prove my point.

His mom's eyes miss nothing, and when she notices Tristan's hand still lingering on my back, she looks strangely pleased. "Capri was telling us about her editing company." Joy lifts the book in her hand, and I want to die where I'm standing. "Apparently her company edits Sunny Palmer's books. Did you know that?"

He shakes his head, and his accusatory gaze slides to me. "I didn't."

I wave away the comment with my hand. "It's really not a big deal. I'm not the one who actually does her edits."

"But it's your company," Tristan says. "And having Sunny Palmer as a client is a big deal." Him just saying my pen name makes me want to turn on my heels and run out of here.

"You know who Sunny Palmer is?" Sandra is suddenly back in the conversation, leaning forward in her chair. I'm not usually someone that forms an instant dislike of a person, but this woman's pushing my limits. Whether it's warranted or not. Which it's not.

"Her books are literally everywhere—including sitting on your desk most days." He gives Sandra a smile that brings immediate color into her cheeks. "I've also been asked, on more than one occasion, if I'm related to her."

I'm no longer chilly. In fact, the heat is moving through my whole body with such intensity, I'm at risk of overheating. To prevent anyone from noticing my splotching décolletage, I wrap my towel around my shoulders, which doesn't help cool me down, but it's worth the tradeoff.

"I actually wondered that at first too," Sandra says. "Until I found out it was a pseudonym. Though I suppose it could still be her real last name. Some authors do that." She quirks her lips up as if considering the likelihood. "But with how little is known about her, I'd guess the whole of the name is made up."

"Here you are, Capri." Walker steps to my other side, holding out a snow cone, and I want to hug him for the interruption and the icy offering. "Half peach, half strawberry."

"You're the best." I shove a bite in my mouth, letting the ice sit on my tongue in an attempt to cool myself down.

"It took you long enough to admit it out loud," Walker says, helping Grandma into a seat near Tala and Sandra. When he makes sure she's good, he joins Mark and Joy. "So, what are you looking forward to most about retirement?" Who is this man and what has he done with my brother?

I listen to the three of them talk for a minute until Tristan leans in close. "You haven't been avoiding me since we've come outside, have you, Capri Sun?"

"It's not my fault you failed to bring a swimsuit to a *swim* party."

He just smiles as though he knows it wouldn't have mattered if he had. He's probably right. With so many people around, it makes sense to keep our distance as much as possible. And considering he currently seems to have no plan to make that happen, I have to do what's best for both of us in order to prevent people from thinking we're anything more than we are.

"Besides, it's not like I could abandon Serenity and Jack's game of Marco Polo, and they needed my *non-partial judging skills* for their ring dive competition."

Tristan chuckles. "You did look like you were having fun out there."

"They're fun kids."

"Well, they're lucky to have you as an aunt."

As if they knew we were speaking about them, Jack and Serenity bound past us, dripping water in their wake. "Mom, can we get something from the vending machine?" Jack asks, bouncing on his toes in front of her.

"You already had two snow cones."

"But I'm hungry. And so is Serenity. We'll get something healthy—like chips."

Tala shakes her head. "This is why you should have eaten more of your dinner."

"That's what I told him." Heath steps into our little circle and grabs a towel, patting himself dry.

"Please?" Jack and Serenity say in unison.

Grandma gestures for them to come closer. "If you can convince your parents to say yes," she whispers loud enough for all of us to hear, "it'll be my treat."

Serenity and Jack's hopeful gazes turn to their mom.

"Grandma, you don't need—" Tala begins.

"I insist." With a hesitant nod of agreement from both Tala and Heath, Grandma points to her purse sitting with our bags. "Jack, if you'll hand me my purse."

Instead of going around, Jack, still dripping, squeezes between the Palmers and grabs the purse.

"Jack!" Tala calls after him, obviously not thrilled with his method.

"He's fine." Joy smiles, scooting away from Mark so there's more room for Jack as he steps between them a second time.

Jack hands Grandma the purse. "Here you are, Grandmama."

She opens it and removes her wallet, but Jack's attention remains fixed on something inside her purse. He leans in, then his eyes brighten. "Auntie Capri," he says, reaching in and pulling out a bundle of keys with a familiar seashell keychain. "Are these yours?"

I stare at Grandma. "You had my keys this whole time?"

She has the decency to look somewhat embarrassed. "How did those get in there?"

"You sneaky little troublemaker," Heath says with a laugh. "We looked for those things for hours. Why would you take them?"

"Desperate times call for desperate measures." Grandma's eyes slide from me to Tristan, and the implication must be excessively clear to anyone nearby who cares to see it. Which, with one glance around, is everyone, the smiling Palmers and gleeful Sandra included.

And just like that, all my friendship progress vanishes, and I'm right back to square one—the love-struck neighbor.

"Do I still get the money for finding them?" Jack asks, handing the keys to me.

I give a small nod, my eyes stinging from embarrassment. It takes every bit of self-control I possess to meet Tristan's gaze. "Looks like you don't need to drive me home Saturday after all."

CHAPTER 19

TRISTAN PULLS Old Bessie into his driveway, and when he turns off the golf cart, neither of us moves. Being alone with just him again has me breathing easier. Which it's kind of crazy that I feel that way, all things considered.

"Sorry I didn't swim tonight," he says, glancing over at me. "I should have clarified that I'd be there as a Seaside Oasis representative."

I turn to face him on the bench seat, tucking my legs beneath me. "It's fine. I was there for the snow cones."

He chuckles. "You and Walker both, apparently."

The image of Walker and Jack racing to see who could eat a snow cone the fastest and both ending up with massive brain freeze warms me straight through. "There's something different about him. I'm not sure what, but it makes me happy."

"He does seem different somehow. In a good way."

"Speaking of different," I can't fight my smile, "he went all protective-older-brother on me the other night and warned me to be careful around you."

"Did he?"

I nod, waiting expectantly for Tristan's defense.

He leans in close. "If you think I'm just going to hand over an answer without a victory, you're very much mistaken."

"I'll exchange you a question for a question," I say, confident he won't refuse me. Not when he still wants the answer to the question I wouldn't give him on our bike ride.

His smile broadens. "Deal."

"So, what caused the rift between you and Walker?"

"You did."

"Me?" I expect him to say he's kidding, but he doesn't. "What did I have to do with it?"

Tristan's hand lifts off the seat behind me, and he mindlessly pushes a hair from my face. It doesn't feel mindless given the focused way he's looking at me, but it's the only thing that my risk-averse brain can latch onto. And it's the only way I can convince my dancing nerve endings to calm themselves down and pay attention. "Do you remember the last day of school your freshman year when we were out chatting on my dock about our summer plans and Walker came out to get you? He'd said that your mom wanted you to ride along with your grandma to the store to help her with her grocery shopping?"

Of course I remember it. Any memory involving Tristan has been safely stored away into a separate compartment of my brain that's only function is to record detailed memories of him. "He'd had a bad day at golf practice."

Tristan nods. "When you headed inside, I told him to ease up on you. He responded that I should mind my own business and started back to the house. I probably should have left it there, but instead, I followed him. I called him some things I regret and said that you didn't deserve to be treated the way he treated you."

My heart swells at the thought of Tristan championing my awkward freshman self, even if it was to my brother. "And that was it?"

"No. In a few choice words of his own, Walker basically said that I was one to talk. He accused me of constantly toying with you while I had a girlfriend." Tristan's gaze goes distant for a brief moment. "Once he shoved me, the rest gets a bit hazy. Thankfully, Beau heard the commotion and broke things up before more than our pride was injured." His eyes return to mine. "I never would have *toyed* with you. Not intentionally. I swear it."

The idea is almost laughable. Sure, Tristan paid more attention to me than any other guy, but he never, not once, did something to lead me on. Trust me, I would have remembered if he had. "I never felt like you did." I reach out to squeeze his hand resting on the seat between us. It's meant as a friendly gesture, but when my hand makes contact with his, he not only welcomes it but intertwines our fingers. What? Last I checked, friends don't hold hands. At least not co-ed friends. But that's very clearly what we're doing, and my brain is going into hyperdrive, trying to figure out what in the world is happening.

"My turn," Tristan says, setting his other hand against my arm, and with both contact points, a surge of excitement flows through me as if he's an energy source and I'm the conductor for it. "What were you thinking about when I found you the day of our boat ride? What *movie* was playing in your head?"

I set myself up for this entirely, and my stomach still flutters with nerves, but Tristan's hands on me make me feel invincible. And a little reckless. "I was thinking about"—I lean in close and put my lips right next to his ear—"Beau."

Tristan glances over at me, his face so close that we're one brief movement away from our smiling lips touching. "You were not," he says. His gaze searches mine as if he's trying to determine if I'm serious.

I shrug, attempting to fight my smile with little success. "That uniform of his—"

"He didn't wear a uniform in high school." And suddenly, Tristan's hands are at my sides, and he's tickling me!

"Okay, okay!" I say through my squirming giggle.

He pauses, his fingers still in position. And I realize I've completely underutilized tickling in my books. Why did I never see it as sexy until now? "You're going to tell me the truth this time?" he says.

I nod, smiling like a smitten little kitten.

"And?" His fingers move just enough that I know he's serious about continuing where he left off if he's forced to.

"You were the one I was thinking about. Are you happy now?"

"Exceptionally." Tristan smiles, his fingers relaxing but staying put exactly where they are. "Which also makes sense with what Heath mentioned to me on our run earlier."

It's my turn to gawk. "I knew it! I knew he told you I had a crush on you."

"*Had*? I'm pretty sure he said *has*. As in present tense."

"Oh, he's in so much trouble."

"So it's true, then?" Tristan smiles. "You have a thing for me?"

"If you think I'm just going to hand over an answer without a victory—"

His fingers tighten again, but before he can tickle me, I spring out of the golf cart and start running, a stream of laughter trailing behind me. I don't get far when Tristan's hand clasps my wrist, and he turns me toward him, pulling me against his body. "Does this count as a victory? Because I think it might."

It does for me. Honestly, I can't think of anything better than Tristan's arms wrapped around me and him staring down at me with a yearning that matches my own. "I might have a little thing for you," I whisper. Apparently my lungs have stopped functioning at full-capacity along with the rest of me.

"That's good, because I might have a thing for you too." His smile widens. "But mine isn't little."

My heart nearly bursts with his declaration. The man I've been pining after for practically my entire life has a thing for me? But it also doesn't entirely make sense. And not just because it's hard to believe it could be true. "But the other night at the villa, you seemed so eager to leave. And then you wanted to drive me back to Naples Saturday, which I assumed was your way of saying you were done with our arrangement—we'd agreed to do it *until* I went home."

Tristan's gaze shifts back and forth between my eyes. "First off, I wasn't taking you home to end our arrangement. I was taking you home in an attempt to be helpful. Honestly, it was an excuse to spend an entire day with you. But I can now see where the confusion came in." His fingertips brush down my left arm, leaving a trail of pleasure behind. "And as for the villa, I guess you're not the only one misinterpreting the other person's motives. I feel like every time I tried to cross the line of friendship we'd established, I made you nervous."

"I was nervous, but not in a bad way."

"My chat with Heath this morning clarified some of that for me. In hindsight, the smart thing to do would have been to simply ask you instead of overanalyzing each one of your reactions. But I felt like it was a conversation we needed to have in private, and then we were alone in the room together after the spa"—he swallows, and his Adam's apple dips—"I really didn't want you to think I brought you to The Belacourt for … well, for anything other than our outing. So honestly, it was probably best we waited until now."

My smile is on the excessive side of big. "I guess that answers for the platonic side hug you gave me before fleeing."

"It was a protective measure. I knew I had to get out of there quick or I wouldn't be able to resist kissing you for another moment. And I really didn't want to scare you away. But now …" His hand comes to my neck, his thumb grazing my jaw, and I know exactly what is about to happen. I've written moments just like this many times—well, maybe not *just like this* because the butterflies I get when I write a kiss scene are not even comparable to the ones exploding through the whole of my body currently—but I'm well aware of what he's about to do. And I'm here for it.

Except I shouldn't be. Not when he doesn't know the truth. But if I tell him, there will never be a kiss. And didn't I decide, when I was young, that I'll die a happier woman having kissed Tristan Palmer? I still stand by that.

His lips graze mine, and the minty smell of him intoxicates me, but not enough to dull my conscience. No matter how much I want this. Stupid conscience. I step back. "I can't do this."

"I'm sorry, I thought …" His words trail off, a look of complete and utter confusion on his face.

"No. It's not you." I pull in a deep breath, longing to be back in his arms. But there's too much to say. Too much that will change everything. "I have to tell you something."

He stands an arm length away, waiting, but I can't figure out how to say what needs to be said. For all my fretting and anxiety about this moment, I should have done a better job at planning out how to go about actually telling him. "Now that I have my keys, I'm going to head back to Naples tomorrow. I have some editing I need to do." A slight trembling has started in my body, and I clasp my hands together to keep Tristan from noticing. "For a book I'm writing." There. That wasn't so hard. A perfect lead-in to the truth bomb I'm about to drop on him. My stomach churns.

He gives a timid smile. "Are you going to publish it?"

"I am. It actually already has a release date and everything."

Tristan's head pulls back slightly and there are conflicting emotions in his expression. "That's incredible. Is that what you needed to tell me?"

"No. Well, kind of." I drop my gaze to the ground in front of me. I honestly feel like I'm going to be sick. *I am Sunny Palmer.* I can do this. But before I can get the words out, a familiar heaviness moves into my chest and tears prick my eyes. No! I refuse to let him witness another floodgate cry session. With the emotional rollercoaster I've been on today, it isn't a surprise I'd be reeling, but I need to calm myself. I shut my eyes and draw in a deep breath. I can do this. I have to do this. "I'm Sunny Palmer," I blurt, ripping the bandaid right off.

Tristan gives an uncertain laugh like he's not sure why I'd joke about that. Then he takes in my expression and his smile fades. "Are you serious?"

I nod. "Only Jane and Tala know."

"Wait. You're Sunny Palmer? As in the best-selling author we were talking about at the pool?"

Again, I nod.

He sits there a minute as if waiting for me to shout 'gotcha' but when I don't, he smiles. Smiles! He obviously didn't pick up on the whole theft of his name situation in the shocking reveal. "That's incredible!" He pauses, his gaze turning thoughtful, and I'm confident the connection has been made. "But why has that kept you away from Sunset Harbor?"

"I'm Sunny ... *Palmer*," I say, accentuating Tristan's last name.

Suddenly there's recognition in his eyes. "You used our last name for your pen name?"

"*Your* last name," I clarify. "And Sunny comes from—"

"Capri *Sun*," he says, finishing for me. Contrary to the disbelief I think will follow this admission, his smile widens. "Heath really undersold the level of your crush. And honestly, so did you." He chuckles to himself. "*I might have a little thing for you*," he repeats my own words back to me. "You used my name for your pen name. That doesn't sound little."

"Fine," I huff. "It was a huge, massive crush. Are you happy?"

The way his whole face is lit with sheer and unadulterated amusement, he doesn't need to answer. "So why are you telling me this now? Haven't you been publishing under that name for years?"

I shift on my feet. "Because that's not all."

"Oh, there's more?" He looks far too delighted, and I have to keep reminding myself that I should be relieved he isn't freaking out.

"My first book—now a *New York Times* Best Seller and the fan favorite—may have *loosely* been based off of a fictional love story"—I swallow—"between us."

Tristan crosses his arms in front of him and narrows his eyes. "How loosely are we talking?"

I shrug and tuck a piece of hair behind my ear. "The main characters are neighbors, their physical descriptions resemble ours, and their names are ... somewhat similar." That is definitely a gross understatement, but it seems like a good place to start. "But they're older than we were at the time. Recently home from college, actually."

Tristan's lips tick upward. "What are their names?"

Why does this feel like some kind of slow torture? I get that I deserve it, but heat has settled into my face and neck, and I can't stop squirming. "Trenton and Cali."

"Trenton and ... Cali?" The way he says Cali, it's clear he didn't miss where the inspiration for that name came from. He covers his mouth with a fist in an attempt to hide his smile. "So, that's it? Outside of those three things, nothing else is *similar*?"

I clear my throat. "I mean, there are probably a few others that could lead someone to make the connection if they knew to look for it." Like the fact that I never changed Bridget's name, the whole football-player-with-the-introverted-book-nerd thing, and basically every minor and major detail included besides a handful of romantically exaggerated interactions between Cali and Trenton, including the fictionalized ending. "Which is the reason why I'm telling you now. With my recent success, if anyone discovers who I am—and there are people actively trying to figure out my real identity—it won't be hard to connect you to all of this."

His gaze goes distant, and he gives a solemn nod as if he's

finally understanding the gravity of the situation. "I guess it would be difficult to be known as the man who inspired Sunny Palmer's first, and apparently most epic, love story. Not to mention the pen name."

I whack my hand into his chest, and he laughs. "This is serious. There's a chance you'll get dragged into the whole mess right along with me."

He shrugs. "I'm not worried."

I lean away from him, appraising his smiling self. How is he not furious? Or at least a little bit mad? Maybe he's in shock. I probably would be if the roles were reversed. "This is not how I expected this conversation going."

"What'd you expect?"

"Honestly? Best case scenario: that you'd be upset and things would become super awkward between us but we'd cope with it by avoiding each other. Worst case scenario: a restraining order and some mortifying court appearances that would bring light to the whole situation."

He chuckles.

I drop my chin, allowing my mind to stray to a place I typically refuse to let it go—how different all of this would be if Bridget and Tristan were still together. My thoughtless choice from years ago would have pulled them both into it. My mistake would have been unpardonable. "If you were married to Bridget right now, the latter wouldn't seem that far-fetched. She would be rightly livid."

His smile lessens some but it doesn't completely vanish. It's just softer now. "I guess there's a reason everything happens the way it does."

"I'm still sorry," I say, glancing up at him. "If I could do it all over again, I'd do it differently."

"Then, it's a good thing you can't." There's no teasing glint in his eye this time.

Instantly, a crushing weight is lifted from me, and I feel at risk of floating away without it. I've spent way too long shouldering the pointless load. I've spent way too long stressing about his possible reactions. But I should have listened to Tala and Jane. Of course Tristan would be generous. That's who he is.

Tristan's gaze settles on me with an intensity that leaves my heart pattering about recklessly. "So, what's next?" he asks.

I give a small shrug, my insides vibrating at the potential of where this conversation might go. But there's also a niggling, unsettling feeling vying for dominance in the pit of my stomach. A realization that with my massive, apparently flattering revelation, Tristan might be swept up in the moment. Or worse, that he feels somehow obligated to try and make something work between us now that he knows the truth. The last thing I want is Tristan to do something that will lead him to feel stuck later. Something that will hinder his ability to choose for himself. Especially now when he's about to leave. So, for his sake, I can put my own reckless desires aside for the time being. Or I hope I can. "Maybe you ... well, we—you and me both—should take a little time to process everything."

Tristan's hand comes to the side of my face, and he rubs his thumb along my jaw, making my legs weak beneath me. "What if I don't need time?"

With his skin on mine and my nerves racing through me, I seem to be short-circuiting. But I'm still cognizant enough to do what's best for Tristan. "With how I've forced you into this ... *situation* without your knowledge or permission, I want to make sure you won't have any regrets. Especially considering how you've mentioned your tendency toward doing what's expected of you." Shoot! That didn't sound like it did in my head. "Not that I expect anything of you. Honestly. I have zero expectations." That somehow sounds worse. And it's not even entirely true. I've developed all sorts of hopes surrounding Tristan. I need to stop talking until I can recalibrate.

His hand drops to his side, and his introspective gaze lowers to the ground at our feet as if he's trying to make sense of the nuanced messages behind my babbling comment.

And suddenly, with the massive void I feel from the loss of physical contact, I'm questioning my altruistic attempts. I'm questioning if I single-handedly ruined my chance to finally kiss Tristan Palmer. To be with him. And not even because he's furious about my big reveal. Of course I'd self-sabotage this moment with my overthinking. I should have just kept quiet and let him kiss me. Embraced this for what it could potentially be —a summer fling. The most wonderful, most anticipated summer fling in the history of summer flings. I'll be beyond crushed when he leaves, but the memories we'll have made can buoy me in the hard times. "I'm not opposed to a summer fling," I blurt before I have a chance to consider what I'm saying. Or that I'm even saying it aloud. My mouth has gone rogue in its desperation to make sure it finally accomplishes it's lifelong goal of having Tristan's lips against it.

His gaze lifts to mine, but instead of the smile I'd hoped to see, his lips are pulled in a straight line and his jaw is taut. It's a look I'm not used to seeing on him. And it's worse because I know I'm the one that caused it. "A summer fling?" he repeats in a way that verifies he isn't a fan of the idea like I am. Or was. I'm definitely not a fan of it now.

"I just meant since I'll be going home for the next few weeks, and then you're leaving at the end of summer. It doesn't make sense—"

"To expect this will go anywhere," he finishes, though it's not exactly what I was going to say. He runs a hand over his stubbled chin. "Maybe you're right."

I don't respond. I don't know what it is I could be right about. Everything I've said has been wrong.

His eyes meet mine, and I don't like the cool resolve in them. "Let's take some time to think through things."

Despite that I've achieved my original intent, my heart deflates and sinks to the bottom of my chest cavity, and I'm not sure I'll ever be able to revive it. "Yeah. Okay."

He hesitates, then takes a step back. "Let me know when you're back in town."

Tears prick my eyes, but I nod. "I will."

Tristan lifts a parting hand, but before he can turn to leave, I move in front of him and lift onto my toes, placing a light kiss on his cheek. It's impulsive and slightly reckless, but I can't just let him walk away without some kind of indication of how I feel about him. Even if it's super minor and way too brief. "Thanks for understanding," I whisper.

For once, I can't quite decipher the mix of emotions in his eyes, but when he brushes his fingers across my cheek, the slightest flicker of hope is reignited within me. "See you soon, Capri Sun."

I don't look back as I start up the stairs. I've used up all of my strength, and I'm worried that one backward glance will break open the floodgates. So I slip inside the front door and pull out my phone:

CAPRI

I told Tristan.

JANE

I'm assuming you aren't with him anymore since you're texting?

CAPRI

I'm back at Tala's.

JANE

I'm headed over now!

CHAPTER 20

TWO WEEKS LATER

I GLANCE around my office floor at the scattered boxes of unpacked books. The morning I drove back to Naples, Tristan and Heath had skipped their run to load my boxes into my jeep. I hadn't realized they were planning on doing it, so by the time I woke up and got going, Tristan was already at work. Keith, my neighbor, unloaded them for me when I got home, and now they're sitting on my floor like a painful reminder as to how those stinking boxes uprooted my entire life. And that the only place I want to be right now is with Tristan. I'm pathetic.

It's not that I haven't heard from Tristan. We've texted back and forth a few times, but I can tell he's trying to give me space —whether to allow me to concentrate on work or because it was my idea to take time to process, I'm not sure. And with how we left things—well, how I left things—I'm confident he requires a little space himself.

If only I hadn't mentioned the *summer fling* comment. It clearly didn't go over well. Which shouldn't surprise me with Tristan—he's an all-in kind of guy. But the last thing I want is for him to feel obligated to be with me. Ever. Let alone when he's about to move across the country in pursuit of choosing his own path in life. Of doing what he wants without thinking of anyone else. That's a huge deal for him. I won't stand in his way.

If we had more time to see if things could work, I'd absolutely take it. But we don't. In fact, he texted two days ago to inform me they found a buyer for all four of the centers, including Seaside Oasis, and that the sale should be finalized the first week of July. So as much as I actually don't want a summer fling either, I also don't see another option currently. Besides us not being together at all. And I really, *really* hate that idea. Because real life Tristan is even better than fictional Tristan. Like so entirely better. Even with his tendency to assume meetings are shorter than they'll be, his subtle insecurities (like riding a bike with a bell) along with his less-than-subtle jealousy, his overly competitive nature, and his professed dislike of reading (which I still can't understand) —even with all that, I'm falling harder for him. He's perfectly imperfect. He's real.

My gaze catches on the flashing cursor on my screen, and I shake Tristan from my thoughts for the millionth time. No wonder these edits are taking exponentially longer than I'd expected. The only thing I seem to be able to focus on is Tristan, and our almost kiss, and where he's emotionally at in his processing, and how I probably ruined everything, and then right back to our almost kiss.

Concentrate, Capri.

I skim the last paragraph of changes I made, trying to determine the next logical place to add this new character. I know the addition will make my book better, but more than once, I've considered my sanity at attempting such a significant change this late in the process. What if I mess it up? There will be no time to fix it.

My phone buzzes, and my gaze shoots to the screen. The fact that my phone has remained off concentration mode for the last two weeks has definitely not helped my productivity, but when I see Tristan's name, I feel the compromise was worth it.

TRISTAN

How's the editing going?

CAPRI

Super slow. How are you?

TRISTAN

Good. Do you have a minute to chat?

My heart rate doubles instantly and my chest tightens. What does he want to say that he can't over text?

CAPRI

Sure.

My phone rings and I pick it up. "Hey."

"It's good to hear your voice," he says, releasing a quick breath that makes my ear rattle.

"Same," I say like my insides aren't dancing some kind of tumultuous jig. "So what's up?"

"I was sitting here thinking about our competition. How we never chose a winner before you left."

That's it? That's what he wanted to talk to me about? My next inhale comes more easily though my body is now buzzing with anticipation. Surely this is a good sign, right? Maybe he's gotten on board with the whole summer fling idea. "I'm extremely confident you won."

"Well, hold off on making out that dedication page to me for the time being."

"And why's that?"

"Because it wouldn't be fair to choose a winner before you have a chance to plan another date."

I don't miss the way he calls it a date instead of an outing. Another good sign. "That does make sense." I pause as if I'm considering what to do. "I guess, for the sake of fairness, I'll have to."

"Any idea when it'll be? Not because I'm desperate to see you or anything. I'm just curious."

I laugh. It's a mix of relief and excitement. If I could just bottle up Tristan to use for all my male characters, my books would sell like hotcakes. But now that I think about it, that's basically what I've done and why my books do sell like hotcakes. My characters aren't necessarily Tristan, but they each have pieces of him. Besides my first book. That's all Tristan. Hence why it's the readers' favorite. "Considering the latest I can have the manuscript to my editor is July first and I have to get a few things done here, I'll plan to head that way the afternoon of the second. So how about the third?"

"I'm in a meeting until four that day, but any time after that works."

"Great. Whenever you're done, I'll be ready."

There's a lull in the conversation, but I don't want to get off yet. I search my mind for another topic, but my hasty attempt proves unnecessary when his voice comes over the speaker again. "So, did you finally get to go on that date you were looking forward to?"

His question surprises me, but so does the way he asked it—like he's not sure he'll like my answer but still really needs to know. And I kind of love it. "Yeah, I did. It was actually pretty amazing."

He's silent for a whole breath cycle. "Oh. What'd you do?"

"You know—dinner, a movie, and ended the night with a bubble bath." I'm doing my best not to laugh, but I can't hold out much longer.

"You're kidding, right?"

And there it goes, my laughter breaks free. "Mostly. The date I first mentioned was a celebratory tradition I do when I get a manuscript off to the editor. But with the timing of everything and my new deadline, I forewent the movie and settled for takeout from my favorite Cuban place along with a quick bubble bath. It was a party of one."

He gives an airy chuckle. "You think you're so funny."

"One of us has to."

We chat for a while about the buyers for the retirement centers and what my editing process entails when I hear Sandra step into his office and say something about a meeting.

"Sounds like you've got to go," I offer before he says anything. "But I'll see you in a week for our date. Get ready to have your mind blown."

"I'm looking forward to it."

CHAPTER 21

"THE KIDS ARE IN BED," Tala says on our way inside her house. "They wanted to stay up, but I wasn't sure what time you'd get here."

I glance at the clock on my phone. Whoa, it's already nine-thirty. "Good call."

She drops her golf cart keys in the drawer and looks at me. "You look tired."

"That round of edits kicked my butt. I made my deadline by four minutes with a time-stamp of 11:56 PM to prove it." I don't mention it took another three hours to get myself to fall asleep after the desperate scramble to finish on time. I was hoping I'd crash, but it seemed to have the opposite effect on me. Then I spent all day today doing the stuff I've been putting off until my edits were done—like laundry and cleaning and packing.

Tala rubs a hand down my arm. "I'm sorry. But you did it! That has to feel amazing."

I nod, unable to stifle a yawn. "Yeah. It's always a relief to finally hand off my manuscript." And completely nerve-wracking that the story's basically stuck in stone from here on out. Though I can make a few minor changes when I go through my proofread.

"Are you feeling up to celebrating?"

"Tonight?" I ask, hopeful that's not what she means. Right now, all I want to do is fall into bed and not move until morning.

She nods, her eyes alight with excitement, and I know I can't disappoint her.

"Sure. What did you have in mind?"

A knock at the door has her smile brightening. "Nothing," she says, moving to answer it. "But I think someone else might have an idea."

When the door opens, Tristan is standing there in shorts and a t-shirt, a timid smile on his lips. "Hey."

With the way my body overreacts to the sight of him, there's no longer a trace of tiredness left in me. "Tristan, what are you doing here?"

"If you're feeling up to it, I was hoping to take you out to celebrate you turning in your manuscript."

Tala's blinding smile in my periphery is excessively distracting, so I step toward Tristan so she's behind me. Or maybe I'm just using it as an excuse to get closer to him. "Yeah, that sounds great," I say, glancing down at my outfit. "Can I go like this or should I change?"

His gaze trails over me slowly. "That's perfect."

I grab my phone. "Is there anything else I need?"

"Nope."

I glance at Tala, who looks like she might explode with joy. "You two have fun," Tala says, ushering me out the door and shutting it behind us. Wow. Talk about overly eager. It must run in the family.

"Where are we headed?" I ask, stepping in next to him.

Tristan's smile sends a trill of happiness to my core. "You'll see."

While in the golf cart, we make small talk. I explain the next stages for my manuscript—proofreading and formatting—but that those will be a breeze compared to my edits, and Tristan updates me about Seaside Oasis. Apparently, the people buying it are a family very similar to the Palmers and who already own a few other retirement centers scattered around Florida. He says they don't intend to change anything and seem to run their other centers similarly—with a resident-first mentality—but with the way his thumb is tapping on the golf cart steering wheel, I can tell he's slightly unsettled. Probably because once the sale goes through, he'll have to make the announcement, and as I'm well aware, the task is a rather daunting one. Sunset Harbor is a small-town island that's not big on change. Especially when it'll involve an unknown family coming in to run Seaside Oasis where several of our residents work and live.

When we pull up to the gate outside of Jane's house, I look over at Tristan. "What are we doing here?"

He just smiles. "I assume you have the code? Jane let me in earlier."

Attempting to guess what he's up to, I lean over him and type it in, relishing the proximity to Tristan that the task requires. He parks the golf cart on the far side of Jane's massive two-story home, grabs a large bag, and leads me through the arched side gate, past the pool, and toward the beach behind the Hayes' house. Technically, it's still a public beach, but because the Belacourt Resort owns the land north of here, not many public beach goers make it up this way. And I doubt we'll see anyone else at this hour since we're getting close to the weeknight curfew. Not that it'll matter here.

When we step out onto the sand, my gaze catches on a large white screen and a blow-up pool that's not filled with water but is brimming with pillows and blankets. "What's all this?"

"I figured since your last celebration wasn't what you hoped it would be, we needed to have a proper one now that your edits are in." He lifts the bag off his shoulder and sets it down, gesturing to it, then the screen. "Dinner and a movie. Oh, and a pool of pillows instead of a bubble bath. I felt like that was an appropriate replacement."

My smile is stretched to maximum capacity. "It's perfect. All of it."

"The location was Jane's idea. I ran into her a few days ago and told her my plan, and she insisted we do it at the beach behind her house for a little more privacy." I'll definitely remember to thank her later for her forethought. He lifts the bag. "I'm hoping you're hungry."

"I'm starving," I say, and as if on command, my stomach rumbles to prove my point.

I follow Tristan to a small pop-up table with two chairs that's set up on the far side of the blow-up pool. He places the bag on the table and starts rummaging through it. "I know you said you already had Cuban food, but I wasn't sure if that was part of your tradition or not, so I decided to stick with it. I hope that's okay." He lifts out two packaged boxes and opens the one in front of me. The delicious aroma of cooked meat, pickles, and swiss cheese wafts upward.

"Cuban sandwiches. My favorite!"

He pulls out a Diet Coke and hands it to me. Then he moves the bag to the sand next to us before taking his seat.

I take the first bite, and between the toasted Cuban bread and the zesty mayo sauce, the pleasure sensors in my mouth sing their approval. "You aren't trying to get a leg up in our competition with all of this, are you?" I ask, covering my mouth with my hand while I chew. "Or do I need to plan a third outing now?"

"Nope. This one's not in the running."

"Good. It's already going to be difficult enough to try to beat you at this point."

He chuckles. "Though maybe it should count for something considering the movie I brought for us to watch. Jane said I couldn't go wrong with *How to Lose a Guy in Ten Days*."

Okay, apparently my smile can grow wider than I previously thought. "That's what we're watching?"

"I'm glad to see one of us is excited."

"Don't tell me you don't like romcoms either."

He leans back in his chair, studying me. "You're still dwelling on my admission that I'm not much of a reader, aren't you?"

"I'm not dwelling on it. Not really."

Tristan folds his arms over his broad chest. "Would it help my case if I told you I read a book while you were gone?"

"You did?" I ask, taking another bite of my sandwich.

"I did. It was absolutely gripping. Eye-opening even."

See? He just has to catch the bug and he'll be a reader in no time. "Was it fiction or non-fiction?"

"Honestly, I'm not sure. I'd probably say fiction, but it was definitely based on true events." The way Tristan is watching me with a growing smile gives me pause, and suddenly I understand his meaning.

My lips part. "Did you read my book?"

"How could I not? I had to check for accuracy. And can I just say, your whole *loosely based off of us* comment was entirely misleading?"

I cover my face with my hand and groan. "I assumed you'd read it, I just ... can we not talk about it?"

Tristan laughs. "But I have so many questions."

"How about we save them for later? When we're not celebrating?" I hope he'll take pity on me. I get that my reckoning day is coming, but I really don't want it to be tonight. Though I'm not sure tomorrow is much better. Or the day after that.

"It's your night, so I guess I can wait." His head tilts to the side and his smile widens, matching mine. "But just so you know, you're not getting out of this one."

AS I SIT in the cozy little pool with Tristan next to me, my focus is on anything but the movie. Each movement he makes, no matter how small, sends me into a strange anticipatory state.

I'm also excessively aware of the current position of his hand and the exact distance, down to millimeters, between our legs. The levels of flirting we've engaged in tonight is top notch, but I'm still not entirely certain what Tristan wants or where we stand on the whole summer fling concept. Well, I know where I stand, and it doesn't include us sitting four inches and six millimeters apart from each other while I pretend to watch a movie I've seen countless times. Not that I don't love it—it's my absolute favorite—but Tristan's currently taking up every ounce of brain energy I possess. Which, after edits and with how tired I am, isn't much to start with.

About halfway through the movie, he leans back, propping his head on a pillow, and his gaze slides to me. It's only then I realize I'm watching him and not the movie. Quickly, I turn my attention back to the screen, squinting as if I haven't been blessed with near perfect vision. His hand slides around my wrist, and he gives a little tug on my arm.

I glance down at him, and he pats his chest with his other hand invitingly. And like a bug drawn to a bright, beautiful light, my path is set. I lay down next to him, and he wraps his arm behind me, guiding me against his side. Timidly, I set my hand on his chest, and his other hand settles over mine. I'm pretty sure I've died and gone to heaven.

"Comfortable?" he asks, and I nod. "Good."

I'm so comfortable, in fact, I could fall asleep right here. Not that I will. I want to enjoy every moment I'm in his arms. But with how perfectly content I am and how heavy my eyes suddenly are, it's going to take a massive effort to stay awake. An effort I'm willing to undertake.

"CAPRI?" Tristan's voice is so close, I'm sure I'm dreaming.

"Hmmm ..." There's no way I'm so much as cracking an eye open if I'm having a Tristan dream.

"Let's get you home." Fingertips that feel far too real for a dream brush across my cheek. I peek open an eye to find Tristan smiling down at me with an amused smile. "Hey, you."

My lips part when I realize exactly where I am. "I fell asleep? I'm so sorry."

"I'm not complaining."

I rub a hand over my eyes, glancing at the blank movie screen and blinking a couple times to try and get it into focus. "But the celebration and the movie. I—"

"Nope. It was absolutely perfect." His fingers brush against my cheek again. "You smile in your sleep. Did you know that?"

I shake my head, feeling my face warm beneath his attentive regard.

"Just every once in a while, your lips curl into a small little smile."

"Did you dislike the movie so much that you had to watch me instead?"

"The parts I saw I actually liked. But you were a lot more fun to watch." His gaze moves across my face. "You're beautiful, you know. Stunning." Then his eyes lower to my lips.

My stomach lifts in anticipation, and I realize the moment I've waited years for has finally come. I'm going to kiss Tristan Palmer! And cuddled up next to him with his adoring gaze on me, it all feels too perfect.

He leans in, making my breath catch, but pauses, as if to see if I'm okay with it. Before I can hint that I am, his brow lowers and he looks away.

I'm reeling, not exactly sure what's happening, when Tristan's attention returns to me. "Do you hear voices?"

I still, attempting to decipher whatever it is Tristan's hearing. "No." But then I hear them. "Oh, I do."

"It's probably just a couple out for a midnight stroll," Tristan says, but I can tell he's still focused on the voices. Whoever it is, they're getting closer. Then suddenly, a bright light shines on the pool, making the soft blue plastic glow.

"What do we have going on here?" The masculine voice is oddly familiar, and I glance at Tristan.

He releases a breath and rests his palm on his forehead. "You've got to be kidding me."

"Is that Beau?" I whisper, drawing closer to Tristan to keep the light from hitting me.

"I'll handle this." Tristan sits up, and the beam of light hits him square in the face. He squints and covers his eyes. "What are you doing, Beau?"

"If it isn't Tristan," Beau laughs. "And I'll be the one asking the questions. Do you know how many ordinances you're breaking right now?"

"No, but can you enlighten me later? And can you put down that flashlight? I can't see a thing."

"I'll put it down once the interrogation's over. I need to know who you have in that cute little blow-up pool with you so I can verify she's there of her own free will and choice."

I moan, covering my face with a pillow.

"It's really none of your business," Tristan says.

"My job is the public safety of Sunset Harbor's residents." He pauses, a light chuckle making its way to where we are. "Capri, my brother isn't taking advantage of you, is he?"

I don't know whether to laugh or cry, so I sit up, joining Tristan in the line of fire. The flashlight is super bright. "Hey, Beau."

Beau chuckles again. "How's your night going, Capri?"

I squint in the direction of the light. "It's been good."

"We're just watching a movie," Tristan offers, and Beau's flashlight swings to the now blank screen and back to us before I can so much as catch a glimpse of him.

"I'm not a qualified detective, but I'm going to call your bluff on that one."

"It just finished."

"Sure it did." The amusement in Beau's voice is palpable.

Tristan's holding out his hand in front of him to block the light. "Can you stop it with the light now?"

Beau lowers his flashlight, but it takes a few seconds for my eyes to adjust to the darkness, and it's only then that I realize Beau's not alone. A tall, slender woman with a slicked-back, dark ponytail is standing next to Beau, looking like she's not quite certain what to do. She's vaguely familiar, but I can't place her.

"You two remember Gemma Sawyer?"

Oh! Gemma. Virginia's granddaughter. Wow, the more the bright circle in my eyesight fades, the more of her I can see, and she is gorgeous. Is it petty of me that I'm extremely grateful she moved away from Sunset Harbor before high school?

"Hey, Gemma." Tristan lifts a hand. "Good to see you again."

"Capri is a Collins," Beau says, attempting to spark her memory. Though I doubt she'll remember me regardless. "Deedee's granddaughter."

I give a little wave.

"I remember Capri." Gemma's gaze settles on me. "I haven't had a chance to thank you for offering to help move my grandma into Seaside Oasis. I obviously didn't need to take you up on it, but I appreciate you being willing."

"Of course."

"Why don't we continue your patrol of the beach?" Gemma looks at Beau and gestures in the direction they came from. "That way Tristan and Capri can enjoy their night together without any further interrogations or flashlights blinding them."

"I'd like to, but they're out past curfew."

"Are you kidding me right now?" Tristan says, shaking his head.

"What kind of officer would I be if I look the other way every time my own brother breaks a law?"

"It's like an hour after curfew."

"Which is a ticketable offense, Tristan. And your casual attitude about law-breaking is honestly a bit concerning." Laughter is brimming in Beau's voice when he points at me. "I'm not sure my brother is the sort of guy you should be hanging out with, Capri."

I can't hide my smile. "I appreciate your concern, Beau."

His gaze returns to Tristan and he heaves a heavy breath. "Because I like Capri so much, and because I'm feeling charitable, I'll let you off with a warning. But this is the last time."

Even Tristan's fighting a smile now. "I can't wait to repay you for your generosity."

Beau's laughter finally breaks free. "Threatening an officer?"

"I wouldn't dream of it."

"Come on," Gemma says, tugging him back the direction they came. "Enjoy the rest of your evening together," she calls.

Beau takes a few backwards steps, allowing Gemma to keep hold of his arm. "You two better not dawdle too long. If I get a complaint from one of the neighbors about you being out here, my hands will be tied."

Gemma gives one more tug that has him turning and walking away with her.

"Sorry about him," Tristan says.

I give an absent smile, my gaze following Beau and Gemma. "Do you think they like each other?"

Tristan chuckles. "A Sawyer and a Palmer? There's no way. She's just helping him with a project, so she's been tagging along with him while he's on duty."

"I don't know. They have incredible star-crossed lover vibes."

Even in the darkness, I can see humor shining in Tristan's eyes. "That imagination of yours is really something."

Without warning, a yawn surfaces, and I put a hand over my mouth. "Sorry."

He stands up, steps out of the pool, and holds out his hand for mine. "It's late. Let's get you home."

A wave of disappointment settles over me, and I wonder if my lifelong desire to kiss Tristan will ever be actualized. Though with our little run-in with Beau, the opportunity definitely seems to have passed. I suppose I've waited this long; I can wait one more day. But I'm not sure I can be any more patient than that.

I put my hand in Tristan's and allow him to pull me to my feet. "That's probably best. I'd hate to mar my pristine record with a ticket."

WELCOME TO
SUNSET
HARBO

BELACOURT RESORT

GOLF COURSE

NOAH'S HOUSE

JANE'S HOUSE

NATURE PRESERVE

OAX'S DUPLEX

SEASIDE OASIS RETIREMENT HOME

SUNSET REPAIRS

PHOENIX'S OFFICE

CITY OFFICES

SCOOPS AHOY ICE CREAM

SUNRISE CAFE

KEENE B&B

TOWN SQUARE

BAKERY

BRIGGS'S APARTMENT

THE BOOK ISLE

CUTS AND CURLS

GULF OF MEXICO

TRISTAN & BEAU'S HOUSE

CAPRI'S HOUSE

GEMMA'S HOUSE

HOLLAND'S HOUSE

BEACH BREAK BAR & GRILL

PUBLIC BEACH

N
W E
S

CHAPTER 22

WIND TOSSES my hair and the whirring of the motor is loud in my ears as I steer the boat through the bright greenish-blue water. The sight of Tristan lounging against the bow of the old fishing boat with closed eyes and a contented grin sends a trill of excitement down my spine. "We're here."

"Where's here?" he asks, sitting up. There's still land in the distance to the east, but besides that and the small, sandy islet we're moving toward, it's only ocean as far as the eye can see. Thankfully, there are no other boats anchored nearby, which isn't super common. People love this secret little spot. Though their absence probably has to do with how late in the day it is. So maybe it's a good thing Tristan's meeting went a little later than expected again.

"Winn Island." I rev the motor a touch until the boat's nose beaches, then cut the engine. "Technically it's an islet, but *Winn Islet* doesn't have the same ring to it."

He's still taking in the sandy strip of land that's really just a long, narrow sandbar without vegetation. "So your Grandpa Winn discovered it?"

"That's what he always told us. Though whenever other people are here, I've never heard one of them call it Winn Island. Make of that what you will."

Tristan chuckles and stands up, glancing at the floor of the fishing boat. "What in here needs to come out?"

"All of it."

"Aye, aye, Captain." Tristan grabs the beach chairs and cooler, and I grab the towels and my tote. "I'll come back for the paddleboards," he says, helping me out of the boat.

"It's high tide, so we can set up camp right by the edge of the water."

"Camp?" Tristan asks, setting down his load and coming to take mine from me. "This isn't another of your attempts to seduce me, is it?"

Despite the rush of nerves his question causes, I send him a playful scowl.

"You are an acclaimed romance writer. Who knows what's going on in that head of yours."

He's one to talk. I'm still not sure what he's thinking when it comes to us, and each time I've thought to broach the subject since he came by after work, my courage wanes before I can.

He walks back to the boat, grabbing the paddle board cases and hauling them over. "I assume you want these pumped up?"

"Yep." I lean over and unzip one of the cases, pulling out the long, deflated board and rolling it out flat on the sand.

With Tristan as the muscle behind the pump, he has them both filled in less than twenty minutes, and we head out. The clear water around the islet is shallow enough to see the bottom, causing a greenish blue hue in the late afternoon light. An occasional fish darts beneath us and, more than a few times, the shadow of our boards makes me startle. Personally, I've never seen a shark at Winn Island, but once the thought is there, I can't unthink it.

We haven't been out very long when my paddleboard starts veering to whatever side my paddle is submerged on. "I think something's wrong with my board."

Tristan watches me attempt a few more strokes before paddling his own board over to where I am. "I hope your fin didn't fall off." He drops down onto his knees and puts his hand into the water beneath the end of my board. "Darn. It did. We must not have locked it in." By *we* he means *me*, but it's nice of him to make it a collective blame.

"Did I ruin Tala's board?"

"No, you can get a replacement fin for like ten bucks." He stands back up. "But we'll probably want to beach it for the rest of the evening. If you want, we can switch boards and I can paddle it in, then we can head out on this one together."

Why does that sound like the most wonderful yet nerve-wracking situation of my life? "Sure."

He holds out his hand, and we do an awkward maneuver that leaves him on the dunce board and the lingering effect of his warm skin against mine. I get the sense he wouldn't have minded the transition taking a bit longer, but with nerves bouncing through me, I suddenly feel like a young, inexperienced teenager all over again.

He dips his paddle a few times, and though he definitely has a little more control than I did, there's no way he'll be able to keep up with me. So I take advantage. "First one back to the island gets the extra brownie I brought for dessert," I call over my shoulder.

Tristan says something, but I can't make it out because I'm already several board lengths in front of him. When I pull my board onto the beach, I'm holding my paddle horizontally above my head, gloating over my victory.

"You're a sneaky one," he calls, making his way toward me one wobbly paddle at a time.

"Remember, I prefer smart," I say with a laugh.

When the water's about chest deep, Tristan jumps off the board and pulls it to the beach, dragging it out of the water before heading straight toward me. "Let's see how those smarts will work for you now."

I drop my paddle and start backing up. "Okay, you can have the extra brownie."

He shakes his head, and I recognize that playful glint in his eyes. "It's too late for concessions."

With his next step, I take off running in the opposite direction, but as we're on a narrow strip of sand in the middle of the ocean, there really isn't anywhere to go. I can hear his thudding footsteps getting closer, so I veer into the water on the other side, my laughter thwarting my efforts to move faster. Salty water is splashing everywhere, but I don't stop until Tristan's strong arms slide around my stomach and he lifts me into the air.

He moves a little deeper as if he's going to dunk me, and my squealish giggle would put a little pink piglet to shame. "Okay, okay," I say. "I'm sorry, I'm sorry, I'm sorry!"

Tristan pauses, but he doesn't release me. "Do you mean it?"

"I mean it."

"And do I get the brownie?"

I nod.

"And an extra question?"

I don't respond to his demand until he takes another few steps. "Fine. I'll answer another question."

Tristan's chest rumbles with laughter against my back, and when he slowly lowers me down, the water reaches my stomach. But what leaves me gasping for air is how he keeps his arms around me. I don't turn to face him immediately, but I set my hands on top of his, and the entire mood shifts. All the splashing and laughing from moments before is replaced with anticipation and nervous energy.

"I've taken some time to think about things …" Despite that we're the only two people here, Tristan's mouth is right next to my ear, his voice just above a whisper. "And I'll have no regrets when it comes to you, Capri Sun."

I suck in a quick breath to compensate for my shallow breathing, and then slowly, timidly, I turn around. Our eyes meet, and his match the sea-green tones of the water surrounding us with a hint of golden sunlight. My fingertips seem to be acting of their own accord when they settle on his abs, then trail upward along his bare chest. My heart is thudding wildly, and I fully embrace it. I've waited a lifetime for this moment, and I mean to enjoy every aspect of it.

Tristan's lips pull into a small smile, and there's a question in his eyes. Never have I been more confident of any answer than I am of this one. "Kiss me," I whisper, settling a hand behind his neck and guiding him toward me, and that's all the encouragement he needs before his lips are against mine. Fireworks erupt, exactly like I always suspected would happen if I was ever lucky enough to kiss Tristan Palmer. His movements are slow—full of tenderness and restraint—and it's as if Tristan intrinsically knows how I always envisioned our first kiss.

And I'm memorizing each detail—from the feel of his stubbled jaw beneath my hand and the pressure of his hands on my lower back to the salty taste on his lips and the closeness of our bodies—so I can finally write that chapter in my autobiography that outlines The Kiss and the monumental impact it's had on me. Because, even while experiencing it, I'm absolutely positive this kiss will affect every single thing about my life moving forward. That's how incredible it is.

Tristan's hold on my lower back intensifies, and the overpowering urge to lift onto my toes and deepen the kiss is all but actualized when something brushes against my leg in the water. I break away and look down, seeing a shadow whip past our feet. Without taking a moment to process, I jump onto Tristan and wrap my legs around his waist.

"What is it?" he asks, securing me against him with his arms and following my frantic gaze into the water.

"Something brushed against my leg." I don't see anything. Not anymore. "It was probably just a fish or ray."

Tristan shrugs and pulls me closer. "Whatever it was, I won't complain."

This time when our lips meet, it's not nearly as restrained.

I POP the rest of my brownie in my mouth, then lean back on my towel and close my eyes, letting the last rays of sunlight touch my skin.

"Well, this officially puts an end to our competition," Tristan says, moving in behind me and making my skin tingle with that familiar anticipation. He wraps his arms around my waist and I lean against him.

"The date's not even over yet."

"Either way, there's an obvious winner and my vote is cast."

"Which did you vote for?" I ask, already knowing his answer.

"This one," he says, resting his chin on my shoulder as we watch the colors of the sky shift into sunset.

I smile. "This beats manatees? All we did was paddleboard around a sandbar."

"That was the worst undersell in the history of underselling." His hands come to my arms, his fingers trailing up and down them slowly, causing goosebumps to erupt on my entire body. "And that's definitely not all we did."

My cheeks burn at the mention. "I suppose that's true."

"Which is exactly why no other outing can even come close to winning. At least for me."

"Well,"—I lift one shoulder in a partial shrug—"it's a relief to hear that all that kissing wasn't for nothing."

"Right?" Tristan's laugh rumbles around us, then he leans me to the side and bestows the most breath-stealing, dream-filling, toe-curling, heart-strumming kiss on me, and I nearly swoon on the spot. He pulls away, lingering just out of reach with a knowing smile on his lips. He's clearly aware he just rocked my entire world. "Otherwise, what would be the point?"

"Exactly." My gaze flits to his lips, before returning to his eyes again. "I'm glad we're in agreement."

"About the winner?"

"No, about the kissing. But now that you mention it, I do think the other outings have an unfair disadvantage competing with our first kiss. So for the sake of fairness, maybe we need to remove it—well, all of the kissing—to make an accurate judgment."

"I can't uncast my vote. It's the rule."

I laugh. "Fine. Then I'll vote for the kayaking ... and the spa day."

"So half a vote for kayaking and half a vote for spa day? Got it." Tristan lifts my arm at my side as though I'm a WWE wrestler that just body slammed her opponent into submission. "And the winner is Capri with one full vote for her Winn Island excursion."

"What about your dedication page? You're willing to give it up just like that?"

"The only victory I actually cared about was getting you to do the competition. Besides, I got my dedication." Tristan's smile is full of mischief. "'To the protagonist of my own love story. Thanks for the inspiration.'" He repeats the dedication page of *Secret Crush* verbatim. "I assume that's me? The protagonist?"

Immediately, I feel my skin start to splotch, and I know my reckoning has come. "Possibly."

He chuckles. "So, about this book ..."

"How about we talk about something else? Like work. I didn't even get a chance to ask you how the meeting with the buyers went today."

His fingers brush over the skin of my reddened décolletage before his gaze lifts to my eyes. "You really don't like talking about your books, do you?"

"Not even a little." I shake my head. "And I'm pretty sure

even less so when that conversation's with the real-life guy from my fictional story."

"So I can't mention how long Capri—sorry, I mean, Cali had a crush on ... Trenton? Because it was a long time. Like a lot longer than I initially thought."

"Oh my gosh, stop!"

"Okay. But technically, I do have another question I get to ask, and I was super curious about the exchange between—"

I pounce on him like a love-crazed lioness, knocking him onto his back and stopping his words by pressing my lips against his. He is smiling beneath my kiss, but I don't give up, and it's not long until his lips become pliable against mine. I know the pause of questioning is only temporary, but I also don't mind in the least utilizing this diversionary tactic. I've missed out on years of kissing Tristan, and I fully intend to make up for lost time.

After a few glorious minutes, I pull back. "Are you done?"

"Nope." He pulls me to him again, and I don't mind at all. Because kissing Tristan is my new favorite thing ever.

After one more dizzying kiss, I lean back again. "Though I loved your enthusiastic response, I meant are you done with the questions?"

Tristan's lips quirk upward as if he knew exactly what I meant, and he lifts on his elbows. "If people discover you're Sunny Palmer, are you going to make a habit of stopping them from talking about your books like this?"

"It really depends," I deadpan as if the vast majority of my readers are men and not women. "I'll have to gauge it reader by reader."

"Noted." Tristan laughs. "So, now that you've won, what is it you want for your prize?"

"I already got it." I grin up at him. "It's the same thing that won me the competition—a kiss."

"I thought that's what you were going to ask for."

"No, you didn't."

"The night of the swim party, when we were talking by the front desk, and I asked you what you wanted, you couldn't keep your eyes off of my lips."

My mouth opens, and I give him a little push that makes him smile. "I wasn't that obvious."

"You were so obvious. If your brother hadn't walked in, our first kiss very well could have been right there in the lobby at Seaside Oasis."

"Then you would have won the competition."

Tristan shrugs. "It would've been a much closer call, for sure."

"Well, considering how things turned out, I'm confident we both won."

His narrowed eyes hold mine like he doesn't want to agree to accepting his participation-award, but then he nods. "We definitely both won." Tristan drops his gaze briefly before looking back at me in a way that causes my nerves to flare.

"What is it?" I ask.

"I just want to make sure we're on the same page with everything."

My pulse quickens. "What page are you on?"

"Not on the summer fling page. I'm on the page where I really like you. Where I want to see if this can work out. I'm not exactly sure what that looks like with me leaving in August, but we can figure that out when it comes." He pauses. "Are you anywhere close to that page?"

I roll my lips inward, trying to prevent the obnoxiously large smile that's attempting to break free. "I've been on that page for an exceptionally long time, just waiting to see if you'd ever pick up the darn book."

Tristan's whole face lights up with his smile. "You want to do this, then? You want to make things public between us?"

My mouth opens, then closes again, and my shoulders fall.

Up to this point, Tristan and I have been in our own little Sunset Harbor universe. We've crossed paths with a few people here and there, but no one outside of my family and Jane would suspect that Tristan and I were anything more than friends. Well, and Beau and Noah. And possibly Gemma now. But other than that, if people know …

He lifts my chin, so I'm looking him in the eye. "What is it?"

"If people see us together—if they know we're together—I worry they'll start to make the connection between us and the characters in my book. Especially since two different book clubs on the island are currently reading *Secret Crush*." Even saying the name of the book in front of Tristan makes me feel all sorts of self-conscious.

"Can I ask why you don't want people to find out? I understand why you didn't, but do you still have reasons to keep your pen name a secret?"

"I've thought about announcing it. More in the last few weeks since telling you than I've ever allowed myself. I even spoke with my manager about what it could potentially look like if I did. But there are so many unknowns. And so many things I'm not sure how I'd handle." I shake my head, not certain where to start. "Gossip. About me … and you. How awful it was that I made Bridget the antagonist in my book." I wince. Even speaking the reminder out loud is uncomfortable, but to acknowledge my pettiness in front of Tristan is physically painful. "The fact that I write romance at all. That I didn't tell anyone."

I slowly exhale. "There's also the fact that being an author is difficult enough when I have a pen name to hide behind. Most readers are kind and wonderful, but some aren't. Some are awful. The separation between who I am and the author version of myself allows me to cope with the negativity. To keep creating in the face of it." I lower my gaze from his, my fingers mindlessly brushing across Tristan's bare skin. "And what if I let everyone down when they find out I'm Sunny Palmer? I've been a mystery for so long that I'm not sure I can live up to the expectations. I'm good at being invisible. I'm comfortable being invisible," I whisper. "It's easier this way."

Tristan wraps his arms around me, and I melt into him. We don't talk but just sit there, watching the sunset together.

"Thanks for helping me to understand," he finally says, still holding me to him. "And I get it. I'm not looking forward to making the announcement that we're selling Seaside Oasis, and this is a lot more personal than that. But I wish you could see what I do when I look at you. I can't think that anyone would feel differently once they were given the privilege to know you better. Including your readers." He places a soft kiss on my temple, and I feel so seen. So adored. "But I also think it's okay if you decide not to share that part of yourself with the world. Especially if you go around kissing people to stop them from talking about your books."

I give a small laugh but quickly sober again when I consider the reality. "The problem is, I'm not sure I'll have a choice soon."

He pulls back slightly and looks down with those captivating eyes of his. "Capri, if being with me could cause—"

"No." I turn my upper body more toward him. Instantly, I know if I have to choose between Tristan and keeping my anonymity, I'll call the Associated Press myself and hand over my name. Though I'm thankful that's not actually something I have to do. "I want this."

He grabs my face with both hands. "Which is why I was going to say that if being with me could cause someone to find out before you're ready, we don't have to go public with things yet. We can just keep it between us until you feel the time is right. Maybe once the book clubs are over and people aren't in the midst of reading our story? Or … even longer if you need."

I smile at the way he calls it *our* story. "That could work. But can I tell Jane and Tala about us? And my mom?"

"I'll follow your lead on this one."

I shift to face forward again, pulling my hair to one shoulder and leaning back against him. His lips settle on my neck just beneath my ear, making me light-headed and giddy. "That was nice," I say, smiling up at him. "I'll have to remember that for my next book."

He kisses my neck again, a little lower this time, and I feel it all the way to my toes. "If you ever need inspiration, I'm your guy."

He has no idea how true that statement is. "I appreciate your willingness to sacrifice for the greater good. My readers thank you."

"What can I say? I've always been a supporter of the arts." His thumb caresses the same place on my neck his lips just were, and my heart pounds like it's recently taken up clogging. Or maybe that's because I already know how I intend to respond.

"Then let's see what else you've got," I say, pulling him toward me again.

Tristan is ready and waiting for my command. The minute our lips touch, he's all in. My sensory receptors are in overload, and I'm trying to memorize each pleasurable sensation as his fingers move into my hair. His kiss is more certain. More intentional. And all teasing aside, this moment will provide a lifetime of inspiration for all future kiss scenes.

CHAPTER 23

"I KNEW IT!" Jane's squeal has me holding the phone away from my ear. "I told you Tristan would be smitten with you by the end of summer, and we're barely into July. Now you're going to get married and have lots of babies. I'm so happy for you. And only a little jealous."

My smile is ridiculously big. "Let's not get ahead of ourselves. There's still a lot to figure out."

"Oh, please. You two have known each other your whole lives. Everyone knows that relationships founded on a lifelong friendship turned to love are a *kiss on Monday, married by Sunday* sort of deal. And I'd argue that the same goes for lifelong crushes." Jane's ability to apply fictional truths to real life is astonishing.

"I think we both want to take things slow," I say. I haven't told Jane about the Palmers selling Seaside Oasis because it's not my place, but I don't want her to get her expectations set on a happily-ever-after between us that happens to land us here on Sunset Harbor. At least not any time soon. The assistant coaching position is just a rung on the ladder when it comes to a career in coaching. Besides, there aren't any colleges near enough to Sunset Harbor to make a commute possible even if Tristan eventually finds a position in Florida. Which is sort of my hope since California is way too far from me. "And we're not telling anyone we're dating yet. With so many people currently reading *Secret Crush* for their book clubs, we don't need anyone making connections between us and Trenton and Cali."

"Book clubs? As in plural?"

I frown. "Sandra informed me there's another book club on Sunset Harbor also reading it right now."

She releases a thoughtful hum. "Well, now that you've told Tristan, why don't you just broadcast to the whole world that you're Sunny Palmer? Can you imagine the hysteria it'll cause? Your fans are going to flip! Especially when you and Tristan get married!"

Oh, sweet Jane. "Unless someone discovers my identity, I'm not sure I want to reveal my identity. Besides to my family." There are too many what-ifs. Too many unknowns. And with things being so new with Tristan, I worry ... whatever this is between us... might be more fragile than it currently feels. I don't want anything to ruin it.

"But you're going to tell your family?"

"Yeah. At least my mom, Grandma, and Heath. Walker has to wait until I'm not livid at him anymore. Speaking of, he hasn't tried to kiss you again, has he?" A week ago, while I was home editing, Jane texted to inform me that my freaking, womanizing brother kissed her! Not just a peck either. A *kiss* kiss. Which, in hindsight, I'm actually not that surprised about. Jane is gorgeous and fun and incredible, and Walker ... well, Walker is a well-known ladies' man who's obviously used to women fawning over him. It's been that way since we were preteens—girls at school and in our neighborhood pretending to be my friend just so they could get close to Walker. Jane is the first friend I've had who's been immune to Walker's charms. And now the jerk went and kissed her! And to make things worse, she admitted to having a small crush on him. Ugh! I'm so mad at my brother! Here I thought he was changing, but apparently he's not changed at all. He's only thinking about himself, and if Jane's not careful, he's going to break her heart when he leaves.

"No. That was just a one-time thing." She hesitates. There's more she wants to say, and I wish she'd just say it. "But I'd rather keep talking about you and this monumental accomplishment in your life. How does it feel to fulfill the lifelong dream of kissing Tristan Palmer? Was it everything you expected?"

I contemplate pressing her about Walker, but I know she'll talk to me when she's ready. She always does. So I let my thoughts shift back to Tristan, and my chest buzzes just thinking about earlier. "It was more amazing than anything I ever imagined." And that's saying something with how vivid and capable my imagination is.

I STEP into the front room, the first hints of sunlight illuminating the morning sky out the window. A robe-clad Tala glances up from the couch with my most recent comb-bound manuscript lying open on her lap. I think to mention how she's not supposed to read it while I'm still here, but since I don't have current departure plans, I decide to let it go. Plus, I'm too tired to say anything.

"You're up early," she says, eyeing me.

I drop down onto the couch next to her. "I just got off the phone with Mom."

Tala closes the manuscript and turns to face me. "You told her?"

I nod. "I started with the Tristan confession before dropping the whole Sunny Palmer thing on her."

"What did she say?"

I give an overdone smile. "She was thrilled about the Tristan part."

"And the Sunny Palmer part?"

I drop my gaze to my lap, fidgeting with a loose thread on

my pajama pants. "Surprised. And hurt. Not that she said it, but I could just tell." I release a slow breath. "I should have told her a long time ago."

"I'll talk to her." Tala wraps her arm around me, and I lean my head onto her shoulder. "Once she hears the only reason I know is because I eavesdropped on a conversation between you and Jane, the two of us can commiserate together."

"As a reminder, it's not that I didn't want to tell you."

"I know why you didn't say anything. But you can stop worrying about that now. Considering how things went on the doorstep last night when Tristan dropped you off, he seems more than fine with your revelation."

I pull out of her arm, my mouth gaping. "You spied on us?"

"It was Heath's idea."

"What am I being thrown under the bus for now?" Heath says, stepping into the front entryway and grabbing his golf cart keys from the table drawer. He's already dressed, but not in his work clothes.

"I just mentioned that we saw her and Tristan on the doorstep last night."

"Oh yeah, that was totally my idea."

I shake my head in disbelief. "You two are the worst."

Heath steps into the room. "Actually, we're the best. Until I had that chat with Tristan, he was convinced he was firmly in the friend zone with you."

"You mean the chat where you told him I had a huge crush on him?"

He points at me. "*Has.* I said 'Capri *has* a huge crush on you.' It's all in the details."

I roll my eyes, but I can't conceal my smile. "I guess I won't have to name a villain after you in my next book after all."

Heath's eyes light with excitement. "No, you totally should. Then one day when it's published, I can use it as bragging rights." He glances at his watch. "But we can discuss exactly how you can thank me later because I have to get to the town square and help set up for the Fourth of July breakfast. I'm already late." So that's where he's headed. He hurries over and gives Tala a kiss, then she pulls him back for a second.

He throws a satisfied smirk in my direction, and I roll my eyes like a very mature adult.

"Oh, Heath," I say, right before he steps out of the room. "I've been meaning to tell you that I already have published a book. Sixteen actually. And I'm about to release my seventeenth."

"Funny." He laughs, disappearing from view. "I'll see you two later," he says, his footsteps moving away from us.

"She's Sunny Palmer," Tala calls. Silence follows, then his footsteps grow louder and his shocked expression reappears. Tala lifts the manuscript from her lap as proof.

He glances from me to the manuscript to the bookshelf. "You're for real right now?" We both nod, and his smile returns in full force. "You're Sunny Palmer?"

I lift a hand in a small wave.

His gaze slides to Tala. "Wait, does that mean you knew?"

"I made her swear she wouldn't tell anyone, including you," I say, coming to Tala's defense.

He stares at us, his jaw slackened. "I'm offended you didn't think you could trust me."

"You told Tristan about my crush."

Heath's head shifts from side to side as though he's considering the evidence. "Point made. But that was for your own good. And his."

"So I can trust you not to tell anyone about this outside of our family?"

"Am I the last to know?" he asks. I pin him with a look that must match Tala's because he looks back and forth between us and lifts his hands like he's innocent. "What? I'm just curious."

"Tala, Jane, Tristan, and Mom know," I say. "... and now

probably Stan. I'm also going to tell Grandma soon … and eventually Walker. Though we'll hold off telling Serenity and Jack for the time being."

"I knew I was your"—he raises his fingers one at a time, counting—"fifth favorite. I guess sixth if you count Stan, but I'm thinking you would have told me before him if you'd had the option."

Tala laughs. "Tell yourself whatever you need to, my love."

"Oh, I will." He glances at his watch again. "I've got to go." His footsteps sound in the hallway, but then they stop and he pokes his head around the corner one last time. "That really is incredible, Capri. I'm proud of you."

If Tala is a hybrid sibling, Heath is equally so. And since my dad isn't here to tease me and heckle me and be proud of me, I'm glad Heath is. "Thanks."

With one more wave, he's gone.

I look over at Tala. "You don't think he'll tell anyone?"

"No. Not with this." She rests her head back on mine. "And I know you hate when I gush about your books, so I'll very casually say that I'm absolutely loving the changes you've made. Brant might just be my new favorite book boyfriend."

I truly won the lottery getting Tala for a sister.

CHAPTER 24

IT SEEMS the whole island plus some have come out for the annual Fourth of July breakfast in town square, and it takes me a minute to locate my family stationed at one of the many tables set up throughout the central area surrounding the fountain. Grandma's next to Tala and Heath, who seem to be attempting to get the kids to focus on eating instead of watching everything else going on around them.

"How are the pancakes?" I ask when I approach, kissing Grandma on the cheek.

She pats my hand that's resting on the back of her chair. "Delicious."

"Deliciously cold," Heath says with an overdone grimace.

I swipe Lucas from Tala's arms so she can eat with both hands. "I forgot you're kind of a diva about your warm syrup preference."

"He totally is," Tala laughs, glancing over her shoulder at me. "I'm glad you found us. I was trying to text but you didn't answer."

"Sorry. I realized while walking up that I left my phone at home."

"Where's Tristan?"

"He dropped me off before attempting to find a place to park in all this madness." I don't mention it's part of our plan to avoid being seen together too much throughout the day. It's not that we can't see each other at all, but we decided the less we see of each other, the easier it will be to keep things platonic between us. Had Tala and Heath had room for me on their golf cart with all the kids and having to pick up Grandma, I would have kept things simple and ridden with them. But that wasn't an option, and I can't say I minded the extra time spent with Tristan at his house this morning before we left. Not that I should be thinking about that right now.

"Look at you!" I say to Serenity, taking her darling big bow and red, white, and blue sundress. "You look amazing!" My gaze slides to Jack. "And you. Nice shirt."

Serenity points to my cute little armful. "Lucas has the same one as Jack."

I turn Lucas around to face me, and he gives a gummy smile. "Oh, you do! Aren't you a dapper man? Speaking of dapper men," I say with a hint of sarcasm no one else will likely pick up on, "isn't Walker supposed to be here?"

Tala gestures to the line of people waiting for pancakes, and I assume she means he's getting food, but then my gaze settles on him behind the griddle. Serving eggs? Seriously? What's up with my brother? But then I see Jane zipping around behind him. He must be trying to make a good impression on her. Which I'm not sure how I feel about because he looks genuinely happy—almost like the old Walker I miss so much. But he's just going to leave, and he'll break her heart when he does. Kind of like my heart's going to break when Tristan leaves next month. My heart sinks at the poignant reminder.

"You'd better get the kids to the start of the parade," Tala says, looking at Heath. "They're having the bikes first this year so when the kids finish, they can watch the rest of it." She pauses. "Unless you'd prefer I take them? I'm happy to."

"No, I can." Heath stands up, clearly not the least bit sad about leaving his partially finished pancake uneaten. "Let's get going, you two." He clears the remaining plates and dumps them in the trash nearby, then holds out his hands for Serenity and Jack.

The moment their backs are to us, Joy Palmer steps up to our table, her bright, smiling eyes moving over Grandma and Tala before landing on me. "Are you saving these seats?"

"No," Tala says, gesturing for her to take them. "But I can't promise there won't be lingering drops of syrup, so watch yourself."

Joy signals to Mark who's at the front of the line, having just finished filling two plates. He catches her eye and lifts the plates in acknowledgment. "Is Tristan not here yet?" Joy asks. "He said he was planning to eat breakfast with us, but I assumed he'd be with you."

Her assumption causes my cheeks to burn. "He's parking the golf cart. He dropped me off so I wouldn't have to walk." And to limit the time we're seen together.

"Of course he did. He's always been such a thoughtful boy." She gives a small laugh as though embarrassed about her pride in Tristan. "Not that you wouldn't all know that. We've basically been neighbors our whole lives."

She's staring at me, and I shift my gaze back to Lucas, laying him down in my lap and propping his chubby thighs against my torso. "I wholeheartedly agree," I say, feeling like she's expecting some kind of response.

Mark steps up to the table, setting one plate in front of his wife and the other next to it so he can sit. "You picked a great table, Joy."

"Didn't I?" she says, mirroring his smile with one of her own.

I don't miss the knowing look that passes between them, and I get the distinct impression that Joy's arrival at our table immediately after Heath and the kids left was a little more than coincidence. "That smells amazing," I say, looking at their loaded plates—pancakes, eggs, and bacon. My stomach rumbles. "I think I'm going to go get in line."

"Here," Mark slides his plate toward me, standing up again. "They're dishing up the same thing for everyone."

I'm handing Lucas to Tala. "You don't have to do that. I can—"

"I insist," he says, pointing to the plate and then walking away before I can protest his thoughtful act again. Like father, like son.

"Grab a plate for Tristan too," Joy calls after him. Her gaze returns to me, her expression brightening. "That way, he won't have to waste any time in line when he gets here."

Tala glances down at Lucas to hide her smile, but Grandma doesn't even attempt to conceal hers.

"So, I was finally able to start the book for book club," Joy says, nearly causing my heart to fly out of my chest. "Secret Crush."

Tala doesn't miss a beat and gives a causal smile. "It's good, isn't it?" It's a wise move with the yes or no question. Less opportunity for expounding.

I shove a piece of pancake in my mouth, attempting to appear uninterested in the conversation.

"It really is … riveting." And this time, with the way she's looking at me, I'm décolletage-splotching-aware that she suspects something. I settle a hand over the skin beneath my neck, hoping to hide it as best as I can.

"If you think that one's riveting," Tala says, "you should read Summer Fling. I finished the whole book in one sitting."

"You can't go wrong with any Sunny Palmer books," Grandma chimes in. "But Secret Crush is my absolute favorite. Trenton and Cali just have so much pent-up chemistry. It leapt right off the page." And I'm suddenly really glad I haven't had the opportunity to tell Grandma that I'm Sunny Palmer yet. I love her, but she's so easily excitable, and her privacy filter isn't always functioning. "You know what I think she should write next?" Grandma continues, returning her attention to Joy. "A cowboy romance. The only things that could level up her stories are some Wrangler jeans, boots, and a cowboy hat."

With how intently I'm staring at my plate, I'm likely only strengthening any suspicions Joy has.

"Hey, there you are, Mom." Tristan approaches the table and greets his mom with a kiss on the cheek before sending me a brief, apologetic smile. "How'd we get so lucky in our seat selection?"

Joy beams up at Tristan. "I saw Heath and the kids finish and thought: 'Well, isn't that perfect timing? Three newly vacant chairs for the three of us, and next to our old neighbors.' It was meant to be."

"Sounds like it." Tristan glances toward the line.

"Dad's in line. I told him to get you a plate so you can sit down."

"Where's Grandpa? I thought he was coming."

"He called to say that, with all the people headed to Sunset Harbor, the parking garage is full and he has to find somewhere else to park. He'll be here soon, though."

Tristan's hands go to the back of the chair like he's about to pull it out to sit, but he pauses. "You know what? I'll go keep Dad company."

"You don't need to, sweetie." Joy points to the open seat nearest me.

It's apparent Tristan's trying not to smile, though I'm not sure if it's at his mom's blatant intentions or that within the first few minutes of him getting here, our attempts to limit our time together today are already being foiled. At this rate, it's going to be a very long day.

"I've actually been meaning to ask him—"

"Sit," she says, her voice firmer than before. I try not to

laugh at how fast he drops into the seat next to me. Mama Joy still holds sway over him, and it's absolutely adorable.

When Joy turns her attention to Grandma, Tristan leans in. "Sorry, she's a stubborn one."

"It's fine. We're just old neighbors catching up over breakfast." I take another bite of eggs, and I don't miss how he eyes them.

"That's definitely all that's going on here." His knee brushes against mine, and my heart rate increases tenfold. "Oops," he says, sending me a cautious smile. "Habit."

Which is exactly why we'll do better keeping our distance today. It's amazing that in such a brief amount of time, it's becoming second-nature giving in to any impulse to touch him —to hold his hand or run my fingertips along his arm. To nestle my head against that place in his chest that feels like it was made for me. But this—sitting next to him but resisting his magnetic field that is constantly pulling me to him—is pure agony. "Do you want any?" I ask, pointing to my plate. "I'm not going to eat it all."

"I can wait."

I glance around to make sure no one is paying us any interest, then hand him my fork. "You know you want some."

He leans in close. "I want something else more."

My eyes widen, and he just laughs, taking the offered fork from me to scoop up a bite of eggs before starting on the pancake.

And again, I'm all too aware of how today is going to go. It might be easier if we just avoid each other completely. Otherwise, we might as well ride on a float in the parade and hold a poster that announces our relationship and that I'm Sunny Palmer to all of Sunset Harbor.

"Beau said he ran into the two of you the other night?" Joy says, pulling our attention back to her.

"Did he say anything else?" Tristan asks, sounding casual enough to hopefully not raise suspicion.

"No. Why?" Her smiling eyes move back and forth between us. "Was there more to say?"

Tristan and I look at each other, both of us trying to train our expressions. "Not really," I say since he looks like he's closer to laughter than I am.

"Did he tell you he was with Gemma Sawyer?" Tristan offers in an obvious attempt to redirect her interest.

Joy gives a lift of her eyebrows. "No, he didn't."

With the way Tristan shifts in his seat, I know he must feel bad for saying something, despite how Beau ratted us out. "It's nothing. She's just helping him with a work project," he says.

Joy nods. "Well, it's about time the Palmers and Sawyers figure out how to work together."

"Hear, hear!" Grandma interjects, and Tala nods, bouncing Lucas on her knees.

Mark sets down a plate in front of Tristan and glances at the fork in his hand hovering over my plate. "Or maybe I should give this one to Capri," he says, his gaze sliding to me. "Did you even get any of your own breakfast?"

"I wasn't going to eat it all," I say, reaching out to pat Tristan's cheek playfully and ignoring the delightful way his whiskers tickle my palm. "And he just looked like such a sad, hungry little puppy. I couldn't resist his begging eyes."

Everyone laughs, including Tristan.

"That boy has always loved his food," Mark says, moving to his seat with his own plate.

"Did he use your same fork?" Grandma asks, leaning forward in her seat. Both of us sit there, unsure of what to say with only one fork in sight besides the one Mark just brought. Grandma smiles at our apparent inability to answer. "How interesting that you feel comfortable enough to share the same utensil. It makes me wonder what else the two of you've been sharing."

Tala is literally shaking with laughter at my side, covering her lowered face with the hand not supporting her son. This is not going at all how I planned. But Tristan looks completely delighted by this strange turn of events. A turn of events that was entirely my fault.

Joy glances back and forth between us with a hopeful look. "Do the two of you have something you want to tell us?"

Tristan finds my hand beneath the table, and I give it a gentle squeeze.

"We aren't telling anyone yet," I say. "But ..." I look to Tristan.

"But what?" Joy asks, eagerness saturating her voice.

"It turns out Capri has a massive crush on me." Tristan smiles, and I nudge my elbow into him. "Fine. And I have an even bigger one on her."

Joy squeals, clapping her hands together like we just announced our engagement instead of a new relationship. "I knew it."

Mark puts a hand on his wife's shoulder, wearing a wide smile that very much resembles hers. "You did hear the part about them not telling anyone yet? I'm guessing we should probably keep our celebrations to ourselves for now."

Joy clasps a hand over her mouth and glances around as if to make sure she didn't single-handedly expose our secret. "Why exactly can't we say anything?"

"We need to figure out a few things first," Tristan says.

I nod, tightening my fingers in his, thankful for the table-cloth that conceals it from view. "But we hope it won't be too much longer."

We just have to get through the next couple of weeks until *Secret Crush* isn't fresh in anyone's mind. Starting with today.

Which means we're going to have to keep our distance from each other. Once breakfast is done, that is.

TO KEEP myself busy and my mind distracted from how much I want to be with Tristan, I volunteer to help Jane by passing out extra decorative ribbons for the bike parade. When my bag is empty, I search for Jane to see if there's anything else I can do, but she's flying about on her rollerblades, getting everything ready for the parade to begin. She's laser focused and totally in her zone, so I decide to catch up with her later.

As I weave through the crowded town square, I avoid looking toward The Book Isle. Earlier, in the front window of the bookshop, I saw a poster with my next release on it that read: *Order your copy now!* I don't need the reminder of how close I'm cutting it with my submission this time around, considering I don't even have my proofread back yet, or that people on Sunset Harbor might be pre-ordering my book.

Someone grabs my arm, and I startle before I realize it's Tristan. Apparently, I was so thorough in my attempts to disregard the bookshop that I missed seeing him standing on the sidewalk nearby. "Hey," he says, looking oddly relieved to see me.

I'm slightly confused at Tristan's greeting since we parted ways after breakfast with the understanding of intentionally avoiding each other until we meet back at Tala's this afternoon. But that doesn't keep me from smiling up at him in a way I probably shouldn't with so many people as potential witnesses. "Hey."

"We were just talking about you."

My brow lowers, and I peek around him to see who he means by *we*, and my whole body goes rigid when I catch sight of Bridget Hall!

Her golden blond hair is thrown back in a ponytail, but unlike mine, the top of hers is smooth and the ends are curled in a loose spiral that defies the laws of humidity. Her little white halter dress is a stark contrast against her tanned skin but matches her bright white teeth perfectly. My gaze flies back to Tristan's.

He gives one subtle shake of his head as if to say he doesn't know why she's here either. Or maybe it's something else he's trying to tell me, but my head feels suddenly cloudy and there's a slight ringing in my ears. His brief touch to the small of my back, probably as encouragement for me to step forward, grounds me enough that I can drag a smile to my lips and offer a quick wave. "Hey, Bridget."

"Capri," Bridget surprisingly says my name correctly, and I force myself to hold her gaze. She does a quick once-over of me and smiles, but I'm not sure how genuine it is. "Wow, I can hardly believe it's you. You look all grown up."

Considering she's a year older than me, it feels like a back-handed, patronizing compliment, but there's nothing to do but smile and accept it. "Thanks." My eyes instinctively drop to her left hand, and to my horror, she's not wearing a ring on her finger. I assure myself it's because she left it at home for the day as a precaution, but the way she's smiling at Tristan seems to counter that reasoning.

"She was asking which of our friends I've seen, and I mentioned you were here," Tristan says, subtly informing me of their previous conversation. "And Noah."

She glances around. "Cat and Ivy are here somewhere too. Cat told me to meet her in front of the bookshop." Her smile brightens. "Oh, there she is," Bridget says, waving a hand.

My gaze follows hers to where Cat Keene and Holland Blakely are making their way toward us through the crowd. Their smiling gazes pause on me, and suddenly, I feel like seventeen-year-old Capri again—panicked and out of place. These were the popular girls in school, except for Holland since she's a Sunset Harbor implant. But had she gone to Beachside with us, she definitely would have been one of the cool kids. Unlike me. Even with Jane as my best friend to act as mediator, I never fit in with them. And in those instances when I was around them, I was a mere shadow on the wall.

"Hey," Cat says, hugging Bridget. "It's good to see you." With her blue eyes and the red scarf that's tied up in her platinum blond hair, she looks beautifully patriotic. Suddenly, I realize that every person in this group is blond except me. If that isn't symbolic of how I feel—the black sheep of the herd—I don't know what is. "Hey, Tristan," she says with a smile, then her gaze pauses on me. "And Capri! I heard you were visiting."

"I am," I say, realizing how obvious that now is since I'm standing here. Heat creeps into my chest and neck.

"I don't think we've met. I'm Holland." Holland is absolutely darling, and though she's several inches shorter than me, I'm completely intimidated by her unassuming charisma. So I don't tell her we have met before. Besides, it was only in passing, and I don't expect her to remember. If it weren't for Jane always keeping me up-to-date about what's happening with everyone on the island, I probably wouldn't feel like I knew her either.

"Capri Collins," I say.

Recognition lights her features. "Oh, you're Walker's sister … so Jane's best friend. I think we have met. Sorry about that."

"It's fine," I say, barely stopping myself from assuring her that I'm used to not being remembered. Tristan shifts at my side, but thankfully, he doesn't say anything.

"So how long will you be in town?" Holland asks.

"Ummm …" I resist looking at Tristan for an answer. Though Tala insisted I stay through July, I'm not sure I'll take her up on it. Even with my constant attempts to be helpful, I'm still a guest, and she'll need to recoup at some point. But for now, I'm happy to stay. Especially considering I don't have that much longer with Tristan before he leaves. "A week or two probably."

"We should all get together while you're here." Her eyes glisten in the sunlight. "And I'm assuming you're coming to book club with Tala and Jane?"

My head is shaking of its own accord. "No, it's been a long time since I've read the book."

Holland gives a dismissive wave. "That doesn't matter. We mainly chat and eat snacks. You have to come." She turns to Bridget. "And you should also come. It's Saturday night at seven. We meet at Seaside Oasis."

The collective gaze shifts to Bridget, and I'm silently pleading that she'll say no. With a dainty swat at her ponytail, she shakes her head. "I'm not really one for book clubs."

"Oh, but this one's so much fun. You won't regret going." Holland's energy is contagious enough that she nearly has me wanting to go. Which I absolutely will not be doing. "The old ladies reminisce and tell the craziest stories about when they were young. I seriously look forward to it every single month."

Bridget shrugs like she's far from sold on the idea, and I try not to appear too relieved.

"We're reading a Sunny Palmer book," Cat offers as though that might hold sway over her decision.

Tristan straightens next to me, and I know he's thinking what I'm thinking—Bridget cannot read that book.

"I've actually never read a Sunny Palmer book." Bridget says it as if it's a point of pride.

Before I have a moment to celebrate the phenomenal news, Holland continues. "Well, you should right that wrong and join us. It's a super-fast read." She points at the bookshop behind Tristan and me. "I was just in The Book Isle yesterday, and they still have two copies in stock. Or you can borrow mine."

"What's the book called?" Bridget asks.

I force myself not to glance at Tristan in my desperation, but

I'm spiraling. It's like I'm living out one of my nightmares in real life.

"*Secret Crush*. And it takes place on an island just like Suns—"

"Is that the parade starting?" Tristan interrupts, and all the ladies turn in the direction he's looking. He takes the opportunity to glance down at me, apparently gauging how I'm doing. Or maybe he's hoping for some kind of hint on how to proceed.

I've got nothing for him but a blank stare.

"I don't think so." Cat drops down from her toes and glances at her watch. "But we probably need to get going since Ivy's holding our spots." Cat directs her smile at me. "You should come sit with us, Capri."

The offer sounds sincere, but I'm already shaking my head. "Thanks so much, but my family's saving me a seat." I take a step away from the group and lift a stiff hand in farewell. "It was good seeing all of you."

"Hopefully we'll see you at book club," Holland says, optimistically.

I force a smile but don't respond verbally.

Tristan shifts as though he intends to come with me, but I meet his eye, willing him to stay for at least a couple more minutes. These ladies cannot suspect anything is happening between me and Tristan. Even if Bridget, the woman he nearly married a few years ago, is touching his arm with her ringless hand to pull his attention back to her.

And I hate that it works.

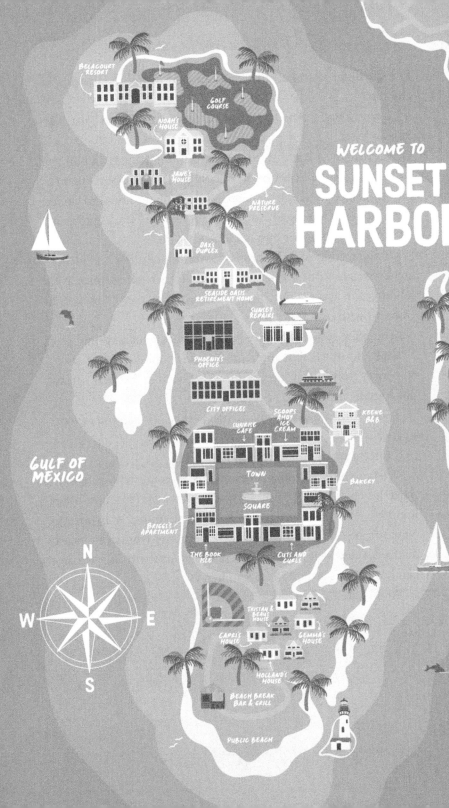

CHAPTER 25

A SLIGHT BREEZE has me digging my toes into the warm sand, and I cover my eyes with my hand, glancing around the crowded beach. I don't know if I've ever seen this many people on Sunset Harbor. There aren't a lot of familiar faces in the crowd, so most of them must be mainlanders that came over for the Fourth of July Bash. And I can see why. With food trucks and beach games and music blaring over the speakers, Jane and the City Council have really outdone themselves this year. Though for that very reason, I can also see why Grandma wanted to head back to Seaside Oasis with Virginia after the parade. She's never been one for big crowds while I thoroughly enjoy them. Not because I care to interact with anyone, but because it's so easy to go unnoticed and people-watch to my heart's content.

And at this moment, I need all the distraction I can get. I haven't seen Tristan since I left him with Bridget, and my fiction-creating mind is weaving all sorts of potential stories. The problem is, being a romance writer, I'm well aware that there is something undeniably strong about the attachment to one's first love. I'm also aware how, in real life, women like Bridget Hall always win. A few weeks ago, I would have gladly taken just a brief fling with Tristan and counted myself blessed, but now ... now I want more. The thought of losing him already is wrecking me.

"Are you sure you're okay staying with Serenity and Jack?"

Tala asks, lifting the diaper bag onto her shoulder. "Because one of us can stay with you."

"We're fine. You two deserve a rest while Lucas sleeps."

Heath smirks and wraps the arm not holding Lucas around Tala's back. "Isn't she cute? Capri thinks we're going to *rest*."

I make a disgusted face, and Tala shoots him a look. "Unless you're planning to fix that plank on the dock like you said you were, maybe you should stay here," she says. "Because I'm taking a nap."

"Sure, you are." Heath sends Tala a wink that makes her cheeks pink.

"Okay." I shoo the two of them away. "You two have fun whatever it is you're going to be doing. We'll be home in a couple of hours, and I'll knock before we come in."

Heath laughs. "You're the best, Capri."

"Thanks again," Tala says, and the three of them head toward the boardwalk.

I locate Jack and Serenity each hauling a bucket of water and wait for them by the large pile of sand they've created near our towels. "Can I help with your castle?"

Jack dumps out his water, causing blobs of wet sand to fly in all directions. "We're actually making an alligator. But you can help."

Serenity dumps out her haul as well. "That's enough water."

I drop to my knees, and the three of us begin pushing and moving sand until it resembles a long, flat log. Then, beginning with the head, we start to shape it. We're nearly done with the alligator's midsection when a shadow falls across the part we're working on. I set my sandy hand over my brow to block the sun and look up to find Tristan watching us.

"Hey." I sit back onto my heels.

"You're not an easy one to locate."

I stand and wipe my hands on my shorts. "Invisibility is one of my talents."

His smile doesn't reach his eyes. "Have you not been getting my text messages?"

"No, sorry. I forgot my phone this morning."

He gives a slow nod. "I thought you were avoiding me."

"Well, that is kind of the plan."

This time, he doesn't so much as crack a smile. "Can we talk?"

My heart plummets at his serious tone, and my imagination is unhinged with potential scenarios as to why that might be. "Right now?" I glance back toward Serenity and Jack. "I'm watching the kids for Tala."

He hesitates, his gaze flicking to them. "Would it be breaking today's protocol if I joined you?"

"Hey, Tristan," Jack says before I can answer. "Want to help us with our alligator?"

Tristan's gaze shifts back to me as if seeking permission, and I give a nod. It's not that we can't be seen together at all. We just need to be careful.

"How can I be most useful?" he asks, kicking off his flip-flops and dropping down next to us.

"You and Jack can work on the tail while Auntie Capri finishes the middle," Serenity says. "I'll start gathering seashells to decorate it."

"Don't go too far," I say as she picks up the bucket.

"I won't."

The three of us start on our assigned tasks, Jack rattling on to Tristan about the parade and how he was the sixth boy to cross the finish line, despite that I'm certain there actually was no finish line. Serenity comes up to show Tristan and me a shell she found, then goes back to her shell hunt. I love how comfortable Jack and Serenity are around Tristan, but I also feel I might burst from all the unspoken questions filling my mind. With Jack's next pause in his story, I can't stop myself. "So, Bridget is in town?"

Tristan's gaze flicks to Jack and back to me like he isn't sure if he wants to have this conversation in front of my nephew. The thought makes my stomach drop, but I can't put it off any longer.

"Hey Jack, want to help your sister look for shells? I'm thinking we need a whole bunch of little white ones for the teeth. Maybe broken pieces?"

"That's a great idea." He jumps to his feet and looks toward the water. "Where's Serenity?"

I point to the shoreline where the tide is moving out and Serenity is gathering shells along the wet sand. "Right there."

His gaze is still flitting about until he locks in on her. "I see her," he says and takes off running.

I begin shaping the alligator's front leg, alternating my attention between it and Serenity and Jack. "So?"

"Apparently she and Logan split, so she's back on Sunset Harbor for a while."

The news is a kick to the gut. The worst of the worst. A catastrophic change in trajectory. But I should have expected it. Of course Bridget will win. It's in her DNA. "Oh, that's unfortunate." It sounds as if I mean it's unfortunate for her, but really, I mean that it's unfortunate for me. There's a reason why second chance romances are a reader favorite. It's hard to move on from a first love. I keep my focus on my hands, trying to fight the tears that are stinging my eyes. "I guess it's good we didn't make things public between us, then. I just wish we wouldn't have said anything to our families this morning."

He doesn't speak. He probably doesn't know what to say. I don't want to see the pity in his eyes, but I can't help but glance up because my curiosity demands it. When my gaze meets his, it's not pity I see in his expression, it's hurt. "This is exactly why we need to talk. I'm not sure we're on the same page right now. Actually, I'm not sure we're even in the same book."

I swallow against the tightness in my throat. "And what book are you in?"

"I'll tell you what one I'm not in—the one where Bridget and I get back together."

Now it's my turn to stare. "If this is because of me—"

"Capri." He says my name with a sternness I'm not used to, stopping me mid-sentence. "It's absolutely because of you. Earlier, when I saw Bridget again, I felt nothing outside of a general desire for her happiness. She was a big part of my life, but I've realized we were together because people expected us to be together. They expected us to end up together. Being the status quo type of guy that I am, I do what's expected of me. I come to expect of myself what it is others want from me. Neither Bridget or I could even see how discontent we'd become over the years—how much we deviated in what we wanted— because for so long, she was what I was supposed to want. And I was what she was supposed to want. Which is why when she broke things off, I felt lost. Anchorless. But I don't feel that way anymore. Not since you came back to the island."

The lightness inside me makes me worry I'll drift away at the slightest hint of a sea breeze. Or maybe I'm dreaming. I discreetly pinch myself on the outside of my calf, just to be certain. Ouch! I'm definitely awake.

Tristan isn't choosing Bridget.

He's choosing me.

In real life.

"Did I shock you into silence?" he asks, and it's only then I realize I haven't spoken.

I nod, attempting to find words. Any words. "I'm sorry ... I ..." I draw in a slow breath, a ridiculous smile breaking onto my face. "Ever since seeing Bridget, I've been preparing myself for a much different conversation."

"I assumed that story-creating brain of yours might be up to some kind of mischief." He quirks his head to the side, appraising me in a way that sends heat pulsing through me. "I'd come kiss you senseless to prove my point, but that's currently not allowed."

I glance at the shoreline where Jack and Serenity are happily filling the bucket with shells, and I wonder how soon is too soon to leave. "We won't be here all afternoon, so I expect you to make good on that offer when we're alone again."

He chuckles. "I'm very much looking forward to it."

TRISTAN and I show up at the dance together. Not only because we've spent the afternoon and evening hanging out but because we're neighbors. And neighbors ride together to things. At least that's how I justify it to myself.

Mo and the Kokomos are playing on a makeshift stage set up in the beach parking lot. Strings of bulbs light the area where some people are dancing, but the majority are standing around talking or swaying to the music. Kids are running and giggling as they dodge in and out of the crowds, Jack and Serenity being two of them.

"It's about time you made it here." Heath steps up to us with two drinks in hand. "I can't imagine what kept you."

"Shhh," I say, my cheeks reddening. "We're not telling anyone we're together yet."

Heath grins. "I don't mean to be the bearer of bad news, but you might want to rethink your plan. You two can't keep your hands off each other for a whole minute. You're definitely not going to be able to manage an entire night of it."

Tristan's smile broadens. "That sounds like a challenge."

"Oh, it is." Heath steps closer to him, his voice lowered. "If you and Capri kiss even once while you're here tonight, Tala and

I get to go out every Friday night for the next month while you two watch our kids."

Tristan nods, accepting the terms. "If we don't kiss, I get your bike."

Heath quirks his brow. "The beach cruiser?"

"With the bell."

Heath laughs. "Deal. And for the record, I'm not even worried. Though since I have to keep my eyes on my kids, we're working on the honor system." He glances around. "Speaking of … Where did those two get off to?"

I point out where Serenity and Jack are standing near the edge of the parking lot closest to the beach, talking to a few other neighborhood kids.

"Ah." He takes a step away, his gaze sliding between us. "Tala's going to be thrilled to hear we're getting a free month of babysitting."

Tristan shakes his head. "My guess is she's not going to be happy you agreed to give me your bike."

Heath just laughs and turns in the other direction.

"We've got this." I say it mostly to myself as a little pep talk because with how bad I want to slide my hands around Tristan and touch his glorious, smiling lips to mine, I worry Heath might be right. But he can't be. I can be strong for a couple of hours.

"Absolutely," Tristan says, sounding as hesitant as I feel. "Should we go find some of our friends? Make a quick appearance in case we need to get out of here early? Heath never stipulated how long we have to stay."

"You stole the words from my mouth."

His gaze flicks to my lips, and he breathes out a slow exhale. "Let's get this over with."

I laugh and step in next to him but at a distance that shouts: *Nothing to see here! We're just friends.*

After a minute of making our way through the crowd, Tristan

glances over at me. "I think we've been spotted," he says, and I notice the group of our peers several paces away. Jane breaks away from the others and hurries over to me. By her panicked expression, she must be coming to warn me about Bridget.

"Can I speak with you, Capri?" she asks, already latching on to my arm.

Tristan gives a smile. "I'll see you over there."

Jane pulls me in the opposite direction. "Okay. Don't freak out, but you'll never guess who's here."

"Bridget Hall."

Her eyes widen. "You already know?"

My stomach knots at the reminder. "I ran into her before the parade."

"And did you hear she and Logan split?"

"Tristan mentioned it."

She leans in close, making sure no one will overhear her. "Apparently, Mr. Pro Football cheated on her, and rumors are that it wasn't a one-time event but that it's been going on for months." Jane's lips form into a straight line, and I'm confident she wants to say something else but is deciding how to go about it.

"And … ?" I say, encouraging her.

Her shoulders fall. "Speculation is that she regrets ending things with Tristan and that's why she's back. Not that you need to be worried, I just …"

I take her hand. "I'm not worried."

Jane's gaze searches mine. "He really does love you, doesn't he?"

I laugh. "I don't think he loves me, but he told me he has no intention of getting back together with Bridget. Then, after having dinner at Tala and Heath's, we went back to his house, and he spent the last hour kissing me senseless."

Jane squeals. "Oh my gosh! I'm going to need all the details later."

"And I want to hear all about your day." I glance around at the crowded beach, people laughing and talking, and some even dancing near the stage where Mo and the Kokomos are rocking out. "Look at everything you pulled off. I'm so proud of you."

"It's not over yet," she says dismissively, but her smile is full of pride. "But with Mayor Barnes in charge of fireworks, I get to simply enjoy the dance."

I pause, not sure exactly how to broach the next subject I want to speak with her about. "I saw Walker helping today."

Jane's smile falters briefly before brightening again. "Yeah. I think he doesn't quite know what to do with himself, so he asked to be put to work."

I want Jane to be as happy as I am, and I honestly wish my brother was the answer. But I really don't think he's what she needs. "Is he still here?"

"I have no clue. I haven't seen him for a while. But let's not ruin the night talking about him."

Jane is definitely not telling me something, and I don't know what to do about it. Not even a little. We never keep secrets from each other. "Okay."

She starts leading me back toward the group. "So, is your relationship with Tristan still hush-hush?"

"For now."

Jane's gaze goes to the others. "Maybe you should at least tell Bridget so she can back up off your man."

I follow her line of sight, and sure enough, Bridget is standing in front of Tristan, smiling up at him and touching his arm to excess. His hands are shoved in his pocket, but he's nodding at whatever she's saying.

I'm not worried. And then one more time so I believe it: *I'm not worried.*

But I am glad when Jane steers us toward Cat and Gemma, so I don't have to face Bridget. Even if I kind of want to intrude on her and Tristan's conversation.

"Hey, Capri," Cat says with a smile when Jane and I step up next to them. "We were wondering when you'd get here." Her gaze slides to Tristan, then Bridget. "Did you come with Tristan?"

"Yeah. He gave me a ride." I say it like it's the most insignificant news in the history of all news, but Gemma's twitching lips are evidence she isn't fooled. She saw exactly what we were up to the other night. Thankfully, she doesn't say anything. "Where's Beau?" I ask, mainly because I need something else to talk about and it's the first thing that pops into my head. With the way she blushes, I'm now fighting my own smile. There's definitely something going on between the two of them even if Tristan refuses to believe it.

"He got a call about some kids letting off fireworks, but he'll be back soon."

"Can we join you?" Tristan asks, stepping up behind me. We all instinctively spread out, and Tristan moves in next to me, his arm brushing against mine. He sends me a brief conspiratorial smile that reminds me what it is we're hiding. A jolt of pleasure surges through me until it's immediately extinguished when Bridget steps to his other side. Noah Belacourt joins the circle as well and glances at Cat in a way that catches my attention. She meets his gaze momentarily before intentionally dropping hers to the ground. My romance-author senses are buzzing with the tension I'm picking up on, but I quiet my thoughts. With Bridget's focus on Tristan, I don't want to get distracted with potential story ideas.

"Well, isn't this just like old times?" Bridget's smiling eyes move across the other faces, pausing briefly on me as if she's not certain why I'm here. Then she looks up at Tristan. "It's crazy how little has changed."

A few nods and awkward glances pass between the group, or maybe I'm just projecting that on the others with how completely out of sorts I'm feeling.

"I don't know," Tristan says. "I feel like a lot has changed."

She flutters her thick eyelashes. "Not the important things."

My face begins to warm. Not from jealousy (not entirely, anyway) but from indignation. And it's aimed at myself. How can I even be frustrated at Bridget when she has no idea about me and Tristan? I mean, yeah, it's annoying that she thinks she can treat him the way she did and then show up and bat her long, gorgeous eyelashes and stroke his arm with those lovely, manicured fingers of hers and he'll instantly forgive her. But even there, I can't blame her for trying. Tristan is incredible. And sometimes it takes a huge reality check to realize what it is we gave up. Which apparently is exactly what Bridget's gotten by choosing Logan over him.

But ultimately, it's Tristan who's in this tricky position because of my fear of being discovered. Because he can't simply wrap his arm around me or plant a kiss on me to make his point.

His hand closest to me is hanging by his side, so I subtly reach over and loop my index finger with his pinkie. His gaze slides to me, then drops down to our hands, a smile forming on his lips. It's a small gesture. A teeny tiny baby step, but it's something. He shifts toward me, the closeness of our bodies concealing our subtle hint from those around us.

We spend the next hour or so in this way—sharing secret touches as we sing along with the band, dance as a group, and chat with old friends (well, as I mostly listen). Even Walker comes and hangs out with me for a bit, and it's hard to stay mad at him. So I don't. Instead, we talk about his upcoming trip to Scotland and how his golf game is going. Apparently, it's improved a lot since he's come back to Sunset Harbor, which is amazing. I hope he'll remember that the next time he doesn't want to come home. I also dance with Tala, Serenity, and Grandma (I have no idea how Virginia convinced her to come), and I have a great chat with Gemma about what she's been up to since her family moved away.

It isn't until Tristan is returning with a drink for me that I take the opportunity to slip away from my current conversation with Jane and Cat.

He holds out my drink as I approach him. "One Diet Coke."

Before I can thank him, Bridget steps up next to us and gives Tristan a smile meant solely for him. "I didn't realize you were taking drink orders."

Tristan hesitates, obviously not sure what to say. "I overheard Capri say she was thirsty, and I was getting myself a drink, so I thought I'd grab her something."

"And you knew exactly what she wanted?" When neither of us respond, her lips part slightly. "Are the two of you—"

"Hey, Tristan." Noah slaps a hand on Tristan's shoulder before pausing, his gaze shifting between the three of us. "Sorry, did I interrupt?"

"Not at all," Tristan says. "Did you need something?"

Noah blows out a breath. "It can wait."

Tristan looks from Noah to Bridget, then to me. Sensing his question, I give a subtle nod. For me, him leaving me alone with Bridget is preferable to her interrogating the two of us together, especially with Noah as witness. He likely knows more than I care for Bridget to. "Let's chat." Tristan gestures to Noah, and the two of them walk a few paces away.

"So," Bridget says, drawing a step closer. "What's up with you and Tristan?"

My throat feels dry, so I take a drink, but the fizz of the soda is far from relieving. "We're friends."

She quirks one of her perfectly shaped brows, exactly like the action beat I regularly put in my books but always wonder if it's even possible. It is. "Really?"

"Yep. Good friends." Plus a little more. I glance over my shoulder to see if I can catch Jane's eye so she'll come and rescue me, but she's not at the table with Cat anymore. My gaze skirts the dance floor, and there she is, being swung around by none other than Walker. My attention lingers on them, and if they weren't so entirely wrong for each other, I think I'd be thrilled with the idea of my best friend falling in love with my brother. But that can't happen. He'll break her wonderful, enormous heart.

"Walker and Jane seem to be getting along really well," Bridget says with what seems like a genuine smile. "She's a lucky girl."

"They're also just friends," I say, taking another swig of my Diet Coke, uncomfortably aware I'm in denial but having no clue what to do about it.

Bridget gives a tight laugh. "You may need to reconsider your definition of friendship. Because that"—she lifts her chin toward them—"is more than friendship. And the way Tristan has been hanging around you all night ..."

Her gaze sweeps over my expression, and I feel like I'm a page of a book being read. Or, more precisely, an encyclopedia since my emotions are completely written out for her to study at will.

Her shoulders fall slightly, and she looks over at Tristan with a resigned glance. "I thought so."

I don't deny it. It seems counterintuitive when she'll figure out the truth soon enough. And maybe it'll save Tristan from having to say something to her.

"He's the best guy I've ever known," she says, her eyes glistening when she meets my gaze again. "Don't take him for granted or you'll probably regret it for the rest of your life."

I stare at Bridget as if I've never seen her before. And I guess, in a way, I haven't. I always saw her as my enemy—my arch nemesis—because she had Tristan. But suddenly, I'm getting a glimpse of someone else. Likely the person that first captured Tristan's attention all those years ago. Which, now that I think about it, isn't surprising considering Tristan loved her for so long. My fictionalized version of her only includes the parts that made sense with my narrative. The villainized parts. But I have an unsettling feeling that there's a whole different side to Bridget Hall I've allowed myself to be blinded to. "I won't."

She gives a small clearing of her throat and exhales a quick breath. "I think I'm gonna head home."

I give a weak wave goodbye and watch as she passes out a few hugs, then leaves. My thoughts are spinning as I stand alone and finish drinking my soda.

Mo's voice comes over the speakers. "We've got one last song to play for you before the big firework show. We hope you don't mind, but it's a slow one."

A movement in my periphery has me looking to my right, but it isn't Tristan standing there smiling at me, it's a guy with a boyishly handsome face I've never seen before. Likely a main-lander here for the celebration. "Hey. I'm Todd."

"Capri."

He flicks his head in the direction of the stage. "I was wondering if you'd like to dance?"

I glance over my shoulder to where Tristan is still talking to Noah, and his gaze meets mine. "With me?" I ask, realizing how stupid that must sound after having just exchanged names and being that there's no one else around, but I'm not sure what to say.

His smile broadens, and I'm guessing he's managed to get himself several dance partners tonight with that trait alone. "With you."

For a brief moment, I hesitate. I don't want to say no. Todd looks like a great guy, but if I'm going to dance this last dance, I want it to be with Tristan. "I would, except—"

"She promised me this one." Tristan steps up behind me. "I'm really sorry, man. But you can't understand the effort it took to convince her to let me have one dance tonight."

"Whatever you had to do, I'm guessing it was worth it," Todd says, dipping his chin to us and taking a step away. "Happy 4th."

"It was great meeting you, Todd," I say as Tristan grabs the empty cup from me and tosses it in the trash. Then he takes my hand and leads me toward the dance floor.

Tristan sends me a look of mock disbelief over his shoulder. "You were going to say yes to him, weren't you?"

"He seemed nice, and no one else had asked me."

Tristan shakes his head. "Does a promise mean nothing to you?"

I tighten my hold on his hand. "I'm pretty sure I said I'd try to squeeze you in. Besides, weren't you supposed to be in a uniform?"

Tristan laughs, leading me toward the stage. When we find a space on the fringe of the other dancing couples, he turns to face me, his hands coming to my hips. "Is this breaking protocol?"

I wrap my arms around his neck. "I honestly don't mind."

A mischievous smile forms on his lips. "You don't mind?"

I give a little shrug, savoring the sensation of his body against mine and the pressure of his strong hands sliding along my waist until they possessively settle on my lower back. "All of these secrets are getting exhausting."

"*All* of them? Are there more than the two I'm aware of?"

I laugh, shaking my head. "No, but those two seem to affect every aspect of my life currently."

He nods, and his fingers curl into the fabric of my dress. "Considering how much effort it's taking to not kiss you in front of everyone, I can't even imagine. And that's with Heath's bet on the forefront of my mind."

My cheeks pink, but I hold his gaze. "The not kissing you right now honestly might be the worst part." His laugh vibrates in his chest, and I barely resist leaning my head against him to more fully absorb the feel it. "What did Noah need to talk to you about?" I ask, needing to change the subject or risk losing Tristan Heath's bike.

"Cat Keene."

I smile. "I thought there was something going on between them."

"*Was* being the key word. Poor guy. He's had a thing for her for a long time."

"I feel his pain."

Tristan pins me with a look. "That's enough of that. I'm already kicking myself for not seeing what was right in front of me this whole time. And for not reaching out to you after Bridget and I broke up."

"You thought about reaching out to me?"

"So many times. Especially once I moved back to Sunset Harbor. Between all the memories of you that being in my old house brought and the fact that Tala and Heath constantly mentioned you... and so did Jane ... and your grandma and your mom ... and my mom"—he gives a small laugh, shaking his head, and my heart soars thinking about our own little group of haphazardly blatant matchmakers—"I almost did reach out to you. But I'd always talk myself out of it. I hadn't seen you in years, and with how things ended before I left for college—for how I got back together with Bridget that night, for not correcting her when she intentionally said your name wrong..." He blows out a breath, as though his next admission is a painful one. "...for letting you walk away without an apology or explanation. I'd convinced myself you'd want nothing to do with me. Or, if you somehow didn't hate me, you'd wrongly assume you were an afterthought if I attempted to get a hold of you, which is the last thing I'd ever want you to think. So with all of that and how I'd accepted the assistant coaching position in California, I kept dismissing the urge to reach out to you."

The frown pulling at his lips convinces me to work past my shock at his revelation and respond. "So, what I'm hearing is that I'm not the only one who imagines false reactions for other people and fully convinces myself they're real?"

Tristan's frown lessens but doesn't disappear entirely. "In my defense, those first few times I saw you this summer seemed to confirm my conclusions."

My heart aches remembering the look of confusion and hurt on his face when I'd abruptly ended those first brief conversations. "I am sorry about that, even if my quick retreats weren't for the reasons you thought."

"I'm sorry ... for everything. Particularly for being so blind." His gaze sweeps over me. "But I see you now. Every beautiful facet of you."

If he keeps saying stuff like this, there's no way I'm going to be able to keep resisting him. Protocol or no protocol. Bet or no bet. "I'll need to write that line down," I tease in a desperate attempt to lighten the mood. "My readers will love it."

His eyes twinkle. "Oh, there's more where that came from."

I'm all but staring at his lips now. Actually, I'm staring. He opens his mouth, but I reach up to cover it. Mainly so I can touch his lips, but the moment I do, I realize what a bad idea it is. My resolve to keep things platonic is quickly crumbling. "How about we save those nuggets of inspiration for later when I can fully appreciate them."

With his lips concealed, he kisses my palm, and I'm glad he still has a hold of me because I might swoon right there. Or throw all caution to the wind and jump attack him.

But Mo's voice comes over the microphone to close out the dancing, and a loud boom overhead has the collective gaze looking up at the sky. An explosion of golden light sparkles in the darkness a couple hundred feet above us. The suspended lights that have been strung around the stage dim, and the traditional patriotic firework music begins to blare over the speakers.

Another firework whistles and explodes, followed by

another. Wide-eyed, I look at Tristan to catch his expression, but his gaze is on me.

"You're going to miss the fireworks," I tease.

His mouth quirks into a smile, and he brushes a hair from my face. "I've experienced plenty of fireworks today, thanks to you."

With everyone's attention on the sky and Tristan's adoring gaze still on me, I can't stop myself. Anticipation lifts my stomach, and a sense of reckless abandonment takes over my fear of being discovered. I raise onto my toes and press my lips to Tristan's. He seems surprised at first, but then his hands come to my face, his palms on my jaws and his fingertips light on my neck. I linger a bit longer than I initially intended. But how can I not? Each kiss with Tristan is new and different, and I want to experience them all for as long as I'm able. And I don't care who's watching. I'm done hiding.

He's smiling when I finally pull away. "Okay, that was definitely worth a month of babysitting. Though it may have broken protocol."

"Maybe we need to adjust our protocol, then. Or get rid of it altogether."

"I like the sound of that," he says, but then genuine concern fills his expression. "But what about people finding out that you're ... ?" He doesn't finish, probably worried someone might overhear him.

With Tristan's arms around me, my fears seem to scatter. "At this point, it's only a matter of time until they do. I might as well come clean while it's still on my terms."

He lifts his brow. "You're going to tell people? Outside of your family?"

I nod, strangely resolved. "Once I tell Grandma and Walker since I didn't get a chance today."

Tristan's smile widens. "Do you know how you'll go about it?"

"Not exactly. I'll call Maven, my agent, regarding the official announcement, but I wonder if I should tell a few people on the island first. Let the news start to spread organically before the media gets a hold of it." An idea pops into my head that causes my stomach to twist with nerves, but probably because it's a decent option. "I could always attend the Seaside Oasis book club Saturday night. Tala, Jane, and my Grandma make up half of it, so it shouldn't be difficult to tell a couple of others. And, if anyone is going to help spread the word in a positive light, I'd think it's those ladies." At least I hope it is.

"That does make sense."

"And as for tonight …" I lift on my toes again, guiding him forward until his lips are against mine. Then, after a brief kiss, I lean back slightly, just out of reach, and I love the way he involuntarily leans toward me as if he can't help himself. "Let's stop pretending that we aren't obsessed with each other."

Fireworks are still booming overhead, but nothing can compare to the smile on Tristan's face. Or the way he kisses me again, for anyone to see.

WELCOME TO
SUNSET
HARBOR

BELACOURT RESORT

GOLF COURSE

NOAH'S HOUSE

JANE'S HOUSE

NATURE PRESERVE

DAX'S DUPLEX

SEASIDE OASIS RETIREMENT HOME

SUNSET REPAIRS

PHOENIX'S OFFICE

CITY OFFICES

KEENE B&B

SUNRISE CAFE

SCOOPS AHOY ICE CREAM

TOWN SQUARE

BAKERY

BRIGGS'S APARTMENT

THE BOOK ISLE

CUTS AND CURLS

TRISTAN & BEAU'S HOUSE

GEMMA'S HOUSE

CAPRI'S HOUSE

HOLLAND'S HOUSE

BEACH BREAK BAR & GRILL

PUBLIC BEACH

GULF OF MEXICO

N
W   E
S

CHAPTER 26

I'M SITTING on the dock with my notebook in hand, jotting down a few story ideas, when I hear Tristan's back door open. I glance behind me and smile when I see him headed my way, but he looks upset.

"Hey," I say, standing up to join him. "You okay?"

"The paperwork for the sale's all signed." He lets out a heavy breath and runs a hand through his hair. "It looks like we both have big confessions coming up."

I take in his tight jaw and the heaviness in his gaze. "You don't look thrilled."

Tristan's gaze turns distant. "You should have seen my dad's face. He looked like he was going to break down at any minute. And I don't blame him. He's given his whole life to our retirement centers. To Seaside Oasis. I feel like I'm disappointing him. That I'm being selfish and ungrateful for everything he's done for me."

I wrap my arms around his waist, my notebook in my hand making it slightly awkward, but I manage. "You're the least selfish man I know, Tristan. And your dad wants you to be happy."

"I know, I just ..." He shakes his head. "What if I don't enjoy coaching? What if I gave up all of this"—he gestures around us —"for some vague hope that choosing my own path will bring me the fulfillment I'm searching for?"

I don't say anything this time. I just hold him, letting him talk.

"I've always wanted to coach. And I know I could be good at it, but the tradeoff suddenly feels a lot steeper—a lot more permanent—than I thought it would." His gaze drops to me. "And California's a long way from here. From my family. And from you."

I let go of him and take a small step back so he can't feel the slight trembling of my hands. "I know something that could maybe help."

His brow drops, his eyes narrowing slightly. "What's that?"

My heart is trembling inside me, and I hope I'm not being reckless. That he won't think I'm pressuring him to move quicker in our relationship than he's ready to. "It occurred to me that as an author, I can work from anywhere. Including California." There. It's an offer to go with him, but a vague one. He can make of it what he will.

Tristan searches my expression so intently I'm pretty sure he's trying to decide if I'm serious. "You'd move to California?"

I give a small shrug like I didn't just suggest I'd pack up my entire life and move across the country for him. "If you're there, that's where I want to be."

Tristan's lips break into the most glorious smile I've ever seen, and I breathe a little easier. "You're serious right now?"

"I am."

"But you love it here. And your family's here."

"But you'll be there."

He stares at me, his smile locked in place. Then his finger slips through the beltloop of my pants, and he pulls me against him, pressing his lips to mine. His arms engulf me, and our kiss is deep and full of all the best feelings that love encompasses—hope, joy, excitement, understanding, and even a bit of uncertainty.

"Ewwwww." Jack's voice forces us from each other's

embrace, and we see not only Jack but also Serenity and Walker standing on the back porch, sporting an array of expressions.

"Eww is right," Walker says, but his lips are noticeably lifted upward at the corners. "You two go inside and tell your mom we'll be there soon. I'm going to have a chat with Auntie Capri and her *boyfriend*."

"They aren't in trouble, are they?" Serenity asks, her big doe eyes turning on us.

"I'm not ruling out anything yet," he says.

I scrunch up my nose and shake my head to indicate to her that Walker's teasing, and that seems to pacify her.

"In you go," Walker says, opening the door, and Serenity and Jack file inside obediently. He adjusts his hat and stuffs his hands in his pockets, then starts in our direction. When he gets close, he flicks his head in the house. "Since Tala and Heath have their hot date tonight courtesy of you two babysitting, I think they want to get the kids fed so they can head out right after."

"Are Grandma and Jane here, yet?"

"Yeah, they're in talking to Tala," he says, momentarily dropping his gaze. "And, to make things easy on you, I overheard Grandma mention how you're Sunny Palmer. I don't think she realized I didn't know, but Jane and Tala ended up filling me in on everything."

Tala and I had taken Grandma out to lunch today to tell her the news. She giggled like a mad woman and then claimed she suspected as much all along. I informed her that she's not supposed to tell anyone until I give her the go ahead, but my guess is at least Virginia already has the full scoop. And apparently Walker now too. So it's a good thing I'm coming clean with my secret. "Wow, that was easy. And, since it's confession time, you should probably also know that Tristan and I are dating."

Walker is noticeably avoiding eye contact with Tristan. "Yeah, that one was pretty obvious."

We stand a moment in awkward silence when Tristan's hand settles on my back. "I'll head inside. Give you two a minute to talk."

I squeeze his hand as he passes. "Thanks. Tell them they can start eating and we'll be right in."

"Hey, Tristan," Walker says, pausing him before he can get far. He clears his throat. Then he clears it again. "I just want to say that I was wrong about you."

Tristan's gaze slides to me as though he's second-guessing what he just heard and needs confirmation I heard it too.

Walker blows out a breath like this is painful for him. "With a little *assistance*," he says, and I'm certain the assistance he's referring to is Jane, "I realized you always had my sister's best interest at heart. I just couldn't see it." He takes off his hat, runs a hand over his dark curls, then puts it back on again. "Probably because I disregarded anyone's needs but my own. But you were there for her. Not romantically like she wanted at the time, but you were a friend when I wasn't."

Tristan sticks out his hand and the two of them shake. "I appreciate that," Tristan says. "And I was wrong about those things I said—"

Walker grimaces. "No, you weren't."

Tristan leans his head from one side to the other. "Maybe not all of them, but some were definitely uncalled for. And I'm sorry."

Walker lifts his chin in acknowledgment, and they drop their hands. Then, in sync, their gazes turn to me.

"I'm not going to lie," I say, glancing between them. "That was the cutest bro apology I've ever seen."

Tristan chuckles, and Walker gestures to the notebook in my hand. "Why don't you jot it down in there? You can use it for one of your books."

"I honestly might have to."

Walker looks at Tristan. "Have you gotten a glimpse inside one of her top-secret notebooks yet? Because, at least when she was younger, you made countless appearances. And there were Capri Palmer signatures all over those pages."

My mouth gapes open. "You looked in my notebooks?"

"What?" He lifts his hands at his side. "You literally left them everywhere in our house, Capri. Trust me, I didn't want to see half the stuff I saw in there."

Tristan laughs. "I did glimpse a few of those signatures once."

My gaze flies to him. "When?"

"Right before our sunset boat ride, you dropped your notebook."

"But it was closed."

Tristan grins. "When I handed it back it was."

A blush seeps into my cheeks, though I have no idea why. It's not like he doesn't know how obsessed with him I was. How obsessed with him I still am.

"The only problem was I didn't know which Palmer brother you were crushing on at the time. I secretly hoped it was me, but Beau's a hard one to compete with." I wonder if that's why he asked me about Beau on the boat that day and on our bike ride home from the lighthouse. I have a sudden urge to tease him, but when I open my mouth, Tristan points at me. "Don't say it."

I give an innocent smile as though I have no clue what he's talking about.

"Are you guys coming?" Tala calls from the door, and Tristan takes a few backwards steps, still eyeing me before he turns and starts toward her.

His long strides make quick work of the distance. "Capri said to start eating. She and Walker will be in soon."

Tala nods, letting Tristan through to the kitchen and then shutting the door behind them.

Walker's hands are tucked in his pockets again, but he meets my gaze without reserve this time. "The whole Sunny Palmer thing is pretty darn cool, Capri."

"I'm sorry I didn't tell—"

"I don't blame you for not telling me. I've basically been the world's suckiest brother. So I'm the one who's sorry. Moving forward, I hope to be closer to the brother I should have been since Dad died. The brother that you deserve." He gives a hint of a smile. "Though don't set your expectations too high."

Without thinking, I wrap my arms around him. His body is stiff at first, but then he relaxes and returns my embrace. "I've missed you, Walker." And I don't just mean I've missed seeing him but that I miss the old Walker from when we were children. The one that I'm beginning to see again. I can't help but think this has something to do with Jane bringing him back to us.

"I've missed you too." Walker allows my hug for longer than I think he will before he finally pulls away.

"Maybe you should stick around."

Walker shrugs. "Maybe I should."

I don't know if he means it, but as we head inside, I hope he does. Not that I'll be here, but Jane will be. And I'm sort of coming around to the idea of my brother and my best friend falling in love. Sort of.

CHAPTER 27

WHEN TRISTAN PULLS into the Seaside Oasis parking lot, my entire body is buzzing from nerves. I'm still trying to figure out exactly how I want to tell the small group of women that I'm Sunny Palmer. I stand by the decision. Outside of my family, these are the most obvious people to share the news with. And they'll definitely help spread the word, so it won't come as a total shock to Sunset Harbor residents when Maven drops the official announcement in a couple of days.

He puts the golf cart in park and glances over at me. "You ready for this?"

I turn to face him, propping up my knee on the seat. "What if, instead of me telling people, we just sail away into the sunset together?"

He chuckles.

"No, really. If you think about it, it's the obvious answer here."

His arm settles around me, and he mindlessly plays with the ends of my hair. "How big is this boat? Because it'd have to be big enough to fit your entire family plus my family. And Jane too."

I purse my lips. "If my suspicions are correct, possibly Gemma as well."

Tristan just shakes his head, smiling. "I suppose if that's true, Virginia Sawyer will insist on coming, and I'm not sure how well she'll fare being stuck on a boat with several Palmers.

Though we might save on food rations if she leads another hunger strike."

I give an airy laugh and take hold of Tristan's hand, intertwining his fingers with mine. "You're positive you don't want to come inside with me? I'm confident all the ladies would love you being there. Plus you've read the book."

"If I remember correctly, you were the one who said it would be weird if I came."

"I take it back. It wouldn't be weird at all."

He laughs again. "I'll be at my parents' house right there. I have something important I want to talk with my dad about anyway." He tips his head toward their lovely one-story, red-brick home with bright white shutters just across from Seaside Oasis. "If you need me for anything or want to leave earlier than you planned, I can be here in a few minutes."

"Is your mom coming tonight?" The more familiar faces, the better.

"Yep." Tristan tucks his lips inward as if he's attempting not to smile.

"What is it?"

"She finished your book."

"She suspects it's me, doesn't she?"

Tristan nods. "Right after you came to visit me at work yesterday, she stopped by with a brand-new copy from The Book Isle. She made me swear on pains of death that I'd read it."

"Did you tell her?"

"I didn't really need to. I simply confirmed I've read the book already." He pauses. "Which I hope is okay? I knew she'd be here for the reveal today, so I figured it might be good to have one more person who already knows."

"That's completely fine." I drop my gaze from his, my nerves getting the better of me. "What was her reaction?"

Tristan's hand moves beneath my chin, and he lifts my face

to his. "She was beyond thrilled. And if I had to guess, most of the people at the book club will feel the same."

The thought does ease my worry some. Not much, but a little. It also verifies what I've been thinking—with Tristan and me paired together in people's minds, my confession isn't coming a moment too soon.

Tristan's watch beeps seven, and I groan. I close my eyes, pulling in a long, slow breath, and then Tristan's there, wrapping his arms around me and reminding me exactly why I'm about to do this.

I'm done living a secret life.

I'm done hiding.

Even if telling people is going to suck. Super bad.

"You've got this." Tristan tilts my chin up so I'm looking at him, and his eyes are so full of warmth that I believe him. "And I'll be waiting to hear all about it when it's over."

"Let's just hope everyone laughs off the news like you did." His fingers brush across my cheek.

"However they react, you're worth being seen."

I lean in for one last bolstering kiss before I step out of old Bessie and start toward the front entrance.

"Capri!" Holland is several paces behind me when I glance back, and I wait for her to catch up. With her level of excitement at seeing me, it's obvious she didn't go to school with us to realize where I stood on the social ladder. "I didn't think you were going to make it!"

"I changed my mind."

"Well, I'm so glad." When she reaches me, she loops her arm through mine as if we've been friends our whole lives. "You're going to love it."

I highly doubt that, but I appreciate her enthusiasm.

The automatic doors to the lobby open. "I saw that Tristan dropped you off." She grins, her eyes searching my profile for any hints I might give. "Are the two of you dating?"

I meet her gaze, relieved I don't have to keep it a secret anymore. "We are."

Her face lights up. "I knew it! You two were looking pretty cozy the night of the Fourth. Even when we spoke with you before the parade, he couldn't get out of there fast enough after you walked away." Holland breathes a contended sigh. "You two are absolutely adorable together. Seriously."

"Thanks." I pause, but before I come up with something to say in return, we step into the large sitting room. Cat and Jane are here already, along with Tristan's mom who's speaking to Sandra—the receptionist and Sunny Palmer's self-proclaimed number one fan—and another lady that looks a lot like her. Probably her sister if I had to guess. Virginia's also camped out on the couch, her purse intentionally positioned next to her, likely saving the spot for my grandma. But what I wasn't expecting is for there to be several other women standing around talking in small groups.

Cat and Jane wave at us and head in our direction. "Hey!" Jane pulls me in for a hug, and with the tightness of it, I can tell it's a you-can-do-this-and-I'm-so-proud-of-you support hug.

"I'm so glad you came," Cat says, offering me a kind smile.

"I'm excited to be here," I say, though it's only because I'm excited to get this whole thing over with. My gaze sweeps the room again. I count seventeen people, and that doesn't even include Grandma and Tala who aren't here yet. "Don't you usually only have seven or eight women show up?"

Cat nods. "It's because we're reading a Sunny Palmer book. Those always draw a few extra."

Joy comes over to give me a hug, and Sandra tags along with her, as does the look-alike woman who wears a similar bun though hers is more densely streaked with grey.

"You made it!" Sandra claps her hands. "I was so excited when I saw you walk in." She glances at the woman standing next to her. "Kathy, this is Capri. The one I was telling you about who owns the editing company Sunny Palmer uses." She looks back at me. "This is my sister, Kathy."

I give a small wave. "Hey, Kathy. It's nice to meet you."

"Wait," Holland says, her head quirking to one side. "Your company edits for Sunny Palmer?"

The din of voices silences, and the collective gaze shifts in my direction. "One of my editors works with her."

"How cool is that, though?" Holland appears as impressed as all the others do.

I briefly contemplate if I should use this opportunity to blurt out the truth, but without Tala and Grandma here, I decide to wait. Postponing the inevitable a little longer.

"Kathy is also a huge Sunny Palmer fan." Sandra looks at her sister. "She'd argue she's an even bigger fan than I am."

"I'm just louder about my love for her," Kathy says with a proud smile. "In fact, a few days after her next release, I'm hosting a Sunny Palmer trivia event at our local library. There will be some pretty awesome prizes, so if anyone wants information on it, I brought some flyers with me to pass out."

"That sounds fun." Jane glances around. "Who are we still missing?"

"I think we're just waiting for Deedee and Tala," Cat says.

Since Tala left the house before me—and since I see the lemon bars we made are already on the snack table—I assume she must be getting Grandma. "I can go check where they are." But right then, Tala and Grandma walk into the room.

Their gazes lift to us, and Tala waves. "Sorry. Were you waiting on us?"

Jane smiles. "You're totally fine."

Grandma gives me a kiss on the cheek and a conspiratorial grin as she passes, then she joins Virginia on the couch. The other women begin to take their seats, and I grab a chair by Tala, across from where Jane is sitting so I don't have to be next to her while she moderates the discussion. I want everyone looking in the opposite direction until I make my confession.

"How you feeling?" Tala whispers.

"Like I'm going to vomit."

She gives me a pitying smile. "Just think how nice it'll be once it's over with."

I nod, trying to hold on to that idea, because right now, all I'm aware of is how bad it's going to suck to fess up. And my author brain is not the least bit helpful at rallying my courage despite that I'm confident none of the scenarios playing out in my mind will actually happen.

"Okay," Jane says, smiling at the group of ladies gathered, her gaze pausing on me. "Should we get started?"

I understand the question behind her question, and the buzzing in my chest doubles. Now?! I suppose it makes sense. Just get it over with. I just need to say the words: *I'm Sunny Palmer.* "If it's okay, I did have one thing to say quick ..."

The sound of clicking heels on tile pulls my gaze over my shoulder. My pounding heart stops mid-beat, plummeting downward.

Bridget Hall is standing on the threshold of the room like some kind of goddess descended with her perfectly curled blond hair and off-white flowing jumper with matching wedged sandals. And, for the first time in a long while, my imagination has failed me. Not even my worst-case-scenario thinking conjured up Bridget at book club.

"Bridget!" Cat says, waving. "You came."

Bridget shrugs her shoulders in response, and Holland squeezes closer to Cat on the couch, then pats the seat next to her. "Come sit by us." When Bridget does, Holland points toward me. "Capri was just about to say something."

All twenty sets of eyes return to me, and my mouth goes dry. With Bridget's sudden appearance, my resolve hasn't only wavered, it's disappeared completely. It's one thing to tell the truth to a small group of women I know fairly well, but it's a different thing entirely to make a confession of this caliber when Bridget Hall is here. I can't do it. I'll just find another way to tell people—maybe in smaller groups. Like over lunch with Holland and Cat. Jane's been trying to get me to go out with the three of them for a while, and this seems like the perfect reason to finally make it happen. I'll also find a time to explain to Bridget and apologize. Eventually. Just not right now.

Because right now, I need to get through the next hour attempting to hide my secret identity and simply fly under the radar. Which, for me, usually isn't difficult. "Sorry, I forgot what I was going to say."

Jane reads me perfectly and gives a wave of her hand. "That's okay. But feel free to chime in if you remember. Let's go ahead and start the discussion."

Listening to people talk about my book is its own form of torture. But I suppose I deserve it, so I train my expression as people say the things they enjoyed and, on occasion, didn't enjoy about the book (though Jane moves on quickly from those). I can also tell, with Bridget here, Jane's doing her best to brush over the real-life connections, but it's hard when there are so many.

"Bridget is the worst," Holland says after a comment about a run-in where fictional Bridget pretends not to know Cali's name, and the familiar prickling of heat starts on my chest. Thankfully, I had the foresight to wear a high neckline and keep my hair down to minimize the visible splotching, but I'm sure my exposed neck is already showing signs of my discomfort. "Not, you," she says to Bridget with a little laugh. "The book Bridget."

In my periphery, Bridget's gaze slides to me, and I go statue still. Like a flock of pigeons could land on me right now, and I wouldn't budge.

"I started the book this afternoon," Bridget says, stunning me with the revelation. With how quiet she's been, I assumed (or really, really hoped) that she hadn't read it. That she'd held firm to her resolution to not read a Sunny Palmer book. And I've never felt so much dread at being wrong. "I'm only about halfway through, but there seem to be a lot of similarities between Sunset Harbor and Coral Cove. Like the golf carts and the canals and how the houses back up to them with docks along the bay-side yards. It's almost like the author has been here." Bridget glances around, avoiding eye contact with me. "Or am I the only one who sees all the connections?"

"No, I've always thought the same thing," Cat says. "Which is probably one of the reasons I enjoy it. It feels like I'm reading about home."

I shift in my seat to stave off my discomfort.

"Maybe the author visited at some point," Jane says dismissively.

"Maybe," Bridget looks directly at me this time. "Or maybe she's from here. Maybe her characters aren't as fictionalized as we think."

With her direct stare, the gaze of the entire room shifts to me again, and with the way my face is burning, I'm positive I'm lobster red. I try to swallow, but the tightness in my throat won't relent. I can't outright lie to these women when they'll know the truth soon. And with Bridget seemingly fixed on forcing my hand, the time has apparently come. "Bridget's right," I manage to get out. "Sunny Palmer is from Sunset Harbor."

Everyone looks slightly confused except the people who already know—Tala, Jane, Grandma, and Joy. As well as Virginia, judging by her unfazed expression. No surprise there. Grandma can't keep anything from her.

Joy's smile dims when she glances toward Bridget. She's obviously concerned with how this situation is going to play out. As am I.

"So you do know her?" Sandra asks.

Panic rises in my chest, but Tala's hand settles on top of mine, offering me the strength I need. "I am her." I clear the emotion from my throat. "I'm Sunny Palmer."

A collective gasp moves through the room, and I can feel tears pricking my eyes. No! No floodgate crying. I absolutely have to hold myself together.

"You're Sunny Palmer?" Holland's brows are raised high and her lips are parted at first, but then she smiles. "Like, for real?"

I nod. "I wrote *Secret Crush* years ago, when I was young and naive, and I never thought there was a chance anyone would read it. Let alone all of you."

"But why write under a pen name?" Holland's tone is more curious than condemning. "At least at this point in your career."

My gaze drops to the floor. "Because of my pen name and—"

"Sunny *Palmer*," Hollands says, interrupting my confession. She sends an uncertain glance toward Joy. "As in Tristan *Palmer*?"

I give a sheepish nod. "I had a bit of a crush on him."

"It sounds like more than a bit," Virginia says under her breath.

I take a deep breath, ready to have this over with. "My first story is also based off a fictionalized version of real life. And real people. And I didn't want anyone to discover the truth." I finally force my gaze upward again. "About any of it."

"Wait." Cat looks completely dumbfounded. "Cali and Trenton are ... you and Tristan?" I give another slow nod, and Cat's widened eyes shift to Bridget, but she doesn't ask her next question.

I follow her gaze to Bridget. "I don't even know what to say besides how sorry I am." My voice trembles. "I regret how I handled so many things. Most especially using your name."

She pulls in a quick breath, and with the way her nostrils flare, it's obvious how upset she is. And I don't blame her at all. What I did was beyond foolish. It was reckless. "Does Tristan know? Or have you lied to him too?"

"He knows."

Her eyes narrow as if she's trying to determine if I'm being honest or not. Which makes sense. "Considering your track record, I'm not sure how valid your word is."

"He knows," Joy says, sending me a reassuring look.

Bridget glances between the two of us, her lips pursed. "And has he thought about the fact that you're hoping to get another best-selling book by coming back to Sunset Harbor?"

Her comment hits like a fist to my stomach. The idea of anyone thinking that's why I'm here—or that's why I'm with Tristan—makes my insides twist into knots. "I wouldn't do that," I say, tears blurring my vision.

"You wouldn't?" she asks, lifting an eyebrow. "Forgive me for not believing you. You've obviously used him once. What's stopping you from doing it a second time?"

"She's not using me." Tristan's voice comes from behind, and my head whips to where he's standing. His gaze is fixed on me. I have no idea why he's here, but the sight of him is like stumbling on an oasis in the middle of a sweltering desert. "The first three times I ran into her, she was desperate to get away from me. I actually had to sit outside the mainland store for over twenty minutes waiting just so I could talk to her when she came out. My plan had been to ask her out, but it didn't take long to realize she wasn't going to agree to that, so I was forced to use the guise of friendship to convince her to hang out with me."

My heart swells briefly at his admission before Bridget's voice deflates it.

"Or maybe she's good at acting." Bridget's glare is so intense when it shifts to me that I want to look away, but I don't. "She's done it for long enough."

Jane shakes her head. "The whole reason she left Sunset Harbor in the first place is because she hated hiding the truth, but she didn't know how to tell everyone."

"It's true," Tala says. "We only managed to get her home by forcing her to come get some boxes that we were storing. I didn't tell her that Tristan had moved back in next door or she never would have come."

"And, to keep her here, I stole her keys," Grandma says proudly.

Virginia smirks and raises a hand. "I gave Deedee the idea."

Tristan moves behind my chair, resting his hands on the back of it, and he glances down at me with a smile. "I'm happy to say we all eventually won her over to our cause."

Bridget sits a moment in silence, her gaze distant, then she stands up. "Well, this has been a blast, but I'm gonna head home."

"I'll walk you out." Cat stands, following Bridget as she makes her way across the inside of the circle we've formed.

"I really am sorry, Bridget," I say as she passes.

She pauses, meeting my gaze, and I can see I'm not the only one on the verge of tears. "How would you feel if you were immortalized in a book as a villain?"

Her words are a direct hit, knocking the wind from my lungs. I never would have thought a flippant choice I made years ago could do such damage. That it would come to cause someone else pain.

A tear breaks free, and Bridget swipes it before stepping past me with Cat at her side.

The entire room is unnervingly quiet with their exit, and everyone is staring at me.

The only movement is Virginia removing her coke bottle glasses, rubbing the hem of her shirt across her lenses, and placing them back on. "Whoa, talk about awkward." She clears her throat and lifts the book from her lap. "But any chance I can get you to sign my copy?"

"Same!" Sandra and Kathy say in unison, their faces beaming

with an excitement that contradicts the scene they were witness to.

I stand up, a flood of emotion welling inside of me. "I'm sorry. I need to go."

TEARS ARE ALREADY STREAMING DOWN my cheeks when Tristan leads me into his office. He closes the door behind us and pulls me into his embrace. I bury my face into his chest. I can't talk through my sobs, but Tristan holds me, allowing me as long as I need.

Several minutes later, there's a knock on his door, and he glances down at me. "Do you want me to get that?"

I nod, a shuddering breath escaping me. "It's probably Tala or Jane."

Sure enough, when he opens it, both Tala and Jane step inside, their looks of pity doing nothing to ease my distress.

"Oh, sweetie." Tala wraps her arms around me, and Jane does likewise, the two of them sandwiching me in a hug that manages to refill my depleted reservoir of tears.

"At least the hardest part is over," Jane says. "And once the initial shock settles, everyone will be more than fine with it. Most of them already are."

I shake my head. "I don't know why I thought this was going to be a good idea. I shouldn't have come tonight."

Tala runs a hand through my hair. "Whether you were here or not, Bridget would have been, and she would have said something."

Jane nods. "It was better that you were able to say something. To apologize. And it didn't hurt that Tristan was there."

"How did you know to come when you did?" Tala asks before I have a chance to.

"I texted my mom to see how book club was going. She replied that she thought Capri was about to tell everyone she was Sunny Palmer, but Bridget showed up. When I heard that, I decided to head over from my parents' in case Capri ended up wanting to leave earlier than she'd anticipated. So I was actually in my office when my mom texted a second time to say Bridget had read the book. That's when I figured I might be needed. Not that Capri couldn't hold her own, but I worried Bridget might attempt to make me out to be the victim. I wanted her and everyone else to know that isn't the case."

I take hold of Tristan's hand, excessively grateful for his forethought. "All things considered, Bridget handled everything fairly well." Apparently I feel the need to defend Bridget after what I just put her through.

"She tends to be quick to anger, but she's relatively level-headed once those feelings pass," Tristan says, and I try not to care that he knows her so well. "Not that she'll come around to the idea, but she'll move on."

"And, so you know," Jane says, "Cat came back inside. I think she just wanted Bridget to feel supported, but she also asked how you're doing. And Holland asked me to give you a hug for her."

Another knock sends Tala to the door this time, and she cracks it open. "It's Grandma," she says, glancing back at me as though she's asking for permission, but she's already opened the door wide enough to let her in. And Virginia with her.

"How are you, my love?" Grandma says, running a hand over my tear-streaked face. "You were so brave."

My shoulders drop. "It's not bravery when you're forced into a confession."

"And what a confession that was," Virginia says with a little laugh. "With how it all played out, it's going to spread through the island like wildfire."

Jane winces. "Probably more than just the island."

Before dread at the thought fully consumes me, Tala points at me. "Don't think about that. What's the game plan?"

"It had been to make the announcement in a few days—giving some time for the news to spread organically so it doesn't take the island by surprise when it hits social media and news outlets. But now ..." I shrug. "I'll call Maven to see what she suggests." I pull in a slow breath. Whatever she says, I'm guessing life as I know it is about to implode.

CHAPTER 28

SUNLIGHT IS SEEPING through the edges of the blinds, but I don't get out of bed. I want to put off the reality of today as long as possible. Late last night, with the help of my support team—Tala, Jane, and Tristan—I drafted an announcement for Maven to send out to her news sources and to post on social media and to my newsletter. Once she looks it over (she likely already has but I haven't checked my email yet) and modifies anything that needs changing, I'll give her the green light to share my secret identity. And the thought is terrifying. I'm a creature of habit and comfort, and the prospect of being known is entirely unsettling. Especially since I have no idea what to expect, and my mind is far too willing to fill in the blanks.

But I can't put off the inevitable forever, so I grab my phone and turn off airplane mode.

My phone dings with an incoming text. I'm expecting it to be from Tristan or Jane, but it's a text from Lacy, my neighbor in Naples.

> LACY
>
> Hey. I know you're in Sunset Harbor, but I wanted to give you a head's up that there are a few people outside your house here. With cameras. I'm guessing they're reporters of some kind. Is everything okay?

Before I even finish reading the first message, another text comes in from her.

LACY

Keith is outside asking.

Yep. They're reporters.

Oh my gosh! Are you Sunny Palmer? Because
that's what Keith said they're claiming.

I throw the sheet off and hurry from the room, texting a
quick response back to Lacy that I'm okay and I'll explain everything soon.

"Morning." Tala's in her bathrobe, sitting at the kitchen table
with a mug of tea and a piece of toast while Serenity and Jack
watch cartoons in the family room. "Can I get you something to
eat?"

"Look at this," I say, handing my phone to Tala so she can
read the text exchange. "There are reporters at my house
already."

Her gaze skims over the messages, her eyes widening. "But
the announcement hasn't gone out yet, has it?"

"It has to be someone from book club." Or, more particularly, Bridget, because who else would it be? She probably wants
to preempt the announcement to get her sob story out first. And
the truth is, I don't even blame her. "How else would it spread
so quickly?"

The back door opens, and Heath and Tristan step in. They're
both wearing running clothes, sweat is glistening on their skin,
and their breathing is labored.

"How was the run?" Tala asks, tightening her robe.

Heath holds up a finger, leaning over to catch his breath.

Tristan's gaze falls on me, his chest raising and falling in
rapid succession. "There are people outside."

"What do you mean?"

"Reporters," Heath gets out. "Several of them. That's why
we came in through the back."

I hurry to the front window, the others following me, and

sure enough, over half a dozen people with cameras hanging around their necks and a man setting up a large video camera onto a tripod are lining the sidewalk. I close the blinds all the way. "Are they allowed to be here?"

"I'm not sure." Tala says.

"Beau will know." Tristan pulls out his phone. "He's in Miami for a few days, but I'll call and ask. I'll be right back." He disappears into the kitchen, the soft hum of his words barely distinguishable over my rushing thoughts.

Heath's chest is still heaving up and down when he steps next to me. "Pretty cool, huh? You're going to be famous."

I lift my palms to the ceiling in a you-have-to-be-kidding-me motion. "Yeah, famous for being the woman that wrote a fictional relationship involving real-life people. One in particular whose name I was dumb enough not to change." And who most likely already went to the media with her side of the story.

"Stop," Tala says, pinning me with a look. "For the most part, people are going to find the whole thing endearing." She leans in, lowering her voice. "Especially because you and Tristan ended up together."

I gesture to the reporters outside, matching her hushed tone. "Unless this is the reality check that forces him to realize he wants nothing to do with any of this."

"Yeah right," Heath laughs, but thankfully he also lowers his voice. "That guy's so head over heels for you it even makes me uncomfortable."

Despite that my life seems to be unraveling at the edges in this exact moment, I can't stop my smile. "I'm not sure you're a reputable source."

"No, I'm serious, Capri. It's disgusting how in love he is. He's like a love-struck little puppy."

Tala nudges her elbow into him. "Takes one to know one."

"Exactly." Heath reaches out and grabs Tala, pulling her toward his sweat-drenched body while she attempts to push him away, but her laughing doesn't help, and he plants a big kiss on her.

"Go shower," she says, swatting at him. "You're all sweaty and you smell awful."

"According to your romances, women go feral for this musky smell." He holds out his saturated shirt and takes a whiff. "Raw manliness."

Tala shakes her head. "This"—she pinches his shirt between two fingers, her arm straight, and she leans away from him as though repulsed—"is not that."

Footsteps echo in the hallway before Tristan reemerges, and he glances at each of our amused expressions. "What'd I miss?"

"Tala was just appreciating my *musky* scent." Heath slings an arm around her shoulder. "She can't get enough of it."

"Clearly," Tala says, dryly, turning her head away from him. "So what did Beau say?"

Tristan's gaze settles on me, and I can tell he isn't thrilled by the news. "Basically, that as long as they remain on public property, in this case the sidewalk, and don't heckle or harass anyone, they're allowed to be here."

Tala lets out a breath. "Maybe I should send Heath out there to see if he can get a few to heckle him."

We all laugh, but Heath nods his head. "You know I'm game."

Tristan moves to where I'm standing, and it's only then I realize I'm still in pajamas with no makeup on and my hair in a falling-out pile on top of my head. "Good morning, by the way," he says, leaning down for a kiss.

I offer him my cheek so I don't kill him with my morning breath. I have enough working against me right now with the whole reporters-standing-outside-our-door. I don't need anything else to weaken his desire to be with me.

"Too musky for you?" he asks with a laugh.

I wrap my arms around him, inhaling his wonderful, salty,

sweaty self. "No, I just need to brush my teeth. And I should probably go get ready."

He pulls me closer. "No way. You look absolutely gorgeous."

"See," Heath says, pointing at Tristan. "Love is blind."

My lips part in feigned offense. "Is that how you're going to treat me after we babysat your kids for you Friday night?" I'm glad Heath's here to lighten the heaviness of the moment, even if he just playfully mentioned that Tristan loves me in front of him.

"You look beautiful," he says, and once again, he's the ten-year-old little boy being forced to apologize.

"That's what I thought." My phone buzzes in my hand, and I look down at it. "It's Maven." I click accept, and with how intently everyone's watching me, I put it on speaker so they can all hear. "Hey, Maven!"

"Capri, I'm not sure if you're aware yet or not, but your name was leaked on social media. Your actual name—Capri Collins."

"Yeah, we figured as much. We have a few reporters outside, and my neighbor texted to say there are reporters at my house in Naples."

"I worried that might be the case. I've been bombarded with calls and emails all morning asking if I can verify the source. Which I haven't done since I wanted to talk to you first. I did try to call you several times earlier, but it went directly to voicemail."

"I'm sorry. My phone was on airplane mode."

"Honestly, it's fine. It gave me time to figure out exactly what we're dealing with, and I managed to find the original post—"

"Do you know who posted it?" I ask, nervous for my assumption to be confirmed.

"Yeah ... a Kathy Lance."

I stare at the phone. "Kathy Lance?" I repeat, positive I've never heard that name.

"Sandra's sister," Tala whispers. "She was there last night."

I give a slow nod, trying to make sense of the fact that it wasn't Bridget. How many times can I make her out to be the villain before I learn my lesson? I mean, she did call me out in front of a roomful of people, but honestly, who wouldn't have? Especially after seeing their name as the antagonist in a fictionalized story with their ex as the love interest. A *New York Times* best-selling story at that. Again, the reminder gives me that uncomfortable feeling as if my insides are itching.

"Yeah, apparently, she posted about it in a private Facebook group for local librarians last night around nine. The original post seems innocent enough. It's a picture of her holding up a copy of *Secret Crush,* and the caption reads: Best night ever for this Sunny Palmer fan. I got to meet her! And can I just say, her real-life story is better than fiction. As is the man who inspired Trenton. *fire emoji* I can't say more since she hasn't revealed her identity to the public yet, but it's coming. So get excited!"

"So how did someone figure it out from that? It doesn't seem like that much to go on."

"I'm not exactly sure. Even with the GPS settings on the pictures, which pull up Seaside Oasis, it must have taken quite a bit of sleuthing. But one of the group members—a Lilah York?—seemed to be the one to do it. She copied and pasted the original post along with her conclusions, and it spread from there."

I exhale a long, slow breath, staring at the phone in my hand. "Do we change our course now?"

"I don't think so. We're fortunate since the leaks aren't malicious in intent. If we release our own announcement to verify your identity, we can start to paint the narrative before someone else does."

"And how does one paint a narrative?" I ask hesitantly.

"Kind of what we discussed last night. Interviews—lots of interviews, especially at first—social media videos where you introduce yourself and talk about your story. You need to explain why you've decided to share your identity with the world now after remaining anonymous for so long. Stuff like that. Be open and authentic. And it wouldn't hurt to have … Tristan is the name of the guy you used for Trenton's inspiration, right? The one you're dating now?"

I glance at him, my cheeks heating. "Yeah."

"Well, readers are going to go ballistic when they realize the two of you are together in real life, so if you could get him on board, it'd be great to utilize the relationship as much as you're both comfortable with." With Bridget's accusation still fresh in my mind—that I'm using Tristan to advance my career—I inwardly cringe at Maven's word choice. I'm not in this relationship to *utilize* it to my advantage. Not even a little bit.

"Let me talk to him and I'll get back to you." I don't look at Tristan, because I don't want him to feel pressured to agree to anything. Honestly, I'm not even sure how I feel about it. I'm just getting used to having him to myself. I don't know if I'm ready to share him with the world.

"One last thing. I know you're not going to like this, like at all, but I really, really think an impromptu book tour for this upcoming release could be huge. And I don't just mean success-wise, though that's a given, but it'll be a way for you to get in front of your readers and connect. Many of them have been waiting years to meet you. If I can be so bold, this is an important moment to step out of your comfort zone and let them get to know the real Sunny Palmer. For you to get to know them in return."

"Isn't it too late for something like that?" I ask, hoping she's neglected to consider the logistics. "My release is in a couple of weeks."

"Not for Sunny Palmer. In fact, I've been brainstorming some different venues we could potentially use, so please, think about it."

"I will. And I'll call you right back."

"Am I good to post the announcement in the meantime?"

My stomach balls in a clenching, uncomfortable mass. "Yeah. Go ahead."

"Sounds good. I'll be in touch."

I hang up the phone, attempting not to panic. The whole world will soon know that I'm Sunny Palmer. "So ..."

"Heath and I are going to go get Lucas up and let the two of you have some time to talk things through," Tala says. "But can I just say, really quick, that I think you should do it. All of it. The book tour, the videos, everything Maven said. You'll be amazing, Capri. And before you say no, I'm just going to put it out there that I can come along as your emotional support human if you need me to. I'll have to bring Lucas, but I'm sure Heath wouldn't mind, especially once the kids are back in school." Tala glances at her husband, nodding her head in encouragement. "Would you, honey?"

Heath looks as though he needs a little more convincing. "Tell me how good I smell."

"How about instead, we go get you in a shower?"

"We, huh?" Heath gives a victorious smile. "I like the sound of that."

"That's not what I meant," Tala says, pulling him from the room. "We'll be upstairs if you need us."

"Yes, *we* will," Heath calls over his shoulder.

I'm covering my growing smile. "I'd apologize, but if you're going to be sticking around, you'll have to get used to them. They're gross."

"*If* I'm sticking around?" Tristan's brow is lifted. "Are you doubting me again, Capri Sun?"

"No." I set my hand on his bearded jawline. "It's just we

haven't been dating very long, and I don't want you to feel pressured into any of this. It's a lot."

Tristan's eyes narrow, but his mouth twitches at the corners. "Are you going to force me to take time to consider it? Because I already know my answer."

I pin him with a look, knowing exactly what he's going to say. This is so Tristan of him. "You don't have to do this. Any of it."

"What if I want to? What if I can't think of anything I want more than to be at your side through all of this? The world needs to see you, Capri. And I want to be there when they do. I want to be holding your hand and calming you down and telling you that you're enough and that they'll love you exactly as you are. That even when you can't see it, they'll be falling in love with you. Like I am."

Emotion wells in my throat and my heart is pounding. "You're falling in love with me?"

Tristan draws closer and his hands settle on my waist. "I've—"

A thump nearby draws both of our attention, but before I can even process what it could have been, I hear Heath's voice. "What? There was a bug." The sound is muted, but it's not because it's far away. He's whispering from somewhere much closer—like the other side of the wall.

"Heath," Tala hisses. "Are you kidding me? Right now?"

"What was I supposed to do?" he whispers.

"You do know we can hear you, right?" I say, loudly enough to stop their whispered conversation.

When Tala peeks around the corner, her face is bright red and she's wearing an apologetic expression. "I'm so sorry."

"She's only sorry because we got caught," Heath pops his head around the corner. "But it's fine because now I can give you this." He tosses something at us, and I flinch away from it thinking it's the bug he apparently squashed, but Tristan catches whatever it is in the palm of his hand, looks down at it, and glances back at Heath with an uncertain expression. "It's for her," Heath says, pointing to me.

"What is it?" I ask warily, and Tristan opens his hand to reveal a stick of gum. I glare at Heath.

"Oh, come on." Heath gestures to Tristan. "That man deserves a minty-fresh kiss after a declaration like that."

I actually more than agree, though I have no intention of telling Heath that, so I take the gum and pop it in my mouth. "There. Now will you go away so we can kiss in private?"

"Okay. Okay." He lifts his hands, his palms to us. "Just trying to make sure you don't leave a bad taste in Tristan's mouth."

"Oh my gosh, Heath!" Tala somehow turns a brighter shade of red.

"No. It's a play on words. Bad taste in the mouth ..." Heath points at me. "She's an author, she gets is. Don't you, Capri?" I don't answer, but he just grins.

Tristan's laughter is not the least bit helpful to my maintaining a straight face. "We shouldn't be encouraging him," I say. "He's like a stray cat. If you laugh at his jokes once, he never stops coming back." I gesture to him with my hand. "Case in point."

"Ouch." He throws a hand over his heart. "Capri, you wound me."

It's no use. His dramatized delivery finally does me in, and my smiles breaks free. Though I throw in an eye-roll and a shake of my head for good measure.

Tala grabs his arm. "I'll make sure we get all the way upstairs this time."

When both sets of footsteps can be heard on the stairs, I turn back to Tristan, still smiling at Heath's ridiculousness. "So, back to this falling in love comment. How close are we talking?"

Tristan pulls me to him with his strong arms. "Like, as soon as I'm done kissing you, you should call Maven back and tell her

I'm in. And then we should probably go outside and talk to those reporters together."

I lift onto my toes and press my lips against his briefly before pulling just out of reach again. "That does kind of sound like you love me."

"You know what else might make it sound like I love you?"

"What's that?"

"My family's decided not to sell Seaside Oasis."

The smile drops from my lips, and I'm searching his sea-green eyes. I don't allow myself to hope just yet. "I thought the sale already went through?"

"The paperwork was all signed, but thankfully, there's a 72-hour cooling-off rule that allows both sellers and buyers some wiggle room to change their minds. After speaking with my dad yesterday, he contacted our buyers. He explained we'll still sell the other three centers, but that it took his son almost losing the inheritance he was handed to realize it's actually exactly what he wants." Tristan's gaze softens. "This is the life I choose."

I can't suppress my smile. "But what about the assistant coaching position?"

"I called to tell them I couldn't take it." He tucks a piece of hair behind my ear. "I'd still love to try coaching, but I'm thinking I'll start with something local I can do on the side. Jack was saying he wants to play pee-wee football this fall. Maybe I'll see if his team needs a coach."

I'm biting at my lip to keep myself from giggling in delight.

"I hope you didn't have your heart set on California too much."

"My heart is way too preoccupied with you to be set on anything else. Besides, this is *our* home."

He smiles. "That's exactly what I was hoping you'd say." The back of his fingers brush downward along my jaw, pausing on my chin. Then his thumb settles on my lip.

I close my eyes, relishing the sensation, when my phone dings in my hand. We both glance at the screen and read Maven's incoming text, then our eyes meet.

"Well, it's official," I say, trying to breathe through the constricting feeling in my chest. "The world now knows that I'm Sunny Palmer."

"What's *official* is that the world's about to fall in love with Capri Collins. Because you make it exceptionally effortless."

I grin up at him, allowing his reassurance to calm me. "So you do love me?"

"I love you, Capri Sun."

I slide my arm around his neck. "That's good. Because I kind of love you too."

Tristan shakes his head, smiling. But before he can comment on my very apparent understatement, I lift onto my toes and give him the most minty-fresh kiss of his life.

CHAPTER 29

SEVERAL MONTHS LATER

I PULL my Jeep into a spot in the parking garage and glance over at Jane, who looks as excited to be home as I am. After a week away, it feels good to be back on the island. Almost, anyway. A short boat ride away.

Over the past several months, I've been all over the country doing signings and interviews and even speaking at a few conferences. It's been so incredibly fulfilling and so insanely exhausting. Thankfully, Maven's kept my schedule doable with a lot of recouping time between tours and enough downtime while on them to restore my introverted battery. Meeting my readers has been more rewarding than I could ever have imagined, and I keep thinking what a waste of energy it was to spend years worrying about letting them down. Go figure. They are kind and gracious and encouraging and have filled a part of me as an author that I didn't even know needed to be filled.

Did I say stupid things in front of hundreds of people? More times than I can count. Did I have a floodgate cry on two separate occasions in front of a similar number of people? Absolutely I did. Do I regret any of it? Not a minute.

And the fact that I got to have my people with me throughout the experience made it all the better. Between Tala, Jane, and my mom (once she got home from Europe) taking the longer distance trips, and Tristan joining me wherever he could manage, I often had someone in my corner. Even Grandma, Heath, Walker, and Stan made it to a few events. As did Joy and Mark. And for the first time in my life, I feel as though I'm being seen. By my family. By my community. By my readers.

"I'm still reeling that *Secret Crush* is going to be a movie," Jane says, her bright eyes settling on me. "And that Presley James is going to play Cali! She's going to be perfect."

Jane and I give dreamy sighs in unison.

"She really is," I say. "And I hope it'll be the comeback role for her that all the magazines are claiming it will be."

"I'm positive it will be. It hasn't even been filmed yet, and it's already the most anticipated upcoming movie release." I'm not sure where Jane gets her information, but I don't say anything. "And the fact that Presley James literally spent all summer hiding out on Sunset Harbor means she's totally going to nail the part."

Suddenly overwhelmed by how grateful I am for Jane, I reach across the middle console and grab her hand. "Thanks again for coming with me."

"Are you kidding? It was the best week ever! I loved every moment. Meeting more of my fellow Sunny Palmer fans, all the incredible food, and watching you step into the role I always knew you could fill. You're amazing, Capri."

"You're amazing. I'll forever be grateful that you forced me to publish my first book all those years ago. And even more so, that you came and introduced yourself to the quiet, awkward new girl in seventh grade."

"Best friends ever since," she says.

"And with the way things are going between you and Walker, maybe we'll be sisters soon."

The smile she gives me is so brilliant and full of excitement that tears prick my eyes. "It does feel right, doesn't it?"

"It probably is the reason you fell in love with my brother."

"Oh, definitely."

We laugh until a loud bang on her window makes us both scream. Walker's laughing face pops up on the outside of the window.

"Sheesh," Jane says, opening the door with that same bright smile. "Talk about a welcome."

"I'm guessing you'd prefer this?" Walker grabs her face and kisses her in a way that has me opening my own door to flee. After an exceptionally wild ride, the Summer of Jane Hayes was obviously a complete success, at least in the end. But if I'm being honest, I'm still getting used to the idea of Walker and Jane together. Not because I don't absolutely love it, because I do—in theory. It's just a little weird to have my best friend and my brother kissing every time I turn around. And sometimes when I'm just sitting there minding my own business. But I'm sure they feel the same way about me and Tristan.

I grab my luggage and Jane's from the trunk, poking my head around the corner to see if the two of them are finished yet. They're not, but because I'm eager to see Tristan and he should be getting off work soon, I can't help myself. "There will be time for that later," I say, offering Walker a bright smile when he glances over at me.

Walker smirks. "What's the hurry, Capri? Excited to see someone?"

I shrug. "I have no idea who you're talking about."

"I'll try not to be offended by that." Tristan's voice comes from behind me, and I spin around to find that glorious smile of his aimed right at me.

"What are you doing here?" I ask, jumping on him and wrapping my legs around his waist before kissing him a week-away-level kind of kiss that prevents him from answering.

When Walker grumbles something under his breath, I drop down and shoot him a smile. "You're one to talk."

"I'm well aware of the hypocrisy, but still …"

I ignore him and turn back to Tristan. "I thought you had a meeting and then football practice."

He pulls me into his arms. "Turns out if you know the right people, you can reschedule both a meeting and practice to pick up your girlfriend who's been gone for way too long."

"Aw. Remind me to thank *those people* later."

"Oh, I will definitely be reminding you."

"Okay, you two." Walker steps next to me. "I don't need any other images of you guys stuck in my head."

"I think it's sweet," Jane says, placing a kiss on his cheek that instantly makes him look as smitten as the rest of us.

Tristan grabs my luggage while Walker grabs Jane's, and the four of us head to the docks. After Tristan helps me onto his boat, he walks over to Jane's boat where she and Walker are, and he hands Walker my luggage. He says something I can't hear, and Jane's gaze flicks to me before she nods.

"What was that about?" I ask when he steps into the boat and starts his engine.

"What was what about?" he asks, his slight smile making it obvious he knows exactly what I'm talking about.

"Why did you give them my luggage?"

"Oh, they're headed to Tala and Heath's and said they'd drop it off for us."

"And where are we headed?"

"You'll see."

I watch for manatees as we move across the bay, but when Tristan gets to open ocean, I move onto his lap. It's my new favorite seat with the way Tristan's arm is wrapped tightly around me as we fly over the water. After several minutes, he slows the boat, then stops it, cutting the motor.

I glance around, but besides the shoreline in the distance, there's nothing but ocean and sky. The sun is dipping into the horizon, causing an array of pinks and oranges, purples and blues, and it reminds me of that time over ten years ago when

Tristan brought me out on his boat at sunset. The evening of The Incident and the night I decided to start writing my first book. It was that experience—the fictionalized version I created in my head of it, anyway—that acted as inspiration for the scene in *Secret Crush* when Trenton proposes to Cali. A book Tristan has read. Suddenly, my heart is pounding and my mind is reeling with how this could potentially play out. But I quiet my thoughts, wanting to live in this moment.

"I have something for you," Tristan says, and I force myself to take a deep, calming breath.

"What's that?"

"Let me get it."

I stand up, and he grabs a rectangular package in brown paper wrapping out of the dashboard compartment on the passenger side. He takes a seat in the front and gestures for me to sit by him. When I do, he hands me the present. "What's this for?"

"Open it."

My hands have a slight tremble, but I run my fingers along the taped edge to undo the wrapping. When I see what's inside, I glance up. "*Secret Crush?*" I ask, not quite understanding why he'd gift me a copy of my own book.

"Just open it," he says again, his smile widening.

I pull the book out and flip the first page open. On the dedication page, in Tristan's writing, it has his name written out above my dedication with a caret pointing to it: *To (Tristan Palmer) the protagonist of my love story, thanks for the inspiration.*

"The prize from our competition?" I ask, still completely lost.

"Keep reading."

I turn the page to the prologue, and in the first paragraph next to the description of young Cali watching her neighbor, Trenton, fish off his back dock, it says: *I saw you in the tree. I knew you were there the whole time, but I was too nervous to come talk to you.*

My gaze lifts to his. "You knew I was there?"

Tristan's eyes twinkle and he nods. "You were wearing that striped navy-blue jumper, and your mom had done your hair in two long braids tied with bright pink ribbons."

"I can't believe you remember that." I didn't even remember until he brought it up. "The ribbons were our compromise. I hated that jumper, but my mom loved it, so she'd let me pick out my ribbons when I wore it. They never matched, but I didn't care."

I flip the next page, reading each of the little notes Tristan inserted, and with each word I read, the size of my smile increases until I'm not sure it can grow any larger. It's painfully big. The details he's included make it apparent that Tristan always saw me. My greedy eyes want to take in every note and personal message, but to read and truly appreciate them all will take hours. Probably longer. But I fully intend to do just that once I'm back at Tala's. I close the book and look at him. "I can't believe you annotated my book."

"Is that what it's called?"

"Yeah. And I can't wait to read every last comment."

"It gave me something to do while you were gone. And it was shocking how much I remembered. How a lot of the things you wrote about in your book are actually shared memories between us. Especially the flashbacks."

"Like the time the neighborhood kids convinced us to play spin the bottle, and when it was your turn, it landed on me?"

"And how you literally ran away, crushing my young-boy heart."

I laugh. "That's not true. You wanted it to land on Cat Keene. I remember Beau saying so."

"Beau said that because he wanted his spin to land on Cat. I was secretly hoping mine would land on you. Not that it paid off for me when it did."

"You should have stuck with Cat if you were wanting a kiss."

"There are lots of things I regret, but that's not one of them." Tristan takes the book from me and sets it on the seat before pulling me to my feet and wrapping a hand around my waist to steady me against the slight rocking of the boat. "Do you know what I regret more than anything?"

I shake my head, hardly able to think with the way I'm getting lost in his sea-green eyes.

"Not kissing you that day I took you out on my boat to watch the sunset."

"You weren't going to kiss me."

"Oh, I very much was."

I still, meeting his gaze straight on. "Then why didn't you?"

"Because Bridget and I had just broken up, and I didn't want you to think that was the reason I'd kiss you—that you were some rebound for me. Then there was the fact that I was leaving for college. I knew I didn't want to do anything that might hurt you, so despite how much I wanted to, I resisted." He runs his fingers through my hair, his fingertips grazing my neck as he lowers them. "I can't tell you how many times I've thought about that boat ride. Wondering what would have changed if I'd just kissed you. What path my life would have taken. So when I saw you on Sunset Harbor at the beginning of summer, my excuses of why I hadn't reached out completely vanished. All I knew was I couldn't miss the chance for a do-over. To have this moment again and get it right this time."

The sky is ablaze around us, but I can't pull my eyes from Tristan to admire it. My heart thumps in my chest, a hopeful, anticipatory rhythm.

"Capri Palmer," Tristan says slowly, intentionally, as though he's trying out the name on his tongue to see how he likes it, and I still. He gives a slow nod, his lips curving into a smile. "It has a nice ring to it. No wonder you spent so much time practicing that signature in those notebooks of yours. And while in some respects, you have your own claim to Palmer now, I want to officially give you my name."

And then suddenly, Tristan is down on one knee, pulling a ring from his pocket. The most perfect ring I've ever seen—a circular yellow diamond surrounded by a halo of smaller diamonds. It resembles a sun. "I love you, Capri. I'm pretty sure I've loved you for most of my life even if it took me until this past summer to realize it. But now that I have, I know this is what I want. This is the life I want. I feel it with my whole soul. Will you marry me?"

I can't find the words, but I'm nodding my head in excess so he knows my answer. A swell of waves sends the boat swaying, so to prevent my trembling self from spending the night with a concussion or missing even one glorious second of this, I sit on the bench behind me.

When he slides the ring on my finger, I pause, creating a mental image of this moment to store away for the rest of my life. To replay time and time again. Then suddenly, it's as if the emotions from a lifetime of loving Tristan seem to culminate. I let out a half laugh, half sob. With tears streaming down my face, I kiss him as though he's my reason for everything. For being the man that has always seen me. The man that made me brave enough to be seen. The man that chooses me now and for always. And, just like so many of the moments I've had with Tristan these past several months, I'm fully aware that this one is better than anything my imagination could ever create.

IT'S dark by the time we pull up to the dock. Tristan helps me out of the boat. "I have one more little surprise for you," he says, leading me toward his and Beau's place.

"And what's that?" I ask, already knowing his answer. Or, more accurately, his lack of an answer.

"You'll see." Oh, Tristan and his surprises. I don't think I'll ever grow tired of them. He opens the back door, and there, filling his kitchen, are the faces of all of my favorite people. He lifts my hand up for them to see. "She said yes!"

Cheers erupt, and I'm being hugged by my mom, whose eyes are filled with tears just like mine, and Tala and Jane. Then Grandma is pressing kisses against my cheek.

"We are so thrilled for you both," Joy says, wrapping me in one of her famous hugs. Then Serenity and Jack's little arms are around my waist.

Once the delighted squeals and excitement over the gorgeous ring die down a little, I make my way toward the rest of the group, getting a congratulatory hug from Walker, Heath, and Stan, then Beau and Mark.

"Are you sure about this guy?" Beau asks, flicking his head in Tristan's direction. Tristan's taking baby Lucas from Heath and making my heart melt all over again.

"Yeah," I say, unable to restrain my smile. "I've been sure about that guy for a very long time."

"Okay, then." Beau nods, a huge grin on his face. "I have another question I've been meaning to ask you. In Secret Crush, the extremely attractive, exceptionally charming brother of Trenton—that's me, right?"

Beau's read my book?

Mark laughs. "You mean the trouble-making brother?"

Apparently, reading my book has become a family affair, and the thought makes me squirm and turns my cheeks pink. And also makes my heart happy.

Beau does a forward circular motion with his hand. "Yes, but he, most importantly, is extremely attractive and exceptionally charming."

"That was definitely what I was going for with him," I say, sending Mark a knowing smile.

"It was pretty obvious," Beau says with a wink. "But I'm glad we had this conversation for clarification purposes. I've also been thinking that he seems like a worthy leading man for a future story." He gives a casual shrug. "That is, if you were looking for your next book idea."

I give a thoughtful hum. "I'll have to keep that in mind. Once I finish Bridget's story."

"Bridget's getting a story?" Beau asks, sharing a look with Mark.

"She deserves a redemption." And honestly, it's part of my own redemption arc. It can't make up for what I did, but I hope it's a step in the right direction.

Mark sets a hand on my arm. "You're a real special woman, Capri."

"It's true," Beau says. "How Tristan ever caught your eye is beyond me."

We all spend the next hour together, laughing and chatting and eating the yummy food people brought, before everyone starts to head out. After a farewell hug from each of the Palmers, Tristan walks his family to the door.

"We're going to head out too," Jane says with a mischievous glint in her eye. "Give you and Tristan a little time alone to celebrate."

"Did you need to say it like that?" Walker asks with a huff.

"Absolutely." Jane hugs me, the two of us lingering in shared excitement, then Walker pulls me in for a hug. There's no stiffness to it this time. It's natural and sweet and makes my sisterly heart squeeze with joy.

"I'm happy for you, Capri," he says, a grin pulling onto his lips. "Tristan's an okay guy."

I laugh. "You're a pretty okay-ish guy yourself."

He smiles, his gaze sliding to Jane. "Did you hear that? That's a real solid endorsement right there."

Jane laughs. "I definitely heard it."

The two of them head to the front door, and Jack and Serenity step into the spots they vacated. "Are we still going to go to your house like you promised?" Jack asks. "To do the arcade and go bowling?"

"And get an ice cream?" Serenity adds.

I lean down, glancing between them. "Absolutely. I'll talk to your mom about when your next school break is, and we'll make it happen."

They share a smile. Then, apparently appeased with my answer, Jack strolls away.

Serenity's still looking up at me. "When are you and Tristan getting married?"

"I'm not sure. We haven't talked about it yet."

"Well, when you do, can I be your flower girl? I've wanted to be a flower girl since I was little."

I pull her in for a hug, smiling to myself at her *lifelong* dream. But then I think about my own lifelong dream I had at her age— the one where I'd grow up and marry Tristan—and I'm suddenly in awe that young Capri's dream came true. "Of course you'll be my flower girl," I say, because who am I to deny a little girl her dream?

She stays in my embrace but cranes her neck up to see me. "And Jack should be the one who carries the rings down the aisle."

"Serenity," Tala says, stepping up next to us. "Stop hounding Auntie Capri. She literally just got engaged." Her gaze lifts to me. "It's all she's been able to talk about since Tristan told us he was going to propose."

"My own family keeping secrets from me," I say with a smile.

"Tell me about it." Tala pins me with a mock glare. "But ours was only for a couple of weeks. Jane and I went ring shopping with him while you and Mom were in California for your tour at the beginning of the month. Not that we did anything because the moment he saw your ring, he was sold." She grabs my hand, lifting the ring up to get a closer look, and the diamonds sparkle in the light. "It's perfect, isn't it?"

"It really is."

"Did you have any idea he was going to propose?"

"Not until we got on his boat and he said we were going for a ride. And even then, I didn't think ... I more hoped."

"What did you hope?" Tristan slides his arms around my waist, nuzzling his chin into me and tickling my neck with his beard.

"That you'd finally stop being stingy with your last name and share it with me."

Tristan's fingers tighten on my stomach, and I let out a squeal that makes Serenity giggle.

Tala looks between us, doing a subpar job at hiding her amusement. "I think we'd better go get these kids to bed." She steers Serenity by her shoulders toward the back door. "Heath, are you ready to go?"

Heath and Stan glance in our direction. "Yeah," they say in unison, standing up from the table where they've been chatting about European infrastructure or something along those lines. "Faye and I can take Grandma back to Seaside Oasis on our way," Stan says, helping Grandma up from her chair.

Mom's rocking a sleeping Lucas but comes to give me one more kiss on my cheek. "Congratulations, you two. You can't possibly know how thrilled we all are for you. When you were young, Joy and I used to tease about the two of you growing up and getting married. And now here we are."

Tristan and I share a smile.

"But we'll let the two of you have a quiet moment together." Her gaze settles on Tristan. "Thanks for letting us celebrate with you."

"We wouldn't have it any other way."

"Oh, and Heath," I say, catching his attention. "I'm only going to say this once and then pretend it never happened, but thanks for your help. You and Tala both."

Heath grins, glancing around at the few people still standing here. "You're all witness to that. Capri is grateful for my meddling." His gaze returns to me. "So grateful that she's probably going to name a character in her next book after me."

"There's a slight possibility," I say, not yet informing him I already named the hero's debonair friend and comedic relief in my next book after him. I don't want to inflate his ego before it's absolutely necessary.

He gives a victorious fist pump. "That's what I'm talking about."

Tristan and I walk the group to the back door, and once they exit, Heath turns toward us, taking a few backward steps. "You two behave yourselves now. I'll be expecting Capri back by midnight." He points at Tristan. "Don't make me come get her."

"Heath, you're ridiculous," Tala says, tugging on Heath and sending us her customary apologetic smile. "We'll leave the door unlocked, Capri. And I'll keep Heath entertained so you don't have to worry about him."

Heath wraps an arm around Tala. "That's what I like to hear. Taking one for the team."

"I meant I'd turn on a movie for us," Tala says, throwing him a playful look.

"Don't play coy," Grandma says. "We all know exactly what you meant, you little minx."

The whole group laughs, including a blushing Tala.

When they head inside, I close the door and turn to face Tristan. His warm gaze is on me, and I can't help but go directly into his arms. "I loved the surprise of celebrating with our families," I say with a timid smile. "Thanks for planning it."

"Oh, that wasn't the surprise," Tristan says, taking my hand in his. "This is."

He leads me from the kitchen, down the hallway, and up the stairs. The Palmer's layout is a near replica to Tala's house, and when we climb the stairs, Tristan stops me. "This is the surprise."

I glance around, again not exactly sure what I'm supposed to be looking at, when my gaze falls on a framed gallery wall that wasn't there before. I step closer, studying the picture in the frame closest to me. It's of me and Tristan at the lighthouse. And the one next to it is us with the kayak, my frown and lowered shoulders making me smile. And there's one with our robes and my gigantic smile at the spa. And on Winn Island. And watching fireworks on the Fourth. But as I continue to look at the pictures, not all of them are of the two of us.

"Where did you get these?" I ask, my hand settling on a picture of Beau, Walker, Jane, Tristan, and me when we were still in middle school, eating popsicles on the back porch together. Another one at a neighborhood BBQ where I'm sandwiched between Beau and Tristan, a bashful smile on my face and my body awkwardly stiff. And Grandpa, Dad, and me sitting on the back dock with our feet dangling in the water. The classic photo of Tala, Walker, and me with our Fourth of July sparklers that hung on my grandma's wall for years. Along with the fishing one. One of the Palmer family at the beach. And a picture of young Beau and Tristan with their arms slung around each other and gaps of missing teeth in their big smiles.

"Gathering the pictures was a team effort between Tala, our moms, and your grandma, then I had them printed out and framed." He glances over the gallery wall, a satisfied smile on his lips. "Tala also hung them up because it was proving a lot harder than I was thinking it'd be."

Tears prick my eyes. "You did this for me?"

"That day we saw the manatees, you said you weren't sure

where you belonged anymore. That your memories of your life on Sunset Harbor were either fading away or packed in boxes." Tristan runs his hands down my arms, causing a shiver to move through me. "So, I decided to unpack your old memories and display the new ones along with them. Because this is where you belong, Capri. With me. On *our* little island."

I cover my mouth with my hand, glancing at the wall again, and I'm certain my heart is on the brink of exploding. I've never felt so understood. And loved. And cherished. But emotion is choking out all the words I want to say, so instead, I throw my arms around him and kiss him like he deserves to be kissed.

After several glorious minutes, I pull back. My gaze falls on the pictures again, and I still can't believe Tristan made a gallery wall of us. "How does Beau feel about this montage being here?"

"You would be thinking about Beau right now."

I laugh. "I just can't help myself."

Tristan chuckles. "I bought out Beau's interest in the house. He moved out this last week."

I stare at him. "Where's he going?"

"He's making plans of his own."

"So the house is yours?"

"It's ours, Capri. If this is where you want to be. If it's not, we can rent it and figure the rest out."

My smile is so big I'm certain I've stretched it to a new limit. "This is exactly where I want to be. And you're exactly who I want to be here with."

"Good. Because it turns out all of my best memories on this island are with you. And I can't wait to keep making more."

WELCOME TO
SUNSET HARBOR

BELACOURT RESORT

GOLF COURSE

NOAH'S HOUSE

JANE'S HOUSE

NATURE PRESERVE

DAX'S DUPLEX

SEASIDE OASIS RETIREMENT HOME

SUNSET REPAIRS

PHOENIX'S OFFICE

CITY OFFICES

SUNRISE CAFE

SCOOPS AHOY ICE CREAM

KEENE B&B

GULF OF MEXICO

TOWN SQUARE

BAKERY

BRIGGS'S APARTMENT

THE BOOK ISLE

CUTS AND CURLS

TRISTAN & BEAU'S HOUSE

CAPRI'S HOUSE

GEMMA'S HOUSE

HOLLAND'S HOUSE

BEACH BREAK BAR & GRILL

PUBLIC BEACH

N
W   E
S

EPILOGUE

ONE YEAR LATER

I'M SITTING inside a back room at The Book Isle with Tristan in the chair beside me, his arm casually draped behind me and his other hand reaching across his body to hold mine, as we listen to dear Mrs. McMannus explain how things are going to work for the book signing tonight. It's for my upcoming release, *Along for the Tide*, which is a sequel to *Secret Crush*. Tristan and I dropped off a copy at Bridget's parents' house a few days ago with an apology letter tucked inside. They said they'd be willing to get it to her and even congratulated us on getting married before we left.

Mrs. McMannus's graying hair is short and styled around her face in curls, and her light eyes sparkle as she talks with animated gestures. "Tickets sold out so quickly that we decided to move it to the town square to accommodate more people." Mrs. McMannus's round cheeks lift, and she looks near giddy with excitement. "And that sold out too. Not that I'm surprised considering you're doing an early release for us. It has put our online sales through the roof." She glances down at my ink-stained hand. "But I'm sure you're well aware with how many books you already had to sign this week."

Tristan's thumb rubs along the outside of my palm, and it makes my hand tingle all the way up into my arm. "I'm so happy to hear that," I say. "Thanks for setting this whole thing up."

"Of course! We all absolutely love you. Our own Sunset Harbor celebrity." She gives a little laugh. "Well, we have a few of those, don't we?"

Most locals would assume she's referring to Noah and the Belacourt clan, though I suspect she's talking about Presley James—America's darling—who is not only starring in *Secret Crush* (I can hardly believe the movie's premiere is next month!), but was rumored to have spent quite a bit of time at The Book Isle while she was hiding out on the island. Whether Mrs. McMannus's son running the bookshop had anything to do with her frequent visits, is up for debate. But my writer's brain is keen to assume that behind the rumors is a really great story worth knowing.

Mrs. McMannus glances at her watch and lets out a little gasp. "Oh, I'd better go get this thing started. Once I welcome everyone and we explain the raffle, you can come outside for the Q&A."

"And does Capri come back in here for the signing after?" Tristan asks. "In the air conditioning?"

I squeeze Tristan's hand, barely restraining my eye roll at his question.

"Yes. We'll have her at a table near the back of the store so we can fit as many people inside as possible. Not everyone is used to this humidity. In fact, several of the people who came in before we closed the shop mentioned that they traveled in for this. One gal came all the way from Alberta, Canada. Oh, and one from … Idaho or was it Iowa? Anyway, it's not close." She glances at her watch again. "But there I go rattling on. If you need anything during any part of the evening, don't hesitate to ask."

"Thank you, Mrs. McMannus," I say.

"Call me Marianne." We follow her into the main area of the bookshop, and she stops us next to the door. "You can wait here until I introduce you. Otherwise, no one will listen to a thing I say." Then she slides out the door.

I scan the crowd of faces from behind the glass door, picking out several familiar ones all sitting together: Cat, Holland, Gemma, and Ivy. I also know my whole family and Jane are here somewhere, but I can't see them from where I'm standing. And Joy texted to say her and Mark are on the third row toward the middle, and that Beau's the on-duty officer for the event.

A few women seated close to the shop glance in this direction, then their gazes shift to me and smiles light their faces. Several wave, and I wave back.

Tristan steps up behind me, his laughter rumbling through the quiet space. "It's like they don't get that I'm married."

"Seriously. I'll probably have to fight them now."

His hands slide around my waist and settle on my stomach. "Oh, there won't be any fighting for you. Not for the next six months, anyway."

I look over my shoulder to where he's nuzzling into me. "You'd let me fight someone if I wasn't pregnant?"

"Someone has to defend my honor, Capri Sun. It really isn't easy being the man who inspires Sunny Palmer. The one that gave her his name. The man who fathered her child."

Why am I smiling like a love-struck teenager? Probably because Tristan constantly makes me feel exactly like I still am one. "With comments like that and ensuring I'll have air conditioning during my signing"—I glance down at his hands, his palms pressed against my belly protectively despite that I'm just barely starting to show. I'm still in the I-ate-one-too-many-pieces-of-cake-so-I-can't-fasten-the-top-button-on-my-pants phase of the pregnancy—"and with the way you keep placing your hands over my stomach, people outside of our family are going to figure out our little secret before we're ready to tell them."

Tristan places a kiss on my neck that sends a shiver of pleasure through me. "That kind of seems par for the course, doesn't it?"

"Walker would appreciate your golf reference," I say to keep my wits about me instead of allowing Tristan's touch to be my undoing. I probably need to tell him to stop so I'm not too frazzled before I have to go answer questions in front of hundreds of people, many that I actually know in real life. But I'd rather not.

"Not as much as Jane."

I laugh because it's true. Jane does nothing half-heartedly, so she's officially the most invested golf-lover of all time now. Walker couldn't be luckier. I guess, she's pretty darn lucky too.

"Are you nervous?" Tristan asks, as Mrs. McMannus (I can't bring myself to call her Marianne) begins to explain the raffle tickets.

"Of course. But at least I don't feel like I'm going to vomit this time."

"In your defense, that was morning sickness at the last event. You just didn't know it yet."

"Still. There's nothing like speaking to a roomful of people after having spent the thirty minutes prior being sick into a toilet."

"But you did an amazing job."

"Because you're not at all biased."

He glances down at me, his expression sober. "Look at this audience, Capri. Look how many people came to hear you speak. To get your new book. To meet you. I'm clearly not biased."

Tears prick my eyes, and I start fanning my face. "You're going to make me cry." My hormones are already all over the place, and I don't want to get on stage and have a babbling fit in front of half of the people on Sunset Harbor. "Quick, tell me something funny."

"On the way home the other day, I saw Beau on a bike ride. Guess who had a bell and a basket on his beach cruiser?"

"You're lying."

"Not even a little." Tristan leans in, his breath tickling my neck.

I laugh, leaning in to Tristan when I see Mrs. McMannus gesture in our direction and the crowd's collective gaze shifts to the bookshop. I crack the door open, so I can hear what she's saying. "And now, let's give a warm welcome to our very own Capri Palmer. Or, as most of you know her, Sunny Palmer."

"Go get 'em, my love," Tristan says, opening the door for me.

A surge of nerves rushes through me, but I wave at the countless faces watching me, a huge smile plastered on my face. Before I make my way to the stage, I pause and give Tristan a quick kiss on the lips because I can. The audience goes wild for it with a collective "aww!" along with some hoots and calls for more. These are definitely my people, every romance-loving part of them! And who better than them to appreciate the fact that this quiet, romance-loving-book-nerd got her man. And so, so much more.

Thank you for reading Plotting Summer! Need more of Capri and Tristan? Join my newsletter at www.JessHeileman.com to receive a FREE bonus epilogue from Tristan's perspective.

Read the next book in the Falling for Summer series all about Tristan's brother Beau and his potential rival, Gemma Sawyer.

Falling for Beau Palmer would be the ultimate crime

Wild horses couldn't drag me back to the small island where I grew up, but you know what can? Making sure the Palmer family–aka the worst neighbors ever–show appropriate respect to the newest resident of their retirement center: my grandma.

But as soon as Grams moves in, her shenanigans put her at risk of being kicked out. Since she's set on staying in Sunset Harbor until her last breath and there's no way I'm staying on this nightmare island to take care of her, that's not an option.

Enter Beau Palmer, the infuriatingly charming local cop who's got the connections to keep Grams right where she needs to be *and* help me get out of Dodge sooner. But he's got a price, and it requires putting the Sawyer/Palmer drama firmly in the past.

But the drama *isn't* behind us. In fact, it's right in front of me, wearing a police badge and a smirk that's really started disturbing my peace.

FALLING FOR SUMMER

Summer Ever After by Kortney Keisel

Walker + Jane

Beachy Keen by Kasey Stockton

Noah + Cat

Plotting Summer by Jess Heileman

Tristan + Capri

Summer Tease by Martha Keyes

Beau + Gemma

Beauty and the Beach by Gracie Ruth Mitchell

Phoenix + Holland

One Happy Summer by Becky Monson

Briggs + Presley

Rebel Summer by Cindy Steel

Dax + Ivy

ACKNOWLEDGMENTS

You know the saying, 'It takes a village to raise a child'? Well, it also takes a village to write a book (which is probably why we authors talk about our *book babies*, though I digress). And so, that being said, I'd love to thank the numerous people that helped make *Plotting Summer* what it is.

As always, I couldn't do anything I do without the talent I've been given from a loving Heavenly Father and His son, Jesus Christ. They are my business partner, my inspiration, and my strength. They're ever patient with me when my prayers turn into plotting sessions. And when I'm down in the arena, wrestling with self-doubt and fear and anxiety, they're not watching from the stands. They're with me, battling alongside me. Often, battling for me when I can't, and I'm forever grateful for their infinite love!

To my incredible husband. What a strength you are to me. As I've written this book, you've picked up more than your fair share of slack. From making dinners and doing dishes after a long day of work, to playing taxi driver to our kids and making housekeeping your new favorite hobby (okay, it's not your favorite, but that makes me all the more grateful for your efforts). I truly have the best of the best when it comes to husbands. Thank you, Tim, for choosing me to be the person you do this crazy life with!

To my sweet babies (Andrew, Hyrum, Eden, Mary, and Edmund) that aren't babies anymore: your love, encouragement, and understanding have been a motivating factor in getting this book finished. Sorry for all the nights dinner wasn't ready until eight, for the pantry that too often needed restocked, for the unfolded piles of laundry you had to search through to get dressed, and for stepping up to help where it was needed. I'm one lucky momma, and each one of you is my very favorite!

To my community of friends, neighbors, and family, thank you for caring. Thank you for asking how my book is going and stepping up to help with my kids or bring me a treat when I'm in the thick of writing and editing. Your support buoys me up and your examples of kindness and service touch my heart in a way that encourages me forward.

Tawnie West, Ashley Weston, and Jennie Goutet—aka the world's best cheerleaders--without your listening ears, calming reason, and constant Marco Polos, I'm not sure I could have gotten through this book. Thank you for your constant positivity, for walking me down from cliffs holding my hand tightly in yours, and for being some of the first people to read my book. This book is so much better because of you (and so is my mental health). Thank you!

To the ladies of the Falling for Summer series. I adore each and every one of you. What a joy it's been working through this intense process with you. There's no other group of ladies I'd want to create a vast web of interconnected characters, schedules, and places with through thousands of text messages, emails, and Marco Polos. We set out to do a really hard thing, and we did it! Even if we are a little worse for wear, developed random eye twitches, and became extremely sleep-deprived because of it. Way to go us!

Melody Jeffries, I'll never cease to be amazed by your talent and your ability to bring characters to life from a brief description and a few vague inspiration pictures. Your sketches of Tristan and Capri have been a constant source of inspiration for me where they hang on my bulletin board, and I am so incredibly in love with my cover! Thank you for sharing your talents with us and helping our series stand out from the crowd!

To Jacque Stevens, my developmental editor at HighTower Editing, you took a mess of a draft and were able to rake through it to find what the story most needed. I'm incredibly thankful for your grasp on story, arcs, and character development. What a privilege it was working with you, and I look forward to working with you again in the future!

Susan Kuechenberg, there's a reason Capri's editor was named after you in my book. You are invaluable to me with your knowledge of story, your eye for detail, and your grasp of grammar. Though I can rarely answer your questions about my comma and ellipses preferences, I know I can trust you to help me put out the cleanest, best version of my story possible. Thanks for working with me time and time again! You are my (not so) secret weapon.

For all of those who read an early and messy draft of my story, I applaud you. It needed a lot of work. My beta readers: Deborah Hathaway, Tawnie West, Jennie Goutet, Ashley Weston, Brooke Losee, Susan Kuechenberg, and Meredith Logan, you gave me the confidence, help, and direction I needed to keep going. The story being published looks quite a bit different (and is thankfully much improved) from the draft I first gave you, and that's in large part thanks to each one of you.

To my favorite traveling companions: Martha Keyes, Ashtyn Newbold, Esther Hatch, and Kasey Stockton, I'm so incredibly grateful for your friendship and for all the memories we've made together. I will treasure them for my whole life. This last research trip was not only full of incredible research opportunities, but it was also exactly the break I needed to clear my mind before hitting my edits hard when I got back. Also, thanks for all the plotting you did with me as we drove, talking through kinks and finding solutions. Your ideas made a huge difference in my finished story.

Ellen Quay, my exceptionally talented narrator, it's a pleasure to be able to work with you again. I cannot wait to hear you bring Capri's story to life. Your voice has the most inviting, calming quality to it, and your pacing is exceptional. With the nuances of your narration, it's clear you are not only a gifted voice talent but you are also a gifted storyteller.

To the team at Dreamscape, thank you for all you do to spread the love of my audiobooks, and for working with our group of authors to promote this series. It's such a pleasure to work with you, and I'm excited to continue the relationship for many years!

Each release comes with its ups and downs, but one of the highlights is working with amazing readers and bookstagrammers. Thank you to the Falling for Summer Cheerleading Squad. Your effort to share both our books and this series has been instrumental to its success. You are the best ever, and I'm blown away by your support and your creativity. Thank you for all you've already done and will continue to do for this series! You ladies rock!

To my amazing ARC team, thank you for loving my books enough to want to be part of my release. Thank you for taking the time to read an early copy, for helping me to catch any lingering errors, and for sharing my book with your friends and followers. It's such an honor and a comfort to have people like you behind me, and I hope you know how grateful I am!

And last, but never least, thank you to my readers who make all of this effort worth it. Thanks for your emails and your messages, for your reviews and your posts, and thank you for sharing my book with others. I wouldn't be where I am without you! And hats off to those of you who've made it this far in the acknowledgments. You are a special kind of reader, and I feel blessed that you care enough to take the time to read my inadequate attempts at expressing my gratitude. Happy reading, friends!

ABOUT THE AUTHOR

Jess Heileman is quite content being an average human being. Besides her five darling children and swoon-worthy husband, she doesn't tout much claim to glory—even her middle name is just plain old Ann with no 'e.'

After a ten-year stint as a portrait photographer where she put her BA in Political Science from Brigham Young University to good use, Jess now spends her time frolicking between this awe-inspiring world and the one in her head where enthralling stories come to life.

Besides her love of storytelling and her deep obsession with her perfectly quirky little family, Jess is an avid reader, proud introvert, collector of awkward moments, shameless people watcher, international café loiterer, and homeschool mama. For sparse updates on what she's up to, sign up for her newsletter at JessHeileman.com or follow her on social media @author-jessheileman. Though know that her presence there is left wanting.

Made in the USA
Monee, IL
25 June 2024

60605560R00204